**CELESTIAL SUN
PUBLISHING**

Picking

the

up
Pieces

A Novel

-By Sungee-

**Celestial Sun
Publishing**

Published by Celestial Sun Publishing

To order books, please write to the following address:

Celestial Sun Publishing
P.O. Box 92114
Atlanta, G.A. 30314-0114
(404) 212-7533

Book cover painting by Paul Griffin, Jr.

Book cover layout and design by Katherine Siegel

Book editing by Ericka Johnson, Kisha Gunter, and Lisa Martin

Printed in the United States of America

ISBN 0-966-73310-X
Library of Congress Catalog Card Number 98-095031

PUBLISHER'S NOTE
This novel is a work of fiction. Names, characters, places, incidents, or locales are a product of the author's imagination and used to give the fiction a sense of authenticity. Any resemblance to actual persons, living or dead, events, or locales is purely coincidental.

LETTER TO THE READER

First, I would like to thank you for purchasing my book. As long as I can remember, reading and writing have both been my first loves. Since reading has always been a pleasure to me, I thought I'd try my hand at writing. It is by the grace of God that I am able to pursue such an exciting and fulfilling career. I love to talk and socialize, but most importantly, I love to smile. I think smiling and laughter can lead to longer, healthier lives.

I am constantly in the "market" to improve my writing as well as myself. So, if you have any constructive criticism, please let me know. I am open to other's opinions and advice. Once you have read my book, please feel free to write with suggestions or comments. But remember, I'm like Erykah Badu, (I'm sensitive about my _ _ _ _. So please be gentle).

Thanks once again for supporting my endeavors. I hope you will enjoy this book and the many others to come in the future. I look forward to hearing from you. I can be reached at the following address:

Sungee
P.O. Box 92114
Atlanta, GA 30314-0114

DEDICATION

Not a day goes by that I don't think of you. Your love has guided me through many safe years on this earth. I can not truly say in words how much I love you because the human language does not expand to such depths. And although I miss you somethin' terrible, I know that you are in good hands. Each night that I pray, I know that you are watching me from above. And this is why I dedicate my first book to a gentle and caring spirit and soul. I love you grandma.

Nancy Momon 1919-1997

THE AUTHOR WANTS TO THANK...

First, thanks go to the Almighty for blessing me with a precious gift. The gift to write, to gab, and the gift to love. Special thanks go out to my parents, Dorothy and Cookie. Thanks for all the support of two loving, hard-working parents. I may have floated through some of life, but believe me-I am truly doing what I love now. With your unconditional love, I have found my way. This is just the beginning. Watch me soar! You two have taught me strength, love, and perseverance. I am extremely blessed to have you as my parents. Thanks. I love you both very much.

To my oh-so interesting and lovable family. I love you all: Jamal, Gin, Nyeka, Vashika, brotha' DeAndre, brotha' Phillip, Neecie, Jr., Manuel, Phyllis, Shirley, Trecinna and Diatra (you guys will make it! I have faith in you. Stay strong, we're soldiers-no limit), Chester, Kisha, Monica, and Willie. Thanks for always being there and knowing the true meaning of "family."

To my girls: Donna, Ericka, and Monique. Thanks for believing in me and hanging in there during my moody times, for hitting the poetry readings with me, for reading *and* re-reading my work, for listening to the poems over the phone, for helping me solve many of life's problems in California *and* Georgia, and for understanding my plight. Basically, thanks for dealing with me. Y'all know how I can get sometimes. I love y'all shawdies!

Another special thanks to my investors Dorothy, Phyllis, and Shirley. Thanks for supporting me and believing in me. If it weren't for you guys, I'd be stuck. Much love. Hopefully soon, I can pay you back (smile).

To my boys: Joe, Rob, and Vamian for "hooking" me up. Maurice for always being there and helping me through those difficult times and making me laugh when I needed to. I appreciate that. George Michael "Mike" Phipps-I still think of you. Thanks guys. I love y'all. You guys are great friends!

Thanks to my editors: Ericka Johnson and Kisha Gunter. My graphic artist: Paul Griffin Jr. And my mentor: Thomas Green,

Love's Home Run and *Courting Miss Thang*. And Ms. Dorothy Allen: One of the best educators I've had thus far.

And finally, 'cause I *can* get long winded, thanks to everyone who has supported me throughout my life, be it financially, emotionally, or spiritually. You know who you are but to name you would take a whole 'nother book. Thanks, with much love.

Sincerely,

Sungee

PIECES

One by one falls,
Shattered lives, shattered dreams, and shattered hopes
With each one, lost children call
For our help, for our love, for our all
Responsible for delicate souls
Precious minds to be nurtured through time
With ruining of these dreams, hopes, and lives
That continue to be shattered
Will leave us in a sick society
Full of sick souls
And like pieces to a puzzle
All articles must fit
But when unexpected shattering occurs
We as a race, human *and* ethnic
Will be forced to face the music
And be left with
Picking up the pieces

-Sungee-

TABLE OF CONTENTS

CAR REPAIRS

"Damn!" Senida hissed as her purse toppled to the asphalt. Her large sharp butcher knife fell out and a bright glimmering beam of moonlight reflected off of the silvery blade. Night air whipped around her body and she shivered. Senida liked Atlanta's night air. It was cool and crisp as it entered her lungs. Tonight it seemed as if each breath lasted an eternity.

Looking around to make sure no one saw her, Senida quickly bent to retrieve the weapon. Her long slender fingers gripped the mahogany colored handle. Each finger fit perfectly around her weapon of choice. Hands trembling, she approached the jeep with caution and kneeled by its side. Senida tucked the leather purse under her left arm and with two quick thrusts of her forearms, she forced the sharp butcher knife into the thick rubber tire.

There were no lights on in any of the houses on Cedar Street. In fact, Senida's eyes had not quite adjusted to the new day. Few cars lined the side streets and there were many trees filling the small subdivision. Brookhaven Subdivision housed mostly young aspiring and prominent African-Americans. However tranquil, Brookhaven's community unleashed itself on Saturday nights. Cars, by the numbers could be seen speeding down the narrow streets, headed towards a night filled with fun. Since the age range of the tiny community ranged between 26-35 years, many residents partied hard on the weekends.

Senida usually enjoyed the constant weekend buzz of Brookhaven. The sounds of music, the chattering, and the clacking of high heeled shoes made her think of when she and Maya were younger. However, tonight, the persistent traffic interfered with her duties. Her ultimate goal on this night was to get revenge.

Slow, low hissing sounds crept from the tires and floated on the cool breeze. A wave of jubilant satisfaction rushed through Senida's veins as she enjoyed the pure act of revenge. She smiled to herself. Senida couldn't believe that she was actually sitting next to *his* jeep, slashing *his* tires. An orange glow still hid behind the faint horizon and Senida could see the reflections of the streetlights across the lawn. The silvery sheath of dew on the grass was reminiscent of a clear ice-skating rink.

Senida looked up into the thick sky. A dark morning embraced her and reminded her of her lover's skin color: a deep, dark, blue-black hue that was smooth and soothing. That color was the very reason that she was bending by his jeep now. It was his blue-black hue that made her lose all of her God-given sense. It made her want him, even when he decided that he couldn't be available for her, like tonight.

Earlier, an excited Senida had planned to surprise her lover with a new teddy and new toys that she'd purchased from Victoria's Secret. But she was the one surprised when she saw the very young, very attractive woman with the overnight duffel bag get out of the burgundy Nissan Sentra and waltz into the house. She didn't even use a key, Senida thought as she watched, stunned from her car. She waited for an hour and when the woman didn't come out, Senida went home.

Later, when she could not reach him on the phone or get any sleep, she went back to his house, ready to act a fool. Her eyes were blood shot from anger and frustration. True he was only her lover. And true he was young. And true he was extremely attractive and could work his hips until you called your mama's name...but *she* didn't want to share him with anybody else.

Senida put her hand over the slash and could feel the air seeping out of his tires. His prized possession would be sitting on rims soon, she thought as she pushed the knife farther into the tire and pulled down harder to make a bigger gash. At three-thirty, the morning air whipped around the jeep and Senida looked at her watch to estimate the time that she had left. He would be leaving for work around seven, so that gave the tires approximately three and a half hours to leak before he came walking outside to view her artwork.

She leaned back and looked at the burgundy Nissan Sentra parked in the driveway. All four tires were flat. That will teach that man stealing little hussy when her little Nissan is rolling on rims. Senida positioned herself by sitting on her butt and crossing her legs Indian style, like she used to do in kindergarten. Her short hair flowed in a soft pattern to the back. Senida loved to wear her hair short. It complimented the oval shape of her caramel colored face and brought attention to her almond shaped eyes. Men mostly complimented her on how alluring her eyes were.

The hissing came quicker as the jeep began to sag on the left side. She had one more back tire to do but she wanted to ensure that each one died a slow, silent death, so she waited. She waited until all of the air was gone and then commenced to the other side.

Senida could not understand what went wrong. She and her lover had discussed their situation on many occasions. Their agreement was for him to please her when her man couldn't. And she knew that she was more than enough woman for him. There was no need for other women in his life. As far as Senida was concerned, she should have been the only woman that he lusted for. A year and a few weeks, Senida had grown dependent on his gentle touches. But with each month that passed, his attitude had worsened. In the beginning he would pursue her, but now the tables had turned.

She looked at the sagging tire and slowly shook her head back and forth. The things we do for dick, she thought. She didn't want to get rid of him, just teach him a little lesson. Her hands slid up and down her thighs as she waited for the air to escape. Her head tilted back, almost in an orgasmic position. She couldn't get him out of her system, no matter how hard she tried.

Briefly, Senida almost felt sorry for slashing his tires. But her guilt quickly subsided when the wind blew thoughts of the beautiful woman back into her mind. More thrusts of the forearms and sliding of the blade into the final tire. Her right wrist began to hurt and she massaged it with her left fingers. She smiled as the last of the air escaped the last tire.

Suddenly, as if on cue, a flood of light spilled out onto the porch and the young woman walked out into the driveway. Her short-cropped hair was much like the style that Senida wore. She was slim, yet shapely. Her track-like legs were perfectly built and her smooth deep, dark skin had not a blemish. Senida moved in just enough time to see the woman's facial expression change when she saw her burgundy car. Her young attractive face twisted in horror and then in anger at the now squatting Senida.

"Bitch, what the hell is wrong with you?" the young woman yelled.

She lunged towards Senida. The young woman was fast and before Senida could blink, strong blows caught her off guard. Her heart rate raced. She had to think quickly on how to protect herself. Senida talked a good game, but truthfully, she had never really been a fighter. More times than none was she ever called out. Okay, she thought, swing, kick, jab, punch! Do something! Her mind screamed.

Senida's right temple took another blow. Then a third hit to her eye. Arms, fists, and legs were pounding at Senida with a sturdy force. Another blow to her jaw and another to her neck. A sharp pain shot up through Senida's eye and to her brain. Then quick repeated bolts of pain inflamed around her lips. The woman was screaming loudly and swinging wildly. Senida winced in pain as she tried to cover her head with her arms.

Lights came on in the rooms of a few houses. The young woman's attention turned towards the house and Senida found the strength to push the woman off of her. Senida tumbled on top of her. Screams continued to spill out of the young woman's mouth as she struggled with Senida. She let the young woman go and tried to run off but the woman grabbed her by her shirt and snatched her back.

The young woman jumped and bobbed from side to side. Senida swung and her right fist connected to the woman's face. She withdrew from pain. Senida swung again but missed. Senida was fast but the young woman was faster.

"So you want to tear up somebody's car, huh? Well now it's time to tear that *ass* up." The young woman jumped, swung in the air and landed a kick into Senida's chest. Karate?

Air rapidly escaped Senida's lungs. She stumbled backwards and held her chest. Fire surged up through her throat and burned down towards her limbs. Quickly, without thinking, Senida snatched up the knife. Shimmers of light reflected again off the blade and came to a shiny point on the end. The woman's eyes grew wide and she took a few steps back. Senida jabbed the knife at the woman a few times. Damn, she thought, the woman was so young and so attractive. No wonder he had been avoiding her calls lately. Senida hoped he wouldn't come outside and see them fighting.

With the energy of a bull, the young woman flung open her mouth and let out a loud, echoing wail. Lights went on in his bedroom and then in his living room. Senida backed up and started sprinting down the street and around the corner. As she ran, she could hear the woman's screams still echoing behind her. She ran until she got to her car, which was a block away from his house.

Out of breath, she looked at her watch; it was four-forty in the morning. She had to get home before Darrell got worried. Senida turned the key and gave her burgundy Honda Accord some gas, but the engine died quickly. She tried again and realized that she was stuck. Each time she tried to start her car, she would get more and more frustrated at the fact that her engine wouldn't turn over. She checked her rear view window. Nobody was coming. She knew for sure that the woman would have called the cops by now.

"Shit!" Senida said as she hit her fist on her dashboard. Just as she did that, the hand on the gas tank fell down to "E." Her gas hand was stuck again. Darrell had told her earlier that week that she should take her car to the shop, but she was too hardheaded. And there was no way in hell she would call him to come pick her up. How would she be able to explain *this* situation?

"Damn, damn, damn," she said hitting her fists on the steering wheel.

Her only solution was to call Triple A. Senida looked around. She knew the closest gas station was at least two miles. She locked her car doors, wrapped her scarf tight around her neck, and started. As she walked, she thought about the situations that she usually got herself into, like this particular one. All over a man. Senida didn't know why she acted the way she did when it came to men. She had a sweet tooth for chocolate men. Couldn't control herself when she got around them, couldn't stop staring at them, couldn't stop thinking about them. Her friends told her time and time again that she needed to stop. She had a good man at home. A real good man, well pretty much. Outside of his own personal problem, he didn't give her any trouble, usually.

There were always many men in her life. If it weren't the ones that she was interested in, it was the ones that were interested in her. Throughout college, she had a reputation of sleeping around. Although smart, Senida often seemed to mistake lust for love, and usually associated love with sex. Even when she did have a steady boyfriend, like Darrell, Senida would catch herself lusting over someone else, especially if she wasn't satisfied. And that meant satisfaction in every aspect emotionally, mentally, spiritually, and sexually.

She felt bad that there was no one to make her feel whole. She got bored too easily with men who couldn't complete the package. And although she loved Darrell with all her *heart*, her *body* would sometimes forget. So until she got married, she would have all the fun she could. As long as she didn't hurt anyone, she thought that her actions were justifiable.

A small phone booth stood outside of the little gas station mart by the corner of the street. There were usually lights on, but someone had cracked the bulbs. Senida dug through her Dooney and Bourke purse. A pack of gum, a compact, her Teek lipstick by Iman, her checkbook, the thin toothed comb that she bought earlier that week, and her wallet. She pulled her Triple A card out of her wallet and dialed the number. A friendly representative's voice came across the wire, took Senida's information, and told her that the tow truck would be there shortly.

Senida again fumbled through her purse looking for change. She had emptied her change into her ashtray back in the car. Damn, she thought. She had to call Maya. She started to call her collect, but decided against the idea. Senida fumbled through her purse some more and stuck her hands in her jean pockets, where she retrieved an old worn and tattered five-dollar bill. She quickly made her way into the little store and bought another pack of gum to get change to call Maya. Since Maya was her back up for the night she had to let Maya know everything that went down. The phone rang three times and Senida thought the answering machine would pick up, but Maya answered after the fourth ring.

"Maya."

"Senida. Where are you?" Her voice was groggy. Senida looked at her watch. It was well after five-thirty in the morning.

"At the gas station on Jasper and Pines."

"What the hell are you doing there? I've been calling you all night," Maya lifted her head from her pillow to look at her clock. She had to let her eyes focus for a minute and had to give her mind a minute to wake up.

"Girl, I ran out of gas."

"Ran out of gas? You need me to come pick you up?"

"Nah. The tow truck will be here soon. I just need you to cover for me tonight."

She heard Maya sigh.

"I told Darrell I was with you tonight and we went to the club. So just in case he calls, cause he knows I should have been home by now, okay?"

"Yeah."

"Thanks girl. You're the best friend."

"You know I don't like doing this. Darrell is my friend too."

"Yeah, I know. But where does your loyalty lie?"

Maya sighed. "With your raunchy ass."

Senida laughed. "Thanks."

"Next time you plan on doing something like this, at least let me know so I won't be caught off guard if he calls."

"I will."

"So what happened this time?" Maya leaned back in the bed and rested her head on the pillow. She tried to whisper.

"I wanted to surprise him. But I guess I was the one to get surprised."

"How?"

"Another woman."

"Damn. Did you guys have plans for tonight?"

"No."

"Well that's what you get. I told you plenty of times that you don't need to be popping up over his house."

"Girl I can barely hear you."

"Well Michael is here, I can't talk that loud." Maya shifted her weight in bed and turned toward the wall.

"Girl what am I going to do?" Confusion laced Senida's voice. She did not want to tell Maya that she went off the deep end and slashed not only *his* tires but the young woman's tires also.

"You *need* to be worried about Darrell. Ever since he

moved to Atlanta you've been acting crazy. Quit messing around with that young twenty something and get yourself together. You always lose perspective when some new dick walks into your life."

"I know," Senida sighed. She'd heard the lectures on more than a few occasions.

"I thought you and Darrell finally decided to get engaged."

"We did, but I'm not sure I can be faithful with his problem and everything."

"You haven't even tried."

"I have."

"You haven't."

"Well I'll call you tomorrow. I'm sure the tow truck is there by now."

"No, you call me tonight so that I know you made it home safely."

"Okay. Bye."

Senida's walk back to her car wasn't nearly as long as her walk to the gas station. She had plenty of time to reflect on her previous actions. She chuckled to herself when she thought about how the woman had looked when she saw Senida squatting by the jeep. She wondered if she would describe Senida and if he would know that it was she.

She didn't have to wait long for the tow truck to arrive. A tall, lean man jumped out the truck with his gas can. He checked under her hood to be on the safe side. He then flipped open the gas tank and started pouring the gas into her tank. While he stood there, he looked Senida up and down.

"Isn't your name Senida Johnson?"

"Yeah, why?" Senida looked suspiciously.

"We went to high school together. Remember me, James Terry?" He grinned as Senida frowned up her face. She did remember him, but had no interests in playing catch up or name that student.

"Oh yeah, I remember you. Now, how long is it going to take for me to be back in my car rolling?"

"Oh, not that long," he said as he straddled his legs open. "What you doing way out here in Atlanta?"

"Working."

"Where you working at?"

"Smithers' Law Firm."

"Oh, you a lawyer?"

"Yeah."

Silence.

"Good ole A-T-L. You like it out here?"

"Yeah."

"How long you been out here?"

"Not too long."

"I been out here for about five years. I like it. Bought me a house out in Lithonia. Guess who else is out here? Leroy Hines. I saw him at the grocery store. He said he been out here for..."

"I'm not in the mood to hear about anybody. I just want to get home. Are you done?"

"Almost." James ignored her rude disposition and continued talking. "Ms. Senida. Yeah, I remember you in high school. Ambitious, driven. You always knew how to party *and* get good grades. Me myself, I barely made it out. Now, I'm working for this towing company. I'm trying to save up so I can buy me a few of those babies." He nodded towards the tow truck. "I want to start my own towing company."

Senida was not interested in hearing about anyone from California or Georgia for that matter. She was ready to get in her car and go before somebody rode around the corner, noticed her stranded, and realized that she was the one slashing tires. From experience, she knew that the cops would be patrolling the area for a minute to appease the people who called them. Senida thanked the man when he finished putting the gas in her car, declined when he asked for her number and sped off leaving him in the dust. She had to get home to Darrell. He would definitely be calling Maya soon if she didn't get home.

Ambition was the motivating factor behind Senida's climb up the corporate ladder. She was driven by persistence and the overwhelming feeling of being outdone. It was this attitude that drove her straight to the top five percent in her law school class. When she graduated from Georgia State's Law School, she was one of the most sought after African-American females. Her job offers expanded from Georgia to California and she even had a few offers in Florida. It is this very reason that made her feel guilty when she rode home. She knew what she'd just done was against the law. But her guilt quickly subsided when she thought about the young woman at her lover's house. She wished she'd done more to her car. But she'd let out her frustrations the way she needed to.

Senida pressed harder on the pedal, she needed to get home to her man.

SWEET VICTORY,
I'M COMING HOME!

The sun was barely peaking over the land as Maya stood in front of her apartment building stretching. She bent over and touched her toes first and then leaned from one side to the other, stretching out her thighs. Long, lean lunges pulled at her muscles-stretching and releasing them. Maya rolled her head around in circles, releasing tension in her shoulders and shook her head vigorously. She would jog for an hour and head back home to get dressed. This week would be important and exciting for Maya. This week she would start negotiations with the art gallery in San Francisco. Dr. Coleman informed her that she would be traveling to California to represent Sanfords' Gallery. He'd congratulated her with a healthy, warm smile and heart-filled hug.

A cool breeze lightly pushed at her face as she began to run up Westlake Street. Although it was still early, she could tell that the day would be a hot one. Sun beams provided energy for Maya as she ran harder. She would be able to see Aunt Setty when she went to California, she thought. It had been at least two years since she'd set foot in the Golden State and she couldn't wait to get some of those California rays. It was going to be nice getting pampered by her Aunt Setty. She always did make a fuss about Maya. Home cooked meals, long talks at night, and Aunt Setty's famous sweet potato pie.

Maya could hardly wait to make her reservations. Sweet victory I'm coming home, she thought as she rounded the corner and headed toward the cemetery on Martin Luther King Way. Thick asphalt pushed up against her feet and the pounding grew harder, stronger. Her heartbeat grew rapid and her breathing intensified. Sweat started to appear on the bridge of her nose. She felt as if she could run forever on her high. Life was great! Maya's neat ponytail bounced as the elastic rubber band began to give way, allowing a few strands to fall in her face.

As she ran, she could hear traffic gathering over the bridge. Horns honking from the cars filled with people trying to get to early morning services at church, echoed through her body. Atlanta's community rose early on Sundays to commence preparation for church. Women with swollen ankles and heavy breasts, smelling of Ben Gay, would rise to finish up meals that they had begun to prepare the night before. Sunday dinner. But before engaging in feast, these women would have to go to church and praise the Lord, thanking Him for providing food for Sunday's meal. The women would sit in the first few pews, swatting at their granddaughters for untied hair ribbons and at their grandsons for talking or making noise while the preacher preached.

These same women would sing out loud, off key, many not knowing the words to the hymn. Would raise their hands high asking for the Lord to take them and save them. They would stand and shout in front of the congregation, dancing and swinging wide, plump hips to the music of the Holy Ghost. And the Holy Ghost would grab them and swing them around, carrying and pulling them up and down the aisles. Thus, leaving these women drained of energy until they collapsed on the floor or in someone's arms or on their grandchildren.

And after church, the community women would hum and head home to their home cooked meals of chicken, cornbread, and mashed potatoes. They would say how that was a good sermon, how the Reverend knew what he was talking about, and that the Lord was good. And many, but not all, would commence to sinning back on Monday, until it was time for them to repent again on Sunday.

Maya stood at the crosswalk waiting for the light to change. Her body was hot and she could feel heat rushing down to her fingertips. She continued to bounce around to keep her blood flowing until it was time to cross the street. She rounded out a cyclical pattern, as she wove her way past liquor stores, back down through the park, and back to her street. By the time she returned to her apartment building, Mr. Miller was standing in front of his yard sifting through his trash. He waved and immediately smiled as Maya jogged up the parking lot.

"Hey Mr. Miller. You lose something?" Maya smiled. Her maple colored eyes bounced.

"That darn grandchild of mine threw away some important papers. Now I got ta put my hands all through this stuff to find 'em. And we had fish for dinner last night," he said turning up his nose.

"Oh no!" Maya frowned in mock disappointment. "I hope you find them. Good luck."

"How you been Ms. Lady?" Mr. Miller tried to stall Maya's entrance into her building.

"I've been pretty good and you?"

"Still living. Still hanging in there." Mr. Miller began the short walk over to Maya's building. She could tell that he was in the mood for talking. She decided that she would entertain the old man for a little while. She liked Mr. Miller and he was quite taken by her beauty and her genuine personality.

"I was telling my son yesterday that it's time for him to get married."

"Really? How old is your son?" Maya leaned against the trunk of a tree. She was still slightly panting from her run and Mr. Miller watched intensely as her chest was heaving in and out.

"He's hittin' on thirty. I want him to find a nice girl, such as yourself."

"Oh Mr. Miller, you know I'm taken," she smiled as she lied and repositioned herself so her weight would be on her left foot. Mr. Miller laughed a rambunctious, hearty laugh.

"I know your parents must be proud. Your folks still together?"

"No, well I mean yes." Technically they are, she thought. Maya was beginning to feel uncomfortable. She did not make it a habit of discussing her "folks" with just anyone.

"How long you been here in Georgia?"

"I went to high school here. My Aunt Setty raised me since I was sixteen." She looked at her watch. "Whew! Mr. Miller I gotta go. I'm running late," she lied again. Maya waved to Mr. Miller and sauntered quickly toward her building.

Mr. Miller watched Maya's ample behind swish from side to side until she disappeared into her building. It was more excitement than he was used to. Mrs. Miller had long since lost her luster. Her once large, perky breasts were now dragging against her knees, a result of five children suckling from them over the past forty years. Mr. Miller used to like to sneak up behind Mrs. Miller to rub against her round firm backside. Now she was a few sweet potato pies overweight. She had no more desire to be sexy or even *pretend* to be sexy. Many a night Mr. Miller would sleep in the living room because of Mrs. Miller's loud snoring. He would sometimes sleep in the bedroom during the days when she would clip her toenails and lose some in the couch and on the floor.

So every morning and every evening he would have a free show watching Maya. Mr. Miller would often stand below her window, where the large dumpsters were and watch her silhouette as she dressed for bed. Mrs. Miller asked him one night where he went every other night. He would tell her that he was just standing on the corner getting some air.

Michael was sitting on the bed when Maya jogged into her bedroom. His back was turned to her and he had a slight hump on the right side of his shoulder from the heavy book bags he'd carried in medical school. Maya could tell from his position that he was in the process of leaving. Michael hadn't dressed yet but he looked as if he were in his don't-touch-me mood. His curly, sandy colored hair stood in array over his head. Each large curl framed his butter colored yellow face. Usually when he was in a funky mood, his hazel eyes would narrow over his wire-rimmed glasses. Like they were doing now.

Maya usually did not let Michael's mood swings bother her but today was different. Michael had been avoiding their conversation, which was long overdue. Maya knew that he was avoiding the impending conversation because it would most likely end in an argument. Since her early morning jog, Maya was in high spirits and definitely didn't want Michael or anybody else to bring her down.

"Good morning." Maya slightly startled Michael from behind as she slid onto the bed and wrapped her arms around his bare waist. "Did you sleep good last night?"

"Ummm," Michael grumbled as he cupped his hands around her hands.

Maya kissed him on his back. His buttery smooth skin felt like silk under her lips. She moved her head down and continued to kiss him up and down his spine. Michael grumbled and squeezed her hands. He swiveled his body around on the bed to face her, placed a gentle kiss on her forehead, and then on her lips. Their lips locked and then slowly parted. Michael became aroused and his body stiffened. Maya kissed him on his lips again and his eyes softened.

Michael slid his fingers down the front of her shirt and fondled her breasts. Maya's lips slightly parted as Michael caressed her. He pulled at her shirt and she tugged at his boxers. Before they knew it, they were both naked and lusting. Michael fell into Maya and they rolled around in the bed. Panting and sweating, Maya rode Michael as if he were a saddle. Her raggedy ponytail bobbed up and down allowing a few of her thick curls to fall over her light brown eyes.

Her pumping became more vigorous, more intense. Sweat formed on Michael's brows and his upper lip. Maya saw his eyes roll to the back of his head. She felt as though she was really doing something now. With each twist of her small waist and each grind of her hips, Michael's groans became more animated.

He grabbed tightly at Maya. His face was distorted and his lips were poked out in a pout. Michael let out a loud howling noise and his entire body tightened. Maya could see the veins in his neck pop out as he pulled her tight to him.

"Ummm. Don't move," he panted. "Don't move baby."

She did. She moved her hips back and forth. She wanted to see Michael's body squirm. And it did. Maya smiled to herself and climbed off of Michael. They lay side by side for another hour, resting.

"You sure know how to put a smile on my face," Maya said as she ran her fingers through his thin curly hair.

"Like wise, Ms. Dickson."

"It's Maya if you're nasty," she replied in her best Janet Jackson imitation.

Michael swung his legs out of the bed and sat up. He leaned over and kissed Maya on her forehead. Maya sat up next to Michael. She smiled at him and then hugged him. But when he touched the side of Maya's face, she knew what was coming next.

"Baby, I have to go." Michael pulled the rubber band out of her hair, letting the curls fall over her face. He liked the texture of Maya's hair. Her texture was much like his great grandmother's; she was part Creek Indian.

"Now?"

"Yeah. I have some business I need to take care of today." He twirled a few strands of her hair around his finger, making small ringlets.

"I thought we had the whole day to talk about our situation?"

"We did. But I got a page from the hospital while you were out jogging."

Maya looked over at the pager, which sat on her nightstand. Next to Michael's pager was his wedding band. She hated the little gold cyclical reminder that Michael was not completely her man. Each time he would visit he would take off his wedding band and carefully place it onto the nightstand closest to him. One particular night, he forgot to take the band with him. Maya had stared at the band wondering what she would do with the precious metal that haunted her. Her first intention was to flush the band down the toilet, then she thought of hiding it from him, and then she thought about pawning it for a little cash. But before she could make up her mind, Michael had made his way back to her house to retrieve it.

"Michael, we need to talk..."

"Maya not now. We can talk about this later."

"Later. Like when? You've been putting this off for too long. I want to talk about it now." Maya pulled back when he tried to run his fingers through her hair again.

Michael sighed loudly. "Look we'll get together for lunch tomorrow and I'll let you know everything that's going on. But this situation takes some time. I would be doing both of us a disservice if I even began to talk about it now. Something like this can't be interrupted."

"When are the divorce papers going to be finalized?" Maya asked. He had spoiled her mood and she didn't feel like hearing any bullshit from him. It was too early in the morning for bullshit.

"As soon as Glenda signs them, I'll be your man and your man alone." Michael seductively ran his hand down her right arm.

"Well, what's taking her so long to sign them?"

"The woman is stubborn. I don't know why I ever married her," Michael replied as he stood and slipped on his pants. He stepped into his loafers and quickly threw the T-shirt over his head and onto his body. Before he turned to her he reached onto the nightstand and abruptly put the band on his finger. Maya listened to him as he flipped through the numbers on his pager.

"So am I just supposed to wait until you decide that it's cool to talk?"

"I said we could talk later, Maya. Right now, I have a job to do. I have to be at the hospital all night. I have to induce a labor and I may have to perform a C-section. There are supposed to be some interns from Howard University touring today, so I need to get going. I'll leave the BMW and I'll change the oil in your car later tonight or early in the morning. I'll call you later?" Michael cocked his head and smiled at Maya.

"Only if we can talk."

"Tomorrow," he said as he gently kissed her on her mouth. He made his way to the front door. Maya followed. Michael hugged Maya tightly and left her standing at the door, watching. He waved to her when he slipped into her car and sped off around the corner.

Maya slapped the side of the wall with her palm. She couldn't wait until Michael's divorce was finalized. Never had she considered herself to be the type of woman to be involved with a married man. Michael however, had convinced her that his marriage was all a big mistake on his part. He married Glenda for all the wrong reasons, he said. And that he needed a strong black woman by his side while he went through the bullshit that Glenda dished out to him. Maya understood his position and trusted his words. Normally she would investigate, but because Michael was such a charmer, she believed his word. He never truly berated Glenda but he did share the fact that Glenda was insanely jealous and had gone "crazy" shortly after the vows were made.

Maya let the stream of hot water sting her chest as she

leaned against the wall of the shower. Occasionally, she would put her hands up to buffer the force of the showerhead. But mostly, she just leaned there allowing the steam to fill her lungs and cloud her vision. Today was her day. She refused to allow Michael to spoil her Sunday. She'd set aside this Sunday to be spontaneous. And when her body woke her up early, she decided to skip the gym and run through the neighborhood.

She reached for the bottle of Pantene shampoo and bent her neck slightly to let the water wet her hair. Thick dark curls lay in a mass on either side of her head. She lathered and washed her hair three times, before leaving in the conditioner and rinsing that out. Maya despised her thick mane of curls. Only the compliments from the men kept her from cutting it all off again.

Maya stepped out of the shower and dried herself with one of her big, fluffy towels. She would probably read a book today or go shopping. But, she decided on calling her best friend Senida, to see what was on her agenda for the day.

However, when she looked at her clock, she knew it was still too early to call Senida. On Saturdays and Sundays Senida would sleep until she couldn't sleep anymore. Plus, after last night's call from Senida, Maya was sure she would be sleeping in today.

Maya wrapped herself in her robe and wrapped her large, fluffy towel around her head to keep her hair from falling as it dried. She walked into the kitchen and put her bright, red teapot on the stove for some herbal tea. Flipping through her cabinet, she decided that she wanted Sinfully Cinnamon, her favorite. She leaned on the counter and looked out of her window.

Maya could see birds flying and squirrels scampering through the grass and the leaves. As she looked up into the sky, she saw white clouds floating, creating images and then changing, causing a totally different image. First, she saw a dog in the shape of a cloud, then it turned into a dinosaur and then just a large puff of cotton. Then, slowly but surely, she could see her mother. Her mother was dancing with her father in their old living room. Maya could see herself, a little girl with two large ponytails on each side of her head, sitting and laughing, while her parents swayed and sashayed from one side of the room to the other. She saw the smile on her father's face as he dipped her mother and her mother's look of love when he brought her back up. Maya, the little girl, was clapping and laughing.

Then she saw the lights: red, blue, and white. Each color forcefully playing with the other to dominate on the black night. And she heard the sirens too. They were getting louder and closer. The sirens rang and echoed. A long, loud siren, whistling. Whistling to her, long and loud. The whistling siren screamed and whistled, louder and louder. Sounds echoing in her head. Each noise ringing louder and louder inside of her mind. The whistling had haunted her on many nights. She'd think about the loud disturbing whistles. And she heard them now. Loud whistling ringing in her ears.

Maya snapped out of her daze. Her teakettle was whistling. Her water was ready. Maya quickly shook her head and moved over to the stove to receive the screaming kettle. She poured and stirred slowly as she walked into her living room to sit on her couch and think. She thought about her parents and how she loved them and missed them. That's when she decided what she would do today. She would sit and reminisce.

Sungee 20
MEN, MEN, MEN

"What the hell are you doing here?" Senida suspiciously eyed Darrell as he stepped into the cave. A penetrating, musty smell encircled Senida as dust puffed up from the dirty ground. Darrell was still wearing his favorite pajamas and a pair of thick-soled slippers. In his right hand he held a long shiny sword. In his left hand he held a metal shield.

"I came to claim what's mine," Darrell proclaimed as he stepped closer to the astonished Senida. She was standing directly in front of her lover, who at this point had nothing to say. The cave, which held all three of them, was dark and damp.

"Listen here, potna. You gon' have to step with all that. She with me now," the lover finally said. He had on a leather jacket and large dark jeans. Leather straps from the jacket were dangling on both sides of his hips.

"But I love her. She's my woman."

"Boys, boys. Please don't fight," Senida interjected as she stepped in between the two men. She too, like Darrell, was wearing her pajamas.

"Stay out of this Senida. He's bothered us for too long. I'm here to take you back." Darrell held up his shield and positioned his sword. "Unguard," he yelled. He positioned himself in a fighting stance. A shield and a sword appeared in her lover's hands.

Darrell swung his sword at the other man. The lover held up his shield in time to stop the sword from slicing his face. He retaliated quickly and swung his sword at Darrell, cutting into the arm of his pajamas. Trickles of red blood materialized on Darrell's right biceps. Senida gasped as she took a few steps back. Her hands were to her mouth and she didn't know whether to scream or cry.

"Stop, stop!" Senida yelled as the two men swung and jabbed their blades at each other.

Clanking of metal swords echoed in Senida's ears. The two men clashed their weapons together and fell apart. For a split moment it looked as if they were engaging in some type of organized fight. Darrell swung his sword and Senida heard the blade slice through the thick, dark air.

"Give it up old man! Senida belongs to me now!" Her lover forced his sword into Darrell's leg. Darrell's screams echoed throughout the cave. He collapsed to his knees and grabbed his leg. Instantaneously, her lover jumped on Darrell as he crouched on the ground. Metal clanked as Darrell scurried to protect himself with his shield.

"She's mine now," her lover said through clenched teeth as he leaned in close enough for only Darrell to hear. "Do you think I would give up a piece of ass that good?" He began laughing hard.

"You asshole. You don't love her like I do. You're only out for yourself!" With a surge of energy, Darrell sprang from the ground and lunged towards the lover, driving his sword through the leather jacket. Senida's lover sank to the ground in slow motion. Blood gushed from his chest, wetting the front of his jacket. He reached weakly in her direction as she stood wide-eyed and stunned.

"Oh my God!" Senida let out. Darrell hobbled over to Senida and wrapped his arms around her. He smoothed her hair and rubbed his hands up and down her back.

"You don't have to worry anymore baby," Darrell comforted, stroking Senida. "I know you were having trouble deciding between the two of us. But now you don't have to worry about that anymore."

Suddenly, a loud shot rang out and Darrell slowly slipped down to the ground out of Senida's arms. Blood spewed from Darrell's chest. Senida dropped down next to Darrell as he slowly opened and closed his mouth. He was trying to tell Senida that he loved her, but he couldn't get past the first two words when he closed his eyes for the last time. Blood seeped and bubbled from the corners of his mouth. Tears streamed down Senida's face as she looked up to see her lover standing with a small gun in his hands, laughing.

"No! No! You killed him!"

"Isn't that what you wanted?"

"No, no, no!" Senida yelled as her lover grabbed her and they start to wrestle.

Senida jumped out of her sleep. She was screaming and crying and fighting a pair of hands that were pulling on her. All she saw was an image of a broken, bloody, dead Darrell. Someone was gripping her and pulling her down as she fought with them. Finally she was pinned to the bed and she heard Darrell's voice. He was comforting and stroking her hair as he held her tight, until she opened her eyes.

"Shhh, shhh. It was only a dream. I'm here baby. You just had a bad dream that's all." Darrell kissed Senida on her forehead and continued to hold her as she realized that she was in her bed. "It was just a dream."

Darrell held Senida until she calmed down. He held her tightly. Both of their heart rates slowed. Darrell continued to stroke the sides of Senida's head. Slowly, his hand stopped and there was silence. Senida stared out into the darkness until she heard the deep slow snores coming from Darrell.

The previous night's episode replayed in her mind over and over. And when Darrell inquired about her swollen lip and black eye she had to think quick, blurting out a lie about her and Maya getting into a scuffle at the club, which was where they were supposed to be. Senida sighed. Her week had not gone according to plan. She had an enormous amount of work to catch up on. Not to mention that her lover had not called her. She'd wondered when she slipped into the bed next to Darrell, if her lover would know that she had slashed his tires. Her mind would not rest, flipping channels between the other night, work and Darrell. Her job and social life were beginning to exhaust her mentally, physically, and emotionally.

Hours slipped by and Senida lay awake listening to Darrell's snores and feeling the strong thumping of his heart against her chest. She looked over at her digital clock. It was already 11:00 am! Senida wiggled her way out of Darrell's grasp and pulled herself up on her elbows. She let her head fall back between her shoulders and let her thoughts wonder. A tight feeling surrounded her eye and a strong throbbing persisted in her head. Senida gazed down at Darrell still asleep. She sometimes felt sorry for him. He adored the ground she walked on but lacked the capacity to please her the way she needed to be pleased. She started to feel guilty about her dream.

Senida watched as his chest moved up and down under the sheets. She had to remind him of his doctors' appointment today and she had almost forgotten that she promised to go to one of his boring political science seminars tonight. Damn, she thought as she slipped out of her bed and went over to her large window overlooking Piedmont Park. The trees were still displaying a magnificent green despite the sweltering heat. Senida liked the display of natural beauty in Georgia. It was much different than California. The trees were greener and taller and in abundance.

Atlanta's magnetic energy lured Senida. When she visited Maya in Georgia during their years in college, she decided that she did not want to attend Vanderbilt Law School. After graduating from Fisk University, she knew where her destination would be, and was glad that Maya talked her into applying to Georgia State Law School. Her acceptance was all the more reason for her to relocate. Maya, having lived in Atlanta since her senior year in high school, knew all of the hot spots and helped Senida out tremendously when she had to get around and find an apartment. By the time she graduated from law school, Darrell relocated from California. He was a wonderful man and Senida felt bad that she was starting to get bored with him.

The phone rang and Senida jumped at it in fear that it might awaken Darrell.

"Hello," she whispered into the phone.

"Hey girl. Are you still in the bed?" Maya's voice came in loud and clear and if the phone didn't wake Darrell, surely Maya would.

"I was just getting up," Senida whispered. Darrell stirred and wrapped his arms around Senida's waist as she sat down on the end of the bed. He kissed her lightly on the cheek and lay back reaching for his glasses that were on the nightstand next to the bed.

"What are you doing today? I need to go shopping for my trip next month. Did you want to go?"

"I have to go to one of Darrell's seminars with him tonight.

How long did you plan on being out?" Senida was headed for the bathroom. Darrell watched as she shuffled around looking for her slippers.

"Not long. Maybe a couple of hours. Did Darrell find out about last night?"

"No. Thank goodness. You sound restless."

"Oh. I was going to stay in today. But it's such a beautiful day that I couldn't let it pass me up."

"Why would you stay in on a Sunday? I thought Sunday's were your spontaneous Maya days?" Senida asked.

"Just thinking about the folks, ya know. Their anniversary is Tuesday." Maya's spunky voice became soft.

"That's right. Well, have you talked to Aunt Setty?"

"Not yet. She usually calls me on their actual anniversary. But I'm sure she will call me this evening when she gets out of her bingo game. She always calls after Sunday night bingo at the church." They both laughed. "So get dressed. I need some cheering up."

"Okay. I'll come by when I'm done cleaning."

"No. Clean later and I'll drive. I have some stops to make over by your place anyway. I'll see you in about an hour." She hung up.

Senida admired Maya's spunk. Her zest for life was unlike any other she'd known. Senida held the phone tightly in her hand. Her urge to dial her lover's number was strong. She pressed softly on the buttons...404 794-39... Senida looked over at Darrell. He had gone back to sleep with his glasses on. When she dialed the buttons he stirred a little and rolled over on his side. She placed the receiver quietly down on the cradle.

Breakfast was always easy to cook for Darrell. Eggs, bacon, toast, and grits with cheese. He hardly deviated from his everyday routine. The nights he spent over Senida's house were predictable. He'd come over and eat dinner-usually his favorite, steak and potatoes with a salad. They would sit on the couch and watch the news and other worldly event shows until Senida could not take it anymore. Then Senida would tickle his ear and start rubbing the back of his neck. His neck was his sensitive spot. He would look at her and gently kiss her on her forehead. The two would get up and walk into the bedroom. No, he wouldn't pick her up or gently lay her on the floor in the living room. He would meet her in the bedroom. She would undress him and he would watch as she undressed herself. His gentle kisses were laden with love but slacking on the passion. Kissing her breast, but never going below the belly button, he would slowly insert himself and ride until Senida squealed from the release of tension.

Then the ultimate would happen. He would not be able to stay erect or he would ejaculate so fast that she would miss out on the whole ordeal. After the scenario, he would roll over and fall asleep leaving Senida to read or talk on the phone to Maya or her mother. On his good days he could last long enough for her to quickly get what she needed. But, if she concentrated too hard or too long...once again she would miss out.

Frankly, Senida was getting a little tired of the same ole rigmarole. What ever happened to the love making on the beach with water flowing on top of you as you kissed your lover? What ever happened to the men that sung the songs of making love all night long? Where were they? There was no steamy love making in the shower or on the balcony or even in a different room for that matter. And what did those girls sing about, "...going downtown?" White boys weren't the only ones doing that anymore. Why hadn't anyone told Darrell about this new revolution?

Whenever Senida would bring the subject up, Darrell would kiss her lightly on her forehead and say, "You've been reading too many of Terry McMillan's books, watching too many soap operas, and listening to too many of Maya's wild stories." Senida could not take it anymore. He didn't realize how his sexual dysfunction was affecting their relationship. How could she make a life-long commitment to this man if he did not understand her needs? It was beginning to become unbearable. Senida loved Darrell with all of her heart but frankly she needed some excitement in her relationship. She wanted to tell him to pep up but didn't want to hurt his feelings. She knew he could not be held totally responsible for the physical happenings of his body. So she grinned and beared it, without mention of how she was starting to resent him...she didn't want to hurt his feelings.

"How you feeling this morning?" Darrell asked as Senida set his plate of food in front of him.

"I'm fine." She sat down across from him.

"You weren't feeling too hot last night."

"It was just a bad dream."

"You want to talk about it."

"I just want to forget it."

Silence.

"So how is the case coming along? I haven't heard you talk about it lately," Darrell asked as he shoveled grits into his mouth.

"It's moving slowly."

"Isn't this one of the most important cases for Smithers?"

"Yeah. But more importantly, this is one of the most important cases in my career. This case alone could catapult me into a status where I would be able to make partner." Senida buttered her toast and took a big bite.

"Why this particular case?"

"Because it's high profile." She chewed.

"I thought you wanted to start your own practice?"

"I do. But first I want to make partner for the experience. And the Mortin's case just might allow me to do that."

"Aren't the Mortin's pretty well off?" Darrell was now shoveling scrambled eggs into his mouth.

"The Mortin's are a well to do family with old Atlanta money. Mr. Mortin donates money to different charities and school programs. He helped to refurbish part of downtown Atlanta *and* he establishes scholarships for the students in the Atlanta University Center."

"So if he's done all of this, then why is he being dragged into court?"

"Well, Mr. Mortin has a drinking problem..."

"And?"

"And one of his secretaries accused him of sexually harassing her while in one of his drunken stupors."

"And what did he say?"

"He pleaded not guilty. But unfortunately he has no one to account for his where-abouts on the night in question."

"No family or friends?"

"His wife died a few years back, his daughter has relocated, and his son is an attorney in Maryland, so..."

"Poor guy."

"Poor guy? Why is it that every time there is a sexual harassment case the guy is the one getting the sympathy?"

"Because, Senida. Some of these women are out for money. And with Mr. Mortin being as wealthy as he is, he's automatically a target for money hungry gold diggers," he calmly responded and took large gulps from his glass of milk.

"Not every woman is out for money though, Darrell."

"I'm not saying they are. I'm saying that Mr. Mortin is easy prey for those who are. I'm not siding with him *or* the woman. But I've seen my share of men taken through the wringer by those type of women."

"And I've seen my share of wealthy men who think because of their money that they are above the law. And then the public subjects the women to embarrassing interrogation and more harassment. It's hard for women to press charges when they feel that the law is not on their side. Now don't get me wrong, I know of some scheming, conniving women who would stoop this low, and those are the ones who are out for blood."

"It's a shame."

"What is?"

"That black men and black women carry on like they do with each other."

"I know."

"So do you think he did it?"

Senida hesitated for a moment. She took a sip from her coffee.

"No," she finally responded.

"Are you sure?"

"Yes I'm sure." Senida paused for a minute. "Sure that he's innocent or sure that I believe he's innocent?"

"What's the difference? If you're defending him then you need to believe that he's innocent. No, I take that back. You need to *know* that he's innocent."

"He's innocent. Ms. Daphnee Latimore is as conniving as they come. I've got a gut feeling about that woman." Senida narrowed her eyes as she took another sip from her now cold coffee.

When Mr. Mortin hired Ms. Daphnee Latimore, he did not know that he was hiring one of the best con women around. Her motto was "get in quick and get out rich." Ms. Daphnee Latimore was a strikingly attractive woman who was known to be a gold-digger and would scam for money. A native of Alabama, she was biracial and would not let you forget it. Her green eyes caught the attention of too many men and they loved the way she whined through her nose in her Alabama accent. Her long, thin, sandy brown hair was always slicked down with gel. She'd obviously baited, hooked, and reeled in Mr. Mortin. And although her allegations seemed legitimate, Mr. Mortin swore on his wife's grave that he committed no such crime. The back and forth with Mr. Mortin had given Senida more than enough headaches, not to mention the one she had from last night's blows to the head.

"How's your paper coming along?" Senida asked.

"Uhh. I'm almost finished. I've got some more research that needs to be done."

"And then you have to defend it in front of the board?"

"Yes."

"Are you excited?"

"I'm tired. Exhausted to be exact."

"Hang in there. Soon you'll be Dr. Darrell Mason, Ph.D. in Political Science."

"I'm hanging. Some of us are doing what we have to do."

"And what does that mean?"

"You really need to get that eye looked at," he commented on Senida's swollen eye.

"I will, but I want to know what that comment was for?"

"I don't understand why you and Maya act the way you do sometimes," he said setting his fork on his empty plate.

She sighed.

"I need to run some errands before the seminar tonight." Darrell stood and walked over to the sink. "I can't believe that we'll be going out in public with your face like that."

"Darrell don't start. If you don't want to be seen with me, then I'll stay home."

"I don't mind being seen with you, you're my fiancée. But you look like a damn hoodlum with that fat lip and swollen black eye."

Senida did not respond. She knew that she was in the wrong.

"I'll pick you up at six-thirty," he said as she handed him his overnight bag and stuck her face out so he could kiss her on her cheek. His large muscular body leaned sideways at the perfect angle to do so. "And you really should get that eye checked out, it's swelling." He sighed. "You and Maya need to start acting like you have some sense and stop all this fighting and clubbing. Frankly Senida, you're getting too old for that. When we get married, I can't have you hanging all out in the clubs."

"That's why I'm getting it all out of my system now," she replied with a look of disgust.

Senida sighed. She missed the good ole' days when dating Darrell was fresh and new and the world was their oyster. Now it seemed more like their clam. But Darrell reminded Senida of her old, warm quilt that she slept with as a child. Her grandmother made the quilt for her when she was born. It was old and comfortable and familiar...just like Darrell. Maya, her mother, and her other girlfriends agreed unanimously that she should be grateful to have Darrell. They said he was a prized possession. With the exception of Maya, no one else knew of Darrell's sexual shortcomings. However, Senida did agree that he was extremely handsome. She was not oblivious to the women watching and flashing their smiles at Darrell when they went to the mall or the grocery store. His charming smile, deep, dark, sexy eyes, and boyish mannerism attracted many women.

Senida stood in the doorway until Darrell disappeared down the steps. How she hated that she had to go to his seminar. She walked back into her bedroom and flopped onto her bed. Thoughts of her conversation with her mother replayed itself in her head. She was thirty years old and everyone in her family wanted to know why she wasn't married yet, with children. It's not as if she never wanted to get married and have children, but it seemed as if life was just passing her by.

Spending the majority of her life in school, Senida felt as though she was trying to play catch up with everyone else. There was so much more to life than working the everyday nine to five. She hadn't had a chance to travel to exotic places like Maya. Last year Maya took a cruise to Nassau, Bahamas and was planning another trip next year to the Caribbean Islands. She envied the freedom that Maya seemed to possess and the unencumbered spirit within her soul. There was nobody else who could live life the way she's lived it so far. Maya had always been the type to venture out on some adventurous event. All Senida asked is that she has a chance to live a little life before she was ninety years old. The most excitement she got in her life was the gossip that she lived for, and the sneaking around she prayed that she didn't get caught doing.

There was a void that was not filled in Senida's relationship with Darrell. The fire was gone and the spark in the novelty of a new relationship had dwindled. At her age she was ready for a new beginning, a rebirth full of life's pleasantries and beauty. She wanted to travel and see what else was out in the world. Inevitably, her next major step would be marriage. And she was tired of playing these games with other men just to be sexually satisfied. She was educated, her car was paid for, and she had a wonderful job, and was in the process of saving to buy a house. Darrell was almost complete with his doctorate. He owned a nice car, had a good job, and was stable. What more could she want or need? Excitement, that's what! And even if she ended up marrying Darrell, would she still have a wonderful lover on the side? He didn't always act right, but he was definitely good at what he did...making her holler.

Senida began the process of getting ready. Stroking the right side of her head with the brush, Senida sighed at her reflection. She wondered how it would be to take a break from Darrell. She loved him, but she felt as though she was missing something or someone out there that was perfect for her. Maya said she was crazy for even thinking about leaving a good man like Darrell. "When somebody else comes and snatches him, then you'll be sorry," she told Senida. Darrell was a good man, but every time Senida got that feeling in between her legs, she didn't think of Darrell, she thought of someone else.

Maya wore her sunglasses and her hair up. Her mission was to "shop 'til she dropped." She leaned on the horn a little longer this time; to ensure that Senida heard her. Georgia's sun was shining and she could feel the heat. Sun often put Maya in good spirits. She checked the rear view mirror, patting, tucking, and trying to smooth out the rough edges of her ponytail. A reflection of a red jeep appeared from the driveway. Stopping directly behind Maya, two young boys jumped from the back seat and onto the sidewalk. One waltzed into Senida's apartment building, and the other, noticing Maya, "pimp walked" over to the side of her car.

"What up shawdy, what yo' name is?" Sun gleamed off of his gold teeth, which seemed to be about all thirty-two of them.

"Maya. And how old are you?" she asked looking back in the rear view mirror, brushing the curls out of her face and checking her lipstick.

"Nineteen. Why? How old you is?"

"Too old for you sweetheart." Maya smiled at the young man.

"Ah, it's like dat shawdy? Age ain't nuttin' but a number. You can't be dat old any way."

"I'm twenty-nine." Maya was getting impatient as she looked around for Senida. She leaned on her horn for a few more seconds.

"Damn shawdy, you look good. But what dat mean. We can still hook up." She admired his tenacity, or ignorance, whichever one it was, that made him stand there and continue to try to talk to her.

"Sweetheart you are cute." Maya lied. "And if I had a little sister, I would hook you up with her. But I am old enough to be your mother. There is no way we can hook up. Okay?"

Senida walked up to the car with a puzzled look and let herself in on the passenger side.

"A'ight then," he said as he walked back to the jeep with his friend laughing at him.

"Hey girl!" Maya chimed out without looking at Senida. She pulled away from the curve and headed for the freeway. Senida could tell she was in a good mood and decided not to spoil her friends' spirit with sob stories of Darrell. She had hoped today would be a good day.

"What was that all about?" Senida scoffed, as she nodded toward the jeep.

"Girl, nothing. What happened to your lip, and your eye?" Maya had just turned her attention to her friend.

"Girl, don't ask. Who's car are you driving?" Senida questioned about the convertible BMW that they were riding in.

"It's Michael's." Maya yelled from the wind whipping through the top, as they entered Interstate 75/85 North headed to Lenox Mall. Maya was riding with the top down. Loose curls danced around her face. Her ponytail bounced and flipped from the oscillating movements of the air.

"Where's the Camry?"

"He's changing the oil for me."

"You mean, you got that man working for you on his days off...as *hard* as he works at his *real* job."

"He owes me big time. I haven't been putting up with Glenda for free."

"She's still bothering you guys?" Senida asked. "We ought to go over there and whoop that hoe's ass."

Maya laughed. She knew Senida talked a good game, but Senida couldn't bust a grape. Shit look at her eye, Maya thought.

Maya steered Michael's car towards the freeway and took the 10th/14th street exit. She had to drop off some of her artwork to one of her graphic artist friends at Turner's Broadcasting System. Maya drove through the security check and parked by the mansion.

"I'll be right back." She hopped out of the car and went around to the trunk. Carrying her portfolio, she winked at Senida as she briskly walked to the front of the building and disappeared.

Twenty minutes later, they were back on the road headed for Lenox Mall. Maya drove the car as if she was the owner. Senida laid her head back and closed her eyes. The sun warmed the top of her head. Sweat trickled down her back and she could feel her blouse starting to stick to her body. When they arrived at the mall, the place was crowded, but that didn't stop Maya from trying to take full advantage of her credit card. Senida did not purchase anything. She just enjoyed Maya's company and watched her shop for her California trip. On the way home, Maya seemed unusually quiet.

"What's up?" Senida inquired.

"Oh nothing." Maya looked straight ahead.

"Maya. Do I know you or what? It's me Senida," she said pointing to herself.

"Just thinking about my folks. Every year around this time, I get in this kinda mood."

"You're supposed to think about them. They were your parents. You're only human."

"I know. It's just that I miss them so much. Not only can I not see them anymore, but their graves are way in California."

"Yeah, but you'll get a chance to go by their graves when you go visit Aunt Setty."

"Yeah."

Maya turned the car into a gas station and handed Senida a ten-dollar bill. She then got out, waited for Senida to go pay at the window, and began pumping gas. When the two women were back on the road, Senida started again.

"Just keep their memory alive."

"I often wonder how my life would be had they not died. I feel bad because they were so young when the car accident happened. I think about them all the time."

"Well, Maya. You never truly grieved for your parents. Do you know that since the accident, I've never seen you cry."

"I guess my body and mind was in shock."

"For all of these years though?"

"I guess. It hurts like hell, even after this long, but...everybody deals with death differently."

"You know I'm here for you right? If you need anything don't hesitate."

"I know, thanks." Maya smiled. "Have you talked to your mother lately?"

"Just yesterday. She said Kevon came to visit them. They weren't too thrilled."

"Why?"

"Apparently he met someone that he's fallen in love with and is seriously thinking about marriage."

"But he's so young."

"Bingo."

"Your brother is too funny to me. Didn't he want to marry the last girl he was with?"

"Yeah, that's why my parents aren't taking him seriously. He's only twenty years old and he's been engaged at least three times. But he says this one is for real." Senida checked her make-up in the side view mirror. "Oh yeah, before I forget, my mother wants you to stop by when you get to California."

"Definitely. Speaking of marriage, is she still pestering you about getting married?"

"Not since I told her that me and Darrell got engaged."

Maya exited the freeway early and decided to take the street the rest of the way to Senida's apartment complex.

"So what are you going to do about your little young tender when you and Darrell get married?"

Senida shrugged her shoulders.

"Do you plan on keeping him?"

She shrugged again.

"Take it from me, marriage is nothing to play with. I wish I hadn't gotten involved with Michael."

"Yeah, but Michael was in a bad marriage and in the process of getting a divorce when you met him."

"Yeah and almost a year later? Is the divorce final?" Maya responded a little irritated.

"True." Senida thought about Maya's questions. "I don't know what I'm going to do. I figure I'll think about it when the time comes. For now I'm having fun."

"Just be careful."

"I will."

When Maya dropped Senida off at her apartment complex, she gave her a kiss on the cheek and a warm hug. Senida waved bye to Maya and went upstairs to prepare for Darrell's seminar. The first thing Senida did when she walked into her apartment was call her lover. She let the phone ring four times before she hung up. She couldn't help herself. That young boy has got me in a bad way, she thought. Then she thought about Maya's question. What *would* she do with him when she married Darrell?

NEW TERRITORY

The twenty or so passengers stood in the small cabin aisle waiting for the stewardess to open the door. Chattering rose from the crowd, filled with different conversations and laughter. Mandla reached over-head to retrieve his large, blue duffel bag. A small framed white woman slipped by him, leaving the seat empty. Mandla plopped down in the seat, still waiting for the line to move out of the plane. He gazed out of the window and saw the skycaps grabbing the passenger's suitcases from the conveyer belt and tossing them onto the waiting vehicles. He sighed. It was a short, but bumpy trip from Washington D.C. to Atlanta, but he had finally made it. Within the next few months, he would have to make some life altering decisions. Leaving behind mom and the girls was the hardest one yet.

Just a few hours earlier, the twins had tears in their eyes, trying their damnedest not to cry. But Mandla had seen his little sisters' tears. He even saw the tears in his mother's eyes as he boarded the plane in D.C. He couldn't even help but mist himself, as he sat straight up in the seat next to the small framed white woman who smiled and talked the entire ride.

Slowly, the crowd flowed forward and Mandla jumped from his seat to quickly get off of the stuffy plane. His head was pounding and he just wanted to meet Todd so he could go to his house and rest. Once off of the plane, Mandla could see Todd leaning against the opposite wall. He was talking to an attractive young woman, who seemed as if she'd just walked off the same plane as Mandla, but he didn't remember seeing her on his flight. Todd was thin like Mandla and just as tall. Todd's dark skin was flawless and his baldhead shone under the airport lights. Mandla watched Todd, as the young woman wrote her number on a piece of paper and walked off with her bag.

"Still pimpin', huh?" Mandla asked as he walked up beside Todd.

"Whaz up man? Yeah you know," he said as he lifted the piece of paper in his hand and shoved it into his pocket. "Baby was fine tho'. Said her and some friends was throwing a party tonight. You down?" he asked, grabbing Mandla, giving him the Kappa grip.

"That's cool, but I need to rest for a minute. I got this headache that's fucking with me."

"A'ight. That's cool. You better get all the rest you need today, 'cause tonight we gon' set it off like we used to do," Todd said as he began to laugh.

"Aw shit, brotha you a fool. So what's up for tonight?" They began walking toward the small inter-airport train that would take them to baggage claim.

"First, I thought we'd go see what baby was talking about, then we could hit Atlanta Live. Man, you should see the women in there. Mad ass everywhere! Then tomorrow, we could hit Magic City."

"Ah word? Yeah, that'll be cool," Mandla hit his right fist into his left palm.

"Man we gon' set it off!" Todd hollered. He grabbed Mandla's luggage and headed quickly to his jeep.

"Man this shit is phat!" Mandla whooped referring to Todd's jeep. They both slid into the seats.

Todd and Mandla laughed and made plans all the way to Todd's house, which was in an all black subdivision. The homes were one and two stories and lavish. Todd pulled into the driveway of a two-story home. Lightly decorated from the outside, the grass was cut short and neat. No flowers, but there were small shiny white rocks that outlined the small patch of lawn. Inside was large and moderately decorated with black couches, a large stereo system and television, Sega, and a coffee table in the middle.

"Damn, brah, you the man. Shit, how can I be down?" Mandla smiled. He was glad to see his friends successful. Todd was one of the many who everyone knew would land a good job. Although he loved to party, when it was time to get down to business, Todd was the man.

"Maybe I should have majored in computers too. IBM must be treating you real good." Mandla continued.

"Shit, you the big time gonna-be lawyer. You gon' be the next fuckin' Johnnie Cochran. Hell, with the luck I'm having with women, I'ma need you *soon*." Todd laughed. "Have a seat man, I'ma take these things up to the guest room." Todd slipped up the stairs with Mandla's luggage.

Mandla eased onto the large cushioned sofa and kicked off his shoes. He was beginning to feel a little better about Atlanta. If Todd could make a nice living, then he should have no problems. Mandla reached for the remote control and flicked on the television. Todd trotted downstairs, plopped onto the couch, and went straight into the question session.

"What's up with Howard?" Todd slouched down into the thick sofa cushions.

"Man, same ole' Howard University. Same ole' shit."

"Word? You ever see...uh what's that girls name that used to try to hang around with the football team?"

"Uh Raylene? She still going to school there."

"Still fuckin' everybody?"

"Yeah."

"Damn. Wish I was there." Todd chuckled. "Same ole' Howard."

"Ain't nothing changed." Mandla flipped through channels.

"So what's up with this internship?"

"Man, once I'm finished with this, I'ma take the LSAT's and try my luck in getting into law school."

"Is the shit phat?"

"Yeah. The shit gon' give me mad experience, so when I get ready to apply for some real jobs..." Mandla smiled and nodded his head.

"So what's up with Atlanta?" Todd smiled wide. "If you move here, we could turn Atlanta out!"

"I don't know. We'll see," Mandla chuckled. "I'll either stay here and go to Georgia State Law or head back to D.C. You know I can't stay too far from moms and the girls."

"How is moms?"

"Cool. She be asking 'bout you all the time. I don't know why she love your ass."

"Baby, cause I'm from the South. And women love Southern men. I'm po-lite when I'm in the presence of a real woman."

"You could have fooled me," Mandla grinned as he leaned back into the large cushions.

"Hey," Todd replied. "I *do* have respect for *real* women."

"I don't think you attract real women." Mandla laughed.

Todd did not respond. He just smiled.

"What's up with the women out here anyway?" Mandla continued.

"Shit. Fine as hell. You'll see tonight when we go out. I'ma show you a good ass time. After tonight, baby boy…you gon' want to move to this bitch." Todd smiled, showing his wonderful row of incredibly white, straight teeth. In the darkness of the den Todd's teeth were about the only features that Mandla could see. Todd's deep dark skin faded into the background. Fade to black!

"Terrance called me last week…"

"Collect?" Todd asked.

"Yeah."

"That nigga still in jail?"

"Hell yeah. He got another two years before he get out."

"Crazy fool. Didn't nobody tell him to try to rob a liquor sto'. Hell what the fuck was he trying to get anyway? Some Hen dawg? Them mothafuckin' Arabs don't keep no money up in that store. I coulda told him that."

Mandla laughed hard. He was used to Todd's in-your-face humor. It was the one characteristic about Todd that you had to like.

After an hour of talking passed, Mandla and Todd played Sega and watched a couple of hours of television. Mandla eventually went upstairs to shower, rest and wait for later that night. Todd leaned back on his couch, kicked his feet up on the table and began making calls to "hook it up" for later that night.

Todd's body glistened as he stepped from the shower. Mandla was dressing in the guestroom and singing louder than the radio. Todd smiled and began to dry off and lotion himself. He was glad his friend was in town. He would be even happier if he decided to move to Atlanta permanently. He smoothed at his white shirt and reached for one of his T-shirts. He vowed he would show Mandla a good time. A few good drinks and an abundance of fine women should convince Mandla to move to Atlanta, it had convinced him.

Todd walked into his bathroom and splashed on a few fingertips full of Tommy Hilfiger cologne. He wanted to smell good for the women at the club. He enjoyed how they would stand real close to him, sniffing his neck. His dark skin would gleam and his baldhead would shine. Todd not only looked good, but he was a charmer *and* he was smart. He made his own money and even bought his own house.

All his life, growing up poor, Todd had decided early that he would be among the ones to go to college. Working hard at academics and athletics, Todd won a football scholarship that paid his way through four years of college-until he got hurt. A knee injury, the worst kind. One that still made him wince if he stepped down wrong or pushed his body too hard. One that the doctors said would never allow him to play again. But he was one of the smart ones. He knew computers would be a hit. So he practiced hard *and* studied hard. Working for IBM had been a dream come true for Todd. At IBM he had produced more money than he'd ever seen. More money than anyone in his neighborhood had ever seen.

Todd finished dressing and went downstairs to open the bottle of Korbel he'd bought for him and Mandla, who was still in the guest bedroom dressing. Todd broke ice-cubes and pulled down two glasses. He was looking forward to getting out into Atlanta's nightlife. It had been a little while since he'd perused the streets. Maybe he would see some of his old friends.

Mandla felt good and he smelled good. He winked his gray eyes at himself in the mirror and turned to the side to get a better look at himself.

"Damn you's a fine ass brotha," he said, as he buttoned up his shirt and tucked it into his pants. "Women betta' watch out tonight!"

Mandla stood glaring into the mirror smoothing his goatee with his right hand. He'd just gotten a cut and a shave before he left D.C. His deep-set gray eyes complimented his honey brown skin tone. Mandla ran his palms across his wavy hair. His good looks and charming smile attracted a plethora of women. But most importantly, his audacious personality usually put him over the top. He smoothed at his shirt and stepped into his shoes. From where he stood, he could hear Todd in the kitchen and then in the living room, turning on the C.D. player. Minute's later, "All Eyes on Me," blared through the house. Mandla's Snoop Doggie Dog was no match for the loud speakers downstairs, so he turned his portable radio off and headed downstairs to get ready for his night on the town. Who knew, he might even decide to move to Atlanta. Mandla could not wait to taste a little of Atlanta's nightlife. He'd heard so much from his other friends that he could hardly contain himself.

"Damn boy, what you trying to do to the ladies tonight?" Todd laughed as Mandla glided down the stairs.

"The same thang you been doing to them since you been here," Mandla responded, as he took the extra glass of Korbel from the counter and threw it down his throat. He squinted and shook his head vigorously. The alcohol stung going down and he had to let out a small breath.

"Potna. You can't do nearly as much damage as I have in Atlanta." Todd was slowly sipping from his glass. He was leaning against the counter. His baldhead was shining and his dark outfit made his skin color more apparent. He was a handsome man. Women knew he was, but his attitude about women was cold. He thought of many of them as bitches and hoes, and was only out to get as much as he could from them. Todd had many women hating him and taking time out of their busy schedules to get revenge on him, one way or another.

"Don't playa hate," Mandla responded, as he poured himself another glass of Korbel.

The two men, stood drinking and listening to music until the bottle of Korbel was depleted. They stumbled into Todd's jeep and headed to the party first, then to the club; Atlanta Live to be exact. Their night was to be filled with one of the wildest parties around. Mandla was buzzing from the Korbel, but Todd assured him that they had just begun.

*****

Senida watched the clock intently. Ever so often, she would smile at Darrell and nod in the direction of the boring political science speaker. Why did she let Darrell drag her to these ghastly events? The only people who really went were the show offs and the wanna be's. Senida scanned the audience, watching the other people. Many of them were attentive and taking notes. Others sipped coffee and nibbled on the fruit and cheese that was offered on a tray near the entrance.

Most of the audience were students, friends of students, and mates of students. Darrell had become comfortable with the lectures and enjoyed the many speakers at the events. If only she could fake sick. Or even if she could just tell Darrell how much she hated these events, without hurting his feelings. He looked so proud to be a part of the function. Senida tried to look as interested as possible, without constantly looking at the clock. Each time she concentrated on how much time had passed, Mrs. Livingston would interrupt her thoughts.

"So how's the family doing?"

"Everyone's fine." Senida smiled her most fake smile. Why couldn't this lady leave her alone? She already didn't want to be there.

"That's fine dear. And how's the law business?"

"Fine."

"Good. And when's the wedding?"

"We haven't set a date," Senida replied, rolling her eyes. She hated when people asked her about her wedding date.

"Well, I was just talking to James last night and he told me..."

"How is Dr. Livingston doing?" Senida interrupted, throwing Mrs. Livingston off guard. "I mean how is his health?"

"Oh he's feeling much better. Ever since the operation he's been doing great."

"That's good. I love this speaker. Have you ever heard her speak before?" Senida said, as she turned her chair in the direction of the speaker. She was trying to hint to Mrs. Livingston to shut up.

"No. I can't say that I have ever heard her speak."

"Oh she's good. Just listen to what she's saying. It's so much more interesting than the other speakers," Senida focused her attention on the speaker and tried to think of a way to get away from the woman. Mrs. Livingston took the hint and focused her attention on the speaker for a minute. Once Mrs. Livingston had heard enough, she focused her attention back on Senida.

Mrs. Livingston was the wife of one of Darrell's favorite professor. She was close to twenty years older than Darrell and Senida, but was convinced that she could "swing" with the youngest of them. Dr. James Livingston and Alice Livingston were married for thirty wonderful years. They raised three lovely children and had numerous dogs. Mrs. Livingston would tell the story of how she and her husband were the envy of their neighborhood. Both possessed fair complexions and wavy hair.

Dr. Livingston had a pair of light green eyes that "drove those other women wild," as Mrs. Livingston would say. But nobody was a match for her, she would continue. She wore her thick, wavy ponytail down the middle of her back, with one big bow half way down the braid. "I didn't even have to press my hair. The other little Black girls would pull my hair and call me names because I was prettier than they were."

Back in those days, their appearances were considered the epitome of beauty, grace, and wealth. Mrs. Livingston felt as though the standards were still intact. Senida hated to sit and talk to the older woman. She did not understand why a woman that was supposed to have such high standards could be so ignorant. Most of the time during the seminars Senida would block out the woman only listening for breaks in the woman's voice, nodding, and smiling when appropriate.

Dr. Livingston was the total opposite of his wife. He did not talk to you unless it was absolutely necessary. In fact, the only person Senida ever saw him talk to was Darrell. That was also the only time she'd seen him smile. They were like two peas in a pod. Mrs. Livingston would do the majority of the talking when they would be introduced or attended any of the functions or gatherings. She would run her mouth until Dr. Livingston would shoot her a warning look. Then she would trot off somewhere, to pounce on some unsuspecting person and bore them with her stories of "back in the day," or "how wonderful her children turned out" or "that her daughter was so beautiful because they mixed the right amount of blackness" or "how her modeling career was really taking off, because nobody had seen such a beautiful girl with light green eyes before," and blah blah blah. She could wear a hole in your ear in one sitting.

Mrs. Livingston looked forward to Senida and Darrell attending the lectures and seminars. Senida was usually the only person silly enough to sit and listen to the woman. She smiled at Mrs. Livingston and excused herself to go to the restroom. She quickly got up from the table to avoid Mrs. Livingston trying to follow her.

The loud clanking of her heels echoed Senida's fast steps down the hall. Instead of taking the right at the end of the hall to get to the restroom, Senida took a left and went out onto the balcony. Georgia's magnificent scenery astounded her. The multicolored environment was enough to take her breath away. Heat rose from the streets below. There was a quiet hum to the lifestyles that carried out daily routines. She leaned forward onto the railing and took in a deep breath. It smelled like rain. If she looked hard enough she could see the clouds that were starting to form in the sky. Georgia weather. Senida didn't think she would ever get used to it. But how beautiful the land of Georgia was.

There was so much green out there. Senida wished she could stay on the balcony until the seminar was over, but that would be hours from now. And Mrs. Livingston...if she had to listen to one more of her ridiculous stories, she would scream. Senida realized why Dr. Livingston never said anything...he didn't have a chance. Mrs. Livingston could talk! For all the suffering that she was going through now, she should make Darrell take her somewhere special. She did want to try the bed and breakfast that Cindy talked about at work. Maybe she could talk him into taking a couple of days off and spending them with her and only her. No seminars, no banquets, no papers, no computers, no nothing. Just her. How hard would that be to get Darrell to take a few days off? Probably impossible.

"Looks like it's going to rain," a white man stepped onto the balcony and scared the living day lights out of Senida.

"Yeah, it sure does." She smiled

"You must be in that boring seminar," he said with a chuckle and a once over of Senida's outfit. His thick, white beard touched the top of his suit tie. His beady, blue eyes narrowed as he concentrated on Senida's reaction to his statement.

"Yeah. How about you?"

"Yeah. My wife is the speaker." He smiled and chuckled again.

"Oh. Well I'm sure she's a great speaker...it's just that the..."

"You don't need to lie sweetheart. I've been to enough seminars in my marriage to know that they're boring."

He struck a match and lit his cigar. Glancing quickly at his watch, he flicked the used match over the balcony. Senida continued to look out into the sky at the colors. The sun was beginning to set. Orange and yellow overcast of the sun glowed and made Atlanta look like heaven on earth. She could smell the cigar that the man sucked on beside her. He puffed like an old train. He was staring off into the sunset as well. Probably wishing he wasn't here either, Senida thought. She could see his wrinkled forehead from the side. He must have been at least fifty years old. She hoped she wouldn't be that old, still confined to attending these events.

"Well I better get back in there. I don't want to miss your wife speaking." Senida smiled as she brushed past the old man sniffing his cigar scent. He grunted and continued to puff on the nasty smelling cigar.

Darrell sat unmoved. He was still listening attentively, periodically whispering back and forth to Dr. Livingston. The audience peered at the speaker who rambled on about cost effectiveness. Mrs. Livingston was leaning across the table talking to a young woman, who had an uninterested look on her face. Good, Senida thought, she's found her another victim.

Darrell winked at Senida as she took her seat next to motor mouth. The seminar lasted for another two hours and the crowd was dismissed. Darrell wanted to stay behind and talk to the speaker and the other colleagues who lagged behind, but Senida faked a headache and asked to be taken home immediately. Darrell shot Senida a sideways look, but obliged to her request. Senida wanted quality time alone with Darrell, and she sure in hell was not going to get it by standing around talking to the political science people.

The car ride home may as well have been another seminar, because that's all that Darrell talked about. Senida gazed out of the passenger window, watching cars drive by. Interstate 285 was usually dark; there were no streetlights. Tomorrow would be full of paper work that she'd brought home. Lord, Senida thought, please let tonight be satisfactory.

"Are you okay?" Darrell asked, as he pressed the back of his hand to her forehead.

"Yeah, I took some Excedrin before we left the hotel."

"That eye is starting to look a little better too."

Darrell continued to drive oblivious to Senida's gazing.

"Darrell?" Senida sighed.

"Humm."

"I talked to my mother today. She said that they were going on a cruise to Jamaica."

"Mmmm. That's nice. They deserve to go. They've worked hard all of their lives." Darrell did not look at Senida as he exited from the freeway.

"I was thinking...wouldn't it be nice if we could go on a trip somewhere?"

"Yeah that would be nice," he said turning to smile at her. His glasses reflected on-coming headlights.

"So when do you think we would be able to go on something like that?"

"When we're their age," he commented and erupted in laughter. He laughed long and hard until he noticed that he was the only one in the car laughing. Senida twisted her face and squinted her eyes.

"That's not funny, Darrell. When can we go on a trip? Everyone has gone on an excursion but us. Maya just got back from the Bahamas last year, and Tammy just left for Hawaii last week."

"Good for them. But they don't own their own consulting business. I have to work around the clock...even when I'm at home. Plus, how am I going to take time off? I still got to work on my exit paper." Darrell frowned and focused his attention on the road.

Senida did not speak for the remainder of the ride. Darrell periodically glanced at her. He was drained from her constant whining. She never seemed satisfied with his accomplishments. Darrell turned his silver SAAB into Senida's complex and parked in the visitor's space. He walked her to her apartment door and kissed her lightly on the forehead. Dim lights caste a shadow of Darrell's large body behind Senida as he hugged her.

"I'll call you tomorrow," she said as she started into the apartment.

"Call me tomorrow? I take it you don't want me to come in?" Darrell responded, slightly irritated.

"Well Darrell. I do have a headache and you know how I get when my head hurts." Senida shifted from one foot to the other. She really was not in the mood to deal with Darrell and his problem tonight. She needed a sure-fire stress reliever, not a sure fire stress causer.

"That's never stopped me before from spending the night."

"Darrell..."

"What? I don't know why you're bullshitting Senida. You've been acting funny for the last few months. I haven't said anything about it before because I thought you were just stressed about this upcoming trial. But I'm getting tired of this bullshit." Darrell's voice rose and Senida looked around to see if anyone was in the hallway.

"Could you lower your voice?"

"Hell no I can't lower my voice!"

Senida pushed the door open and motioned for Darrell to follow. He did. Once inside, Darrell let go of all of his pinned up frustration.

"You've been inconsiderate and ungrateful. I can't take time off. You just don't seem to understand that. I'm tired of repeating this to you, like you're a little child!"

"I'm just tired of sitting around bored!"

"How are you bored? You got one of the most important cases of your career coming up. Don't you think you need to be preparing for that?"

"I am, but I want to go somewhere. I'm ready for a vacation."

"Hell, people in hell want ice-water Senida. When it's time for you to take a vacation then you'll take it. Obviously it's not time yet. You need to really sit down and get your priorities straight."

"I *have* my priorities straight!"

"No you don't! You're a grown ass woman. Start acting like one. You need to concentrate on Mr. Mortin's case. And on getting your life together. At least for us. In less than a year, we're supposed to start making wedding plans and you're still too busy running around with Maya. Get your shit straight Senida. You'll get your vacation in due time."

"And when the hell will that be?"

"Senida, I'm tired of arguing with you over something so trivial. Lately you've been acting like a little spoiled bitch!"

"How dare you call me a bitch!" Senida yelled.

"I said you've been acting like one! And I'm tired of it! You need to make up your mind what you want Senida. Do you want a man or do you want some little boy that's going to do whatever the hell you want? 'Cause I've just about had it with your ways. It's time for you to *grow up*. Keep on acting a fool. You gon' look around and find me gone."

"So what are you saying Darrell? Are you leaving me? 'Cause if you are, good! Do you think you're the only one tired? Well I'm tired too. I'm tired of your selfishness. I'm tired of your cheap ass. And most importantly, I'm tired of not being satisfied..."

Senida stopped. Darrell's face went from angry to hurt. Senida wished she could have eaten those last few words, but they slipped out too fast for even her. Darrell sat down on the couch. He looked defeated. His large shoulders hunched over. Senida sat down next to him and tried to put her arms around his shoulders, but he pulled away from her. She felt bad.

"Is that what all this shit is about?"

"Baby...I didn't mean to..."

"Nah you meant it. Don't apologize...if you didn't mean it, you wouldn't have said it."

"But I didn't mean...."

"So you're not satisfied? That's what this is all about. I don't need this shit. I've given you too much. And now you want to bring my personal problems up. You want to insult my manhood. I can't believe this shit."

"Well sweetie you can always go to the doctor or something..." Senida started.

"Fuck a doctor!" Darrell jumped up from the couch. He was tired of her bringing his problem up in every argument they had. "And fuck you! Every time we have an argument, you bring that up. That's not something you do to someone you supposedly love. I can't believe that you even had the balls to suggest that shit." Darrell stood abruptly and stormed out of Senida's front door.

Senida sat perplexed for awhile. She couldn't believe that those words came out of Darrell's mouth. Her eyes began to mist and she cried. She rolled over on the couch, balled her knees to her chest and cried. She laid there for a couple of hours, thinking.

The night seemed to drag on forever. Senida tossed and turned throughout the night, still not sexually satisfied. She looked over at the clock, which read four thirty-seven. She picked up the phone and dialed the number. Automatically he was on the phone.

"You sound wide awake." She sighed sleepily into the phone.

"I just walked in the door." He replied.

"Where have you been?"

"I went out with some friends, why? Your man didn't satisfy you tonight?" He asked, chuckling.

"No. Can I come over?" She whined.

"Yeah, but you need to be quiet, 'cause I got out of town company. I'll leave the keys in their usual spot and you just come straight in and up to my room."

"Okay. Let me take a shower and then I'll be on my way."

"Yeah," he said, as he hung up the phone.

Senida hung up the phone and instantly felt relieved. She usually felt as though she had a snack. She could barely contain her excitement. She quickly showered, dressed, and headed out for her meal.

HOT, SWEATY, RELATIONS

Black was Maya's favorite color. Not only did she think that the color was bold, strong, and beautiful, but it was a reminder of her people and their struggle, her struggle. Black represented strength in her will and her heart. She could remember the color in her mother's face and the color in her father's eyes. Most people thought black to be morbid, but Maya's energy seemed to emanate from the color.

Today, Maya wore black because she was feeling good; it made her look slim and fit. The black hip huggers and black shirt, with only one button in the middle, exposing her navel, was Michael's favorite outfit. Maya wore it because she felt that Michael had good news for her about Glenda. Her tall, high-heeled sandals were complimenting her perfectly painted, red toenails and her right ankle was adorned with a tiny silver anklet. She'd worn her hair down and curly, just how he liked it.

All throughout Michael's marriage Maya stood by his side, first as a friend and then as a lover. Michael's stories of how crazy his wife was and how he'd made a major mistake in his life by marrying her would melt Maya's heart. She could feel his pain and she fell for the old okie-doke. It was Michael who eventually filed for divorce after Glenda slashed his tires, broke out the windows in his house, and burned his clothes. But, it was Glenda who found the woman's underwear and lipstick in the wastebasket in their home before she went into action.

Barnes and Nobles intrigued Maya. Nothing could get her

in a better mood than to finish a good book. When Michael suggested that they meet there, she became ecstatic. Maya walked into the bookstore in Buckhead and scoped out the crowd. Large groups of people sat and talked in whispered hushes, discussing books and jotting words down on notepads. Michael was sitting at the Starbucks cafe, sipping from a styrofoam cup of hot cappuccino mocha. He was easy to spot. His bright yellow complexion contrasted starkly with the dark blue shirt he wore. His glasses perched on the tip of his nose and encircled his dazzling eyes. Michael was absorbed in Walter Mosley's, *Gone Fishin'*.

Maya did not have to say anything to get Michael's attention. When she walked up behind him, he recognized her perfume. Her familiar smell had permeated his nostrils on many a nights. Maya's smell instantly turned Michael on. She was much sweeter than Glenda, much smoother, and much more feminine.

Michael knew that he married Glenda for all the wrong reasons. She was considered one of the prettiest women at his college. Her family had money, she drove an expensive car and all of his buddies stood in line, just to get some attention from Glenda. And when she found out that Michael was the star of the football team and smart to boot, Glenda was just as taken by him as he was of her. She'd also caught wind that he was a prime candidate for medical school. Glenda had her eyes on getting her M.R.S. degree *along* with her BA degree.

Michael turned just as Maya tried to cover his eyes and play peek-a-boo. Her smile was wide and she bent to give him a kiss on his cheek. Maya walked over to the counter and ordered herself a regular size mocha. She paid the young girl and sat down across from Michael. He did not look up from his book. Maya cleared her throat and Michael put the book down. Maya took a few sips from her mocha while watching Michael. He did not smile.

"You look nice today," he said to her.

"Thanks. You look nice too." She smiled and he smiled back.

"So?" Maya asked as she sat her cup on the table.

"Glenda refuses to sign the papers." His face did not change.

Maya sat back in the chair. Heat began to rise in her body.

She could feel herself ready to explode!

"So what does that mean?" Maya asked, agitated. She'd been hanging in there with Michael for almost a year and now he was telling her *this* bullshit.

"It means that we're still married."

"And?"

"And there is really nothing I can do right now."

"What do you mean, nothing you can do? Michael what the hell are you trying to tell me?" Maya yelled.

Michael looked around the little shop to see if anyone was listening. He leaned close to Maya.

"Could you please keep your voice down. She told the judge and her lawyer that she wants to give our marriage another try," he whispered.

"And what do you say, Michael?"

"Well, I really thought about it and if I get a divorce, then I'd have to give her half of my hard earned money."

"So?"

"So? Maya do you know how hard I've worked to get to the financial status where I am now? Hard. Damn hard."

"And just how hard do you think it's been for me to hang in there with our relationship? Damn hard too, Michael."

"I understand it's been hard..."

"No I really don't think you understand. I've given up morals to be with you. Never in a thousand years would I have ever thought that I would mess with a...", Maya looked around and tried to whisper through clenched teeth, "...a married man. Never!"

"Baby, I'm sorry. I know this has been hard on you. But Maya you got to know that I care."

"So what are you going to do now?"

"I've been thinking..."

"*What are you going to do Michael?*"

"I think I'm going to give it another try," he said.

"I can't believe you're telling me this." Maya felt tears welling up in her eyes. "What about me, what about us? All that damn time I invested in us."

"Things don't really have to change between us."

"You bastard! Things *can't* be the same, Michael. I thought we were working on *us*. What about *us*? Why would you stay in a situation if you're not happy?"

"Only because she wants to work it out for the baby."

"The baby? What baby?"

"Glenda is pregnant." Maya's mouth flew open. She jumped up from the table and slapped Michael across his face. A loud sound echoed through the building. A red hand mark rose quickly across Michael's left cheek. Tears were streaming down Maya's face. The bookstore became silent. People in Barnes and Nobles started staring at them. Michael grabbed her to calm her.

"Maya please calm down," Michael said rubbing the side of his face and pulling Maya back down into her seat. "I don't even know if it's mine. Glenda has done this before. She's tried to pin pregnancies on me and I found out that she wasn't even pregnant. I *need* you right now. I need you to trust in me and know that things are going to work out."

"How am I supposed to do that Michael when you are talking about giving your marriage another chance." Maya pulled her arm away from him.

"I'm only doing this for my investment. My money. Glenda doesn't want to be married to me. She just doesn't want to see me with anyone else. She'll play the game until I give in. But I have news for her this time. I'm going to play her game. If I seem like I'm attempting to give it a try, then she'll eventually back down. But I need you to believe in me," he said as he reached to caress her hand.

"How can I trust you? How can I believe that?" Maya pulled her hand away from his reach.

"Because you know that I love you. You know that Glenda is crazy. Baby, she's been trying to break us up ever since she found out about us."

"I don't know Michael. It's been almost a year. I've been there for you during this whole ordeal..."

"I know baby. And you will get your reward, I promise," Michael interrupted.

Maya thought for a moment. She looked into Michael's eyes. He seemed sincere, but Maya was tired of being the other woman. She needed someone to want her and only her. Michael stood and hugged Maya while she still sat in the chair. She could feel his heart beating against her eardrum. Maya could feel her emotions melt as Michael rubbed his hands up and down her back.

The drive from Barnes and Nobles was quick. Michael and Maya parked their cars in Michael's garage. Maya slipped out of her Camry and Michael slid out of his BMW. He walked around to her, put his arms around her back and pulled her closer to him.

"We're going to work this out, you and I. I know it's been rough, but I need you to hang in there with me, like I did for you."

Maya took in a long, deep breath. Whenever he wanted her to wait for him, he would bring up the time when her ex-boyfriend wanted to marry her. Michael waited for Maya to make her decision, and when she turned the other guy down, he continued to love her. This was how he kept her hanging in there with him, by making her feel guilty.

"That's not fair Michael."

"Baby, I need you now. I'm just asking that you support me the way I supported you. You know I care about you right?" He pushed his glasses up on the bridge of his nose.

"But I...," she began.

"Shhh." He put his finger to her mouth. "Okay? I need you."

Maya nodded. Michael kissed her on the mouth and unlocked the door to his house. Once inside, Michael went to the kitchen, washed his hands and pulled two wineglasses from the cabinet. He turned and smiled at Maya. She knew this meant to get the wine out of the refrigerator. Maya poured a glass of red wine for Michael and then for herself. She followed him into the den and kicked off her shoes. They both sat on the floor, in front of the couch and watched television until the entire bottle of wine was gone.

"You know that you owe me?" Maya slurred. Her head spun and her vision became blurry.

"How do I owe you?" Michael smiled at Maya. He knew that she was buzzing.

"I've been dealing with Glenda for quite some time now."

"*You've* been dealing with Glenda?"

"Yes!"

"I think I've been dealing with her crazy ass a little more than you have."

"Hell, that's because you're the one who said 'I do'."

Michael chuckled. He found Maya quite amusing when she'd been drinking.

"So you owe me!" she practically yelled.

"Okay. I do." Michael stood to get another bottle of wine from the kitchen.

"See that's what got you into this mess in the first place!"

"What?" he asked. Michael picked up the empty bottle and glasses.

"I do. Saying 'I do'. That's what got you into trouble."

"I wouldn't call it trouble." Michael looked at her, glasses and bottle still in his hand. Maya gave him a strange glance and rolled her eyes.

"Okay." He continued. "Maybe a little. But you know why I married her?"

"Because sometimes Michael, I think you're just as crazy as Glenda."

Michael walked into the kitchen without responding. He grabbed another bottle of wine. Michael reached in the back of his refrigerator and pulled out fresh strawberries. He washed the strawberries and plopped one in each glass. On top of the strawberries, he poured a generous supply of wine. Effervescent bubbles floated to the top of the glass and covered the fruit.

"Oooh baller baller!" Maya giggled as Michael handed her a glass.

"You like that?" he asked referring to the strawberry.

"Uh huh."

"You look so damn good today." Michael swallowed almost half of his wine in one gulp.

"Thanks." Maya sipped her wine.

"I thought I was going to pass out when you walked into Barnes and Nobles. With your belly button all showing." He touched her lightly on her stomach and caressed her waistline with his fingers.

"How 'bout now?"

"I *still* might pass out." He kissed her, forcing his tongue in and out of her mouth.

"Uhmmm." Maya pulled away from him. "I gotta use the commode." She jumped up quickly and ran to the restroom.

When she returned, Michael had finished his wine and was working on her glass.

"Don't keep me waiting." Michael motioned for Maya to come close. He was smiling.

Maya switched over to Michael and kissed him feverishly. Michael began peeling off her clothes one-by-one. He was trying to find as much skin as he possibly could. Maya kissed Michael as if she needed him for the very air that she breathed. He responded to her lead. He threw her clothes onto the couch and continued the descent into Maya's body.

"Ohh yes! Yes Michael, yes!"

"Ooooh girl. Shit you feel good. Whose is it, huh? Whose is it?"

"Baby it's yours if you want it." Maya liked playing sex games with Michael.

"Yeah? It's mine?" he asked as he began to pump faster. Maya's legs wrapped around his firm slim waist.

"Yeah baby. It's yours Michael."

"Do you love me? Huh Maya? Do you love me baby?" Michael rotated his hips and thrust them deeper into Maya.

Did she love him? She cared a whole hell-of-a-lot for him but did she *love* him? Maya listened to Michael as he moaned and groaned. He asked her again and the question bounced around in her head. She didn't answer him.

*****

Mandla yawned and stretched but the pain in his head made him wince. His mouth was dry and grimy. The sun spilled in through the window and lit up the small guest bedroom. Mandla's whole body felt numb as he swung his legs over the side of the bed and leaned over, letting his head fall into his hands. He sat there for a few minutes until he felt movement in the bed beside him.

He turned slowly, as if to not stir his head anymore than it already had. A large lump was snuggled in a ball in the middle of the bed. Mandla slowly pulled the covers back and revealed a beautiful young woman. He rubbed his chin with his hand and frowned. He'd never seen the woman before in his life. He tried to remember how she got in his bed.

Mandla looked around the room and noticed three condom wrappers strung on the floor. There were clothes laying over the bed and empty bottles of Dom Perigon on the dresser. The party. All he could remember was the party. They went, he and Todd, to the party and then to the club with the girls from the party. He looked back over at the bed. But this woman was not one of the girls from the party *or* the club. He would have remembered her; she was a dark, creamy color, with long hair. He leaned over her side of the bed and nudged her with his palms. She did not stir. He pushed harder and she rolled from her right side to her left side, but she still did not wake up. Mandla ran his palm across the top of his head and hung his head. His eyes were squeezed tight. He leaned back over the woman and pushed her hard in her back. She jumped and her eyes popped open, as she began scrambling, trying to cover her naked breasts that had fallen out when she jumped. Her eyes were red and swollen. Mandla could smell stale alcohol on her breath when she yawned.

"Oh. Hi Mandla. Are you feeling better this morning?" she asked as she lay back down on the bed. Mandla narrowed his eyes into dangerous slits.

"Who the hell are you?" Mandla asked, irritated that this woman knew his name, but he couldn't figure out who the hell *she* was.

"Oh, so I give you a little sugar and now you don't know who I am, huh?" She smiled an evil, seductive smile. Her eyes were almond shaped and bright. They shone despite their redness.

"What the fuck are you talking about? I don't know you. How the hell did you get in my bed and where did you come from?" Mandla was now standing at the foot of the bed.

"Sweetie, calm down. You don't remember me from the club last night? You damn near spent your entire paycheck on me." She leaned up exposing her breasts and swung her legs over the side of the bed.

Obviously not ashamed of being nude, she padded her way into the bathroom. Mandla could see one tattoo on the right side of her butt, which read "shuga" in script and had a sugar cane behind the letters. He sat back down on the bed and rubbed his hands over his face. He could not remember the woman. It was probably some trick that Todd was playing on him. Todd was good for playing practical jokes on people.

Mandla heard the water in the sink running. He stooped on the floor and searched for his pants. Once he found them, he pulled out his wallet and looked inside. There were some bills missing, but he didn't know how much.

"You don't mind if I take a quick shower, do you?" the woman asked, poking her head around the bathroom door.

"Uh, nah."

She closed the bathroom door and shortly, Mandla heard the shower water. He reached in the closet and pulled on some sweat pants, put his wallet in the pockets and walked out of the bedroom. Mandla pushed the door to Todd's room, but it was locked. He banged hard on the solid door with his fist, until Todd opened it just a crack.

"What the hell?" Todd asked, as he squinted at Mandla.

"Man, who is that girl in my room?"

Todd smiled, crept out of his room and quickly closed the door behind him. He stood in the hallway, in front of Mandla, with yellow, leopard skin print underwear on. Mandla looked down and raised his eyebrows. Todd shrugged.

"Man, don't act like you ain't got none," he responded.

"Potna. Who is that girl in my room?" Mandla asked again.

"Man, you don't remember? That's one of the strippers from Magic City. Man you was all in her ass last night, now you can't remember her?" He laughed.

Mandla vaguely remembered the young woman. Most of the night before was a blur. His head pounded. He had promised himself the last time that he wouldn't get himself into these types of situations anymore.

He couldn't look at the face of another woman for months, almost a year, when he made Chandra get an abortion three years ago. She'd cried for weeks, until Mandla drove her to the clinic himself to make sure that the procedure would be performed. And after the abortion, Chandra never looked the same. Her eyes became vacant and hallow. Her voice had lost its shine, and her walk lost its bounce. She no longer smiled, at anything. She didn't go back to school or work. Shame too, because Chandra was a beautiful, young woman with a promising future. She'd won a scholarship to Howard University to study pre-law. She was homecoming queen at their high school and on the cheerleading squad. Most everyone liked her.

And almost everyone told her not to mess around with

Mandla. He was too wild and would break her heart, they would say. But Mandla was not worried about her heart, he was young and injected full of hormones, he only cared about what was in her pants or up under her skirt.

Mandla hadn't really noticed Chandra until that summer when he'd talked her into going behind the tree, behind the house, up under the bridge, or in her parent's room when they were at work, or anywhere he could talk her into going. And he really didn't have feelings for her, until after he'd brought her home from the clinic. He thought they might have made a mistake and removed her soul instead of removing a baby. Her spirit was lost and left behind, when they drove away in the car. Chandra had lost her spirit in the clinic and never went back to find it. Mandla would try to talk to her and assure her that it was for the best. He wasn't ready to be a father and she knew it, he would say. But she would just stare through him, as if he weren't there.

Months went by and Chandra did not return to school. Many of the women at Howard ostracized him, once they'd caught word of what happened over the summer break. He became more of an outcast when Todd came to his Law and Government class to tell him that Chandra had shot herself.

Chandra sat at her mother's dining table, writing notes to her mother and father, best friend, and Mandla. She sealed each one with a kiss and tear, and hand delivered them to the places where they would be able to get them. She left her parents note on their bed. Tonya, her best friend, would have to get her letter in the mail. Mandla would have to get his from his dear, old, sweet unsuspecting grandmother.

She then borrowed her father's revolver and walked into the garage. She didn't want her mother to have to clean any blood from her carpet. Blood was hard to get out of carpet and her mother worked hard enough. So she went into the garage, so her father would only have to wash the blood away with the water hose, like he did when the dog peed on the cement floor. Just wash it away with the water hose. Chandra stood in the middle of the garage and looked around her. She put the gun to her head and prayed. Click!

Mandla didn't read the note immediately. He knew why

she killed herself, because of the baby. He knew the moment Todd told him. The pit of his stomach swirled and turned inside out. He threw up right on Todd's shoes and had to steady himself on the nearest wall. He didn't want to go to the funeral. So he didn't. He didn't go. He couldn't face the pain on her parents' faces. They never knew about the baby but he was sure they would know by now. He stayed away for almost two years. He didn't hang out like he was accustomed to hanging out. He studied hard. He vowed he would be more careful when it came to other people's lives. And two years later, when he finally had the courage to read the letter that he'd tucked under his mattress; he actually fainted, blacked out.

Dear Mandla:
    If I've completed my mission, then I'm gone by now. But I wanted to tell you how I felt before I left this place. You were the first guy that I've really cared about. I loved you. And I'm sorry that you could not love me the way that I loved you. But you stole something away from me, when you forced me to get rid of my baby. Our baby. And I can never forgive you for that. It hurt me more than anything I've ever felt before. I know killing myself is not the answer, but I don't know where else to go or where to turn. I hate you Mandla. I hate you for ever walking into my life. I hate you for doing it to me. I hate you for killing our baby and I hate you for killing me. And since suicide is a sin, then I'll see you in HELL!

And it was signed Chandra. Mandla cried. He cried large tears. His heart opened up and poured out tears and sulked in a pain it's never felt before. He tried to move on with his life, but the memory of Chandra and what he did, haunted him. It haunted him every time he met a sweet, young woman, like Chandra. And this was partly the reason why he dated the women whose souls and spirits were already dead. Someone else had taken them away, and *he* wouldn't have to feel responsible for stealing their souls.

Todd slapped him on his back, bringing Mandla back to the present. He hadn't heard a word Todd said about their adventure the night before.
    "Potna are you listening to me?" Todd finally asked when he noticed the far away look in Mandla's gray eyes.
    "Yeah. Yeah I heard you. Damn," he responded, as he ran his palms down his face.

"Don't tell me you tripping off of Chandra still. Man you always start tripping. I thought you'd moved on?"

"I did man. I did." Mandla walked back to the guestroom. He looked back at Todd, who had not moved. "Hey it's me. I'm cool. Just still buzzing from last night, I guess."

"Good. Cause I got me a friend up in here, so I ain't got time to be counseling your ass."

"You brought home a stripper too?" Mandla asked.

"Nah. This some of my personal shit." Todd laughed. Mandla did not laugh. Sometimes he did not understand his friend. He rubbed his face with his hands. His gray eyes looked more pale than usual.

"Potna, you all right?" Todd asked.

"Yeah, man. You just remember that we was supposed to go looking for my apartment today, so don't be laid up all damn day," Mandla said, as he put his hand on the door knob. "Cause I'm about to kick *her* ass out."

"A'ight baby boy," Todd said, smiling at Mandla. He knew what was bothering his friend. He was too damn sensitive. He cared too much for women.

"Aye, yo Mandla," Todd yelled after him. Mandla stuck his head back out of the door. "Don't trip baby...it ain't nothing wrong with having hot, sweaty relations," Todd said, as he slipped back into his room.

*****

"A little more to the left Stephen!" Maya yelled from the bottom of the ladder. Stephen looked down and moved the painting a slight bit to the left.

"No! Now it's crooked!" she yelled as she subconsciously tilted her head to the right, distorting her face to show her disapproval.

Stephen rolled his eyes to the ceiling. He had been through this too many times with Maya. She was never satisfied. And when she wasn't satisfied everyone had to pay, especially him. His position was to assist Maya in anything she needed done, to ensure the success of the new art gallery just outside of Atlanta, Georgia.

"Stephen! Did you hear me? The picture is crooked now!"

She turned to one of the workers and whispered something in her ear.

Stephen stood staring down at the two women giggling. Maya touched the other woman softly on her back as she signed her name on the woman's notepad. The two looked up squinting and pointing, as he balanced himself on the ladder. Their obvious disapproval mirrored their distorted faces. Maria, the Spanish woman, was often near Maya when she made decisions. The two were close friends. They shared jokes, went to lunch, and on occasion, shopped together. Between him and the seven other women, Maya and Maria were the closest, personally. Professionally, Stephen helped to make the major decisions, with Maya being the final obstacle. He was one of the most creative assets to the gallery's production.

Dr. Coleman invested in Sanfords' Gallery, but left all major decision making endeavors to Maya. Working as a professor at Spelman College, he bought the old warehouse and turned it into an art gallery, naming it after his late father. Stephen had worked for Dr. Coleman as an assistant before Maya graduated from Spelman. Impressed with her natural talent and eye for beauty, Dr. Coleman offered her the position of operating the entire gallery for him. He wanted a cultural feel for the place. He felt that Maya was the perfect person to add a little spunk and color to the drab warehouse. When she was his student, he noticed how she took her work a little more seriously than the other students. She went out of her way to make sure that a color scheme was right, or that a painting or portrait really came to life for its viewer.

Sounds of the Interstate 285 traffic could be heard echoing throughout the huge gallery, as well as the thunder and lighting. The weather was horrible. There were no customers on this particular day. Maya was remodeling for a big art exhibit featuring South African portraits. She took the liberty to close the gallery for an entire two days. Much to Stephen's dismay.

His feelings for Ms. Dickson, so he called her, were not obscure. All of the employees of the gallery were aware of Stephen's envy of Maya. It was not unusual to catch Stephen watching Maya from afar when customers were relishing in her radiate glow of kindness. There were no gray areas with Maya; either you loved her or you hated her. Straight black or white. Stephen turned to glare at the portrait. The black and white was a likeness of an old woman with a patterned head wrap. Her large, dark eyes were a reflection of a painful life. Her image was startling. It captured Stephen's attention for the first time. He had to admit one thing about Ms. Maya Dickson...she knew how to pick them.

Maya sat at her desk, gazing out of the open window of her small office. Stephen was still fumbling with the portrait. One thing she had to give to him was that he was tenacious. And tenacity was a criterion for being a winner. Maya played with the pencil on her desk, rolling it back and forth with the tips of her fingers. She looked around her office and decided that it was definitely time to do some rearranging. She had a few cultural items that she wanted to bring in to work.

In the corner there was a dead plant that, for the life of her, she could not bring back to life. She would replace the old plant with a new bookshelf and her little African Heritage dolls handmade by Dorothy Jones. Maya met the woman during a doll fair in California. She was immediately impressed with the carefully hand painted faces of the dolls and their realistic personalities. Each doll obviously was cared for and Dorothy had to have put a lot of love and effort into them. She remembered buying one for Aunt Setty, Senida and Senida's mother. For herself, she bought two clowns, a bride, and an African couple.

Maya leaned back in her chair. Today was such an ugly day. She almost called Senida to cancel their lunch date but decided against the idea. Besides, she could tell that her best friend needed to talk. She missed that quality time with her. Maya slid her fingers across the top of her brown organizer and opened to Thursday. Red stars marked the most important tasks to be completed before the end of the day. She also had a date with Donald, but decided to cancel, because she was developing a headache. Maya knew he would not be thrilled, since she had to cancel last week also. Hopefully, he would understand again. Besides, he probably needed to study anyway.

Donald was working on his MBA at Clark Atlanta University. He aspired to start his own business. Maya cared about Donald tremendously, but for some reason they could not seem to get along. On certain days, they would get along perfectly, but the majority of the time, they were fighting like cats and dogs. She hadn't heard from Michael and decided to let him call her when he was ready to see her again.

Maya let out a sigh and rotated her rolodex.

"D...D...D..," she said out loud, as her fingers stopped at Donald's number. Dialing the number, she peered out of the window and watched the cars drive by. She wondered where they were going and decided that she needed a vacation soon. Donald's answering machine came on and Maya hung up. She hated talking to those things. They were so impersonal.

There was too much work to be done before the exhibit next week, but she could not motivate herself to get on the ball. Every year around this time, she became depressed. July was her worst month. Her parents' wedding anniversary was in July. She could never forget them going out on that day, to the Ginger Bread House for dinner and never returning.

Maya shook the thoughts out of her head and headed towards the front of the gallery. She refused to get depressed here at work. That was something she did in private. She would sulk later. She walked through the first two halls, to make sure that all of the art was in order and all of her demands were met. Maya strolled down each hall, impressed by Stephen's work. Each portrait represented exactly what she intended. She looked at her watch. Senida would be strolling in any minute for their lunch date.

By the time Senida arrived, Maya had made it back around to the front of the gallery.

"Stephen! I'm about to go to lunch. I'll check on the portrait when I get back. Don't forget to make those flyers for next weekend, okay?" Stephen rolled his eyes and nodded his head. With that, Maya waved her hand and disappeared.

"Hey girl, let me get my purse," Maya chirped, as she brushed past Senida.

Senida stood, looking at the work that Maya had accomplished on the old building. Maya's eye for art and color schemes had won her recognition within the Black community of Atlanta. Senida walked around the gallery, admiring how well the decorum was put together.

Maya strolled from the back of the gallery with her purse and portfolio in arm. Her five-foot five-inch shapely build had been poured into a long, black, chiffon dress, spilling cleavage from the top. She elegantly draped a red, orange, and yellow silk scarf around her neck and smiled at Senida. Across her arm was a thick black coat. Her hair was neatly pulled back into a bun, and one twisted ringlet of hair fell from the right side of her head. She wore no make-up but continued to be as radiant as ever. Senida could not compare herself to Maya as she stood waiting in her two piece gray attorney clothing. Her short cut hair was accented by a pair of circular wire rimmed glasses.

"I'm gone to lunch!" she yelled to no one in particular. "Stephen! I'll be back in about an hour or so."

Stephen sucked his teeth and rolled his crystal blue eyes in the back of his head. Senida could not help but to snicker at how much Maya continued to get under Stephen's skin.

"Are you ready?" Maya smiled, turning towards Senida.

"Stephen seems to be getting worse," Senida commented on the progression of Stephen's jealousy. "Why do you keep him around? Why don't you just fire him?" Senida said, ignoring Maya's question.

They waltzed out of the building.

"Because he's a good artist. He loves what he does. He just doesn't love working for me. Or for that matter, for any woman, especially a Black woman." Maya put up her umbrella and stepped closer to Senida so she could get under. Maya didn't seem to be bothered by Stephen and his constant defiance. She looped her arms through Senida's arm and they both walked under the umbrella together.

"Besides," Maya started again, "his finished products are always excellent. I think I give him enough competition to keep him on his toes."

Maya began popping her gum in rhythm to the clacking of their heels on the wet pavement.

"Cut that out. You know that irritates me," Senida quickly blurted out.

Maya laughed.

"Are you ready for your trip home?" Senida continued.

"Almost. I still have some things I got to pick up. I wanted to buy something for Aunt Setty but I don't know what to get her." Maya responded.

Senida and Maya entered the small restaurant leaving their

umbrellas by the door with the rest of the bunch.

A young man seated them. He handed them both menus and proceeded to busy himself with wiping off the table next to them. He left and quickly returned with two glasses of water.

"Your waiter will be with your shortly," he said and disappeared.

"How's that Mortin account coming along?" Maya asked as she scanned the menu.

"It's going okay, so far. I might have to get them to hire some extra help for me. It's a pretty big account. If we win this case we could be talking about millions of dollars for our firm. Not to mention the acclaim that I would receive from a case this big."

"Well good luck. I'm sure you'll kick some ass." Maya's large brown eyes searched the room for the waiter.

"What are you getting?"

"I'm getting the New Orleans platter."

"Well I don't know what I'm getting yet."

"Well you better hurry up. I'm hungry."

"You are so impatient. Just chill."

"So how's Darrell?" Maya asked, coyly ignoring Senida's comment.

"He's the same." The dryness in Senida's voice caught Maya's attention.

"Trouble in paradise?"

"Not really trouble, but..." Her voice trailed off as she tried to concentrate on the menu.

"But what?"

"I'm bored," Senida sighed as she looked up from the menu at her friend.

"Bored?"

"Yes, bored. Darrell's so sweet, and nice, and...predictable. We never have fun. We don't do the typical couple stuff anymore. We don't go to the movies or to the park. We go to those damn political science functions that are boring as hell."

Maya covered her mouth with her right hand and began to laugh.

"What are you laughing at? I'm serious. I don't know how much more of this I can handle." Senida sighed.

"Senida." Maya eyed her incredulously. "Darrell is a good

man. I know a hell of a lot of women who wouldn't mind changing places with you. He worships the ground that you walk on. Shoot, you lucky we're best friends or I would have snatched him a long time ago." Maya teased.

"I know. I hear that all the time."

"You need to take heed. Give him a call tonight and tell him how much you appreciate him."

"I don't even know if he'll talk to me anymore."

"Why would you say that?" Maya asked, still looking around for the waiter.

"He cussed me out."

"No!" Maya's large eyes widened. "Not Darrell. Did he find out?"

"About? No." Senida thought for a moment. "No he couldn't have."

"Well it would serve you right. You need to quit tripping."

"I'm sure he'll come around. Our relationship is like an old pair of shoes. You get tired of them sometimes but you still need them. He'll *have* to come around. I can't imagine Darrell with another woman. It takes him too long to get used to people."

"*He's* not the one that needs to come around. *You* need to come around. Who's cheating on who?"

Senida rolled her eyes. She wasn't in the mood to hear mama Maya's lectures.

"I think I might have that New Orleans platter also."

"Oh no. Don't try to change the subject. You really need to evaluate your relationship with Darrell."

"Okay Doctor Ruth. What about doing some evaluating of your own?"

"Who? Me?" Maya said pointing at herself in astonishment that Senida would even imply such a thing.

"Yes Mother Teresa."

"Are you talking about Michael?"

"And Donald."

"I'm in the process of getting rid of both of them."

"Yeah right."

Maya laughed. "See unlike you Ms. Johnson, I don't need these men to validate myself. I'm special."

"You sure are."

"Shut up girl," Maya responded.

"And just what in the hell do you mean, 'validate me'. I don't need any of them to validate me either. Shoot!"

Maya laughed. It was usually Senida with the in-your-face comments. But today, Maya was the aggressor. She knew that Senida was weak when it came to men. And Senida knew it too.

"Doesn't taste good huh?" Maya asked.

"What?" Senida asked irritated. She scrunched up her nose.

"A dose of your own medicine."

They both laughed.

"So what about Glenda?" Senida carefully sipped from her glass of water, waiting to see the change on Maya's face.

"I do care for Michael, a lot. But truthfully, I'm starting to wonder if that M.D. is really worth the trouble." Maya frowned.

"Doctors are a lot like athletes and entertainers, chile. They can be difficult to deal with. I don't know if I'd date any of them," Senida assured her friend.

"Yeah right."

"I'm serious. I'm having enough problems with these *regular* men."

"*Regular* men?"

"You know, regular jobs."

"You mean to tell me and don't lie, that if Chris Weber with his young, fine, chocolate self walked up to you right now, that you wouldn't get with that?"

"I'd tell him to get ta steppin'! I don't need no more aggravation from you young, fine, chocolate, sweet tasting, fine smelling, good feeling brothas," Senida teased as she waved her finger around. They both laughed.

"I don't know Senida."

"What?"

"You got a pretty hard head."

"And what's that supposed to mean?"

"You know what they say. A hard head makes for a soft...what?" Maya asked and raised her eyebrows.

"A soft ass." Senida responded.

"A soft behind." Maya corrected her.

"Same thang."

"You so crazy."

"You know what I've been thinking about lately?" Senida

continued, "a trip. I want to go on a trip so damn bad."

"Well you know I'm the one. I'm always down to take a trip. Where you wanna go?"

"I don't know. Somewhere. Anywhere. I just need a change of scenery."

"Maybe we can plan something for when I get back from California."

"Sounds good." Senida softened a bit. "We should make a toast."

"With water?"

"Why not? It doesn't matter what's *in* your glass. Just as long as they clink together."

"Like in the movies?"

"Yeah. And then a little has to spill out. For good measure."

"Okay. A toast to friendship," Maya said.

"A strong, long lasting friendship. Like ours," Senida added. She held her glass up. "May we get through this life unscathed by the craziness and the wrath of these men."

"Here, here!" They clashed their glasses together and a little spilled out of the glasses, for good measure.

*****

"And what utilities do you pay?" Mandla asked.

"Water and garbage. You pay Georgia Power and Atlanta Gas and Light," the plump white lady responded in a Georgia accent.

Mandla looked over at Todd. He was leaning against one of the walls. He looked tired. They had been searching for apartments all day. Todd had taken Mandla to as many complexes as he could stand to see in one day. But nothing seemed to jump out at Mandla. He was too picky.

"Would you like an application?" Georgia accent asked.

"Yeah. I'll take one with me. Do you have a card?"

She stapled a card onto the application and handed them both to Mandla. Todd was at the door with his keys in his hand before Mandla realized it.

"Thank you," Mandla said.

"If you have any questions, call me at that number there," she responded and shuffled quickly away to help a couple.

They climbed into Todd's jeep. Todd rubbed his hands across his dark baldhead.

"Man, I know you don't wanna go to no more complexes today do you?"

"Since you put it that way, then no."

"I'm just saying. We been looking at places all day. It's damn near five o'clock. I wanted to get a couple of drinks from Fat Tuesday's."

"That's cool. I'm down. I'm kinda tired of looking today myself. What's up with Fat Tuesday's?"

"People just hang out there. They got these slushy-like drinks. It be a lot of bitches there."

"Man you gon' have to chill on that word."

"My bad. It be a lot of *women* there."

"Is it cool?"

"Yeah. Hell yeah."

"Shit let's go. I can't keep the women waiting."

Todd swung the jeep into a parking space in front of The Underground Mall. The Underground was crowded with people shopping, gazing, and socializing. Todd and Mandla stopped in *Hooters* first.

"What can I get you two handsome men?" A thin white woman with large breasts bursting out of a tight *Hooters* T-shirt approached their table.

"Give me the buffalo wings and a large coke," Todd said watching her breasts closely.

"Do you want fries with that?"

"Yeah."

"And you sir?" she said turning to Mandla.

"I'll have a Philly Cheese-steak and a large coke."

"Fries?"

"Yeah. Curly fries."

"Be back in a second."

Hooters was a popular eatery in The Underground Mall. The waitresses wore small orange polyester booty shorts and thin tight T-shirts or half shirts. Most of the waitresses were expected to be of the bustier persuasion but that was not always the case.

Men came to *Hooters* to ogle at the half naked women and to watch the game on the elevated television. Occasionally, women would come in also. Some came to eat, some came to watch the men and the game, and *some* came to watch the women, ironically.

"Uh." Todd grumbled and looked around the joint.

"Who you looking for?" Mandla asked looking puzzled.

"For the sistahs."

Mandla was glad Todd didn't use the other word.

"Ah, there's one, two..." He looked around. "...And three. Three sistahs working here. And they all look good!"

"Our sistahs always look good. Especially in those little ugly ass shorts."

"But they make them things look good."

"What else they got in this mall?" Mandla asked looking around.

"Shit I don't know. They got all different kind of little shops here. People don't come here to shop. They come here to hang out and get at women. And to go to Hooters and Fat Tuesdays."

"That's cool."

"Tomorrow. We gon' go to Lenox. Women everywhere," Todd said.

OH MY, MY, MY
I'M FEELING HIGH!

Time and space are elements important to man yet insignificant. One waits for no one and the latter is an infinite air of nothingness *and* everything. Maya's space was unlimited as she floated through the clear blue skies. Her body was as light as a feather as she drifted through realms that are usually unknown to most people. A cool breeze filtered itself with sweet scents of relaxation and calm, cool collectedness into her lungs: as anxiety, depression, and stress floated out through her nostrils. Clouds twisted and hugged her legs. Her body dipped slightly from the sky and slowly eased its way into the cool refreshing water below.

Maya could feel the subtle force of the liquid push away her fears and doubts. Thoughts tried to enter her mind, but were not allowed in as she enjoyed the nothing space of comfort. Feelings and emotions were as simple as the beating of a heart or the motion of breath as it enters and exits the soul. For Maya, gravitation had no boundaries in her comfort zone. She was at oneness with the earth, the moon, the sun, and the stars. The universe engulfed her soul and her spirit. Memories of Michael and Glenda sifted out of her system like water through a strainer. Work stress and Stephen floated out of her mind like birds through a cloud. Worries of love and acceptance poured out of her soul like milk out of a pitcher. There was a soothing calm that lulled Maya and encircled around her mind, her heart, her body, and her soul.

Maya opened her eyes and stretched her arms high above her head. She rolled her neck around a few times and got up from her sitting position. Once standing, Maya stood erect, put her hands on her hips, and stretched out her back. She blinked a few times, to moisten her contact lenses and blew out the white candle sitting on her small meditation table. Incense was still burning and she realized that she had been meditating for close to an hour. She felt good. Her soul felt cleansed and her spirit refreshed. She walked over to the coffee table and blew out the other two candles. Finally, she bent forward farther and extinguished the long candle propped in her mother's golden candleholder. As soon as she flicked on the light and turned on the ringer, the phone rang.

"Hey. Just got through meditating?" Senida asked as she looked at her watch. She knew Maya's routine almost as good as Maya.

"Yeah, you know. Six o'clock. I have to have my after work meditation session to get me through the rest of the night."

"Call any spirits today?" Senida chuckled. "Oh my, my, my, I'm feeling high!" Senida sang the Erykah Badu song.

"Oh shut up. You need to try it yourself. It does a world of good. Might even help you work out the mess you call a life. And Lord knows you need some help with that corrupt mind of yours." Maya laughed as she scraped some of the cool candle wax from the bottom of her mother's candleholder.

The candleholder held sentimental value. It had been passed down from generation to generation. Her great grandmother Jenny used it to hold the single candle that she burned every night. She used the candle to get in touch with spirits. When her husband disappeared in the woods, she burned the candle every night to summon his lost spirit back into her home and her heart. Great grandma Jenny's candle burned each night until she died. Her husband never returned home.

"So what's up?" Senida broke into Maya's thoughts.

"Not much. I figured out what I'm going to do with Michael now."

"Did the spirits tell you what to do?"

"If you mean, did I come up with my own solution during meditation, then yes."

"Did the spirits tell you to leave his sorry ass like I told you to do?"

"I think I'm going to play along with his game. I need to buy me some time to let my heart know that he is not the one anymore." Maya picked up the small book by Sri Chinmoy and tossed it onto the couch.

"Why don't you just leave him?" Senida asked, irritated that her friend did not have a hard shell like herself.

"Cause it doesn't work like that with me. I can't just quit cold turkey. I need to ease out of the relationship. Give myself a little time to get over him. The more time I spend with him, the more I'll realize that he's not the man that I want. Then, it will be easy for me to let him go."

"Oh. Well what are you going to do about Glenda?"

"What do you mean, Glenda? She ain't my problem." Maya was irritated. She had tried to keep Glenda out of her mind the best way she knew how.

"Oh but contraire, mon frere. She *is* your problem if she won't leave you two alone."

Maya flopped herself onto the couch. "Can you believe that she's moving back in with him?"

"Shut your mouth. Tell me all about it." Senida pressed the phone harder to her ear. She didn't want to miss any details.

"Yeah. She says she wants to try to work things out," Maya sighed. She purposely did not tell Senida about the baby. She knew that Senida would explode and she was not in the mood to hear a lecture.

"I say we go over there and beat her ass."

"I say we don't."

"Sounds like its time for you to get another Michael. What's up with Donald?"

Maya scrunched up her face. "We argue too much."

"Darrell has some single friends. I could hook you up. Girl I met one a few weeks ago. He was fine. I mean choc-o-late! Plus it would give me a reason to call him."

"You still haven't talked to him?"

"Nope. So you want me to call?"

"No thank you. I'm really about tired of these men," Maya sighed.

"You know you love you some men. Giving up men would be like not having a period, unnatural."

"You know that's right!" Maya laughed out loud. Senida was right. She loved the hell out of some black men. She loved the way they looked, the way they smelled, the way they tasted, and the way they felt.

"Hey. What are you doing tonight? Let's catch that new movie with Denzel Washington. Now, that's one hunk of chocolate I wouldn't mind biting into."

"Hold it now. Don't you think you got enough chocolate on your hands? Remember, too much of that sweet chocolate can make you diabetic."

"Well girl, bring me the insulin shots cause I can't fight the feeling! So what's up, we going to catch that movie or what?"

"Can't. Tonight is Michael's hospital charity function."

"Sounds about as exciting as Darrell's political science seminars."

"They are."

"Well, have fun. Call me tomorrow. Maybe we'll do lunch."

"Bye chile."

Maya knew she looked obvious as she nibbled on the chicken wings and then sucked the sauce from her fingers. She was trying not to look uncouth and trying not to embarrass Michael at the same time. She looked around and tossed the last little chicken bone into the philodendron that she'd been hiding behind half of the night. Michael was good at bringing her to these hospital functions and leaving her alone. He introduced her to most of the men and none of the women. He wanted to show her off. Maya didn't understand why she subjected herself to such torture. She cared for Michael dearly but was tired of him killing two birds with one stone when it came to her. They hardly ever spent quality time together, alone. All of their time was spent either at some type of function or in the presence of other people.

Michael's high profile deliveries were usually the cause of the couple not getting enough privacy. Michael delivered babies for celebrities. He was known as the youngest doctor that the "celebs" trusted. Maya had to admit that the man was brilliant. His brain was what turned her on the most, then it was his body. Or was it his body first, and his brain next? Oh well, she thought, he was gorgeous, witty, intelligent, and had a sense of humor. All the qualities she wanted in a man. But! He was too damn busy at times. Most importantly, he was still married. And although Maya was just as busy, she would squeeze him into her schedule. However, he didn't always do the same for her.

That's where Donald came into the picture. His attention was usually based on academics. It was a little more predictable. Maya knew that during midterms, finals, and major papers, she wouldn't see Donald very much. But during spring break and Christmas break, Donald couldn't get enough of her. And he wasn't half-bad in bed. Always made her holler with delight. But for some odd reason, Maya and Donald could not get along for very long periods. They would have to take breaks from each other, to prevent going to jail.

Maya wiped the rest of the sauce off of her fingers onto the cloth napkin she was holding. She reached in her purse and pulled out her compact. Looking in the mirror, Maya applied one thin coat of lipstick, checked her teeth for meat, and smoothed her tongue across her lips. She looked at her watch; it was already after midnight. She'd told Michael that she had to get up early for an early morning meeting. Maya scoped the room in search of Dr. Social Butterfly. She spotted him in the corner with a congregation of women around him. Maya slipped the strap of her purse higher onto her shoulder and switched over in their direction.

"Dr. Hill, tell Phyllis the story about the twins that you separated," one of the women said as she smiled a wide, toothy smile.

"Oh, nooo. I'm sure Phyllis wouldn't want to hear about some old boring operation story."

"Well, I sure would like to hear the story," Maya interjected as she made her way into the group.

"Oh, hey Maya. I've been looking for you all night. Where have you been?"

Maya smiled a closed mouth smile. "Over in the corner, entertaining myself as usual."

The other women looked from one to the other and then a couple of them began to dissipate back into the middle of the room. Michael smiled and kept his composure.

"Ladies, this is my buddy Maya," Michael introduced her to the other women. Most of them just smiled but nobody said it was nice to meet her. Maya turned to Michael and smiled.

"May I please speak to you in private?" She began to walk over to a more secluded area. The other women just waved at Michael and started mingling amongst the other guests.

"What is wrong with you Maya? I have never seen you act this bad before."

"Michael. I'm tired and I'm cranky. You always do this to me."

"Do what?"

"Every time you bring me to one of these functions, I feel like I shouldn't have come. You leave me alone. Why do you even bring me if you're going to leave me all of the time?" She crossed her arms over her breasts. Michael didn't like when Maya pouted. He felt he was beyond such childish actions.

"Maya I'm sorry if you feel that way. But these are my co-workers. I bring you to these functions because I think you're a classy lady and that you would be able to hold decent conversations with other intelligent professionals."

"Well, Michael. I also told you that I have to get home early tonight. I can't be out too late. Remember I have to be to work early in the morning." She rubbed her fingers up and down the side of his suit, trying to let him know that she was sorry. She smiled up at him. He forced a smile on his face.

"Why don't you just spend the night tonight and I'll take you to work in the morning? Tomorrow is one of my off days. I'll cook you breakfast, if you give me some dessert tonight." He didn't have to force a smile on his face this time.

"Do you want dessert now?"

Michael looked around at his co-workers. "Give me half-an-hour," he quickly said, and kissed her on her cheek. He abruptly walked over to a group of doctors. Maya just sat down in a chair next to the table with the food and helped herself to more chicken wings. The more chicken wings she consumed, the longer it seemed for Michael to come back. She would spot him roaming around in different groups periodically, but he would pretend that he didn't see her staring. Maya helped herself to more punch. She was ready to go. She looked at her watch and realized that it was getting extremely late.

She could remember how excited she was when she met Michael. It was during her gallery picnic for the employees and their family members and friends. He was a co-worker's cousin. He approached her with the right lines and the right looks. They spent the entire picnic talking and getting to know each other. In the beginning, he adored and spent every waking moment with Maya. After a few months of dating, however, his work seemed to become more important to him. Maya didn't mind that he was into his work but *she* made time for him. So she didn't understand why he couldn't *make* time for her.

Dr. Michael Hill was considered a good man. Maya knew that many women wanted him. She cared for Michael and even thought about marriage. Of course these thoughts of marriage were for after his divorce from Glenda. Maya had developed deep emotions for Michael but she did not love him. Her feelings for him could not seem to materialize into love. She loved him as a person, but she couldn't fall in love with him. She couldn't allow herself to fall in love with him because he was still married. And although he constantly claimed that *he* would *fix* the problem, it seemed to Maya that he was dragging his feet on *fixing* the problem. Michael walked over to Maya and kissed Maya on her cheek.

"Are you ready to go?" he asked, as he handed Maya her coat.

"Yes."

"We going to my house right?"

"Yes."

"Good. I'm ready for you." There was a hint of seduction in his eyes.

"I know. I know."

Michael's lovemaking was incredible that night. As soon as they hit the front door of Michael's house, they started kissing and touching and fondling each other. He pulled and tugged at Maya's clothes and she began unzipping his pants. Michael pressed Maya against the wall and passionately kissed her on her mouth, on her neck, and on her face. Their erotic movements aroused them both.

By the time they made it to the bedroom, there was a trail of clothing between the front door and the bed. Michael's stamina was fierce and his back strong, as he twisted Maya into different positions. She squealed with pleasure. Maybe this was the reason why she kept him around. His lovemaking skills were off the hook! Maya could feel herself getting ready to let loose when she felt Michael rocking and pumping inside of her. Her head was spinning and she could feel his sweat spilling onto her back. She put her hand up in front of her to press against the headboard. Maya tried several times to look back at Michael. She liked to see his facial expressions when he was concentrating on her, but every time she tried to turn around, he would gently push her head back towards the headboard.

His large curls bobbed up and down as sweat formed around the rim of his head. She heard his breathing get louder and louder and she could feel her breathing intensify. She swore she heard a door open, but continued to hold on to the great feeling in between her legs. In a matter of minutes, Michael's moans, Maya's groans, and Glenda's screams climaxed throughout the tiny bedroom.

In split seconds, Michael jumped from the bed and Maya scrambled to cover herself with his sheets. Glenda was standing in the frame of the bedroom door, with gun in hand. There was a crazed, glazed-over look in her eyes and she was breathing hard and tightly gripping the gun. Michael sat up on the edge of the bed, while Maya froze. Maya's eyes were as large as saucers. Her heart was pounding and she didn't know what to do. Glenda spoke first, breaking the silence.

"You cheating son-of-a bitch! I ought to shoot your fucking dick off!" Glenda stood in the doorway, her long straight hair in an upheaval about her head. Her eyes were bloodshot red and tears streamed down her cheeks.

"Glenda, what the hell are you doing here?" Michael was trying to ease his way to her but every time he moved she would wave the gun around in a threatening fashion.

"Don't move Michael. I'll kill you and your little bitch friend."

Maya's heart raced. Her mind was clogged with thoughts of escaping. She was praying to God that Glenda was not as crazy as Michael had said she was, and that she would not pull the trigger on that gun. She didn't want to lose her life over some foolishness. And she was beginning to realize, at that very moment, that Michael was not worth the fight anymore. She swore if she ever got out of this mess, he wouldn't have to worry about Glenda signing those divorce papers. Glenda could have Michael for all Maya cared.

"Glenda, baby. You got to trust me."

"Shut up!" she yelled. "I did trust your ass. I thought we were supposed to be working things out. Is this how it's going to be? Is this how it's going to be? I thought we were through with this shit?"

"We are. I don't know what came over me. I think I had too much to drink tonight..," Michael began explaining. Maya looked from one to the other. Her heart vigorously pounded against her chest. Her breathing came in quick small spurts.

"Michael I'm tired of your shit!" Glenda yelled, as she turned the gun up to the ceiling and pulled the trigger.

A loud bang sounded throughout the room and plaster from the ceiling fell to the floor. Maya jumped and pulled the cover tighter to her. This woman really was crazy, and here she was, trapped in the midst of two crazy fools!

"Glenda!" Michael yelled. "What the hell is your problem?"

"What the hell is my problem? My problem?" Glenda cried. "You've been cheating on me again. Is this where you've been when you claimed to be at the hospital, huh? Is it Michael?!"

Glenda wiped her eyes with the back of her hand. Tears continued to flow endlessly. Glenda's attractive face twisted in pain and disgust.

"Listen, why don't you let Maya go and we can talk about this? I promise this won't happen again. Now give me the gun, Glenda. You know I love you."

Maya saw Glenda's eyes soften when Michael said those three deadly words that men play around with.

"You don't love me. You love yourself."

Maya sat frozen. She didn't know whether to move or stay still. She couldn't believe that she'd gotten herself in such a predicament. This type of situation usually happened in Senida's life. Boy, what she wouldn't give to see Senida right about now. Maya silently prayed.

"If you love me then why do we have to constantly go through this Michael?" Glenda continued to cry. Maya really felt as though she shouldn't be there. Glenda was still holding on tight to the gun. Michael eased his way closer to her and put his arm around her. Glenda was trembling and so was Maya. Michael reached for the gun but Glenda would not let go. She continued to cry in his arms but she still had a tight grip on the gun. Maya reached over for her clothes when suddenly there was a pounding at the front door.

"Police! Open up!" two voices boomed from the other side of the front door.

Seconds later there was a loud thud at the door and two police officers rushed into the bedroom.

"Freeze! Put the gun down!" The cops waved their guns around the room.

Glenda dropped to her knees and the gun fell to the floor with a gentle thump. Michael was kneeling beside Glenda, as the officers took the gun and began investigating the three. Michael explained to the officers what had occurred. Glenda was still crying into Michael's chest. Maya wanted to bolt out of the front door into the night. The sight of Michael comforting Glenda infuriated her.

Michael continued to explain the situation to the amused cops. He seemed to be unscathed by the situation. Maya watched as he babbled on about the situation. And no, nobody was hurt. And no he didn't want to press charges. And yes the gun was registered in his name. And no he didn't object to the officers escorting Maya home when she asked. Maya quickly dragged the sheets into the restroom where she threw on her clothes and went straight to the police car.

She was embarrassed and had enough excitement this night to last her a lifetime. She did not look back at Michael. She did not plan on seeing him again, ever. That crazy woman can have that crazy man, she thought to herself, as the police car pulled away from Michael's house.

*****

Senida gazed at the picture of her and Darrell. They were both smiling. It seemed so long ago but when she flipped it to the other side, the date shown was only two years ago. She sighed. He did not return any of her phone calls nor did he come by to visit. Not only that, but her lover was avoiding her like the plague. He must have known that she was the one responsible for his tires.

Loneliness sunk in as she flipped through the newspaper. Maya was working on negotiations for the San Francisco trip and was too busy to talk. Senida never thought that having Darrell out of her hair would be so depressing. She missed him tremendously. Her finger itched each time she looked at the phone and thumbing through their old pictures was not helping one bit with her emotions.

Senida tossed the newspaper onto the opposite couch and reached for the remote. She repositioned herself and covered her body with her favorite blanket. There was nothing on any of the many channels. She clicked off the television and reached onto the floor to retrieve the latest issue of *Essence*. There was an article on "Sex, Love, and Marriage in the 90's" that she wanted to check out. After reading the article, Senida reclined on the couch and closed her eyes. The calming mood did nothing for her incredible, insatiable desire for sex.

Her craving forced her to gyrate her hips as she imagined a big strong man on top of her. Her hands moved slowly towards the top of the cover and slid under the soft material. She positioned her hand and fingers and stopped at the middle of her spot. She'd promised herself that she would not do this anymore. If she couldn't find someone, then she would just wait or dream. But no more. Her appetite was just too strong and she habitually reached for the phone and dialed. On the fourth ring, he answered. His voice was raspy and breathless.

"Hey," she said.

"Who is this?" He inquired in an irritated voice.

"Senida."

"What's up?"

"I've been trying to catch up with you for awhile. What's up? We not kicking it like that anymore?"

"How you gon' ask me a question like that, after you slashed my fucking tires?" He raised his voice.

"I didn't slash your tires." She lied. "I keep trying to tell you that."

"Whatever. I'm not going to be arguing with you. What do you want?"

"For you to come over."

"Oh, your man ain't doing you right, huh?"

"Are you coming over?" Senida pleaded.

"I don't know. I got company. Maybe later on tonight."

"Well, how will I know?"

"I'll call you later."

"Who's your company? Is it that woman?" she asked.

He hung up.

Senida sat for over an hour waiting for his call. When she got tired of waiting she went to bed. Eventually he called her back. But she was so exhausted from crying that she didn't even hear the phone ring.

Pain flashed through Senida's head when the alarm clock went off. It couldn't possibly be six already. She dashed from her bedroom, into the bathroom and switched on the shower. She couldn't be late for work again. All the crying she'd done last night only made her head hurt worse. Senida quickly showered and dressed. She'd dressed faster than she expected so she decided to call Darrell at his job. An early riser, Darrell had probably been at work for at least an hour by now. She let the phone ring at least six times before he answered.

"Hello, Moore Consulting."

"Hi. This is Senida."

Darrell cleared his throat. "How are you today Ms. Johnson?"

"I'm fine. Are you busy today?"

"Yes."

"How about tomorrow?"

"Busy."

"Okay. Next week?"

"I have work to do Senida," he sighed.

"I just wanted to know if you would have some time to sit down and talk."

"I don't have the time. Isn't that what this is all about? Time."

"Darrell..."

"Plus. If I did take the time to talk to you. I'm sure that you wouldn't be satisfied. So at the risk of sounding rude, I have work to do." He was irritated.

"Darrell, please. I'm sorry. We need to talk."

"I really don't think I can right now."

"You can't talk to me anymore?"

"Not now, no."

"Will you call me when you can?"

"Maybe."

"Darrell, I love you," Senida's eyes filled with tears.

"Good-bye Senida." Darrell hung up.

Senida held the phone for a short time, listening to the dial tone. Eventually, she hung up and headed out to work with a broken heart and a broken spirit.

CRASH, BANG, BOOM!

Red wine was virtually impossible to remove from the silk dress that Maya so carefully draped onto her body. Dabbing at the bright stain with a small wash cloth, she realized it was no use. She would have to change. All she wanted was one little glass of red wine and now she was wearing most of it. Not only is the stain distracting but I look bloated in the front and it's that time of the month, making this the worst day to be having my South African Art Exhibit grand opening, she thought. Could anything else go wrong?

She stomped from her kitchen into her bedroom and flung the closet door open. It was already seven thirty in the morning and she had to find something else to wear, fast. Most of her clothes were at the cleaners. It was her routine to drop off her dirty clothes every Friday evening. Wouldn't Stephen love to see her miss an important event such as this one? The preparation had taken months. She had to make sure she had just enough representation from almost all of South Africa, trying to capture the essence of the aftermath of apartheid, as well as the beauty of the land. Months and months had gone into Maya's researching and bargaining for portraits and art paintings to ensure the success of her exhibit.

"Only to be ruined by a glass full of red wine and the bitch that came every month to make my life a living hell! I hate being on the rag," she sighed out loud, as she pulled clothing from her closet and flung the rejects onto her bed.

With a half-empty closet and the majority of her clothes on her bed, she opted for a brown little number that brought out the natural color of her light brown eyes. She carefully slipped on the pants suit and rushed back into the kitchen, where her breakfast was now cold. The cold eggs were not satisfying and Maya thought she would try another glass of red wine to calm her nerves but decided against the idea.

"Mama, if you're looking down on me now and I know you are. Please let today be all right," she said, as she raised her hands and looked up at the ceiling. Pursing her lips together, she trotted into the bathroom to check her make-up and hair. Perfect as usual. Still, there was something about today that just wasn't right.

A number of wrongs had happened in such a short day. First, her clock did not go off, then her nerves caused her to spill the wine on her dress and now, now it was raining...hard. As she slipped on her matching pumps, her phone rang. Maya began to let the answering machine pick up but thought that it might be someone from the art gallery. Flipping dark curls from her face, she answered the phone in an exasperated voice.

"Hello."

"Hey babee." The country voice echoed through the phone. "I just wanted to call and say good luck on that African thang you giving today," Aunt Setty chimed in her motherly, supportive voice and thick Georgia accent.

"It's an exhibit, Aunt Setty, and thanks. I'm real nervous. I hope everything goes okay."

"Oh it will, chile. Just trust in the Lord. Did you pray today?" Maya came close to lying but decided with the way her day was going so far, she couldn't risk it. She said a quick little prayer to herself, asking the Lord to see her through the day.

"Yes, ma'am. I just got through praying." Well, she didn't lie, she thought.

"When are you 'posed to be coming out here to Cali-fornia again?"

"I'll be there sooner than you think. I can't wait to see you. I wanted you to go over to the Johnson's with me. Mrs. Johnson wants to see you."

"Oh that sounds good. I better get out my Sunday dress, cause I know those folks are high stylin'."

"Yeah, well they said they missed you and would love for us to come by to visit. But Aunt Setty I need to get on out of here before I'm late."

"Befo' you head out, where is dat deed to your daddy's

house?"

"I have it here. Why?"

"Some man called 'bout the paperwork we did last year. Something 'bout whose name the house is in."

"Oh yeah. Tell him to call me. Did you send those papers off?"

"Yeah. I think it would be betta' if'n the house was in your name. 'Cause I ain't gon' be 'round forever. And ever since I left Georgia and moved into your daddy house, I realize that thangs would go betta' if'n you was in charge of everythang. Now my death papers say that I want to be buried in Georgia. I don't want to be buried here in Cali-fornia." Maya hated when she talked about death.

"I know Aunt Setty. I have everything under control. Daddy wanted your name to be on the house in case anything happened while I was still a child..."

"He musta known..."

"Well. If you don't want the responsibility anymore, then I'll make sure that everything is properly transferred. And you can just stay in that house as long as you want or I can fly you back out here to Georgia and set you up."

"Nah. I like the weather out here. I just don't wanna meet my maker in no Cali-fonia." She laughed.

"What ever you want Aunt Setty, you can have." Maya looked at her watch. "Whoo Aunt Setty, I gotta go. I'ma be late."

"Okay. Aunt Setty don't wanna hold you. I just wanted to say good luck and I'm sure you'll do fine at yo' African party. You been eatin' right?"

"Yes ma'am."

"Been staying warm? You don't live in Cali-fonia no mo'. Gotta stay warm out dat way."

"Yes ma'am," Maya looked at her watch again. But she knew better than to cut Aunt Setty off.

"How's the love life? You been courtin'? Still courtin' that nice young man? What his name is again, Mark?"

"No ma'am, it's Michael." She decided not to tell Aunt Setty about her ordeal with Michael. Her situation would only worry the old woman and then she would start worrying Maya about finding another decent young man.

"He still doctrin' on those women? You betta' keep that

one. He know mo' 'bout yo' body than you do." She chuckled incidentally. Maya pulled the long cord into the living room hallway to retrieve her coat from the closet. She needed to get out of her apartment in the next fifteen minutes to make it to Decatur on time.

"Well, I gotta go to work. Love you Aunt Setty. I'll call you later on tonight."

"Okay I love you too chile. Don't forget to call your old Aunt Setty."

Maya grabbed her purse and headed for the door. There was so much work to do today that she didn't know where to begin. Calls had to be made, appointments confirmed, travel arrangements reserved, legal papers drawn, portfolios seen, art hung, arrangements rearranged, exhibits organized, and staff ordered...business as usual.

She would have to talk to Aunt Setty later. That woman could keep anyone on the phone for hours, running up the calling card that Maya had bought her the previous year to call all her friends. Aunt Setty still did not understand that the calls were not free, that Maya was paying for each and every one of them. Yet she would still call and say," This free calling stuff is nice."

Maya loved her Aunt Setty and was grateful for the way she raised her after the accident. She was always supportive of Maya's efforts, even the ones she didn't understand. Maya remembered trying to explain to Aunt Setty that soon she would have enough money and credit to start her own art gallery. The far away look, followed by the twisted face, indicated to Maya that Aunt Setty didn't understand or approve. But when she asked her Aunt Setty why she turned her face in such an ugly way, Aunt Setty just looked at Maya and responded, "Don't you have enough pictures in your house already?" After a long bout with laughter, Maya slowly explained what she meant and even Aunt Setty had to laugh at her silly misunderstanding.

Pulling out of her parking space, Maya waved to old Mr. Miller as he waited for his newspaper. Maya pressed hard on the pedal. She could not be late today. Especially after just the other day, when she stressed to the rest of her staff the importance of making it to work on time, directing her looks toward Doris, who was habitually late. She could just hear the whispers and feel the stares, especially Stephen's. She had a long day ahead of herself.

Once she got through this day she would be alright. She would come home after work and have a nice cold glass of red wine. And this time she'd do it right.

Stopping her car on the corner of Martin Luther King and Westlake, Maya waved a dollar at the Muslim man selling fruit in a bag. He occupied the corner faithfully every morning. Maya often wondered if he got paid for selling the fruit. Most mornings she would buy a bag of fruit to eat as a snack at the gallery. But on bad mornings like today, she would sit looking straight ahead, hoping the light would turn green before he had a chance to walk to her car. Although this was a bad day, Maya realized that she had not packed a lunch and would not have time to go out for take-out.

Extensive planning went into giving an exhibit and with Stephen being out sick Friday, she had to do everything herself. One day, she thought, I will own my own art gallery and I won't have to deal with too many assholes like Stephen. Although the man often got under Maya's skin, she refused to let him know, or let him go. He added a little something to the gallery that none of the other women could.

"Good morning sistah." Brother Johnson was a big man with dark curly hair. He wore small wire framed glasses, almost like the pair Senida wore. There were specks of raindrops on his glasses. He took them off and wiped them with a handkerchief he pulled from his front pocket. His crisp, white shirt was tucked neatly into his dark slacks, topped off with a small bow tie.

"Good morning Brother Johnson. I'll take one, no, make that two bags today."

Brother Johnson handed Maya two bags of bananas and plums. She gave him two dollars, nodded and accelerated through the green light. Today just didn't seem to be her day. And to think it was only Tuesday. There was not as much traffic on the freeway as she anticipated for a Tuesday morning. Maya flipped through radio stations and decided there was nothing worth hearing so she popped in her Sade tape. She needed to relax before arriving at the gallery. Sade's soothing croons seeped through the speakers and Maya began to loosen up a bit. Thoughts of Aunt Setty and her parents went through her mind. Their wedding anniversary would have been today.

She could not wait to visit her Aunt Setty. Sadness often

swept over Maya when she thought of her deceased parents. Aunt Setty was the only living family member that she had left. And even she was getting up in age. She'd never forget how Aunt Setty took her in and tried to raise her in the best southern way she could. Aunt Setty had never been used to being around children for more than 24 hours. Maya was well aware of the fact and took advantage of the poor old woman when she could. She regretted being a hell raiser to the sweet woman.

Maya wiped at the front mirror with her hand, smearing frost from the inside. She could barely see in front of her and she was going at an accelerated speed. Very few cars were on the freeway and Maya took full advantage of the fact. Her Toyota Camry began to pull. She shifted gears. Maya eased her car into fifth gear and signaled to change lanes, unaware of the black Range Rover speeding to cut her off.

J.R. was in a hurry to get to his brother's house. He'd talked to him only briefly over the phone but his brother's urgent tone informed him that there was more pertinent news about his father. Between the two of them, they were responsible for dealing with any situation that came into the public eye about their family.

Their stepsister, Brandy, made it completely clear that she didn't care what was said about that side of the family in the media, because she disowned every last one of them. That was the last statement that both of them had heard from her since she moved to Canada with her boyfriend. His other two sisters were usually unaware of whether they were coming or going. Much older than Jelani, they moved out early with boyfriends and did not return. Jelani had seen one hanging on the corner looking for her next hit. He'd pretended that he didn't see her, even when she started yelling and began running after his car as he drove away.

And although J.R. could care less if his father lived or died, he had a lot at stake. He was tired of trying to prevent the press from exposing his family and tired of dealing with defamation of his character. He'd worked too hard, and too long, and gone through too much shit to go back to the way things were. He'd put his life on that!

And when Donnie called him this morning, it didn't take him long to shower, dress and hit the road towards Lithonia to confer with his younger brother. He had so many "steps" and "halves" that it would not surprise him if someone came up to him on the street and claimed to be his brother or sister. Papa was a rolling stone.

Keeping his business from the media was the most challenging aspect of being who he was. Out of all of his "steps" and "halves", Donnie was the only one in his family that he could trust. He was also the only one that Jelani truly loved. With Donnie in his corner he knew that he would be okay. Thoughts raced through his mind. Pressure swelled up in his nasal cavities, something that happened when he was upset. For many years his mother thought it was allergies, but he knew. He knew when his father acted out, that the pressure in his sinuses would start. He knew that when his mother was crying, that it wasn't allergies. It was stress. Too much stress for a little boy.

And Donnie, being only two years younger, did not live with them. He was a "half" that nobody knew of until they were both well into their teens. Jelani envisioned the look on his mother's face the day she finally admitted that his father was sleeping around. She cried that night, more than she'd ever cried over him. Tears filled with misuse, disloyalty, and mistrust. A deadly mixture that Jelani's mother had been carrying in her heart for many years. A beautiful, intelligent woman whose only crime in life was to love his father. And his father just yelled, telling her to shut up. Jelani remembered the night like it was yesterday. Could even feel the room shake as his father slammed the door on his way out, leaving his mother in a clump of mess on the floor. Too many thoughts, too many memories, that made Jelani angry at the world. His mind was in such a whirlwind of thoughts that he didn't even see the small Toyota Camry jet out in front of his truck.

A resounding sound of thunder roared through Maya's car as she was threshed forward, springing back from the force of her seatbelt. Crackling of metal and glass shattering rang from behind. Shattered glass cut into her arms. Maya flung back and forth from the impact. She lost control of her car and was catapulted into the next lane, where her car skidded to a stop. The small Toyota Camry was no match for the massive Range Rover.

Damage to Maya's car was immeasurable. Traffic began to

slow and onlookers gawked as a few drove around the wreck. Others sped by, appearing to be oblivious to the chaos happening in the two far lanes. Rain trickled through the side window, falling onto Maya's left arm. Maya's vision was blurred, as she slowly shook her head, trying to figure out what had just happened. Her slow deep breathing did not keep pace with the rapid thumps of her heart against her chest. She let her head fall back onto the headrest and waited for something else to happen. She could not move.

"Ah, baby I'm sorry. Are you okay?" He was unfamiliar and unrecognizable in Maya's blurred vision. "I didn't even see your blinkers."

Maya tried hard to focus on the dark stranger leaning in her car. His mouth was moving but she did not understand all of what he was saying. All she knew was that she was beginning to feel lightheaded. He reached in to touch her and rubbed her arm.

"It's going to be okay." She heard him tell her. "Don't move. I'm going to call 5-0 on my cell phone," he said in a hurry and dashed off behind Maya to his truck.

Maya let her head fall back onto the headrest, causing some slight pain when it hit the leather. Her heart was beating a thousand miles an hour. She could feel something wet trickle down the side of her face but she dared not touch it, for fear of what she might find. Maya let thoughts wander through her head. Her accident was unlike how her friends described it. Her life didn't pass before her eyes, she didn't see any white lights at the end of a tunnel, and she definitely didn't hear any voices of people familiar to her. All she felt was shock and pain.

She opened her eyes and lifted her head. The stranger had not come back from his truck yet. She pulled down the rear view mirror to check her lipstick and almost cried at her reflection. She had small cuts on the side of her face and there was blood trickling down from them. Her hair, which she had styled less than an hour ago, was in an upheaval about her head and she had glass and rain on her suit.

"Cops said they would be here in a minute." The stranger reappeared at the side of her door. " Do you know where you are? What is your name?" he asked in concern.

Maya just looked at the stranger's deep eyes. The questions and answers floated through her head but for some reason they could not find their way to her mouth.

"Do you have some ID with you?"

Maya slowly turned her head to look at her small purse, which lay on the passenger side seat. The stranger followed her gaze and briskly strode to the other side of her car and let himself in. He made himself comfortable, looking through her purse and through her wallet. He pulled out her driver's license and held it up to read.

"Maya Dickson?" he asked and turned to look at her.

She frowned at his aggressiveness. Who told him to go through her purse? She remembered stuffing two tampons in the corner of the inside of her purse before she left for work. And although they were both grown and this was an emergency, she had an ego that could not stand to allow some stranger to know her personal business. Cars drove by slowly and some honked their horns. The stranger looked up every now and then and yelled to the traffic.

"It's okay! We've got it under control. The cops are on their way."

"It's rude to go through a woman's personal belongings," she heard herself say as her heart rate began to slow and she tried to position herself to get more comfortable.

"Well excuse me. I didn't know rudeness was a factor in emergency cases."

"Rudeness is always a factor," she responded tartly.

"Well at the risk of being rude again. Do you have any insurance?" he asked, his dark eyes focusing on her. When Maya lifted herself up from her slouched position and unbuckled her seatbelt, she saw him looking at her hair and unconsciously raised her hand to her head.

"Yes baby, you look bad," he said, knowing that nobody had ever told her that. Indeed, she was an extremely attractive woman even with her hair flying over her head, blood trickling down her face, and clothes hanging off of her shoulder. Her large, brown, innocent eyes exposed her insecurities about her appearance.

"Excuse me?" Maya could not mask the irritation in her voice.

J.R. shifted his weight from his left side to his right and sat straight up in her small car. He had too much to think about to get into a cat and mouse game with this woman. He leaned his head back onto the rest and closed his eyes.

His day was planned and already there were screws being thrown into his agenda. Not only did he have to meet with his brother but his real estate agent had a family that was interested in buying one of his homes. And after he met with Donnie, he needed to get a hair cut. Not only that, but his plane was leaving at eight thirty that night to fly him into Florida for a game.

J.R. cursed to himself. Why did he constantly end up handling everyone's business? Why didn't he get a family like the Cleavers? His family was the most dysfunctional family in Atlanta. And he wouldn't be surprised if they were the most dysfunctional family in the country.

"When did the police say they were coming?" Maya asked wearily. She still had to get to work and this asshole was making his home in her car.

"You must not be from 'round here. Or else you'd know that we might be waiting here for awhile."

Maya's irritation grew. She had to get to work to prepare for her art gallery exhibit. There was no way she could miss any work for the next few weeks.

"Well, you don't have to sit in the car with me. I'm not a child," she stated, as if trying to reassure herself that she did not need his company.

J.R. just looked at her and laughed. He didn't say a word. He lifted himself out of her car and walked around back to his Range Rover, which was not in the least bit dented.

Shortly after J.R. reclined in his seat, the ambulance came and pried Maya out of the car. The paramedics tied her to a brown wooden board and put a neck brace on her, stabilizing her movements. Then they slid her into the back of the ambulance. J.R. handed the paramedics Maya's purse and watched as they rushed her off to Grady Hospital.

Once inside of the ambulance, Maya allowed herself to close her eyes and lose consciousness. She should have stayed in the bed this morning. She knew this was going to be a bad day.

*****

"How could you say something like that? If a black woman can't find a good black man, then it should be okay for her to venture over into another race," Malaysia said. She was cute with a slightly oval shaped face. Her dark skin had attracted Mandla the first time he saw her at the mall. Her close cut hair complimented her beautiful smile and her slim, curvaceous physique was all Mandla could watch now, as she conversed with Kayla.

Todd recognized Kayla shopping at Lenox Mall. He hadn't seen her in over two years. Kayla seemed thrilled to see Todd and when he had insisted that the two girls join him and Mandla at his house for brunch, they readily agreed.

"I beg to differ. We've struggled too long and hard to shamelessly fall into the hands of the oppressor," responded Kayla. She towered over her friend and she was in much better shape. Her honey blonde hair highlighted her light brown complexion and light brown eyes. She sat Indian style on the floor across from Mandla. Her friend, Malaysia, sat adjacent to Mandla. He watched each motion of her mouth.

"But the struggle is over. It's all about finding a decent man and settling down. It's a lot of women, *black* women who deserve good men. If they can't be found in our race, then why should we walk around being miserable? Don't you think that the black women who can't find that good black man should go for happiness if it presents itself in another race?"

"No. I think that happiness comes from within. It doesn't have anything to do with a man. That's where women go wrong. Thank you," Kayla said taking the glass of wine from Todd. She took a sip.

Todd handed Mandla a wide-mouthed glass of Korbel and gave Malaysia the orange juice she requested. Mandla was impressed with his manners. Certain women demanded respect and he could tell that Kayla and Malaysia were those types of women. Todd first met Kayla at his grandmother's house in Montgomery, Alabama. His grandmother's best friend had dropped by and brought her granddaughter Kayla. Todd and Kayla remained friends for a number of years and were pen pals when Todd attended Howard and Kayla attended UCLA. Eventually, they lost touch and neither one knew that the other was living in Atlanta, until they saw each other at the mall.

"What do you think?" Malaysia asked Mandla. She caught

him off guard.

"Uh, well. I'd have to agree with Kayla. African-Americans have gone through too much together as a race to just give up on each other like that."

"What do you think about women not needing men to ensure their happiness?" Kayla asked.

"Oh, *I* need to comment on that," Todd interjected. He kicked off his shoes and tossed them on the other side of the couch. Everyone was seated on the living-room floor near the fireplace, drinking. "Women *do* need men to make them happy."

"And why is that?" Kayla rolled her head. She was smiling.

"Because. If you..." he pointed to Kayla and then to Malaysia. "Didn't need us then there would be only one gender on this Earth."

"What?" Malaysia squealed.

"Oh *pa-leeeze*! I can't believe you said that. Todd you are so..." Kayla began.

"Hold up now. Give the man a chance. The brotha's spittin' knowledge." Mandla came to Todd's defense.

"For real. Hear me out. Think about how our bodies fit together." Todd moved closer to Kayla. "Like a hand in a glove."

"Todd we're talking relationships here, not sex," Kayla responded.

"I'm talking relationships too. A hand and a glove have a relationship right? You can't have one without the other. Am I right or am I right?"

"You're partially right." Kayla took a long sip from her wineglass. "But you've always been *partially* right."

"Oh low blow!" Todd wailed. All four of them laughed.

"I want to thank you for brunch. It was really good," Malaysia said.

"You welcome. But I have to admit, my man Mandla over there did all of the cooking. I just poured the wine." Todd downed the rest of his drink.

"Girl Todd don't cook." Kayla laughed.

"What you mean I don't cook? Girl please. I can burn."

"I remember when you used to live with your grandmother in Montgomery and she used to try to make you do stuff in the house. You used to always go to hollering about woman's work."

"Hell yeah. Shit I did all the work outside! All that cooking and cleaning and shit, that was for women. And let's not talk about when we were in Montgomery. 'Cause I sure do remember them little nappy afro-puffs you used to wear and all them colorful bows in your head."

"Okay, okay. We don't have to go there." Kayla laughed. "I just used Alabama to show how you don't cook."

"I cook sometimes, shit I live by myself. If I don't cook, then I'll be the one starving. Now if *we* were to get back together..."

"Oh no. I wouldn't get back with you." Kayla chuckled.

"Why the hell not?"

"First of all, I was young. And second of all, Todd you've turned into a D-O-G."

"Ohhh." Malaysia rolled her eyes and neck at Todd. He hung his head down and smiled. "Are you a dog Todd?"

"Don't even fix your mouth to lie," Kayla was watching Todd closely. All eyes were on Todd. He started barking.

"Told you. That's a shame that you would even admit it."

"It's all good," Mandla replied.

"Where's your restroom?" Malaysia asked as she stood.

"It's one right down that hall to your left," Todd responded pointing. Malaysia excused herself and disappeared down the hall. Mandla turned to Kayla.

"So what's up with your girl?"

"What you mean?"

"She cool or what? I wanna holler at her."

"Don't take this the wrong way Mandla." Kayla put her glass on the floor. "But you're not her type."

"Shit baby, I'm everybody's type."

"No really. She's from New York and if you not pulling in at least six digits, she ain't looking in your direction. Sorry."

"Ain't that a bitch," Todd said.

"Nah don't get me wrong. She's cool, but she's just used to certain things. She's dating this older Italian guy."

"That's why she was talking all that interracial shit."

Malaysia sauntered back into the den and resumed her position on the floor. Mandla looked over at Todd who was checking out Kayla's physique. Kayla took her last gulp of wine and handed the glass to Todd. She nodded to Malaysia who smiled and gulped down the rest of her orange juice. She was the only one in the room who wasn't buzzing.

"How long have you two known each other?" Mandla asked Malaysia as soon as she sat down.

"How long have we known each other?" she asked Kayla.

"Maybe about two years," Kayla said.

"Malaysia do you got a man?" Todd asked.

"Somewhat. I date."

"So you don't have a man?"

"I have friends?" She smiled. "Why?"

"Oh we were just wondering," Todd said with a smile.

"Oh."

"So Mandla, are you enjoying Atlanta?" Kayla interjected. She knew how uncomfortable Malaysia got when guys asked her about her status.

"Actually I am."

"Where have you been so far?"

"We've been to Atlanta Live, to The Underground. Uh, I've been to Lenox, to the AUC. Yesterday we went to the CNN center and Olympic Park."

"That's it?"

"Pretty much."

"Nowhere else?" Malaysia inquired.

"I haven't been here that long."

"I know Todd took you to Magic City and Nikki's," Kayla said smiling.

"What do you mean Todd took you to Magic City?" Todd asked.

"'Cause you a freak like that," Kayla responded. "I wouldn't be surprised if you took him to Montre's."

"Not Montre's Adult Entertainment Lounge," Malaysia laughed. They all laughed.

"You want me to replenish that glass girl?" Todd asked Kayla. He reached for her empty glass.

"No actually we're about to go."

"It was nice meeting you two," Mandla said. They all stood.

"Well Todd-ster. It was really nice seeing you again. Let me give you my number so we can stay in touch." Kayla pulled a piece of paper out of her purse and wrote her number down.

"Thanks for brunch. But we gotta get outta here."

"What y'all doing tonight?" Todd asked. Mandla had never seen Todd so concerned about a woman before.

"Oh we have plans," she replied smiling at Malaysia. Malaysia smiled back. "But call me sometime maybe all four of us can get together or something. Mandla how long are you in town?"

"Oh I'm working here. I'll probably be here a few months."

"I'm trying to get him to move out here," Todd said, following behind Kayla as she grabbed her belongings and headed for the door.

"It was nice meeting you. Bye." Malaysia walked behind Kayla. Kayla gave Todd a quick kiss on the lips and then the two women were out of the door.

"Damn potna," Mandla said once Todd had shut the door. "I thought you was gon' try to make love to her right there."

"I used to be *in* love with her back when we were in Montgomery."

Mandla laughed. "What happened?"

"Life."

"Damn."

"She's one of the few that I respect. And since she dogged me, it's on to the bitches!"

ANOTHER DAY
ANOTHER DOLLAR

Senida pulled the collar of her coat up and opened her umbrella. She normally didn't mind the drizzle, but she had just pressed out her edges the night before. She hated this time of the year. Especially when she had to work. The only thing nice about this weather, was her days off. It was unusually cold for July in Atlanta, complete with light drizzles.

She reached in the back seat of her burgundy Honda Accord to pull out her brief case, when she noticed a glitter of light wedged in between the seat cushion. Umph, umph, umph. She thought she had lost the tiny earring that her father had given her on her sixteenth birthday. Everyone was still amazed that she held on to them for all of these years. She carefully slipped the earring into the deep pockets of her brown coat and grabbed her brief case.

Trotting quickly across the company parking lot, Senida vaguely heard her name through the harsh winds. Much to her dismay, it was Cindy, walking a mile a minute and waving frantically to catch up to her. Damn. Why did she even turn around? The thin, white woman had known Senida only a short time, but latched on to her very quickly. Her short, brown hair blew as she swiftly carried herself on two long stiff legs. Senida could hear the clicking of the woman's heels on the wet pavement. She wasn't a bad looking white woman. Her lustrous, blue eyes were full of ambition and motivation. These particular qualities Senida found enchanting.

"Good morning Senida," Cindy chirped. "Boy is it ever cold out here. I don't understand this Georgia weather. I almost didn't make it in this morning. My bed was feeling so good. I told my husband that he's going to have to get a second job, so I can stay home on days like this." Cindy let out a shrilling little laugh as she tossed a few strands of hair out of her face. "So, how was your weekend...did you and Darrell do anything special...wow what happened to your eye?" she asked, with a smirk on her face.

Senida didn't have to think hard on why she hated to talk to Cindy. Or how strongly Cindy got on her nerves. The woman would say the craziest things to a person. She had that white people humor that Senida just didn't understand. One thing that Cindy was good at was keeping Senida informed of the gossip in the office.

"I ran into a wall the other night, and no, me and Darrell just hung around like we always do." Senida refused to let Cindy know that Darrell was not speaking to her or that he wouldn't return any of her phone calls.

"Oh, you ought to put ice on that. Well, Brad and I went to this bed and breakfast place. It was so nice. We spent the whole weekend laying up, eating fruit and enjoying each other...if you know what I mean?" Cindy let out another one of her ear splitting shrieks. Senida couldn't help but envy Cindy. Why couldn't she go to a bed and breakfast with her man? What did Cindy have that she didn't?

"Why don't you and Darrell ever do anything?" Cindy must have read Senida's mind. Her bluntness irritated Senida and she wished she hadn't stopped for the frail, pale lady.

"We enjoy each other at home," Senida replied, in quick, irritated voice.

Cindy did not respond until they reached the crosswalk.

"Oh well, I guess that could be fun too." She smiled weakly and quickly changed the subject. "Did you hear about Linda?"

Linda was the office flirt and was known for sleeping with the boss when his wife was away on business. She wore too short skirts and had cleavage that fell out all over the place. Her bleached blonde hair was usually pulled up in a raggedy bun and it always looked as if she was just waking up. She wore baby blue eye shadow around her gray eyes and her lips were always painted into a bright red pout. Her anorexic frame towered over every other woman in the office. She had to be at least six feet tall.

Linda was usually the main topic for gossip and the butt of

every tall joke, blonde joke, and every bimbo joke. Linda didn't get along well with too many other women in the office. Basically, she frequented herself around the horde of men in the office, laughing, clowning and spilling cleavage all over everybody. Her larger than life breasts announced her entry into every room and was usually followed by those long thin legs. Many of the men loved to see her rounding the corner with meticulous, risqué cat steps. She fulfilled most of their obscured fantasies, without so much as a simple touch.

"She's being transferred to the San Bernadino office." Cindy's diabolic smile crept across her face.

"She's being what? When, why?" Senida stepped up on the curb and stopped in the middle of the sidewalk, approximately ten feet from their office building.

"Yes. Transferred. I heard that Mr. Teft's wife found out about their affair and he's transferring her to save his marriage. His wife made him do it. She gave him an ultimatum." Cindy smiled and waved as a blue corvette slowed to the side of the curb.

"Hi. Good morning. Are we still on for lunch today?" she leaned into the car.

Senida adjusted her position, shifting from her right foot to her left and craned her neck, so she could see who was driving the expensive car. A responding voice was all too familiar to Senida, in an almost repugnant manner. Cindy continued to smile, long after the corvette slid into the opening of the employee parking lot.

"Was that Jeff Manor?" Senida tried to masque the disgust in her voice.

The two women entered the light gray twelve-story building. Jeff Manor was as irritating as white men could be. He constantly whined about his assignments and affirmative action. His favorite topic was welfare and the many recipients that he felt were black.

"Yeah. We're getting together today to discuss our new case. Anyways, like I was saying about Linda." They got on the elevator. "Six please."

Cindy did not notice the warning look that Senida shot her when they boarded the crowded elevator. She continued to ramble off the intimate episodes of Linda and Mr. Teft, totally ambiguous to the advertent ears of the other listeners on board. Senida shifted her eyes to see exactly who was inside of the elevator. Damn, why

didn't this lady shut up?   She had no discretion what so ever.
Umph, umph, umph, white people.   At least when she gossiped,
she was discreet.

Senida shifted her briefcase from her left hand to her right.
She had plenty of catch up work to do. She'd fallen behind in the
insurmountable amount of research that was needed for the Mortin
case. Since the man was known all over Georgia, there was much
work to do.

Lacey was the first person Senida saw when the two
women stepped from the elevator. Senida turned to Cindy in mid-
sentence.

"Okay Cindy, I'll see you later. I really have a lot of work
to catch up on." Senida tried to be nice to Cindy at times because
Lacey told her that she was mean to the woman. But plenty of
times, when Cindy was done gossiping, Senida had no more use
for her.

Cindy shot an almost hardened look in Senida's direction.
Lacey waved at Cindy and the two women exchanged hearty
smiles.

"I got some more stuff to tell you, Cindy. I'll come over to
your office later today, okay?" Lacey was quite fond of Cindy.
They shared many of the same office stories. Between the two of
them, Senida was abreast of every soap opera on television and in
the office. She knew who was sleeping with whose man on *All My
Children*, as well as at work.

Cindy waved bye to Lacey and carried herself away on
those long sticks of hers. Boy, how can she balance on such thin
legs, Senida thought. Lacey turned from Cindy's direction, still
wearing her smile, which slowly disappeared as she concentrated
her sight on Senida's eye.

"How was your weekend? Whoa, what happened to your
eye?"

How many times today were people going to ask her about
her eye? And she didn't do anything exciting this weekend. As a
matter of fact, she didn't do anything *any* weekend. Her highlight
was when she slashed her lover's tires, but she didn't dare say that
aloud. Her business would spread faster than an Arizona wildfire.

Senida started towards her small office, near the back, with
Lacey tagging behind like a lost puppy. The belt on Lacey's dress
was too high on her waist. And with each twisty move, it seemed

to rise higher and higher. Lacey's plump body was squeezed into a red dress with designs on the print and adorned with a shiny black belt that used to be in style. Knowing Lacey, she was trying to bring it back in style.

"I didn't do a damn thing this weekend. And my eye is fine. And if one more person tells me a cheery ass story about how wonderful their weekend was, I'm going to scream!"

"Well enough of that anyway. Girl I got some gossip for you," Lacey joyously sang out. Senida rested her briefcase on her desk and sat down in her chair behind her desk. "Did you hear about Linda Ross?"

Lacey's face was lit up like a Christmas tree.

"Yeah, Cindy told me on the way to the office." Senida hated to burst her bubble. Lacey plopped down in the chair, sitting on the opposite side of Senida's desk. Her once lit up face now looked as though she had been beat to the punch.

"She always beats me to the juicy stuff. She's good." Lacey let out a long sigh and slumped her shoulders in the chair.

Senida giggled at the sight of the woman's body, which could barely fit in the chair.

"Well she does." Lacey sat up straight, smiling back at Senida.

"Girl, you are so crazy. You make me laugh every time I come in this dreadful place."

Lacey leaned forward onto the desk, as if she were about to whisper.

"So did Maya meet any fine guys when she went out on Friday?" She lived for Maya's weekend rendezvous.

"I don't think she went out."

"What! Why not?"

"Since I couldn't go, I think she decided to stay home. Besides, what's out there for her anyway? A bunch of trouble." Senida looked down at her nails and started to pick the polish off of the right index finger.

"Chile that's what I'm talking about. That's the kind of trouble you want to get into." Lacey fell back into the chair and a rumbling laughter came out of her that shook the little office. Senida looked up and had to giggle herself. "Shoot, if I had a body like Maya's, I would be out every weekend looking for trouble...stirring up trouble...hell, I'd *be* trouble."

Senida and Lacey laughed until they felt a wrenching feeling in their guts. They would pause long enough to look at each other and then would start all over again, until they were almost out of breath.

"Whooo! Well chile, let me get back to work. I still got those flyers I need to send out for the annual charity drive. I'll talk to you later." Lacey stood and gave her right hand a little wave as she headed for the door.

"Oh Lacey, before you go, did you get that information for the Mortin case?"

"Yeah, I'm organizing it right now. I'll bring it in as soon as I'm done." She twisted her hippie body out of the office and back to her area. Lacey was a bit nosey at times, but she was a great secretary...and she made for good company when Sénida needed her to be.

Soon after Lacey left Senida's office, the red light on her large square phone lit up. It stayed bright for a few seconds and then began to pulsate. Senida knew what was coming next.

"Senida you have a call on line one. A Dr. Cardell from Howard University."

"Ah yes. Dr. Cardell. Transfer him through Lacey, thanks."

Placing her hand flat on her desk, she reached for a pen and pad to take notes. Lacey transferred Dr. Cardell through to line one and Senida picked up.

"Dr. Cardell, hi how are you?" she warmly answered the phone.

"Ms. Johnson. I'm fine, how are you?" The deep Barry White voice surprised Senida each time she spoke with Dr. Cardell.

"I'm fine. What can I do for you today Dr. Cardell?"

"I'm just making my phone calls to all of the companies that are going to participate in our internship program to remind them that next week our interns will be starting."

"That's right. What day was that again?" Senida pulled her daily planner from her briefcase. Opening the brown book, she noticed that she jotted down the month but not the exact date.

"The third."

"Okay. Got it," she said, as she penciled the date in her planner. "And what is my intern's name?"

"Mandla Jackson. He's a real bright kid. Wants to go to law school. So I would appreciate it if you showed him the ropes, although *you* didn't choose to go here for law school. I still wish I could have talked you into attending Howard." He chuckled. "But Ms. Johnson...I'll let you get back to your business. Tell your mom and dad I said hello. Oh how's that brother of yours doing?"

"He's doing fine. This is his third year at San Francisco State. He's gearing up for Medical School."

"Great! Maybe I can talk him into attending Howard's Medical School." He laughed.

"You might. But you know Kevon's a mama's boy. He won't roam too far from Mrs. Johnson." Both Senida and Dr. Cardell shared a hearty laugh at her younger brother's expense.

"All right Ms. Johnson. You take care, and I'll be in contact in a few weeks."

"Okay Dr. Cardell, you too. I look forward to hearing from you again. Bye."

Dr. Cardell, the internship program coordinator at Howard University, was a friend of Senida's father. His efforts to attract Senida and her brother to Howard were present for as long as they were able to walk. His large, round belly used to stick out, making it hard for Senida or Kevon to hug him when he came to visit her parents.

Dr. Cardell lost the weight a few years ago when he fell ill with pneumonia. Minus the weight, Dr. Cardell was still jolly. He was the epitome of most of Mr. Johnson's friends: successful, great personalities, loyal husbands, and excellent scholars.

Senida stood and walked over to her window. She looked out over the streets at the people and cars below. The scene reminded her of an old western movie she once saw. People scurried as if the sky were falling, nobody looking directly at each other, but looking straight ahead. That's how Senida felt lately since Darrell wasn't around. Even her lover was feeding her with a long handle spoon. Sporadic episodes of lovemaking plagued her. Senida could feel her heart aching every morning that she woke and didn't hear from Darrell. She didn't realize what an important part Darrell played in her life. She would have to try to give him a call when she got home tonight or maybe she would even stop by his house.

Realizing that there was much work to be accomplished

before the five o'clock whistle blew, Senida flopped back on her chair and flipped through the information on the up-coming Mortin case. She would need to contact Mr. Mortin to confirm their meeting. Senida wanted to go over all details with Mr. Mortin before presenting them to the judge. Senida tried to remain objective but she felt sorry for Mr. Mortin. During the same time that Mrs. Mortin died of cancer, Senida also lost her grandfather. Since then she felt that she could relate to his tragic loss. She knew the pain of losing someone dear to the heart.

Senida pressed the intercom button to dial Mr. Mortin's number. She did not bother Lacey, as she wanted to have a private conversation with the man. His phone rang five times before his son George picked up.

"Mortin's residence."

Senida lifted the receiver from the square phone.

"Yes. May I please speak to Mr. James Mortin?"

"Mr. James Mortin is out today. Who may I say is calling?"

"Could you please have him call Ms. Johnson at Smithers' Law Firm. He should have my number but in case he doesn't...it is area code 404, 555-2929."

"I will give him the message."

"When do you expect him in?"

"I expect that he may arrive home around seven tonight."

"Okay. I'll call back tomorrow then. Thank you."

George hung up. Senida sat with the receiver still in her hand. She continued to flip through Mr. Mortin's files. She definitely needed the extra help around the office. Her intern could take on the excess paper work and help do the tedious research involved in trying a case with such public attention.

Lacey's voice echoed through the intercom.

"Ms. Johnson it's Maya on line one and she don't sound too good."

*****

Small abrasions and muscle strain? Maya felt as if she had been on the field with the Raiders, playing without a helmet. There was more tension than anything. Dreary walls in Grady

Hospital were crowded with other patients with similar and even worse problems. Hospital stench permeated the building. Death seeped from the walls and the fresh smell of blood lingered in the air. Hospitals were definitely not on Maya's list of favorite places to spend her day. But her recent car accident had caused her grief and physical pain, leaving her no choice but to remain at Grady for numerous tests.

The black Range Rover had taken her by surprise earlier, when it collided with her small, green Toyota Camry. Tension crept up her neck. She could not believe that the doctor was letting her go home with only a prescription of Trillisate. Her car was demolished and her head was pounding and all he gave her were some little white pills. She missed her South African Art Exhibit grand opening! And all he could give her were pills! Maya pursed her lips as the doctor stood over her gurney, explaining what was happening and going to happen.

"You'll probably feel more pain tomorrow than today. Your muscles will be stiff and your head will hurt some more. Make sure you don't take these on an empty stomach." Dr. Mayfield was a short, white man with graying hair around his temples. His thin nose and square chin made him look like a cartoon character. "As far as your abrasions, try to keep them clean. You don't want them to get infected. Any questions?"

"What the hell am I supposed to do about my car?" Maya fumed.

"Ms. Dickson, you'll have to talk to the insurance company about that," he responded quite annoyed. "Any more questions about your *health*?"

"No," Maya mused.

"Good. If you have any questions you can call me at that number on your prescription. Do you have a ride home?" He seemed genuinely concerned.

"Yes. My friend Senida is on her way from work to pick me up. Thank you doctor."

Dr. Mayfield slipped out of the room and Maya began to get dressed. She had been at Grady for over six hours and she was starving. She wondered how the grand opening went at work, and searched her pockets for some change. Nothing. The nurse was supposed to have her belongings from her car. When the two police officers arrived at the hospital, moments after the accident, they brought her stuff and informed her that the driver of the other vehicle would be paying for all damages to her car. Paying for all of the damages, Maya thought. Sounded a little fishy, but what the hell. She still needed a car while her car would be in the shop. She dreaded getting on the MARTA.

Her art exhibit would last the entire week, and then she had to start planning for her trip to California. This was no time to be without her car. This car accident would set her back financially, professionally, and physically. She knew that her insurance had just expired...why did she refuse to re-new her shit? The pounding in Maya's head began to intensify. She looked down at the bottle of pills in her hand. "Take one tablet orally every four hours for pain and swelling." Maya popped one of the thick white pills into her mouth, searched for a little Dixie cup and swished it down with water from the sink. Now she had business to take care of and she'd better get started.

By the time Maya reached the front of the hospital, Senida was already pulling up in the burgundy Honda. She jumped out of the car and ran to retrieve Maya.

"Girl are you all right? What happened? Can you walk? What did the doctors say?" Senida rambled on in her frantic voice.

"I'm fine. I just want to go home and lie down. My head is killing me."

Senida unlocked the passenger side for Maya and waited until she was sitting, before shutting the door. She ran around the front of the car and climbed into the driver's side. She shifted her car into drive and rounded out of the emergency area. Senida looked over at Maya, who was now reclining in the comfortable chair.

"So what happened? You scared the shit out of me today."

"I'm fine. I think my car suffered more damage than I did."

"Whose fault was it?"

"I'm not sure. But the other driver is supposed to pay for all damages. At least that's what the cops said." Maya looked over at Senida concentrating. "Don't worry about it. If I need a lawyer, I'll call you."

Senida smiled back at Maya.

"You know me too well."

"First I need to find this...Jelani Ransom."

"Jelani Ransom? Why does that name sound familiar?"

"I don't know. I was thinking the same thing when I first heard it."

"Humm...that's strange. Is he from here?" Senida swore she heard the name before...and more than once.

"I don't know. I found his card in my purse when I got to Grady," Maya said as she handed Senida the white business card.

Senida briefly read over the card and handed it back to Maya, who slipped it back into her purse.

"So he's into real-estate, huh?" Senida asked the rhetorical question.

Maya closed her eyes and tried to relax, wishing her head would stop pounding.

"He was a black man?" Senida probed.

"Yeah."

"What does he look like?"

"Very handsome. Tall, dark brown, and muscular." Maya did not open her eyes.

"Hummm."

"I knew today was going to be a bad day. I can't believe this! I have too much work to do. This whole day has been a nightmare."

"It'll work out. You just need some rest." Senida looked over at Maya's frown. "You're not worried about that gallery?"

"Girl I got so much work to do." She winced from the pain in her head.

"Maya. Stephen will take care of everything. Isn't he the person in charge when you're not around?"

"Yes."

"Well chill girlfriend. You just got into a car accident. Give your mind and your body a chance to relax and recoup. I just thank the Lord that the Camry was the only thing broken up."

Traffic lined the 75/85 Interstate. Maya's eyes were closed and soft snoring floated from her calmly, perpetuated mouth. Senida glanced at Maya ever so often to make sure she was relaxing. Senida focused on the road and thought about the last thing that Maya told her, Jelani Ransom. She could not shake the name or the eerie feeling she got when she tried to remember where she'd heard that name. It was a familiar name, but not familiar like she knew him. Just familiar like she'd heard it in bad company.

Senida pulled the car into Maya's parking space and gently shook her friend. She hated to wake her. It seemed as though the ride finally gave her enough peace to fall asleep. Maya did not stir and Senida began calling her name. Maya did not usually sleep this hard. Groggy, Maya woke and looked around like she didn't remember Senida picking her up from the hospital. Her blood shot eyes resembled two large gems. The pills the doctor prescribed worked well at putting Maya to sleep.

"I'm going to walk you up." Senida gathered up Maya's things and walked her up to her third floor apartment.

Maya handed her the keys and Senida quickly let them both in the apartment. Maya's apartment was a mess. Her bedroom had clothes strung all over the bed. Senida pushed the clothes off onto the floor in one swoop and Maya climbed under the covers and fell asleep instantly. Senida turned the ringer of the phone off and went into the kitchen, where she decided to do some cleaning up. She had nothing else planned for the night, so she might as well clean up her friend's house. She finished quickly in the kitchen, as there were not a lot of dishes in the sink. Maya's living room only had a few CD's out of place and a newspaper strung on the floor, where it looked like she sat the night before, watching the news.

Her bedroom was the biggest disaster area. Senida stood in the doorway and looked about the room. Maya must have been in a hurry this morning. There were shoes tossed in the corner, opened lipstick tubes on her dresser, and the clothes that Senida pushed onto the floor. Pillows from the bed were on the floor and papers were piled up in the corner of the room in two unkempt piles. Maya slept soundly on the bed.

"You better be glad we're best friends," Senida said out loud, as she began to pick up the clothes and hang them in the closet. Maya did not stir. Senida finished in Maya's apartment, took her keys and left.

*****

Jelani took in the moderately sized house. Red adobe type shingles offset its beige stucco. It was the only one like it in the neighborhood, and probably in all of Georgia, Jelani thought as he climbed the stairs to the lopsided lawn. A polka-dotted birdhouse perched on top of the long metal pole stood out in the yard. The children had decided on the colors for the birdhouse. When Jelani asked them why polka dots, they replied in unison that birds liked polka dots.

On the porch was a collection of shiny, noisy, tin ornaments that hung and sang out little chimes as the wind blew or whenever Jelani ran his fingers across them. Different colorful plants lined the outside walls of the house; so many colors and patterns. Donnie's wife, Tressy, enjoyed different...as she was different. Her crinkled, red hair untamed and free, confined only on occasion by plaits that flowed straight back astonished Jelani. Sometimes, when they had to go somewhere special, she would braid it into one, thick braid, that would hang just at the middle of her back. She then adorned it with a small bow that would match her outfit. These are the times when she looked the tamest, lest the unpatterned array of red freckles that covered her pale face.

Her audacious freckles were in accord with her wild, colorful personality. Personally, Jelani did not see what attracted Donnie to her. She was not his type. Yet, she kept the house together, in her audacious style, and she took care of their twins.

Jelani would have been fooled into thinking that everything in the house was in order, until that one day, when Donnie pulled him to the back of the house, wrinkles etching across his forehead. His eyes leaned into dangerous slits. That's the day when he told him that Tressy was seeing another man. Jelani laughed out loud at first, but quickly contained himself by pretending to cough, as he saw the seriousness of his brother's pain.

Jelani could not imagine anyone else wanting Tressy. Her wild, crinkled hair would not fit right in any other environment, but this one. But, after Donnie blurted out the story that he'd heard from Stan at the liquor store, about Tressy meeting with the same brown skinned man, three days in a row, at the corner of Ashby, he knew. He could feel it in his bones that Tressy was sneaking around. She had even taken to acting strange around the house when he asked her of her whereabouts. Home all day she would say or that she only went out today to get a few things for the house. Then she would quickly busy herself by cleaning or adding more colors to something that didn't need them.

Jelani assured Donnie that there was no way in hell, and not in a bad or disrespectful way, that Tressy could be sneaking around on him. She loved him and the twins, and adored the ground that he walked on. He was an excellent provider, good husband, wonderful father...and great lover, Donnie would chime in, grabbing and pulling at his crotch. But seriously, Jelani would say, she loves you man. I can't wait until I can be in your shoes. I'm trying to be like you. You the man, he would say, as they would give each other the pound and get back to working on the car, or whatever other business they were doing.

Today they would be discussing their father, not a subject that either one was fond of. But none the less, they were the only two left. Jelani pressed the small doorbell and waited to hear the children. Small feet were heard running towards the door and laughing and yelling came from within. He could also hear Tressy's voice overpowering the two children, daring them to open the door without her.

Tressy opened the door and stood squarely between Jelani and the children. Her red hair was braided in two French braids on either side of her head. Her freckles lit up and danced around when she saw Jelani. She wore a simple, red dress with multi-colored accessories. Her lips were slightly rouge and her appearance looked neater than usual. Donnie must have told her that she had let herself go after the twins were born. A subject that he mentioned on more than one occasion.

"Uncle Jay!" Two little red haired kids ran from around their mother and latched on quickly to each of his legs. Jelani laughed and scooped up the little girl and boy. He kissed both on their cheeks, did the same to their mother and entered the house.

"Uncle Jay I got a new bike," Jah exclaimed. He was slightly smaller than his sister but just as red. Both of them looked so much like Tressy, that outside of their broad noses and thick lips, Jelani would not have believed that they were Donnie's kids. Now Jahrina was scrambling to get down from her uncle's arms and Jah followed.

"Me too. I got a bike too. Wanna see my bike Uncle Jay, huh?" she said as she pulled on his leg, trying to escort him to her room.

"No. He gon' see my bike first. I said it first. Uncle Jay wanna see my bike first?" Jah tugged at his other leg.

Jelani pulled a wad of money from his pocket. He flipped past the fifty and twenty-dollar bills and pulled out two crisp fives.

He handed one to Jah and one to Jahrina.

"Here's a five dollar bill for each of you. Now, whoever can write their ABC's first, gets a twenty dollar bill."

Jahrina's eyes lit up. "I can write my ABC's. Huh, mommy? I learned them in school, but Jah doesn't know all his. Huh, mommy?" she said, looking back and forth from Jelani to Tressy, as Tressy nodded to the little girl and smiled.

"But what about my bike Uncle Jay?"

"Okay. Why don't you both go get your bikes and bring them in the living room, so I can see them both at the same time? But not until you write your ABC's!" Jelani winked at Tressy, who only shook her head before she went back into the kitchen.

The two children raced to please their uncle. Jelani could see Donnie out in the backyard working on his car, as usual. But the smell of collard greens, beans, and cornbread kept him from going out too fast. He tiptoed into the kitchen and stuck a spoon into the pot, while Tressy's back was to him, as she looked for something in the refrigerator. Tressy turned around and swung her towel at him just missing him as he jumped away from the pot laughing.

"Get away from that pot boy! Your hands probably aren't even clean. Ain't no telling where they been either," Tressy said, as she reached for another spoon to stir the beans. She bent to look through the glass window of the oven at her cornbread.

"Almost ready. Now I think I'll make a pie or something," she said, almost forgetting Jelani was still in the kitchen and then she looked at him.

"Are you done pitting my children against each other for your attention?" She leaned her back against the counter and put her right hand on her hip.

"Nothing wrong with a little competition," Jelani replied in a matter of fact tone. "Besides, Jah needs to get used to it now if he's going to play football." Jelani reached into the cabinet above his head and pulled down a small saucer. He would at least be able to taste some of the greens.

"Oh no. You're not corrupting my son. He will be too smart to be a *football* player. He's going to have to learn how to be competitive when he's applying to medical school."

"Medical school?" Jelani dug his fork into the pot of greens and plopped the wet, stringy vegetables onto his plate.

Tressy may be good to his brother, but when it came to cooking, she was good to him too. He reached for the hot sauce and began pouring it on the greens.

"Yes, medical school. Jelani, the world does not revolve around sports. There is more to life than just playing football."

"Like what?" he said as she hit him with the towel that had previously hung over her left shoulder. "Just kidding. But he's a boy. Competition won't hurt no matter what field he goes into. As long as he has his Uncle Jay he'll be all right."

"A boy? So Jahrina doesn't need competition?"

"Yeah I guess." Jelani shoved a large fork full of greens into his mouth and chewed. He wanted to keep Tressy waiting. He knew the conversation would get heated when he talked about the twins. Tressy was a die-hard feminist when it came to her daughter. Her own life was a different story though. Each visit brought about playful teasing between the two. Donnie would sit back and just chuckle as the two went at it on every visit.

And even though Jelani would never date Tressy himself, he liked her. She was spunky. She had a zest for life. And he liked his women that way. But he would never have been able to get past that red hair, that pale skin, and those freaky freckles. He had only prayed that the two little babies would not be born with freckles, like their mother. Even held his breath and did a silent little prayer right there in the hospital.

Much to his joy they were not born with freckles, but the hair was unmistakable and the stalk, pale skin in contrast to their father's deep mahogany color had shocked Jelani. But don't worry Jelani, Tressy would say, I didn't start getting my freckles until I was ten. And then she'd smile. She knew that he did not like the way she looked. Could see it in his eyes when he looked at her. Could see it in his eyes when he looked at her children.

And although he didn't like their appearance, she knew that he loved them dearly. And that's all that counted. She didn't care whether he liked *her* looks. She felt as though she wasn't put on this earth to please Jelani and wasn't about to try. She cared for him as her brother-in-law, but did not agree with the way he thought. Chauvinist, she thought. Too used to women doing for him. He used his good looks and money to claim power.

He would take power and wrestle it to the ground. Grab a hold of its horns and fight with it. Fling its head back and tie it up.

Most of the times he usually won. And Tressy didn't want her kids growing up thinking that money was everything. That it was the cure to all problems. That it was more important than life itself and that it was okay to lie, cheat, steal and kill for it.

At first she didn't want them to become shells, people without insides. No feelings, no remorse, no emotions for others, like she thought Jelani was, until that Sunday when she looked deep into his eyes for the first time. She didn't see coldness there. She didn't see dark, cool coals that were so dull that they did not reflect her image. She saw another side: a side that was uncertain, insecure at times. Someone who was thrust into the world under unstable conditions and has yet to deal with the pain of an uneven, unfair world. A world where brothers are pitted against brothers, sisters against sisters, children against their mothers, and mothers, even, against their own children. Children who did not ask to be born, unknowing of the turmoil that would be hurled at them from the first day. Like Jelani. And that is why Tressy liked Jelani...now. It took awhile, but she saw past his rough exterior, into a heart of pure gold, concealed by pain.

Jelani chewed hard and swallowed hard. He looked over at Tressy and smiled. She did not return his smile.

"Yeah, I guess Jahrina will need competition in her life too. Cheerleaders go through a lot of competition. It's hard to shake those pompoms." He walked out quickly, plate and all, before she could respond. She yelled after him, throwing her towel at him.

"All right Jelani! Don't play with me today!"

Donnie was bent over, tinkering with his old *Sanford and Son* truck. A hobby of his since childhood. His large body was bent at the waist. He wore a dark head rag wrapped around his head. He was a large, dark man, with a broad nose and sleepy eyes. Many women called them bedroom eyes, but Jelani thought he just needed to get in the bed a little earlier than he usually did. He was an attractive man. Most everyone in Jelani's family was attractive. His mother was an extremely attractive woman. Used to turn many heads when she walked down the street or entered a room. Even his father was an extremely attractive man. All the women threw themselves at him. Unfortunately, he was always there to catch them.

Donnie's face had spots of grease smeared on his right cheek. Some of his curls hung from underneath the scarf.

Donnie's hair was naturally dark and curly. He took pride in its texture and took good care of it. Constantly running his fingers through his hair, Donnie would tangle and untangle his hair. The habitual action usually indicated that he was nervous about something. He looked up when Jelani stepped outside. Two tin flats covered the small garage area, supported by four wooden posts. Underneath the truck lay an old, green, worn out blanket that Donnie used to slide under the vehicle. Tools were spread around the outside of the green blanket and grease was everywhere. Jelani stuffed the last of the collard greens into his mouth and set the saucer onto a wooden bench. He leaned into the truck and watched Donnie work his magic.

"You seen Tressy?" He asked as he looked up at Jelani and handed him the wrench that he was working with. "Hand me those pliers. Did you talk to her?" he asked not necessarily waiting for Jelani to respond.

"Yeah, saw her in the kitchen. Talked to her too, for a minute. Why?"

Donnie looked up at Jelani. He stood, pliers still dangling in his hand. His eyes were narrowed and Jelani knew that he was about to lay something heavy on him.

"I think she still stepping out on me," Donnie said, as he removed the rag from his hair and started raking his fingers through his curly mane.

"Man, why you still think that? Stan said he saw her again?" Jelani looked through the sliding glass door. He could see Tressy busying herself with preparing her meal.

"Nah, ain't said he seen her since those three days last week. But sometimes I call her in the middle of the day and she ain't here. When I ask her where she been, she say to the store. I can't call her a lie, cause she usually got something that she done bought from the sto'." He raked more and more.

Curls were falling everywhere. Across his face, around his ears, and back at the center of his head, curls fell all over. Jelani felt sorry for his brother. He was a softhearted man. But before he could get a response out, the sliding door sprung open.

"There you are! I been looking for you. I wrote my ABC's and you have to come see my bike. It's in the kitchen." Jahrina almost sang the words out.

"All right, now let me see here," Jelani said, as he studied the scribbled letters that looked to be quickly thrown together. He said the entire alphabet, while Jahrina danced around twirling her arms, red hair flying left and right, creating an illusion of a flock of red birds flying South for the winter. After telling her how smart she was and seeing her bike, he reached in his pocket and pulled out a twenty-dollar bill, which she quickly grabbed to go show and tease Jah.

"Man those kids are getting bigger and bigger," Jelani finally said, still looking in the direction of where Jahrina dashed.

"Yeah they are. Those my two angels." Donnie beamed proudly, temporarily forgetting about the conversation that they were having about Tressy. He then looked over at Jelani. "Hey man, what took you so long to get over here? I thought you said you was leaving as soon as you hung up the phone."

"I did. I had a little fender bender on the way."

Donnie stopped what he was doing and concentrated on his brother. The one that looked so much like their father. He knew of Jelani's secret desires to get married and have children. Jelani was the son that made every father proud, except their father. He knew of Jelani's inner thoughts, as they had stayed out until all times of night, for years, once they'd met for the first time. A shame, Donnie thought, two brothers with so much thinking in common, living in the same state, the same city for that matter, and didn't know each other until they were teenagers.

But Donnie had known all along. He knew when he would see the man steal away in the middle of the night. Even sometimes spend the night. He knew of the other family, just didn't know who or where they were. Donnie was just a small tot when the man started coming around the one bedroom apartment, sniffing behind his mother's behind like some lost puppy. He hardly ever paid attention to Donnie, who usually had to sleep in the living room on the foldaway bed, when "mommy had company." Tears would stream down his little cheeks, as he covered his ears with his tiny hands, trying to drown out the moans and groans that came from behind the thin door, every time this stranger, came to visit.

It wasn't until he was sixteen that he decided to search for the "other" family. He did this long after the man stopped coming around. Long after the moans and groans behind the door had died down. Long after his mother cried out for the man in the middle the night. Donnie's first intentions were to find this man that caused his mother so much pain.

But later, his intentions were to find the "other" family, when in a drunken stupor his mother let the words slip out, as easily as water dripped from a leaky faucet. Those three words rung through his head with such riveted force that he had to sit down. "He's your father," he heard flow from his mother's mouth. His room had spun, his stomach caved in, and his insides fought and swirled and rushed to get out any way, the quickest way, through his mouth.

Donnie vomited for close to an hour that night, until dehydration, hysteria, and delusion set in. The stranger that had stole away in the night, ignored him sitting on the foldaway bed, hurt his mother, and broke her heart, was his *father*? His *father* sent Donnie's mother to her deathbed when he left her. He left her to search for that moaning and groaning that he'd given her in the middle of the night. And left her to find that satisfaction in first, a bottle, then a joint, and eventually a crack pipe. Left her for dead is what he did.

"Nothing serious though. Well not for me. The other car looked like it might be totaled. Shame too, 'cause the woman driving was fine as wine man. I haven't stopped thinking about her since this morning." Jelani continued with his story, bringing Donnie back from the past.

"Yeah, shame." Donnie continued to twist his wrist inside of the car, seeming a little distracted and aloof.

"I gave her one of my business cards. I wonder if she'll call."

"Cards?"

"For my real-estate business."

"How's that going."

"It's going cool. I'm glad you gave me the idea to buy and sell property. The homes practically sell themselves. It's a lot easier than I thought."

"Yeah, if you play for the NFL and can afford to buy homes like us poor folks buy candy."

Jelani chuckled.

"Daddy, Jahrina did her ABC's first and I didn't get to show mine to Uncle Jay." Jah had slipped through the sliding glass window. He had tears in his eyes. He sniffed and the tears began to fall. He buried his face into his father's pants.

"Get off me now Jah, you see I'm covered wit grease, boy. Go on over there to your Uncle Jay, move now." Donnie lightly pushed Jah from him with his leg and Jah let out a loud wail.

"Come here Jah. Come here boy. Cut all that crying out and let me hear you say your ABC's." Jah walked slowly over to Jelani wiping his tears and nose with the back of his hand. He climbed on top of Jelani and spewed out his rendition of the alphabet. Jelani and Donnie helped him through the rough spots and assured him that he would have them down pat in no time, if he just kept practicing and didn't let Jahrina bother him. Jelani pulled out another twenty-dollar bill and placed it into Jah's tiny hand.

"Now don't go telling your sister that I gave you this. It'll be our little secret okay?" Jah nodded, kissed his uncle and scrambled to the ground. He quickly ran towards the house yelling.

"Jahrina! I got some money too!"

Both Donnie and Jelani laughed at the little boy's quick promises. It made both of them wish that they had the same type of relationship with their own father. This brought them through the past and back to the present and what they needed to do. Everything that needed to be accomplished that day. The whole reason that Jelani was there. Donnie and Jelani entered the house and went straight back into Donnie's den, and closed the door. Tressy knew not to bother them when they shut the door to the den. She kept the children busy so they wouldn't bother them either. She saw the tired, disgusted look on her husband's face when they walked in past their kitchen and into his den. She knew that look. She knew they were going to talk about their father. She hated to see her husband worn down like this. That's why she felt just a little better for not letting him know about the sneaking around she'd been doing.

MALE-BONDING

Mandla could hear Todd as he got ready for work. He could tell that Todd was trying not to wake him, but Mandla had been up for a few hours. He could not sleep. He was too excited about starting his new job next week and even more excited about finding his own spot. Todd was his boy and all, but they were on two different wavelengths nowadays. Mandla was trying his hardest to concentrate on his future. After his mother told him that she would be laid off soon, he knew that he would have to be the sole provider for his family. She warned him before he went to Atlanta to stick to his goals and his dreams would come true.

Mandla swung his legs over the side of the bed and went to the shower. He showered and threw on some sweat pants. He would probably start working out today. Todd had a membership at Run and Shoot, and he was going to use his membership to get his "swoll" on. He looked at the clock, it was almost eight and he could still hear Todd moving around about the house. Mandla knew for sure that Todd had to be at work at seven. He went to the door and slipped down the stairs into the living room, where Todd sat. His head was in his hands and he was bent over, with his elbows on his knees. He looked as if he'd been crying. Mandla cocked his head to one side to make sure he was seeing what he was seeing.

"Potna? You a'ight?"

Todd looked up and Mandla could tell that either he had been crying, or he got a hold of some bad weed. Mandla sat next to Todd.

"Man what's up? I thought you had to be at work by seven."

"I ain't going in today." Todd looked up at Mandla, as if he were waiting for an answer.

"Why not?"

"You know that crazy hoe said she was pregnant?"

"The one that was here the other night?"

"Yeah."

"Damn. I'm sorry to hear that." Mandla thought back to Chandra and what he'd done to her when he made her get an abortion. "Be careful."

"Yeah. I'll be fine. I just need a minute to digest this shit. I mean, she just called a minute ago and told me." He began untying his tie and loosening his shirt.

"What you gon' do?"

"Man, I don't know right now." He leaned back on the couch and then looked at Mandla.

"Where you going today?"

"To Run and Shoot and then to get a few things from Target. Put your shoes on and we'll go shoot some hoop. You can let off some steam."

"Yeah, it might do me some good. Give me a minute to change. I'll be right back." Todd dashed upstairs and dressed. He wasn't in the mood to drive, so he let Mandla handle the jeep.

The gym was crowded with early morning people. Every one had their own hidden agenda to get fit for: the coming summer, the New Year's party, the size five dress, the wedding suit, or just because they pinched a few inches too much. Todd and Mandla played a few games. Todd let out his aggressions on the court and won the game for his team. After a few hours, they both went to watch the women in the aerobics class. When that played out, they decided to go home to shower and then go to Target.

Mandla talked about his future plans and how he couldn't wait to get accepted into law school, so he could gloat to the people who always told him he would never amount to anything. The woman at the corner store, the sixth grade teacher, his math professor, his English professor, his history professor, his ex-girlfriends, and his potnas who chastised him for going to school, all said that he wouldn't amount to anything. And now it was his time to shine and prove them all wrong.

Todd listened to Mandla's stories, but he couldn't get his

mind off of his own situation. He hadn't planned on being a father at such a young age. He couldn't believe his luck, he thought, as he turned the jeep into the driveway of his house.

"Sometimes I wonder what my purpose in life is," Todd said out of the blue. He passed a cold bottle of water to Mandla. "I mean. We really don't have very much time left on this earth."

Mandla watched Todd carefully, as he gulped down part of the water. Mandla knew that Todd would start talking deep, when he'd heard about his situation. Every time a person was faced with life altering predicaments, he would start to wonder about his own purpose in life.

"Man I think about that all the time. Especially lately, since I've moved away from moms and the girls."

"You know me and my mother were never close. My grandmother raised me. I barely even knew my mother before she died. For the longest time, I thought my grandmother was my moms."

"In essence, she is your moms. She raised you didn't she?" Todd nodded and then threw his head back and took another swallow from the bottle. Mandla stood near the entrance of the kitchen. He was leaning on the breakfast bar. Todd was leaning against the kitchen sink. Mandla's gray eyes were solemn. Part of him wanted to stay in Atlanta and make things work out, but the other half didn't know what the hell he was doing in the city. He'd laid awake almost every night since he decided to move, wondering and worrying about his family.

"That's a shame too." Todd was staring off into space.

"What is?" Mandla asked.

"That a child grows up and not really knows who his parents are."

"Shit. I know who my father is and I wish I never met the mothafucka'."

"I feel you. I think I was about seventeen when I finally met my father and that was a waste of my time."

"I swear, when I have kids it ain't going to be like that. It's too many fools out here not taking care of their responsibilities. I hate to see little kids running around not knowing who they daddies are. Even if he is trifling, you should at least know who the mothafucka' is."

"Fo' sho'."

Mandla walked into the den and kicked off his shoes. Todd followed and they both sat on the couch. Todd reached for his remote control and turned on the C.D. player. Tupac Shakur blared through the speakers. Todd was staring off into space. Mandla sat and listened to the lyrics.

"Man, who was baby trying to holla' at you, when we was playing basketball?" Mandla sat up. "She looked so damn good."

"Oh, that was Courtney. She crazy. We fucked a few times and now she don't know how to leave me alone."

"Why would you want to leave something like that alone. Shit, pass her my way. That mothafucka' was phat!"

Todd started laughing.

"So what's up with the women out here? You like what you see?" Todd reached for the remote and turned the music down.

"Yeah what I see, but a lot of these women don't know how to conversate."

"Fuck a conversation. They don't need to know how to conversate. They look good. Got body and everythang."

"See, that's why you be having bad luck. Your standards are too low."

"And what's *your* reason for having bad luck with them?"

"Man, fuck you."

"Yeah, 'cause we ain't gon' talk about that time you was trying to get with that transvestite." Todd laughed. He hadn't laughed all day. It felt good.

"Shit, you can't tell down here in Atlanta."

"The hands and the Adam's apple, baby. The hands and the apple," Todd responded pointing to his throat. He erupted into more laughter.

"Did I tell you that Kayla called yesterday?" Mandla remembered.

"Nah. What she want?"

"She said she wanted to know what we were doing next weekend. She said she would call you back."

"Uh."

"Would you get back with Kayla?"

"Nah."

"Why?"

"Kayla wants too much. Kayla is one of those women that want a relationship. With her it's either relationship or get ta' steppin'." Todd reclined into the large sofa cushions. "She wanted me to go on vacation with her next year."

"Where she trying to go?"

"Jamaica."

"Word. You know that's my thing."

"Oh snap, you still doing that student rep thing?"

"Yeah. It bring in a little money. I already got two clients in Atlanta."

"Bet. Well I'll tell her about it. But I ain't going on no vacation with her. She might get me out there, give me a few drinks, and I'll wake up married."

"Man you stupid." Mandla laughed.

"What's up for tonight? I need to get out of here."

"I'm down."

"Atlanta Live?" Todd stared at the television.

"That's cool." Mandla was in the mood to kick it anyway.

Once he started working, he would calm down on the clubs. He was just ready to make some cheese, so that he could decide if Atlanta was the place for him. Mandla had future plans on becoming a lawyer and the quicker he got started on that, the quicker he could get paid. And that's what it all boiled down to, making that cheddar.

*****

Maya almost took Michael up on his offer when he called. She'd been dressed for almost an hour and now all of a sudden Senida couldn't go out. Maya knew it was that damn man. She didn't understand why Senida would pick a night with a young, strapping, fine man over her. Well then again, maybe she did understand. But when Michael called, Maya was about to tell him to come pick her up. But she thought twice when she remembered the gun that Glenda had waved around her head.

"Baby look, Glenda is finally out of my life. I promise."

"Michael are you crazy? That woman held a gun to us. And you told her you loved her and comforted her. It took you how long to finally call me to see if I was okay? Forget it. I don't ever want to see you again."

"Maya honey, I was only telling Glenda that stuff to get the gun away from her. You got to believe me. We can still work this thing out."

"How can we work this *thing* out? I can't even trust you, Michael. I can't believe anything you say to me."

"Can you believe that I love you?"

Maya hung the phone up in his face. She then turned off her ringer. She knew he would try to come around again. They always did. And she was sure that was not his last attempt at getting her back. Maya looked around her den. Now what was she going to do? She'd finally had a chance to get out of her apartment and that was ruined. She knew for sure that she was going to go crazy being cooped up in her apartment for so long. No car! It was almost impossible to believe that the words Maya and car were separate. Was somebody trying to tell her to stay her fast ass at home?

A week had passed since the accident and her car was still not fixed. The mechanic was never in and when he was in, he wouldn't tell her anything that was of any relevance. She couldn't believe that she had nobody to pick her up and she was dressed and ready to go shake her ass.

Maya went into her bedroom and stood in front of the full-length mirrors on her closet doors. Damn I look good tonight. Maya had worn her red, snug fitting dress, which hung slightly under her well shaped behind. I guess the men in Atlanta are going to miss seeing me tonight, she thought out loud. Maya looked back into the mirror and gave a little twirl. Her shoulder length hair swung, as did her gold, dangling earrings and matching gold necklace. She picked them up at a little boutique in Lenox Mall. Her matching red pumps went perfect with her dress. "And to think I only paid $22.95 on sale," she said aloud to a smiling reflection.

After approximately 15 minutes of cooing to herself in the mirror, Maya's smile disintegrated into an even, non-emotional line. All dressed up and nowhere to go. Umph, umph, umph. It's a shame women can't be more like men, independent. Who was she fooling, she thought, as she looked around at the empty room? She sometimes felt the raft of loneliness, like now. And even though Senida was bored out of her skull with Darrell, Maya wondered if she would meet someone to adore her, the way Darrell had adored Senida. She did have to admit that she's had her share of good men. At the time, she may not have considered them to be good. But reflecting on the past, she thought of how stupid she was to have let some of those men go.

Yeah, she fell into the conglomerated group of women, who wouldn't know a good man if he walked up to her and spanked her on the butt. Women sometimes tend to mess over the good men, creating dogs to mess over some good women, thus creating women dogs. The vicious cycle continues. Maya remembered the many men swooning, as she picked them off one by one, like a group of flies. But tonight she was alone.

Feeling the sudden wave of emotions come over her, she sat with her back against the closet doors, staring off into her room. Senida cleaned her apartment like its never been cleaned before. That was last week. Now the bed was unmade. Her inner covers were on the floor and the top comforter was still intact. How the hell she did that was beyond her. I must fight someone in my sleep, she thought.

The matching dresser drawer, beauty stand, and nightstands were all gifts from Dr. Michael Hill. Why did she always have to accept gifts from men she knew she did not love? Her array of black art on the wall expressed her culture, and the many leafy plants helped her to breathe on those stuffy nights when her asthma was too much to handle. The stark white carpet matched the bedroom set, which was pure white wicker. Why did she have this obsession with matching? She had become a fashion freak once she graduated from Spelman. Up until that point, she was a diehard tomboy. Wearing nothing but jeans, sneakers, T-shirts, and baseball hats, she would often have to diffuse Aunt Setty's pleas to prove to her that she was a female.

Seeing no use in wrinkling a perfectly new dress, Maya decided to do some light reading, or call someone. She glanced at the clock, to the left, on the wall. Ten-thirty. It was still early to her. Everyone else went to sleep early. Maya thought of who would still be awake, Donald. He would be up, working on his thesis paper for graduate school. She was sure he would need a break right about now.

Donald let the phone ring five times before he answered.

"Hello?"

"Hi Donald, are you busy?"

"Oh hey Maya...well at this moment I am." There was soft music in the background. "I'm entertaining a guest right now."

"Guest? Who?" she asked, in her I don't care but it would be nice to know voice. "I thought you had to study?"

"Well Maya, sometimes we men get tired of chasing after one woman, and we decide that there are other fish in the sea."

"I guess it's obvious that your guest is not in the room right now?"

"No. As a matter of fact, she went to the bathroom as soon as the phone rang. Is there anything else, because I *am* busy." Boy. Give a brotha some new stuff and he wants to show his ass.

"Okay Donald, I'll let you go, but I'll be talking to you soon. I'll call you tomorrow? That is, if you won't be entertaining guests then either?"

"Well, I might. You never know."

"I'll just call and find out. You have a good night Donald." She didn't give him the liberty of hanging up first. It was hard for Maya to accept rejection from any man. She had become immune to the word no. Most people seemed to fall under her spell and give her whatever she wanted. Or at least, most stayed out of her way when she wanted something.

Maya felt restless and trapped. She thought about Jelani Ransom. Neither she nor Senida could shake the strange feeling that they got when they said his name. He was quite handsome and had a body that wouldn't quit. Maya thought of how he would feel under her covers at night. With the two large arms wrapped around her tiny waist. She could just imagine how he would run his fingers through her hair and then how his arrogant attitude and overpowering ego would fuck up the whole mood.

"Nah," she said out loud, as she shook her head. "It would never work."

Maya picked up one of her books that had been sitting on the white wicker nightstand for about three weeks. It had been collecting dust and tonight would be the perfect time to catch up on some reading...while she was alone.

IT'S PARTY TIME

Sounds from the building boomed as the crowd spilled inside. Cars lined the side streets of Downtown Atlanta. The night air was warm and the people were hot. It seemed as if the little Atlanta club was rocking from side to side with the beat of the music. It swelled bigger from the people trying to fit in.

Tonight was NFL night at Atlanta Live and the club was packed with groupies and wanna-be's. Jelani gulped his beer down as he watched the crowd move. Smoke filled the loud room and you could faintly hear balls being hit, racked, and broken, from the downstairs pool tables. Donnie was trying to flirt with the waitress, who only seemed interested in how much money he would tip her. Jelani knew Donnie had a few too many already, and that he would probably have to drive them both home.

Donnie leaned farther and farther over the bar, trying to get as close to the woman's breasts as possible. When Jelani looked into her eyes, he could tell she was a little nervous, she also looked quite young, maybe in her early twenties.

"Donnie, brotha chill for a minute and let the lady breathe. How do you expect her to get our drinks if you all up on her?" Jelani said, as he patted his brother on the back pulling him back down on the barstool.

"Ah man, why you hating on me?"

"I ain't hating on you, but let the woman do her job."

The girl nodded towards Jelani, gave a fake smile and quickly went to the other side of the room to take more orders. Jelani watched her from where he sat. Men were grabbing and pulling on her every time she walked by. She was a very attractive young woman. Much too young for his own taste, but none the less attractive. He could probably imagine that Maya looked that way when she was younger. Nice figure, wide, yet demure smile, and innocent eyes. He wondered where she was now. He wondered if he'd ever see her again. Or even if she thought about him. His insurance was supposed to take care of any kind of pain and suffering that she endured. But he hadn't heard from them in several weeks. So he assumed everything was taken care of. He usually didn't deal with those trivial situations. He had bigger fish to fry.

"Man!" Donnie yelled, as another group of half dressed women walked into the club. "This is the motherfucking life! And you sure you tired of this? I'll switch with you any day."

Jelani looked at Donnie. His eyes were red and swollen. Either from the shots that he'd been consuming all night or from crying over Tressy earlier that day. Jelani knew his brother and when he saw his eyes earlier, he knew that he'd been crying over that crazy woman.

"Man it ain't all that. I'd rather have what you have."

"Shit. Look at all these beautiful women. Are you crazy man? And you could have any one you want. All you got to do is snap your fingers," Donnie said snapping his fingers.

Jelani smiled at his brother and shook his head. Donnie laughed out loud and let out a loud whoop. He started bobbing his head to the beat of the music.

"You's a wild man Donnie," Jelani said, as he reached for the same young waitress from earlier.

"Did you forget about us baby?"

"No," she said as she almost lowered her head. "I'm on my way to get your drinks right now. I'll be right back."

"Don't be too long." Jelani winked at her and she briskly slid by him to the bar.

When the young waitress came back, she carried two Miller Genuine Draft beers in bottles. Donnie reached his finger under her skirt and pinched her behind. She almost dropped the tray on Jelani and he had to jump up off of the stool to catch one of the bottles.

"Ah baby. I'm sorry. My hand slipped. I thought you had something on your pantyhose." The young girl rolled her eyes and sucked her teeth.

"What's your name sweetheart?" Jelani asked.

"Deidra." She smiled.

"Deidra? That's a pretty name. You from 'round here?" he asked, as he looked her up and down, taking in the strong track calves and the ample bust.

"No. I'm from Jersey."

"I heard Jersey girls are freaks," Donnie chimed in, as she sucked her teeth at him again. He just smiled and continued to watch her butt, as it shook up and down to the beat of the music.

"Jersey huh? I was just there last month. How old are you sweetheart?" Jelani took her free hand and stroked it as she spoke.

"I'm...I'm...twenty four."

"Damn, you look young in the face. But the rest of your body is slamming," Donnie interrupted again. This time the girl turned her whole back to Donnie as if to cut him off from the conversation, but Donnie didn't mind, this gave him the opportunity to view her whole backside.

"You do look young. You got a man?" She shook her head no. "Well scribble your number on that piece of paper and I'll call you when I'm in town." She did as Jelani said and blushed as he kissed her hand.

"We'll be calling you again when we need some more drinks."

"Yeah, baby. Or when we need a table dance," Donnie yelled to her, as she walked away. She rolled her eyes, tightened her face in disgust and sucked her teeth.

Donnie turned to Jelani.

"She wants me."

The two men laughed, drank their beer and went out on the dance floor, to do it old school style. It was the most fun that Donnie had in awhile. Jelani enjoyed himself also. He liked to spend time with his only brother. On the dance floor, he swore he saw a woman that looked like Maya but by the time he walked up on her, she was gone. He stood in the middle of the dance floor, wondering if it was she. Had he had too much to drink or was she really there? She had become like a reoccurring dream to him.

*****

"Rack 'em up." Mandla said as he put chalk on his cue. Music blared in the background and he was feeling good. Todd had lost the last three games but Mandla felt no mercy.

"Man I think this is the phatest club in Atlanta. I needed to get out of that house. Thinking about that crazy girl would have driven me crazy."

"Yeah, I know what you mean. But don't think that I'ma spare you anymore embarrassment because of that."

"Ah nigga, I'm letting you win."

"Right." Mandla responded as he broke the balls with his stick. A resonant crack filled their ears as different colors rolled ambiguously across the bright green pool table. A few women gathered around the table to watch them play. Of course with an audience, Todd had to make sure that he played his best game. But Mandla was a skillful master at pool. Most of his free time spent at home was either on the basketball court or in the poolhouse down the street from his mother's complex.

"We got next." Two women set their quarters in the change slots on the table.

"How 'bout we got the next dance? I'm ready to get my groove on." Todd responded looking directly into one of the women's eyes. She turned to look at her friend who smiled.

"Okay." She picked up her quarters and her and Todd headed for the dance floor.

"Ah nigga, you just wanted to dance cause I was beatin' your ass," Mandla said as he threw his pool stick down. He mumbled, "Sorry sucka'."

Mandla and the other woman followed close behind them. Both women were bobbing their heads and shaking their butts on the way to the floor.

Crowds of people were gathered around the bar and packed tight on the dance floor. Mandla lost Todd in the crowd of dancing bodies but didn't mind. The woman that he was dancing with was slightly attractive. She smiled the entire time they danced. Four songs were played and Mandla had to get himself something to drink.

"You want something to drink?" he asked the young woman.

"Sure, thanks."

"By the way, what is your name?"

"Ericka."

"I'm Mandla." Mandla pulled out one of the empty barstools for Ericka and then sat himself.

"So, Man-da-la. Are you from here?"

"Nah. I'm from D.C. Where you from?"

"California."

"Oh that's cool." He responded looking around for a waitress.

"What are you and your boy doing tonight?"

"Chilling. Why what you and your girl doing?"

"We're going to IHOP to eat. You guys want to come with us?"

"What are you doing after IHOP?" He moved closer to her. His leg rubbed against her backside and he softly brushed his hand across her bare arm.

"Uhm. I don't know. But I'm only in town for a few days, so..."

"So...what?"

"I need someone to show me around town." Ericka's voice dropped to a deep, seductive tone.

"Cool. I can do that." Mandla reached for the young woman carrying the tray. "Excuse me, but can I get some Korbel. And..."

"I'll take a Brandy separator." Ericka offered. "Hey Deidra."

The waitress looked closer at Ericka and smiled. "Hey girl. What you doing out here?"

"Visiting. How long you been out here?"

"Two years."

"Well it was nice seeing you again. You look the same. I like your hair."

"Thanks." The waitress touched her hair. "I'll be back with your drinks."

The music in the club slowed and many people walked off of the dance floor. Mandla saw Todd walking in their direction but he wasn't with Ericka's friend. Each woman Todd walked by looked at him. Easing up on the stool next to Ericka, Todd gave Mandla a strange look.

"Where's my friend?" Ericka asked.

"She out there dancing, I guess. I ain't seen her in a minute."

"Well you need to find her before the end of the night, cause we going to IHOP." Mandla responded as the waitress came back with their drinks.

Todd leaned back on his elbows. "Aye. Ain't that Jelani Ransom over there?" He pointed to the other side of the bar.

"Yeah, that's that fool." Mandla responded. The waitress nodded her head.

"What does he do?" Ericka asked. She took the drink from the waitress's tray.

"Girl, he play football. And he fine." The waitress responded as she sauntered her way over to Jelani. He was standing next to another man. They were drinking, laughing and talking.

"What's up for tonight? We going to IHOP to eat after this?" Todd asked.

"Yeah." Mandla said. He was licking his lips at Ericka. She smiled.

"Well. I'll meet y'all at the front when the club is over. I see some women who need my company." Todd slipped away and into a group of attractive women.

Mandla and Ericka talked, drank, and laughed for the rest of the night. She enjoyed his company and planned on keeping in touch with him once she returned to California. Mandla enjoyed her company at the club and then later at IHOP. But he especially enjoyed her company at Todd's house, where they drank some more and chilled.

AIN'T CHOO
JELANI RANSOM?

He looked vaguely familiar as he stood in line across the store. Maya had sworn that she'd seen him somewhere. His large, strong build stood erect as he stared ahead, oblivious to her watching him. The strong, dark hands hung by his side gripping the tiny basket. He was attractive. The smooth, medium brown complexion had only a few nicks, which was expected of men. In his left ear was a tiny gold hoop. He towered about six-foot five-inch and weighed about two hundred and twenty pounds. Shifting positions on his legs, his thick muscular thighs pressed through the snug fitting jeans. His small waist expanded upward exposing a broad, even chest.

Kroger's Grocery Store was crowded and he was too far for Maya to initiate a conversation. His familiarity left Maya in awe. If she knew him from somewhere, why hadn't he tried to talk to her? There weren't too many fine looking men like him that slipped through her fingers. She observed him while he carefully placed his fruit onto the register belt. His hand slid into the front of his pockets to pull out change and Maya watched carefully to scan the bulge in front of his jeans. Nice. But where had she seen this God-like figure? His body was on hit! Maya knew he had to work out everyday or she was going to slap his mama for producing such a perfect specimen. His movements were calculated and each motion smooth. The cashier stood smiling as he grabbed his bag of fruit and headed for the door. He slipped out of the sliding glass doors without even noticing Maya *or* the many women watching.

Georgia's weather was humid, but not unbearable. Maya

left early after work to get to the store and back before nightfall. Since her accident, she was footing it and taking MARTA. Today she rode the bus to Kroger to get the fixings for tacos. All this public transportation was supposed to build her character, Aunt Setty told her. Fuck character! I want my car; Maya fumed, as she prepared to cross the parking lot to get to the bus stop.

The handsome figure was standing at his car when Maya started across the lot. Instantly, she remembered where she had seen the mysterious man, as he unlocked the door to his black Range Rover. The clanking of her sandals caught the man's attention and he turned around, squarely facing Maya, as she stopped dead in her tracks. He squinted at her with a puzzled look on his face. She could imagine the wheels rotating in his head. He hadn't recognized her yet. Maya tilted her head to the side and he broke out into a wide smile.

"Well hello stranger. You're looking better." His muscular jaw line flexed as he chewed the gum.

Paralyzed by the deep, dark mysterious eyes, Maya stood hypnotized, as they danced up and down her body in praise. Sparkling with a hint of seduction and danger, his eyes locked with her large round saucers. His nose was contoured like a sculpture, to fit perfectly in between those gorgeous eyes and his mouth. The sexy, full lips were outlined with a thin dark mustache. His lips spread across his white teeth as the wide grin lingered on his face. He was still chewing the hell out of that gum. Maya could not respond.

"Cat got your tongue?" he asked, still smiling and looking straight through her thin silk blouse. Heat from the searing eyes was beginning to arouse Maya's nipples. Each one uncontrollably poked through the thin material.

"No. I just didn't recognize you." Maya responded. She was trying her best to not sound like she was lying.

"I'm just glad we've met again, under prettier circumstances," he said leaning against his car.

"What's your name again sweetheart?"

"It's Maya."

"That's right. Maya Dickson right?"

"Yes. And yours is...Jelani Ransom right?"

"Yeah, baby. You heard?" he chuckled as his ego began to cause an eclipse.

Maya shifted her grocery bag from her right hand to her left and hiked up her purse strap on her shoulder. It was about time for her to leave and let him gloat in his own Holiness. Besides, it would be getting dark soon and she still needed to take the bus all the way up Ralph David Abernathy to the West End Mall, just to get to her apartment.

"You clean up pretty good," he continued. "You look much better without the blood and your hair flying all over the place." His constant chewing did not cease for a moment, not even when he began to chuckle at his own wry joke.

"That's not a very flattering comment," Maya spewed.

"Well you weren't very flattering that day."

"Who in the hell do you think you are..."

"Hold up baby..." Jelani said, as he held up his hands, as if surrendering. "Don't you got a sense of humor? As long as you okay that's what should matter, not what you looked like. 'Cause you know you fine so..."

Heat rose in Maya's cheeks. Just who did he think he was, embarrassing her?

"My car is still not fixed. The cops told me that your insurance was supposed to pay for all damages to my vehicle," she spat.

"But it looks like someone was riding around without insurance too," he said, referring to her canceled insurance.

Maya frowned. The more she stood and talked to him, the angrier she became.

"But your insurance was supposed to fix my car. There was no damage done to your truck." She whined trying to calm herself. She realized that he was an arrogant, pompous asshole and she would have to play his game to get what she wanted.

"No *apparent* damage. But I had to take it in because it was making a strange noise after you ran out in front of me."

"I didn't run out in front of you. You ran into the back of me! If you were paying attention and not speeding..."

"I think you were speeding too." He interrupted. "You were probably too busy looking in the mirror."

"Excuse me? I'm not the arrogant one here."

"Really?"

"I'm not going to stand here and argue with you. If you weren't speeding, this would have never happened."

"But then I wouldn't have had the lovely pleasure of meeting you."

"Listen. I need to get my car fixed!" Maya's rage grew.

"Baby, I'm not trying to talk about all that. Plus, I don't talk to nobody without my lawyer present. What I *am* trying to talk about is me and you. So what's up with that?"

She could not believe this fool. What's up with me and you? She was trying to get her car fixed so she could continue on with her daily routine of going to work. And all he had to say was, what's up with me and you? He had his damn nerve. Here she is *walking* and he riding around in a tight, sporty Range Rover! After all, *he* hit *her*. But *she* was suffering from *his* negligence. And now *he* wanted to talk to her about some bullshit. There was no way in hell that she would continue to stand here and shoot the breeze with this arrogant asshole. Not when it was his fault that she was catching the bus home. Maya tilted her head to look up at Jelani, squinted her eyes and twisted her mouth in the most vindictive way she could muster.

"*I'm not interested.* If you're not talking about fixing my car, then I don't have the time. Now if you would *excuse me*, I have a bus I need to go catch. Thanks to *you*!" She hissed and spun so fast on her sandals that she almost made herself dizzy. Her strides were not long enough and her legs did not carry her fast enough to the bus stop. Each step she took toward the waiting bus stop made her temper flare.

Jelani locked his door and followed behind Maya. He loved his women with a little fire in their ass. Not to mention that baby was fine! He made a mental note to conquer that ass. But when you play games with J.R., he makes the rules. All throughout his high school and college years he made the rules. There weren't too many women he knew that would not die to be with him. Now that he was cleaned up and straightened out, he was a prized possession. And he knew it. Ms. Maya Dickson was not going to get the satisfaction of telling him no. He had a problem with rejection. *He* was too fine and *she* was too fine.

But J.R. knew, eventually, she would have to come around. She seemed like she was one of those uppity women with an education. The kind he dealt with after he graduated from the University of Michigan. After he graduated, however, he fell for the easily accessible women. The one's who were no good for him. The closer he got to the speedy woman, the more he rambled through his mind what his therapist instilled in him. He tried to remember what she had told him. He resisted the urge to reach out and grab her. His therapist's exercises and breathing techniques worked like a charm.

By the time Maya made it to the bus stop, she was out of breath and this Jelani fool was only a few steps behind her. Why didn't he leave her alone? She thought she'd made herself clear, no car, no talk. It was simple. She worked too hard to have some arrogant asshole come flying by in a Range Rover and destroy what she owned. And he thought it was a joke. It wasn't funny when she had to take the bus and MARTA all the way to Decatur, in the rain. Or when night fell and she was still stuck riding public transportation risking her life in her not-so-safe neighborhood, to get home. He laughed and thought that shit was funny.

Maya stood by the side of the bus stop shuttle and looked straight ahead. She didn't want to hear anything that Jelani had to say. He circled around and stood directly in front of her, blocking her view of the street. His arrogance annoyed her and she wished he'd disappear. Jelani looked at the fire in Maya's large, brown eyes. She was gorgeous when she was mad. Hell, she was gorgeous anyway. He thought he might never see her again when they had the accident, but luck and faith brought them together. What were the odds of him meeting her today in the grocery store? He only stopped there on a whim to get some fruit. He'd never shopped there before. It was his first time.

Once he held her gentle hand in the car, he knew she was special. Different from all of the groupies that he was used to dealing with. He knew eventually he had to settle down and there were no prospects until now. At thirty-two, he had the world on his shoulders and no one to share it with. Grinning like a Cheshire cat, Jelani stood staring at Maya.

"Don't be mad at me. I just thought that two fine people such as ourselves, shouldn't let all of these good genes go to waste."

Maya's annoyance grew with every moment that he breathed in the same air.

"Could you please leave me alone?" Maya was close to yelling.

"Why would I leave a beautiful lady, such as yourself,

standing at the bus stop alone? Why don't you let me give you a ride home? Do you live around here?" Jelani smiled, as Maya turned to see if he was arrogant enough to be serious.

"It's because of *you*, that I'm standing at this bus stop in the first place! Now, unless you're talking about fixing my car *today* then we don't have anything else to talk about. So excuse me if I don't go running to your *Range Rover*!"

"Girl quit tripping. I ain't got all day to be arguing with you."

"Are we going to talk about my car?"

"Nah, not now."

"When?"

"I told you I don't discuss that kind of stuff."

"Is that so?"

"Yes."

"Well then I don't have anything else to say to you. Now please leave me alone!" Maya could not believe the rage that she felt well up in her chest. She could have spit on him, if he weren't so big...or good looking.

Heat rose in Jelani. He was not going to be clowned in front of all these on-lookers, who were obviously staring at him. They would have to pick this conversation up another time. Her little hard-to-get game was starting to piss him off. He had definite plans of contacting his insurance agency and lawyer to arrange for something to happen to her car. Although she was fine, she was beginning to work his nerves with her snotty attitude. But still, he didn't think that a young woman should be taking the bus at night, especially in this neighborhood.

A group of young boys swaggered toward the bus stop and stopped in their tracks when they spotted Maya and Jelani talking. Two of the boys stood looking and pointing, and the other three slowly made their way to the end of the corner and stood directly behind Jelani. One of the boys reached in his pockets and gave a pen and a piece of paper to the smallest boy. He tapped Jelani on the small of his back.

"Ain't choo Jelani Ransom?" he said, as he stood wide-eyed. Jelani turned, towering over the small boys.

"Yeah. You know it." Charm seeped through his veins like heroin. The sugary, sweet smile once again replaced the frown that Maya had caused.

"Can I have your autograph, please?" The boy held out the piece of paper and pen for Jelani to sign. Chatter rose from the group of boys as they muttered, "I told choo dat was J.R."

"Who do I make it out to?"

"Anthony." The little boy was obviously in awe with Jelani.

Maya watched in disbelief at what was happening in front of her. The other boys walked over to Jelani and searched for more paper. Digging into their deep pockets, the wide-eyed, awe struck boys pulled out enough paper to accommodate all five of them. Jelani scribbled something on each piece of paper and handed it back to the boys, who mumbled their thank yous and strolled off, periodically looking back at Jelani and Maya.

Turning his attention back to Maya, Jelani was only going to give her one more chance.

"Do you want a ride home?" he asked, exasperated. His six o'clock appointment could not wait for Ms. Maya to go round for round with him. Not only that, but he still had a host of other important projects that needed to be handled.

"I said no. You need to be talking to me about getting my car fixed not about giving me a ride."

"Fine. I've got things to do." And with that Jelani strutted back across the parking lot, hopped into his truck and disappeared down Ralph David Abernathy. By this time, Maya was fuming. How dare he leave her standing at the bus stop like that? Even though she said no, he knew better. His attitude was fucked up and she decided right then and there, that she did not like him. I don't care how good he looks, he's an asshole, she thought.

Maya stood with the frown on her face in disbelief. Although she hoped she never saw him again, his absence held a slight loneliness. Maya sat down on the bench next to an elderly lady. The woman watched the entire ordeal with Jelani earlier, without blinking.

"You and yo' boyfriend make a handsome couple. Y'all shouldn't argue. Me and my husband was together for over fifty-seven yearns before he died, God rest his soul. I likes to see young peoples getting along."

"Excuse me ma'am but he's not my boyfriend."

"When you my age those little things you arguing about don't mean jack. He looked to be a strong, young buck. If you ain't thought about it yet, you might want to make him your husband. I hear the youngins' saying it's hard for them to find a good black man now a days. Well he looked good to me! And he's black!" She waved her crooked finger in the direction where Jelani had disappeared.

Shocked, Maya watched carefully as the woman pulled a bright, orange wrapping from her pocket and popped a hard candy into her mouth. She sucked on the candy before finishing her lecture. Maya stared at the woman as she talked about her husband, her children, and her grandchildren. The woman enchanted Maya with her wisdom. Her eyes were deep with decades creased in between the pupils. She spoke of the hard times that the black men and women of her time endured and how important it was for the whole race to stick together. She talked until Maya's bus came, and when it did, Maya thanked her for the insight and went home.

*****

Mandla gripped the keys tight in his hand as he stepped out onto the sidewalk. His gray eyes took in the large apartment building...his new home. Although he would have to wait before he could actually move in, at least he had the keys.

The stone building was right off of Peachtree Street, near Piedmont Park. Perfect, he thought, I can go jogging in the morning before work. His internship would start soon and he was in much need of a break from Todd. Mandla had been in Atlanta for a little over a month and he knew of all the hot spots, clubs, hangouts, and knew many women. Women would see him in the mall and remember him from a club.

His relentless pursuit of finding an apartment appropriate for his taste had been in vain until he came across this building. Mandla bounced his way back to the street. He felt good. He had exactly two weeks to prepare for his new job. He needed to rest and get his mind clear of all of the dirt that he'd done in Georgia and get back in the mind frame of accomplishing his goals. He checked his face in the side view mirror of Todd's Jeep, licked his fingers and slicked down his eyebrows.

"Damn, you look good," he said out loud. "You gray-eyed mothafucka'." He smiled as he walked in the opposite direction, towards Piedmont. All of a sudden, he decided that he wanted to check out what was going on at the park. There was no hurry getting to Todd's house. Most of his things were still packed.

Mandla thought as he walked. He liked Atlanta but knew he had a greater commitment to his mother and his sisters back in D.C. He was the only man in the family and they depended on his every judgment. As Mandla walked, women drove by and honked, some slowed and stopped. He attracted attention from the older women, walking around the park for exercise and the younger women, there to attract men. But he was not distracted. He had other thoughts in his head. His future would depend on the decisions he made within the next few months and he wanted to make sure that plans went as smoothly as he wanted.

Mandla looked at his watch. He still had a few hours before he was supposed to meet Tressy. He checked his briefcase to make sure that he had her paperwork ready. She was supposed to pay him today, make a deposit. Mandla sat on a nearby bench. He pictured Tressy with her soft, round hips. Hips that told stories of childbirth and tender loving from the top. Mandla wondered how it would feel to be inside of her. To run his fingers through that red frazzled hair. He imagined that he had the power to make her freckles dance on her face.

But he could tell that Tressy wasn't having it. Even her friendly laughs and light touches did not hint of infidelity. Besides, he thought, all of the trouble she was going through, to surprise her husband, was indicative of the love she had for him. Mandla shuddered. He could not imagine being married. To be tied down with just one woman and not be able to roam the stables would be a travesty to him...and the women.

Mandla's body tingled from excitement. He could not believe he would be moving into his own place soon. And just in time. Todd was driving him crazy with all of his late night rendezvous. His headboard lay up against the opposite wall of the guestroom, where Mandla was sleeping. He heard Todd's entire sessions. He heard the women calling out his name, a different voice every weekend. He especially knew of the mystery woman's voice. She was wild and loud. But for some strange reason, Todd never seemed to mention her. He would skirt around the subject.

And come to think of it, Mandla thought to himself, he hadn't heard her voice in awhile.

Perspiration formed on the back of Mandla's neck and on the bridge of his nose. He stood and felt a stream of sweat trickle down his back. He looked again at his watch and decided to head towards Ashby to meet Tressy. He would go to Todd's first, shower, and change his clothes. He wanted to look fresh and presentable, just in case Tressy ever changed her mind.

Ashby Street was crowded with high school children and college kids. Many congregated in different little cliques, playing around, laughing, running across the street, and filing to the McDonald's Express. The sun had no mercy on anyone, forcing the young boys to bare their chests and the young girls to bare as much as they could without getting arrested. Mandla sat on the bench where he usually met Tressy. She picked the location, he just showed up. Usually, it was the same location, right in front of the liquor store, a few blocks away from her home and out of the way of her children's day-care center. Every once and awhile, Tressy would allow Mandla to drive her home, if their sessions had gone over the estimated time.

Mandla saw the red hair before he saw the face. Tressy was walking quickly in a long, pleated, tie-dye skirt. Underneath she had on a bright orange, scoop neck leotard. She bobbed and wove her way through the hordes of children, who were mostly her height or taller. Mandla could see her small breasts slightly bounce, as she walked towards him with a big smile. Her hair was braided into one long braid that swung with each step that she took. She was definitely eccentric, which turned Mandla on. He believed that she would be a wild, passionate lover behind closed doors...with whips and chains and handcuffs.

"Hey there," she exclaimed as she bounced right up to Mandla. "Do you have the stuff?"

Mandla smiled. She was refreshing, like a breath of air.

"Right here." He patted his briefcase. "Do you want to go somewhere or is here okay?"

Tressy looked around her and twisted her mouth. She looked up and down the street and then sat next to Mandla on the bench. She swung her long left leg over and crossed her right.

"This is fine," she replied with a smile.

Mandla reached into his briefcase and pulled out a manila envelope full of brochures. He handed it to Tressy who quickly opened the envelope and began thumbing through the material. She smiled to herself.

"Nassau, Bahamas?"

"Yes. It's beautiful there. I went last year and I had a wonderful time."

"Tell me something. How does a full-time student, such as yourself, afford to go to the Bahamas? Isn't Howard expensive?" Tressy did not look up from the material as she asked him the questions.

"Very." He looked at her. He noticed the soft pink gloss on her lips. "But I got a student discount deal. I'm a student rep. I post flyers all over and wait for people to call me about the discounts."

"And how did you get the job of student rep?" She still did not look up. She was thumbing through the papers.

"They needed a sales rep, they liked me, I needed a job, I applied and that was it," he answered nonchalantly.

Tressy looked up into his soft gray eyes. He was still a baby, she thought, barely twenty-two years old. She smiled. He smiled.

"And you say this is the best price you can get me right now?"

"Yes. Unless you're willing to change the dates."

"Ohh, nooo! That's our anniversary date. Donnie's been wanting to go to the Bahamas for the longest. If I have to sell Girl Scout cookies to take that man on a vacation, I will."

"You'll have to sell a whole hell of a lot of Girl Scout cookies." Mandla laughed.

"Well thanks to you, I've already raised almost half the money. With the odd jobs I've been doing and my personal savings, I should be able to afford this trip. And paying in installments has helped a tremendous amount. I want to thank you again." She reached out to touch his arm. Her eyes softened and her freckles dimmed.

"You're very welcome."

She smiled.

"Yeah, well. Thanks." Tressy continued to thumb through

the brochures. "Are these for me to keep?" she asked.

"Yes. Just let me get my personal paperwork out of the folder and you can have the rest." He reached over her and slightly, but accidentally, brushed his elbow across her breast. Tressy straightened her back and sat up. Her face jutted forward and she took in a deep breath.

"Excuse me," was all Mandla could say, as he watched her freckles turn bright red from embarrassment. He retrieved his papers and bent back on the bench.

"Here is the deposit I promised," she said, as she handed him the white envelope with wrinkled twenty-dollar bills folded in between a few fifties. Mandla quickly counted the money and nodded. Tressy stood and moved directly in front of Mandla.

"Thank you. I'll be calling you when I get the rest of the money. And we'll meet probably same place, same time." She smiled and waved bye as she quickly bounced her way back to the sidewalk and diffused in the mass of high school students. Mandla attempted to yell behind her, to ask if she needed a ride but Tressy was gone.

MO' MONEY, MO' MONEY, MO'MONEY

Lacey did not notice him until he was standing directly in front of her desk. He smelled of freshly used zest and men's Obsession. His cool attitude didn't mesh well with the chaotic happenings about the office. His hairless face exposed years of inexperience but his gray eyes held an understanding of life and the tragedies of day to day living. The innocent, yet malicious smile that grew on his face held an attraction that enticed most women he met. Mandla was slightly inexperienced, but he was sure about his presence and confident in his skills. Not only was he on a mission to make himself and his race proud but he also had responsibilities at home. Mandla stood over Lacey and cleared his throat.

"Excuse me." His deep, melodious voice bellowed from within his hallow throat. "I'm looking for a Ms. Senida Johnson."

Lacey watched his eyes carefully. He was attractive but she wouldn't be fooled. She'd run across men with his attitude in the many years she'd been on this earth. Her first husband, Anthony was fine as wine. And he knew it. He was so fine that other women couldn't seem to keep their hands off of him. Or vice versa. Men that fine only ended up breaking hearts.

"And you are?" Lacey responded as she continued to peer into his gray eyes.

"Mandla Jackson. I'm the new intern from Howard University." His annunciation of each word was clipped with a slight D.C. accent. His short hair faded along the side of his head. There were two holes in his left ear but the earrings were absent. The tailored suit represented taste in fine clothing. Mandla's posture was erect and self-assured.

"Have a seat. I'll let Ms. Johnson know you're here," Lacey instructed, as she pointed her finger behind Mandla to a row of chairs. In two long steps he was at the chairs. Women working in the small office stopped attending to their tasks to find out who he was waiting to see. He sat watching Lacey, as she switched into the tiny office behind her station. Lacey closed the door behind her and sat across from Senida's desk.

"Your intern is here," she said with a sly smile.

Senida looked up from her work to study the smile on Lacey's face. He was early. He wasn't scheduled to arrive until...Senida reached over to the far-left corner of her desk and flipped her daily planner to Wednesday. Written in ink was Mandla Jackson, 11:00 am. She looked at her watch. It was 10:30 am. At least he was punctual. Lacey sat smiling as Senida tossed thoughts around in her head.

"Tell him I'll be with him in a minute." Senida did not encourage Lacey to say anymore as she bent her neck back down to concentrate on her work.

Her thoughts were deep into going over Mr. Mortin's case. There was an abundance of work that needed to be completed and she was far behind. Her recent bouts with Darrell hadn't eased her mind enough to concentrate the way she needed to concentrate to complete her tasks. He hadn't called Senida in days. Whenever she called his house she would get his answering machine but she never left a message. The last time she talked to Darrell on the phone, their conversation was shallow and superficial. Her constant daydreaming and drifting caused her days of research build up.

Senida thanked the Lord that it was hump-day and she was not coming in to work on Friday. Her dentist appointment could not be put off any longer. She had to get her teeth cleaned. Friday was restricted to her only.

"Lacey, you can send Mr. Jackson in now," she said into the intercom.

"I sure will," Lacey retorted.

Two minutes later, a tall, handsome, young man waltzed into Senida's office and stood directly over her holding out his hand. She stood and shook his hand, motioning for him to have a seat. His gray eyes jumped out and grabbed her attention.

"Well, Mr. Jackson, it's finally nice to meet you. Mr. Cardell speaks highly of you."

Mandla shifted his position in the small seat and crossed his legs.

"Yes, Dr. Cardell and I are good friends. He's helped me throughout my four years at Howard." He smiled. His teeth sparkled bright and white.

"So tell me a little something about yourself. Where are you from? What are your plans?"

"I'm originally from Washington D.C. I attended Howard University. Since I've graduated, I want to get a little work experience before I attend law school."

"Which school are you planning on attending?"

"I'm not sure yet. But I'm thinking about applying to some schools on the West Coast."

"Really. That's where I'm from."

"Where?"

"California."

"Oh. I hear it's nice there."

"It is. Listen, you can take your jacket off if you want, this is strictly informal. As my intern, you'll have to represent me, as well as the firm. But when we're in my office, relax. You'll find that this office and the ones outside are really relaxed. We have fun here, as long as our work is completed. Now, I guess I can give you a little tour of the firm and introduce you to some people."

Senida stood and so did Mandla. His gray eyes watched intently at her every move. She slid around from her desk, making sure that her planner was closed and walked out of her office, with Mandla in tow. His tall body floated across the office, revealing long, strong strides.

"Lacey, I'm going to take Mr. Jackson on a little tour. Just take my messages and leave them on my desk please."

Lacey smiled and nodded at Senida and Mandla as they hooked the right, headed toward Cindy's office. The "Firm," as the employees called it, possessed a certain buzz. There was constantly something happening, either a high profile media case, employee participation events, charity events, or just plain old gossip. Senida worked for Smithers since she passed the boards. Her ultimate goal was to become a partner, which wasn't easy. If they didn't make her a partner, then she would eventually start her own firm.

Her job was to work on the local cases that required less political involvement and less media coverage. Senida was not happy with the mediocre cases thrown at her but she had her hidden agenda for the future. Her luck changed with the Mortin case, when Jeff Manor had to leave town on a family emergency. His mother suffered from Alzheimer's Disease, leaving Jeff no choice but to fly to Florida to be with her during her last months. He returned four months later, not mentioning her death, continuing his daily tasks as if nothing ever happened. Nobody questioned him about her or his trip home.

Senida and Mandla headed for Cindy's office. Although she was nosy, Cindy was a great attorney. On the way to her office, Mandla chatted about how he'd wanted to live in Atlanta since he was a kid. He talked a lot about his mother and his three sisters. Senida exchanged stories about her family and her younger brother, Kevon. Mandla's pleasant disposition enchanted Senida. He must be making some mother pretty damn proud, she thought.

Half way to Cindy's office, Linda Ross rounded the corner, breasts first. Her incredulous smile swept across her face like a tornado. Extending her hand, she eyed Mandla up and down. They were close to the same height.

"Oh, we have a new employee I see." Linda shook Mandla's hand.

"He's our new intern." Senida smiled.

"Hi, I'm Mandla Jackson." His gray eyes took in Linda in one glance.

"What a charming name." Her laugh was hearty and fake at the same time. Each time she sucked in breath to laugh, her cleavage would bounce into Mandla's face. The poor boy was hypnotized by the blonde's busty bosom.

"Well, we need to continue on our tour," Senida interjected, bringing Mandla back to reality.

"Oh, well, yes. It was nice to meet you Mandla. I hope to see you around." Linda let go of Mandla's hand and slowly switched a few steps. "He's working over there with you, right Senida? I might need to borrow him to do a few things for me before I transfer." She flipped her long wrist at Mandla and turned to continue switching.

Mandla looked at Senida and raised his eyebrows. She did not feel like bringing him into office drama gossip so early in the game so she looked away continuing to walk. Mandla broke the silence.

"Are all of the women working here that aggressive?"

Senida looked into his eyes and laughed. She didn't mean to laugh but she could see his personality peeking through his stuffy business suit.

"I don't mean to laugh at you brotha but when you get done interning here, you'll have enough stuff to write a book about. Especially about the big bosom blonde."

"I'm cool on that. She's not my flavor."

Mandla laughed with Senida until they reached Cindy's office. Cindy sat in her see-through office with a client. Cindy's client was an Asian woman with a small child. Senida went straight to Janice's desk. Janice had been Cindy's secretary for a number of years. She was the one who informed Cindy of most of the office gossip. But Cindy didn't know that Janice also spread around a fair share of Cindy's business also.

"Hi Janice. This is Mandla our new intern from Howard University."

"Hello. Nice to meet you. I think you'll like it here. Everyone's professional but we have a good time also. Are you originally from D.C.?"

"Yes." Mandla's cool attitude was enough to send Janice into a talking frenzy.

"I brought him over to meet Cindy but I see she's busy." Senida raised her eyebrows and nodded her head in the direction of Cindy's office.

"Yeah, that lady's been in there for awhile." Janice looked over her shoulder at Cindy who was directing her attention to the Asian woman. Janice then leaned closer to Mandla and Senida and whispered. "I think it's something personal. I don't think it has anything to do with work. You know Cindy's been having marital problems, right?"

"No I didn't know that," Senida responded. "Trouble in paradise?"

Mandla stood to her immediate right and did not move the entire time the two women chatted about the white woman's personal life. Out of all the people who worked for Smithers,

Janice was the main person Senida liked to gossip with. Janice graduated from Douglas High School with Maya.

"So how old are you, Mandla? If you don't mind my asking?"

Senida could not believe that Janice was bold enough to ask Mandla that question.

"I'm twenty-two," he said. "How old are you...if you don't mind *my* asking?" Janice sat straight up, cleared her throat, and bucked her eyes. She was in shock and didn't know what to say. So she laughed. Mandla and Senida joined in with her laughter.

"Chile, you sho' ain't from Georgia," she squealed. "I think we gon' get along pretty darn good."

While Janice and Mandla cooed at each other, Senida excused herself to go to the restroom. She had a splitting headache and wanted to take something for it. She knew with Janice's motor mouth, they could be out there talking forever. She would go save the poor boy in a minute. Not only did she have to finish her work but also she had to find something to keep Mandla busy. Something that would teach him and benefit her, like the Mortin case.

Senida could not wait for Cindy to finish her conference. She told Janice to leave her a message to come by her office when she had the time to meet Mandla. Janice waved bye and Senida and Mandla turned the corner, headed back to her office. She could tell he was going to fit into the office fine. There weren't too many black attorneys that worked in the office and definitely not any black men.

Once back in the office, Mandla openly talked about his plans for law school and Senida watched as his gray eyes lit up. She could tell that he was young but he also had a sense of experience about life. The eyes told it all. He could capture someone's heart with those eyes. And he knew it. He knew the power he held in his eyes. He knew that women loved to look in them and he knew that many of them were hypnotized when he stared at them.

Mandla felt comfortable with Senida. He could tell that she was a little less comfortable with him. Each time he opened his mouth to speak, she would hang on to every word, almost forming the words with him. Mandla and Senida talked for over an hour and then went to lunch. They continued talking over lunch and talked even more when they returned from the office. Senida thought he was a pleasant, young man with long strong legs. Mandla thought she was a great mentor and intelligent woman with thick, soft curves. They both smiled at each other.

A NEW VIBE

"But Maya I've tried..."

"You haven't tried hard enough," Maya snapped.

"I have. I just can't seem to get him out of my system. The feelings I have for him just kinda seeped from my heart into my brain and infected it like an insidious disease. Sometimes I can't think straight. I just have to have him no matter what it takes. I'm wondering if I actually love him?" Senida was trying to convince Maya that her crazy ways were a result of uncontrolled emotions.

"No you don't love him. You lust him. *You love* Darrell, remember? Love is not an insidious disease that contaminates your brain. Love is a feeling, an emotion; it's supposed to make you happy." Maya sighed at her pathetic friend. She repositioned herself on her couch and turned on the television with her remote control. Ever since Senida and Darrell broke up, she didn't get any peace from Senida. But this was her best friend and she had to be there for her.

"I do love Darrell. But I don't think that he will ever talk to me again. Actually lately I've been thinking about just stopping over there and having a 'sit down'."

"I would call first. You know what happened the last time you dropped by somebody's house." Maya responded matter-of-factly.

"I've been trying to call but he won't answer or call me back."

"And what about the other dick?" Maya laughed out loud.

"I very rarely hear from him anymore. He won't return my phone calls either." She sighed.

Maya's phone clicked and she put Senida on hold.

"This is Aunt Setty. Let me call you later."

"Tell Aunt Setty I said hello."

She clicked back over.

"Hey Aunt Setty. What's happening?" Maya chirped. Aunt Setty laughed.

"Oh nuthin' much. How you?"

"Fine."

"Well, I just called to see how you was doin'."

"Things are going pretty good Aunt Setty. I made my plane reservations today."

"Good. I can't wait. What was you doin'?"

"I was talking to Senida but she hung up."

"How she doing?"

"Still crazy as ever."

Aunt Setty laughed. "Hold on. I thank somebody calling me on my other line."

Maya leaned back onto the couch and lifted her legs over the armrest. It was about 11:00 p.m. Georgia's time, so it was 8:00 p.m. Aunt Setty's time. Aunt Setty clicked back on the line. Maya was surprised that Aunt Setty knew how to use her two way calling. She usually did not answer the other line. Maya had Pacific Bell give her call waiting because Aunt Setty could tie up a line for hours and sometimes Maya was unable to get through.

"Dat's that ole' crazy fool Margaret. I'ma call you tomorrow. Love ya babee."

When Aunt Setty hung up the other line, Maya tried calling Senida back but did not get an answer. Maya tried to think of where Senida could have run off so quick. As crazy as Senida was, she probably was posted up in front of that man's house. Maya rolled over on her bed and turned her night light out. She had to get some rest. She was tired of trying to keep up with all of the mishap that went on in Senida's life. It was like a soap opera.

*****

Smoke filled the small club. A thick, dismal haze laid heavily on the people, like a wet blanket. Dim lights mulled over and made the crowd high. Poets graced the stage, living, reliving, and pondering life and love. Waiters and waitresses served drinks, as glasses clanked together in unison. The mellow band blended into the background of the scene and caused a melancholy mood. Energetic vibes were strong amongst the artists, as each one had a story to tell. The young woman on stage waved her arms slowly and rocked her head. Eyes closed and mouth partly opened she allowed sour, sweet words to slip from her tongue and land on the ears of those who cared.

Mandla and Todd sat in the back of the room at the bar. Both were drinking Corona with limes floating in the bottles. Todd seemed a little uneasy that Mandla insisted on going to the poetry reading. He damn near had a tantrum. Mandla however, enjoyed the slow, low groove of the band and the sleepy atmosphere of the crowd. He needed to do something on the chill mode. Atlanta's booty shake clubs were beginning to become a bore. He really didn't have any extra money to put in any of the women's panties or any other place they allowed him to slip a bill. His mind swirled earlier and he knew that he wouldn't let Todd drag him off to some crowded club that would cost him an arm and a leg. He still would have to wait awhile to get his first paycheck, and he need not be frivolous with his money.

"Man this shit is wak. What the fuck is she talking about?" Todd shifted in his seat. He took a swig from his bottle of Corona, waiting for a response.

"Man just chill. It's a whole new vibe. I know you ain't used to seeing women with clothes on, but sometimes you need to try some new shit."

"Fo' what?"

"To calm your mind. To chill." Mandla looked around the room. Many of the women wore head wraps. A lot of the men sported locs. He and Todd were two of the most conservatively dressed men in the club. But that didn't stop the vibe from getting up under Mandla's skin. He just hoped Todd would chill and let the smooth taste grab him.

"I'm as calm as they come but I'll tell you, when I go out, I wanna see some ass. I don't want to be surrounded by some women who think they too good to talk to me. Shit. Look at 'em," he said pointing his bottle in the direction of a group of women seated at a nearby table. "I'd turn all of 'em out."

Mandla laughed. Todd smiled.

"You's a wild boy, Todd." Mandla took a long, hard swig from his bottle. Todd finished his beer and sat the bottle on the bar. He stood.

"Man are you ready to go? I want to get to Magic City." Todd looked around the room.

"Potna. Why don't you just go'on without me this time. I'm not feeling Magic City tonight."

"Man. I can't leave you here by yourself."

"Why? I'm a grown ass man. As good as I look, you know I'll get a ride home. Gon' now. I'll see you later. And don't wait up. I don't want you getting jealous, 'cause your women will be looking at me." He hated that he still had to stay a few days with Todd. Right when he was scheduled to move his things into his new apartment, they reminded him that they hadn't sprayed for roaches. So until they did, he kept himself and all of his belongings at Todd's.

"Yeah. A'ight. I'll check you out in the morning." Todd gave Mandla the Kappa grip and then gave him the pound and he was gone.

Mandla sat, watching the crowd and the poets. He liked the soothing croons of the saxophone. It reminded him of a very sexy woman. He closed his eyes and thought about a few of the women who he'd shared himself with. He thought about the ones that meant something to him. It wasn't many but there were a few.

A waitress wearing fitted black pants and a black T-shirt pulled and tied to the back came over to Mandla, disturbing his aura. She had tight slants for eyes and a round, pouty red mouth. Her hair was short and dark and her color copper. She was beautiful.

"You okay over here gray eyes? Can I get you something else?"

"Yeah, baby. Get me another Corona. Betta' yet, get me some Hen dawg," he replied and winked at her. She smiled and left to retrieve his drink.

*****

Senida sat in her car, parked across the street. His jeep was parked in the driveway and so was the burgundy car. His lights were on in the living room, kitchen, and the bedroom. She saw movements in the living room but she couldn't hear anything. Senida did not wait for Maya to call her back. She could be on the phone for hours with Aunt Setty, so Senida decided to give herself advice. And her advice to herself was to go over to his house to find out what he was doing. It was getting quite late and she just knew he would be out partying. But he was *in* partying with that young-faced, little hussy.

Senida slumped down in the driver's side. She reclined so she could lay down and see the ceiling of the car. After forty-five minutes, a few rational thoughts bounced through her head. Why was she there? Why couldn't she just move on with her life? He obviously didn't care much about her, so why should she worry herself with him? It wasn't as if she *couldn't* get anyone. She was smart, funny, witty, and fun to be with. So why was she sitting her ass outside of a youngster's house, knowing he had another woman in there? And waiting for God knows what?

Senida pulled her seat up and started her car. She would go out. That's what she would do. She would go out and meet someone new. Hell, she would replace him, just like he'd replaced her and just like Darrell replaced her. She swerved her car in the direction of a small, little, reclusive club, that was swarming with men. She wasn't ready for the loud, rambunctious crowds that the younger people made up. She needed to start off slow. It had been a long time since she'd been to a club.

Long tunes crept out of the doors to the club as Senida waltzed up the ramp to the entrance. Cover charge was free, much to her liking and the small room seemed packed but really didn't have too many people inside. She slipped passed the bar and sat at a table with two sistahs. They both smiled and turned their attention back to the poet on stage. An older man shouted about racism and sexism. His mouth slowly formed every word:

"It's the pigs that shot my daddy!
The low down, mothafucking pigs!
Why daddy, why did you have to die a brutal death?"

The crowd went wild. Many gave him a standing ovation and others patted him on the back as he walked off of the stage and dissipated into the crowd. Senida ordered herself a drink and tried to loosen up. After gulping down her first drink, she decided to sip on her second drink.

The tunes, the words, the mood all coaxed Senida into a world of euphoria. She didn't think a club could do this to her. But it wasn't the club itself; it was the vibe, a new vibe. The two women sitting at the table gathered their notebooks, smiled at her, and left the building. No sooner did they hit the door, did an intoxicated man approach the table and took himself a seat. At first the man seemed to want to engage in pleasant conversation, but after two more drinks he began to become belligerent.

"Come on girl. Let's dance," he said pulling on Senida's arm. There was no dancing music.

"No thank you, really. I don't think you're supposed to dance while the poets are on stage."

"Ah the hell with them. They ain't talking 'bout shit. I want to dance and you about the finest woman in here."

He continued to pull on Senida's arm and became louder. People started to look in their direction. Senida almost stood to dance with him, just to get the attention off of her and back onto the person on stage. Right when she decided to give in, she heard another masculine voice from behind.

"Excuse me. But she's with me."

The belligerent man turned around and stared into the hard gray eyes.

"Well now she's with me," he responded, looking up at Mandla, who was almost twice as tall.

"Look old man, why don't you go get with some other woman. This is my woman. I don't want to have to start no trouble 'cause I will."

"Young blood. I don't want no trouble. Me and the lady were going to dance."

"That's cool and everythang, but this woman is with me. So you need to find someone else to dance with." Mandla put his hand in his coat pocket as if to pose before pulling his gun out. The old man concentrated on where Mandla's hands were and then just walked away.

"Thank you." Senida sighed.

"What are you doing here by yourself?" he asked her as he sat down in the empty chair.

"Oh I was just restless tonight and I needed to get out.

What about you? What are you doing out by yourself?"

"Saving your behind." He smiled. She smiled. She liked his eyes.

"You come here a lot?" he asked.

"No. This is my first time. How about you? Have you been here before?" She scooted her chair over so she could get a better look into his eyes. The next poet was going on stage.

"Nah. This is my first time too." He turned his attention to the new poet on stage. She was a dark brown sistah with a white wrap. She was gorgeous.

"So have you gotten to see a lot of Atlanta since you've been here?"

"All the parts that I don't need to see," he responded, still looking at the woman on stage. He then turned his attention back to Senida. "How long have you been in Atlanta?"

"Oh, ha a long time." She started to laugh.

"Well maybe you can show me around a little bit, when we're not working. Is that okay with you?" His eyes locked her and she couldn't let go. Her mind was racing a mile a minute. But he wouldn't let her down with his eyes. So she just stayed there until he looked away to give her a chance to talk.

"Sure. That's fine with me."

"Then it's a date." Mandla and Senida turned their attention back to the stage. The sistah had finished her first poem and was preparing to recite her second.

"The vibe feels so good in here." The poet said with a smile. "I'm a virgin to the mic, but I feel so much love coming from the audience, I think I wanna do another one. This next piece is relatively new but I want to dedicate it to all the strong African kings in the house tonight."

Lights lowered and the audience clapped. Music began once the clapping ceased and she grabbed the microphone and began reciting:

"My darling black butterfly
if love was the sun I could melt the sky
upon gallant wings, I would fly
through melodies and endless clouds
my heart would be yours to savor
a measure of flavor

instantly clads grasping tenderly
at my heartstrings
luring wondrous scenes of a sistah
grown to love the black man's gentle touch;
that he could only muster in such a
delicate display of affection
black fingers gripping clit
suckling life
standing beside me through love
proud and tall as a tree
for all to see
made by God miraculously perfect
the black man, just for me."

"That was phat!" Mandla stood to clap for the young woman.

"Yeah that was pretty nice."

"What are you drinking?" he asked sitting back down. He motioned for the waitress.

"Rum and coke."

"Let me get a 151 and coke and for the lady a rum and coke." He winked at the waitress. "So Ms. Johnson. Do you write poetry?"

"No. How about you?"

"Roses are red, violets are blue...I can't think of nothing else to say, so I guess that I'm through." They both laughed. "Nah I don't write poetry. I just started getting into it since the movie *Love Jones*."

"I didn't realize how beautiful poetry could be."

"It's almost as beautiful as you."

The waitress came over and handed Mandla his drink. Senida blushed as the waitress set her drink on the table.

"Thank you."

"I'm sure that's corny enough to work, right?" Mandla gulped his drink.

"Work what?" Senida asked as the alcohol took over once more.

He smiled. "Work us."

"Not quite."

Another poet came on stage and began shouting and screaming about revolution. Mandla took this as his cue to leave. There was a very, sexy woman waiting on the other side of the club for him. He reached into his pocket and pulled out a pen. Mandla scribbled his phone number onto a napkin and pushed it toward Senida.

"Here. Give me a call so we can go out on that date."

"Wait. Let me give you my number too." Senida wrote her number down and handed it to Mandla. He stood and kissed her hand.

"Do you have a ride?" he asked.

"Yes."

"Well I don't. Can you take me home?" He smiled.

"With me?"

He looked at her and his smile widened. "Yeah."

"Do you really need a ride?"

"Nah. Just testing you. I don't need a ride. Someone else said they would take me home." He thought back to the beautiful sistah that promised to take him home and treat him right. She whispered in his ear, right before the commotion happened with Senida. He needed to get back to the other side of the club to meet with her.

"You sure?" she asked a little disappointed.

"Yeah. It's late. I'll walk you to your car though." He handed Senida her jacket and walked her to her car. Senida couldn't remember telling Mandla that she was ready to go home. But she got into her car anyway. She watched him go back into the club and drove away. She knew she would see him on Monday at work. On her way home Senida thought about Mandla. He was definitely a charmer. His good looks only added to his charm. She'd seen the many women at the "firm" watching him as he walked by, or attentively gazing at his gorgeous lips as he talked to them. Senida knew because she was as guilty as sin. She'd carefully watched his every move, since he'd started working for her.

When she arrived home, she showered, ate a frozen pizza, and went to bed. That night she dreamed about Mandla. He was riding a white horse and she was laying in a meadow of green grass and yellow daisies. He swooped by her a couple of times and whisked her up onto the horse. When they rode a few minutes, he gently helped her down from the horse and they made passionate love in the tall grass. Senida awoke the next morning, in a pool of sweat and a smile on her face.

LONELY NIGHTS

Jelani inhaled the smell of the strong coffee. Normally he did not drink the stuff but tonight he needed to stay awake. Thoughts swam around in his head as the stewardess lightly touched him on the shoulder.

"Is everything okay, Mr. Ransom? Would you like something to eat or some more coffee?"

He slowly shook his head and she left him to his thoughts. The other teammates were chattering and laughing amongst themselves about their trip to the West Coast. Many talked about the women they would sleep with, while others talked about the nightlife and the clubs to visit. Jelani looked over at Matt Fullerton sitting next to him. His mouth hung open as he slept soundlessly. Jelani's mind would not allow him to sleep. He would not be able to really rest until he had cleared up his situation.

His father was trying to appeal and he couldn't possibly let that happen. If it took every ounce of energy in his and Donnie's bodies, they would not allow their father to get out of prison. Jelani leaned back and closed his eyes. He thought about his family and how much he desired to have stability in his life. Even the road trips from state to state were starting to take a toll on his spirit. He could barely remember the last serious relationship that he had but could remember the faces of all the main women from his past. There was Sheila, Shatina, Twanisha, Shontell, Sandy, and Gail. He couldn't remember their last names but he did remember their faces. How he'd made their faces twist in distortion from pleasure or pain. And then he thought back to his car accident and the beautiful woman in the Camry...Maya. She had spit fire at him that day at the accident and then again at the grocery store. That fire sent chills up his spine. He admired spunk in a woman, meant they could take care of themselves if the need arose.

Jelani quickly shook his head. He had more important things to think about than some woman he'd probably never see again. He had to figure out the course of fate for his family. After their game against the Oakland Raiders he had to get back to Atlanta and handle his business. Jelani sipped the last of the luke warm coffee and began flipping through one of the *Ebony Man* magazines that sat in the pouch on the seat in front of him.

"Hey J.R. Gonna get you some pussy when we get to California? Or are you still on that respect the women shit?" Curtis Craft yelled from the adjacent seat behind Jelani.

Curtis was a large, burley, white man with a red face and brown hair. Although he was married, Curtis could not wait to take trips away from home to meet new women. He complained to the entire team of his wife's mishaps when it came to sex. She didn't do this or she couldn't do that was usually the beginning of many of his conversations. He would then move on to the out of town games bragging about the exciting and provocative sex he would have. Jelani knew his kind and even used to hang with him a few months ago but had no desire to be a part of that entourage anymore. He usually just smiled at Curtis and ignored him or came back with a witty remark. He knew Curtis didn't mean any harm, it was all in fun.

"Nah," Jelani replied. "I don't need to get any this trip. Your wife hooked me up good last night."

The plane dipped and the crowd roared. Curtis' face turned a deep red. A much brighter color than he usually wore. After so long of laughter, Curtis had to eventually laugh at the joke. He just shook his head and leaned back in his seat with the other men chastising him. Jelani smiled to himself and continued to read the article in *Ebony Man*.

Jelani could feel the heat break through the early morning clouds on his back. He was in the mood for an early morning jog to clear his mind. He'd almost forgotten the refreshed feeling he received from his daily ritual, which had been interrupted, far too long. Most of his teammates were still in bed from the late night partying. As soon as the plane landed in California, many of them, including Curtis, hit the nightclubs in search of their victims. Jelani opted for staying in, much to the dismay and chastising of the other men. For a moment, he felt as though he should have gotten out but he thought about his mother and he was glad that he'd decided to stay in.

His early morning jog helped Jelani to sort out many of his personal problems that he probably couldn't do if he was suffering from a hangover. Although his body was in perfect shape, his mind was a mental mishap waiting to explode. Too much pressure, too much pain.

And no matter what he thought about, he could not keep his mind off of Maya. He would sit in his living room and wonder what she was doing or where she was. He'd often wonder if she was with somebody and if she was thinking about him. Donnie would tell him that he needed to try to find her again because he was definitely pussy whipped and he hadn't even gotten close enough to smell it yet. He would then let out a hearty laugh that would end in a solemn look when he began to think about Tressy again. The even, thin line in his thick lips would indicate to Jelani that he was back at it again. Blaming himself for a marriage, which he thought, was doomed. But Jelani knew that Tressy loved Donnie and couldn't see why he didn't see the same. He'd only wished that he had the same type of love for a woman that his brother had for his wife.

Jelani rounded the corner and headed into the grocery store to buy some fruit. Each morning he would buy a bunch of bananas, a few apples, and some oranges. When he stepped into the grocery store, there was a slight buzz about the building. Cashiers rung their orders a little faster, clerks smiled a little more, and customers spent a little more abundantly.

Jelani stood in the cereal aisle when he smelled a familiar smell. It was Fendi perfume. Nobody in his or her right, classy mind would still wear Fendi perfume, he thought...except Shatina, his California groupie. He hadn't seen her in over a year. Every time they were in town she would find a way to get in contact with Jelani. But since he'd turned his life around, he did not deal too much with any of the women in California who he used to enjoy in the middle of the lonely nights. And as quickly as his mind went back, he heard her voice from behind. Damn, he'd thought her up!

"Umph. Still looking good huh? Body still tight and popping." Shatina wore her hair in a blonde upsweep. Her dark roots spiraled upward into the thin blonde color. Her outfit was a purple jogging suit and she held her son's hand. Teonte looked up at Jelani with a sheepish grin. He had always been a shy little boy. Jelani noticed that he had grown a few inches since the last time they'd seen each other.

"Miss Shatina Moore. Fancy meeting you up so early in the morning. I'd imagine you'd still be getting over your hangover."

Shatina shifted her weight and rolled her eyes. "Anyway. I don't drink anymore. I quit. I'm a different woman now," she said smiling.

Jelani looked her up and down and smiled. She still had the hourglass figure that was for sure. Shatina wasn't an ugly woman. It was the way she carried herself. She had a reputation of sleeping with football players on a regular basis. She hung out in the clubs where she knew they would be and offered to show them a good time while they were in town. But Jelani made the mistake of having too many deep conversations with her and they opened his eyes to a young woman looking for a fantasy in a realistic, cruel world.

"Well look Shatina, I'm not down anymore. I've changed also," he said watching her chest heave in and out. He wondered if she was still a C cup or if she'd grown some. Each time he saw her it seemed as if her body became more curvaceous.

"When you change your mind, call me. I'll bring back some of the good old times we used to have before you became all high and mighty," she said as she leaned forward and kissed him hard. Teonte stood eyes wide, still holding onto his mother's leg. Shatina then pulled out a piece of paper and scribbled her new number on it. Jelani crumbled the paper into a ball and shoved it into his pocket.

"Thanks, but I don't think I'll be needing your services this trip," he responded. Shatina sucked her teeth and rolled her eyes.

"Call me," was all she said as she walked away with Teonte tagging along.

Hot musk emanated from the locker room. The players sat

around looking disgusted as the coach yelled at the top of his lungs. His face turned blue, then white, and then purple as he screamed at the players. Jelani was listening but he didn't hear a word the coach was saying. He couldn't wait to get back to the hotel to take a hot bath in the Jacuzzi, eat and take a long nap. He knew that it would be a while before he could head to the hotel. He first had to sit and endure all of the coach's hot air, then shower, and then go through the horde of reporters, fans, and groupies just to get to the bus.

All the other players had their heads bowed as they listened to their coach. Jelani wondered what many of them were thinking. He looked over at Curtis. He probably was thinking of the night before and the next few nights in town.

Once the coach was done biting into his players he allowed reporters to come into the locker room. The reporters were all over each key player asking questions, taking pictures, and jotting down notes. Jelani tried to be as pleasant as possible. Curtis, however, yelled and cursed out a few reporters.

When Jelani finally made it through the crowd and back to the hotel, he was grateful to have made it through the rough day. He prayed. It had been so long since he prayed but he felt the urge to drop to his knees and give thanks. At first his knees would not bend for lack of practice but eventually gave way as the soulful spirit rising inside of him pulled him closer to the side of the bed.

It was getting dark and he could hear his teammates gearing up to go out and hit the town. Even with the recent loss, the players were whooping and hollering in the halls. Jelani could hear women's voices giggling and moaning in the rooms. By the time he'd ordered room service and pulled himself out of the Jacuzzi, there was a knock at the door. When Jelani opened the door, Curtis and a few other teammates stood with a few half dressed women, both black and white.

"Come on J.R. We're gonna have an orgy," Curtis yelled.

Jelani smiled. It had been a long time. But he couldn't even muster up the energy to participate.

"Nah," he replied. "I'm cool, y'all have fun without me." He shut the door on the now confused looking Curtis. Jelani leaned his back against the door and he heard Curtis yell through the door.

"Prick! You need a drink, J.R. That's what you need!"

And then he heard them go down the hall into the room with the loud music and shut the door. The music became faint.

Hours went by as Jelani sat, flipping through the cable channels. He watched two movies and then watched a late night porno flick. His nature began to rise and he started to think about Maya. He wondered what she was doing at that precise moment. He then thought about how good she would look in his bed next to him. How her curves would accent the thin sheets and how her smell would permeate the room. He could not figure out why he could not get the woman off of his mind. Yes she was fine but so were many of the women he came across. Jelani rolled over on his side and looked at his pants sprawled over the chair. He wanted sex but there was nobody around. The halls had long since been quiet, as the other players were either out at the clubs or out cold.

Jelani leaped to the other side of the room and grabbed his pants. He searched the pockets. He knew Shatina would be down for whatever. She always was. And although he had a feeling he would regret the call, he made it anyway.

"Hello?" Shatina's hoarse voice was almost like a song to the horny Jelani.

"You down for tonight?" he asked.

"J.R?"

He could hear her shifting under her cotton sheets.

"Who else in the hell would it be?" he asked irritated.

"I thought you wouldn't be needing my services," she responded in a sarcastic voice. Jelani ignored her.

"I'm at Sir Francis Drake. Room 1043. I'm not going to be waiting long. If you're not here in a few minutes then don't bother knocking on the door, 'cause it'll be someone else in here."

"But I don't have a sitter for Teonte," she whined.

"Then you must not want to see me."

"No, no, wait. He's asleep. I can't leave him here by himself. Can I bring him?"

"Hell no! What the fuck are we gonna do with him?"

"Is there an extra room or a room that he can sleep in?"

Jelani thought. Rob was staying two doors down and he was one of the few who did not party. He was probably either in there talking on the phone to his wife or watching television.

"Yeah. Bring him. Rob'll watch him. He owes me a favor anyway."

"I'll be there soon. Bye."

Jelani set up the baby-sitting job with Rob and went down to Stan's room to borrow some condoms. Shortly after he returned, Shatina was knocking at his door with Teonte asleep in her arms. Jelani told her what room to drop him off and that he would leave the door unlocked so she could just come back in without knocking.

When Shatina returned, she and Jelani had sex for over two hours. Afterwards Jelani went to take a shower and Shatina waited in the room. She threw on a hotel robe and ran down the hall to check on Teonte, who was still sleeping in the bed next to Rob. When Jelani got out of the shower, Shatina asked him if she could take a shower and he allowed her to do so. Jelani threw himself onto the bed and smiled.

Shatina walked out of the bathroom and spread out next to Jelani on the bed. At first she seemed a little uneasy as if he would make her leave. But Jelani had released so much stress and tension that he actually didn't mind her staying for a while. Besides, he might have the strength to go another round after they'd rested.

"I'm glad you came."

"It's my job. I have to come."

"Do you ever get tired?" she asked shifting all of her weight onto Jelani. He was laying on his back and Shatina snuggled into his torso.

"It's my job."

"Yeah but don't you ever want to just stay in one place? Like California?"

"Sometimes. But I don't think that I would settle down in California."

"Why?"

"I don't like it too much out here. Too much crime."

"Atlanta has a high crime rate too," she replied matter-of-factly.

"At least I'm used to that type of crime. Plus it's too damn expensive out here."

"It ain't like you *can't* afford it out here."

"Are you trying to get me to move out here?"

"Maybe."

"Forget it."

"I would love for you to move out here."

"Forget it Shatina."

"But I miss you. Don't you miss me?"

Jelani did not respond. He didn't ask her to come over to talk. He just needed some sexual company.

"Well?"

"Shatina, you know the extent of our relationship."

Silence. Shatina knew how he felt about her. She'd wished on many nights to catch a professional ball player. She needed someone to take care of her and her son.

"Why do you treat me so bad?" Shatina asked Jelani, throwing him off guard. This is usually why he didn't like fucking with Shatina. She had a soul. She was a really nice woman and she had dreams.

"'Cause sometimes you make me mad. You got a smart ass mouth."

"I don't mean to. I just like to know things, that's all," she said as she snuggled closer to Jelani. He resisted the urge to push her off of him.

"When was the last time I treated you bad anyway? You've always been my favorite groupie." He laughed.

"That's not funny J.R." She did not move. "I guess it's been a while. You have gotten a little better at the way you treat me," she said.

Silence.

"J.R?" She stopped.

"Hummmm?"

"Would you ever marry a woman like me?" She did not look up at him. He could hear her hold her breath, as if waiting for a terrible answer.

"Shatina. You're not my type. And if you really want to know the truth, men don't want women that are easy. You put yourself out there to be used. You're not marriage material."

He could hear her sigh and then felt tiny tear drops on his chest. He knew he shouldn't have called her ass. Now she was getting all sentimental on a brotha. He had to get rid of her. She wasn't going to spoil his orgasmic high on some bullshit that her mama should have told her.

"It's time for you to go. You need to get Teonte home in

his own bed anyway," he said as he hoisted himself up, forcing her to get up also.

"But J.R. I want to stay the night with you. Teonte will be fine in Rob's room."

"How the hell you gon' impose on that man like that Shatina? Get your ass dressed and go get your son so you can go home!" he yelled as he slipped on some shorts.

Shatina dressed, the entire time crying silent tears. Jelani tried to pretend like he didn't see her for fear that he might suffer from flashbacks. He didn't want to relive the past and Shatina was definitely a part of his past. A past that he fought so hard to get away from. A past that haunted him every time he played away from home and a past that churned his stomach every time he made a woman cry.

Shatina went to the door and opened it half way. She didn't go out or look back. She just stood there as if she had something to say but couldn't think of it quick enough.

"When will you be back?" she asked without turning to look at Jelani. Her back was still to him. He stood in the middle of the room. He rubbed his hand down his face.

"You know when we'll be back."

"Jelani. I think I love you."

"You don't love me."

"Really, I do." Tears formed in Shatina's eyes.

"Shatina, come here."

She walked across the floor to Jelani.

"Listen. You're a smart girl. You're attractive and you're sweet. You got a lot going for yourself. Your problem is that you need to keep your legs closed sometimes if you want to be respected. Now," his voice softened. "Go get Teonte so he can sleep in his own bed."

Shatina walked out the door and started to close it behind her.

"Shatina!" Jelani yelled.

She opened the door and looked at the floor.

"How's Teonte doing in school?"

"Fine."

"Does he need anything?"

She slowly shook her head yes, but never looked up from the floor. Jelani reached into his pocket and walked to the door.

He took her hand and placed a neatly folded $100 bill in her palm.

"Get him something nice. Buy him some clothes or some toys or something. Take care of yourself. And take good care of that little boy."

Shatina nodded her head and shut the door. Jelani leaned his back against the door and rubbed his hand down his face. It was a shame that the little boy had to suffer because of his groupie ass mother, he thought. He really liked the little boy too.

*****

"You have reached Mr. Jackson, please leave your phone number and a brief message. Beeeeeeeeeeeep!"

"Mandla, it's me give me a call. I was wondering..."

It was Senida. Mandla jumped from the couch to answer the phone.

"Hello, Senida. Hi." his voice strained.

"Mandla were you asleep?" Her voice was sweet and sincere.

"Ah huh." He tried to gain back his orientation.

"Are we still on for tonight?"

"Tonight?"

"Mandla, did you forget? We were supposed to go out tonight remember?"

"Oh yeah. No I haven't forgotten. What time are you coming to pick me up? You did say that you would drive tonight right?" Mandla said as he remembered making the plans earlier that week.

"Yes. They still haven't delivered your car?" She asked.

"No. I don't know what's taking them so long. And I had to take the rent-a-car back today."

"Okay. I'll be over there in about thirty minutes?"

"That sounds cool. See you then. Bye."

"Mandla."

"Yeah."

"Be ready," she said as she hung up the phone.

She said thirty minutes so I have a minute to chill, Mandla thought to himself as he plopped back down onto the couch and began flipping channels. It felt good to finally have his own place. He'd talked to Todd just yesterday over the phone. Mandla shook his head vigorously. He was still trying to become fully awake so he could launch into motion. He knew that Senida was a fanatic when it came to being on time. She would pout with her gorgeous lips and whine in a "I've been spoiled all my life" whine. Mandla knew when he met her that she was used to getting her way. He could tell in her demeanor and the way that she took control in her office. Realizing that nothing was on the tube, Mandla bounced to the bathroom with his cooler than cool walk. He turned on the shower and let the water get hot enough to form steam. Slowly undressing, he looked at himself in the mirror and blew himself a kiss.

"You fine, young brotha," he said smiling at the reflection, as he stepped his caramel colored, thin, muscular body into the water. He let out a small girlish type yelp when the hot liquid hit his body and then he began to relax.

Mandla was extremely attractive and sure about himself. His six-five frame was smooth and cut. Mandla's muscles were well defined in contrast to his thin body. His smooth, hairless face was enough to expose his twenty-two years on this Earth much to his dismay. But his confidence in his abilities to "please any woman from twenty to one hundred and twenty" was enough to keep the women flocking. Any woman who would not find him attractive, which was virtually impossible, would surely fall in lust with his charming personality and his winning Denzel Washington smile.

After lathering and rinsing twice, he hopped out of the shower with much more zest than when he entered. Smearing the steam from the mirror to ensure a good view of himself, he waltzed into the living room to turn on his stereo. Tupac's "Makaveli" was blaring throughout the speakers.

"Ah that's phat," Mandla said to himself as he entered the bedroom to pick out something suitable to wear to the restaurant.

Senida looked impeccably beautiful as she stood in the doorway waiting for Mandla to let her in. Her scent traveled through the door, filtering into Mandla's brain through his nostrils. He inhaled deeply and let his mind wander. She could tell that the youngster was impressed by the way he stood staring with his mouth open. Senida wore her hip fitting tan dress with slightly darker pumps. Her shapely legs and thighs pressed against all edges of the dress. Each bump and curve moved in the right direction. Her hair was styled into a small, soft flow to the back. Her edges were neatly shaved and the nape, smooth from her visit to the hair shop earlier that day. She wore tiny droplets in her ears and her face was made up with natural colored make-up giving men the illusion that she was naturally beautiful and had no need for make-up, at all. She stepped closer to the awe struck Mandla, her five foot seven body only inches away from him.

"Are you going to let me in? Or are you going to slobber all over the floor like that?" she asked with a sly smile and seduction in her eyes. His gray eyes were intently focused on her beauty. Their contrast with his caramel colored skin held a mystical spell about them. Mandla knew that many women adored his eyes and he used them to his advantage. He smiled a broad smile as he stepped to the side and to let her past the entrance.

"Mandla. You're not even ready yet." Senida pouted in growing agitation.

"I know baby, I'm sorry. I'll be ready in a minute," he said as he seductively kissed her on the cheek and brushed passed her. Looking back he yelled. "Damn girl you looking too good tonight!"

Senida sat on the couch and flipped through channels. The soft brush of his lips on her cheek startled her. Realizing that the television was no match for the stereo that Mandla was blasting, she turned it off.

"Damn, it's already eight and we got reservations for nine thirty," she said out loud to herself.

Senida was usually a punctual person. Years of going to court made her that way. She couldn't fathom the consequences for the lawyer who was late to his own trial. She heard Mandla shuffling around in his room and when he came out, she was almost glad that she waited. He wore a crisp, white shirt and dark blue jeans. Even with his jeans on, he looked good enough to eat. Senida could see the muscles from his legs shape the contours of the jeans. His gray eyes sparkled.

"Well I'm ready."

Senida did not move.

"Why are you still sitting on the couch?" he asked as he grabbed his keys and headed towards the door.

"No reason," she said as she stood. He was just as breathtaking as he was the first day he walked into her office.

Sylvia's Restaurant was crowded as usual and Senida and Mandla had to wait for about twenty minutes. They decided to wait outside since the night air was warm and clear. Men walking by could not help but stare at Senida's perfect shape and women were mesmerized by Mandla's gray eyes. The two talked easily as if they were old friends getting together after a long time. Senida liked the way Mandla could relate to a lot of her situations even though he was only twenty-two years old. She could tell that his mother raised him well.

"Did I thank you for saving me that night at the club?" Senida asked trying to remember if she'd said something to him through her intoxication.

"Yeah. You don't have to thank me. I specialize in saving damsels in distress. You just need to be careful when you go out by yourself. As beautiful as you are, a lot of men will try to get with you." He smiled.

"Thank you." Senida could have sworn that she was blushing.

"So why is it that a woman like yourself doesn't have a man?"

"Ah, well. At the moment I do...but we're separated."

"Is he your husband?" he asked stepping away from her a few steps.

"No." She smiled. "He's my high school sweetheart. But I think we've outgrown each other."

"Do you miss him?"

"Honestly?"

"That's all I ever ask for."

"Yes."

Mandla inhaled the air. He was feeling good. He had moved, his car was soon to arrive, he was working, and he was in the company of what seemed like a nice woman. He knew that she was a little older. He could tell that she just needed someone to bring out the kid in her so she could start enjoying life.

When the hostess called their names, they asked for a table in the back. The pianist bellowed out songs by Luther Vandross and Mandla watched his eyes as they followed Senida to the back. Sylvia's atmosphere held a sense of calm gaiety that enticed the eaters. Mandla pulled out Senida's chair and then sat himself.

"What do you suggest?" he asked as he studied the menu.

"I usually get the catfish. It's pretty good."

"Hummm. I don't like catfish. Maybe I'll check out these ribs." Mandla looked at Senida seductively. She blushed.

Senida knew what she wanted to order, so she looked around the room to see if she saw any familiar faces. That's when she felt a little insecure about being with Mandla. She wondered if she looked like his older sister, his aunt, or worse, his mother! Mandla could sense a type of panic as he watched Senida break her neck to see if anyone was watching them.

"How do you feel about dating someone from the office?" he asked.

"Oh. I didn't really consider it dating. More like I'm showing you around Atlanta," she responded and took a sip of water.

"Oh." He took a large gulp of his water. "So how do you feel about people who work together dating?"

"I don't know. I guess it depends on how far they take it."

"Uh huh."

"Yeah."

"I was looking over the Mortin files. You know we got a long haul with this case." Mandla geared the conversation from personal to professional.

"Why would you say that? I agree but I just want to know why you would say that."

"First of all, the judge is Judge Bates. No offense but she's a woman and she's been known to take the side of the women. We'll have to be extremely convincing."

"I agree."

"Then, Ms. Latimore is a very convincing lady. And she's attractive, which won't hurt."

"True."

"But with Mr. Mortin's reputation, he might be okay." He smiled as if he'd just discovered the cure for cancer.

"I bet your mother is really proud of you."

"She is. I'm the only son. She brags about me all the time."

"Any sisters?"

"Three. One is three years younger than I am and the other two are sixteen-year-old twins. And I have a nephew."

"By the oldest sister?"

"Yes."

"Well I want to tell you how lucky we are to have someone like yourself working for Smithers."

"I'm glad to be working for Smithers, but I'm especially glad to be working for you." He smiled again.

Their waiter slipped up behind them and took their order. He was a young, dark, brother who looked around the same age as Mandla. He looked from Senida to Mandla and then back to Senida. She wondered what he was thinking. He wore a short Afro and a perfect set of white teeth. He placed their salads on the table and left to put in their order.

Senida loosened up after her first glass of Cristal. Mandla's personality helped to put her fears to rest. He laughed and talked about D.C. She told him about her life in California and they compared the differences and the similarities of the East and West Coasts. When the food came, they were both silent long enough to eat and then continued to laugh and talk. The night was perfect, the mood was perfect, Senida felt perfect, Mandla felt perfect, and the *date* was perfect.

I'VE ONLY
SEEN HER TWICE

Bases were loaded and it was top of the fifth inning. Atlanta's baseball team had two strikes on them and their weakest hitter was at bat. The crowd hushed and the stadium quieted. All eyes were on Antonio Geiko, who had the lowest batting average in the league. Many fans wondered why he was still around and hadn't been traded for someone else. A few people started to stand to get a better view. Before Jelani knew it, half the stadium was standing. He looked over at the three occupied seats to his right and the two occupied seats to his left. Jabarie and Jamarie looked over at him while the other three bigger boys tried to stand to see over the grown ups that were standing in front of them.

"Uncle Jay. I can't see," Jabarie whined.

"Me neither. I can't see," his twin brother, Jamarie echoed.

"Here stand up on your seats," Jelani said, as he stood and helped the two boys to stand on the stadium seats, supporting both with each arm, in case they fell.

Geiko hit a pop fly, into center field and the crowd was breathless. For sure Brad Jackson, the center fielder for the Bronner's team, would catch the ball. The ball flew high into the air and glided downward. Nobody moved, not even Geiko, as he stood perplexed. The coach yelled at him to get running and he trotted towards first. All the other players were transfixed on their prospective bases. Jackson ran forward but stopped as if the sun was in his eyes. He put his glove up to block the sun but it was too late. The ball plopped down onto the ground. Jackson scooped up the ball and threw it towards home but the runner slid and the other players were safe on their bases.

Geiko made it to second base and the crowd went wild. All five of Jelani's little brothers yelled and danced and screamed with delight. Jabarie and Jamarie jumped down off of the seats and slapped five with each other. All right they yelled. Taj, Randell, and Mike all gave each other five also. Jelani smiled. He felt good inside when they were happy.

He looked at each one of their faces as they settled back into their seats. He remembered when he decided to be a big brother. The woman he was dating at the time convinced him through sex and coercion that he would make a great big brother. Jelani refused for at least two months before he decided to give it a try. And although they did not date anymore, he kept the same little boys he met when he was with her. When he walked into the recreation room and saw the set of twins and the other three boys, he could not make a decision so he adopted all five of them as his little brothers.

Many times the boys would express how they were glad he decided to be in the 'Big Brother' program. They adored the ground that he walked on and at first this bothered Jelani but now it was the main purpose that kept him to his promise. He promised that he would walk the straight and narrow and try to be the best role model for the five little boys. Lord knew he lacked the good role model in his father while he grew up.

Jelani snapped back to reality when he heard two of the oldest boys arguing. Taj and Mike were both thirteen and had been best friends for years. They often argued and swore. That was how they expressed their love for one another. Mike pushed Taj on the side of his head and Jelani grabbed Taj's fist right before he planted it in Mike's little bird chest.

"Hey. Brothas chill. What's going on here?" he asked as he let Taj's fist drop.

"See that little red head girl up there?" Mike asked Jelani and then pointed to a group of little girls sitting with an older woman. The little girls were looking down at them from their nosebleed seats pointing and giggling.

"Taj likes that girl right there. He said that was his girlfriend," Mike said smiling as Taj folded his arms across his chest and poked out his lips.

"Did not. She like *me*. I don't like her," Taj responded.

"She don't like you boy. I ast her just the other day. She

told me you tried to kiss her," Mike said laughing. Jabarie, Jamarie, and Randell joined in the laughter.

"Did not!" Taj yelled, as he positioned himself to hit Mike.

"Hey. What's wrong with having a girlfriend Mike?" Jelani asked.

"Nothing, but she don't like him." He chuckled. "Plus *you* don't have no girlfriend."

All five of the boys looked directly at Jelani, waiting for him to respond. He rubbed his chin and lifted his hat to get some air to his head. He felt a little awkward. He'd told the boys that if they needed to talk to him about anything to just let him know. But sometimes they probed into his own personal life, and whatever happened in the past would not and could not haunt him. He refused to let that happen. But he did not want to sound like a hypocrite. He wanted to be honest yet sensitive to their ages. Jabarie and Jamarie were only six years old, Mike and Taj thirteen, and Randell nine.

"Well I'm looking for a girlfriend right now." Jabarie and Jamarie smiled at each other. They sunk in their seats and giggled. All six of them were oblivious to the baseball game. "Do you know any that's available?" he asked them.

They all laughed and Mike, the most outspoken, raised his hand as if he were in class. He bounced around in his seat.

"Ooh, ooh, ooh. I know this girl that go to my school. She can be your girlfriend. She's older."

"And how old is that?"

"She 'bout, ummm, probably seventeen," he said as he seriously thought about the match.

"No thank you. I need someone who is at least twenty-seven."

"That's old" Jabarie chimed.

"Yeah! Old!" Agreed Jamarie. They all laughed.

Turning their attention back to the game, they yelled at the umpire together and booed the weak players. Jelani loved to be around little kids. He thought they were at the best years in life, innocent yet impressionable. A dangerous combination, if put into the wrong hands. And that was his job, to make sure that at least these five little boys did not have the type of childhood that he had.

"So for real. Why you ain't got no girlfriend?" Taj finally asked again.

"Haven't found anyone I like yet," Jelani responded without looking at Taj.

"But it's a lot of pretty women in Atlanta. You don't never see them?" he asked with real concern. Jelani looked away from the game and focused intently on the young boys' eyes. He could tell that he was going through that awkward stage.

"At this point in my life, Taj, I'm looking for someone permanent. Do you understand?" He nodded. "I want to settle down with a wife and maybe have some little rugrats like y'all." They smiled and giggled. "But in my profession, it's hard to find a woman that is true. Do you know what I mean by true?"

He shook his head.

"It means someone who likes me for me. Someone I can trust. I meet beautiful women all the time but it's the beauty on the inside that counts the most."

"So have you found anybody with beauty on the inside too?"

"Yes and no."

Taj looked confused. The other boys were into the game and oblivious to the intense conversation.

"I met a woman but I don't know where she is. I think about her all the time but I don't know her."

Taj raised one eyebrow.

"Do you understand?" Jelani asked.

"No."

"I've only seen her twice. I don't know where she lives." Taj continued to stare at Jelani. " You like the little red head girl?"

Taj looked over at Mike who was not paying attention to them. He slowly shook his head.

"There's nothing wrong with that. It's perfectly normal for you to like her. Just don't write a check your ass can't cash."

Taj smiled. "Uncle Jay?" he asked. "Do you like the beautiful lady?"

Jelani smiled and nodded.

"Then you should find her. But don't write no checks either." He smiled and Jelani placed his hand on top of his head and shook it.

Jelani smiled to himself. Imagine him, God's gift to women on Earth and Heaven, getting advice from a thirteen-year-old. Maybe Taj was right; maybe he should find her. He thought about the way she looked up at him in a daze when they had their car accident. She seemed so helpless, like a lost little kitten. Jelani took in a long, deep breath. Ever since he'd met her, he could not stop thinking about her. And although her beauty was uncanny, it was her spirit that eluded him. A strong, yet sensitive spirit, much like his mother's. He dreamed of looking into her large, round, brown eyes and of holding her safely in his arms.

Maybe he would call his insurance company and get her address and phone number. He was sure that if he gave her an opportunity to get to know him, she would fall madly in love with him. Who in their right mind wouldn't? Every woman he'd come across had melted at his feet.

But Jelani was tired of the same old rigmarole. He wanted a woman with just as much intelligence as beauty...spunk, wit, and humor. And she had to love him for him. He didn't think that was too much to ask. After all, he was a prized possession. A thirty-two year old man with a wonderful career, making more than the average Joe, no children, never been married, and college educated. First thing Monday morning, he would call Charlie his insurance agent and get the necessary information. Maybe *he* would try pursuing someone for a change instead of *them* trying to pursue him. It might make for an interesting situation. Maybe he'd be lucky and end up like his brother Donnie, married.

Jelani turned the music down so he could hear Charlie's words. Sade had been crooning all day, allowing Jelani to rest in his Florida beach home. His bowlegs shined and his muscles bulged from his Karl Kani short set. He settled back onto his couch and waited for Charlie to find his files. The ruffling of the papers distracted Jelani and he reached for his remote control and turned Sade completely off.

Charlie was Jelani's right hand man when it came to handling his finances and other legal situations. Charlie had brown hair and green eyes. His stark, white complexion was quite frightening in comparison with the rest of the colors on his face. Jelani often teased him because he couldn't find a girlfriend. Charlie knew that he wasn't the most attractive human being but he kept up the spirit. He would try to talk to any female. White, black, it didn't matter to Charlie. But he did have a preference for some of the sistahs that Jelani would bring around the social gatherings. Jelani had caught him looking on more than enough occasions. At the time Jelani did not care, he was in that mind-set. Many of those women were just groupies.

He then thought of Maya. How would he feel if Charlie made one of those crude comments about Maya and stared at her until his eyes almost popped out? Jelani unconsciously became heated under his collar. He pictured Charlie standing beside Maya looking at her backside. Then he pictured himself breaking Charlie's neck. Jelani repositioned himself on the couch. He needed to calm down.

"Hey, J.R. I got your files right here." Jelani could hear him ruffling through the files. "Her car was totaled out. And her insurance just expired...so..."

"So...what?" Jelani asked.

"So we haven't paid for any damages," he said matter-of-factly.

"No wonder she was so pissed off. That's been well over a month." Jelani scratched his head. "I wonder how she's been getting around?" he asked himself. He couldn't possibly let her continue to take public transportation.

"Well, what did she say when you saw her?" Charlie asked but more for his personal nosiness than business.

"Everything that you just said. But of course, you know, I don't discuss my business without consulting with you first."

"So what are you going to do now? What do you want me to do with your money?"

"Um...I think I might want to handle this differently. Cause I'm not only trying to do what's right, but I'm trying to get with her."

"Oh." Charlie laughed. "You're trying to get some booty." He laughed louder. Jelani did not.

"No Charles. This one's different. I'm not *just* trying to get the booty. I think she might be the one."

"Not the black Fabio. What will all the rest of the women say?"

"Fuck all the rest of those hoes. I think I've found a woman. A real woman."

"Hey, J.R., maybe once you hook up with this real woman, she can hook me up with some of her friends."

"I don't think so pale boy. Strictly for the brothas this time." Jelani laughed. Charlie laughed.

"Well you tell me what you want me to do with the situation so I can get things in motion."

Jelani spilled out his plan to Charlie for about an hour. His body tingled from excitement when he placed the receiver on the cradle. He could hardly wait until he could see the look on her face. His stunt may put him over the top. Reclining in his chair, he thought about the way her body looked in the Kroger parking lot. Her large, brown eyes sucked him into her soul. And the way her nipples poked through the thin blouse. He played it cool, not letting her know that her presence aroused him. He could picture her pitching a fit and stomping off across the lot. He smiled.

He then pictured her laying in his bed under the covers. He imagined her thick hair wild from their passion and her nipples looking directly at him, not hiding behind the blouse this time. Jelani shook his head vigorously. No need in getting riled up tonight tiger, he thought to himself, especially when I'm alone.

Jelani grabbed his keys from the table and headed towards the door. A long walk on the beach might calm his nerves he thought. He bounced down the steps and onto the cool sand. Each grain felt like tiny little fingers massaging his feet as he walked. He looked out into the night and wondered if she was thinking about him.

*****

Senida frowned at Mr. Mortin. Her head pounded, she had menstrual cramps and this man was not making sense. She looked over at Mandla who had a smirk on his face. She knew what he was thinking and she wasn't amused. He knew that Mr. Mortin wasn't making any sense and that Senida was in a bad mood.

"I'm sorry Mr. Mortin but could you please repeat your last statement on your where-abouts that particular night?" Senida rubbed her temples with her fingertips. Where was her Excedrin? She attempted to focus on the tiny man poised in the chair with his over-sized, black suit and his hat with the red feather perched on his lap.

"Do you have a headache?" Mr. Mortin asked.

Mandla smiled.

"Oh a slight one."

"I could come back tomorrow. It would probably be a better time for me anyway." He cocked his head to the side.

Senida thought. Her appointment book was open tomorrow. She looked over at Mandla. He shrugged his shoulders and then smiled at Mr. Mortin.

"Yes, actually Mr. Mortin, tomorrow would be better for me also. Let's say eleven am?" she asked as she pointed her finger at the time in her organizer.

"That will be fine with me. I trust that things will work out better tomorrow Ms. Johnson. I hear you're the best in town right now. And I hear that from a very reliable source. I'll see you tomorrow Ms. Johnson. And once again, I appreciate your time. Have a good day." Mr. Mortin stood. He nodded at Mandla and walked out of the door.

"That man is something else," Mandla said once the door was shut. "He needs our help bad. The jury's gonna chew him up and spit him out if we don't come up with something quick."

"I know. We're going to have to put some long, hard hours into this case. Are you ready for a lot of work?" she asked as she rubbed her temples. She was thinking of all the long, hard hours she had to spend with him in the office.

"Hey. This is my passion. I love this kind of stuff." His gray eyes bounced from excitement.

"Good. Now I want you to pull everything you can on this Ms. Daphnee Latimore. I want to know everything. I want to know what she eats, where she sleeps, and whom she sleeps with. And give me a report by tomorrow on what you find. I have a headache. I'm going home." Senida stood and gathered her briefcase and her coat. Mandla sat with his eyes widened at the amount of work she had just laid on him.

"Well?" she asked.

"It'll be ready tomorrow," he said. "Boss."

Senida smiled. "Call me Ms. Johnson."

She winked at Mandla as she made her way to the door.

"If you need anything just call me at home later. You know the number." She left.

Mandla sat in the office for about fifteen minutes after Senida left contemplating on how he would start his research. His adrenaline was up. The research would take all night but he didn't have any plans anyway so it didn't matter to him. He didn't mind doing overtime for Senida.

Senida turned the burgundy Honda into the parking lot of Jake's Pizza. Jake was one of Senida's new friends. She had met Jake when she first moved to the area surrounding Piedmont Park. Jake's tiny building sat on the corner of Juniper and Piedmont. The white, brick building was surrounded with lush yellow and orange flowers. Jake would plant and water them himself. In front of the building was a large wooden sign that read 'Jake's Pizza' and the phone number underneath the name. Jake had two local teenagers paint the sign for him. The two young boys gave the sign a type of hip-hop look to it, which attracted a lot of young sistahs and brothas to Jake's spot.

When Senida was in the mood for pizza, she bought only Jake's. Not only was Jake one of the nicest and cutest Italian men around but she loved the young, vibrant atmosphere of the small joint. It was Jake's place that Senida met her lover. She remembered meeting him like it was yesterday.

Darrell had been busy all day so she decided to head to Jake's to get a slice of pizza. The sun was out that day and there wasn't a breeze to be found anywhere. Senida was perspiring immensely and even the trees seemed to be suffering from dehydration. When she entered Jake's, the line and crowd was loud, rowdy, and large. Senida almost turned around to go somewhere else but Jake saw her from the corner of his eye. He motioned for her to come to the front of the line and served her as if she were a pizza VIP cardholder. When she sat at one of the empty booths, an attractive young man approached her and asked if he could sit with her.

Senida had eyed him cautiously as he sat without waiting for her to answer. His eyes were deep and his color dark. His broad smile enchanted Senida immediately. After exchanging names they engaged in deep conversation for over an hour. Senida knew that she would have to explain to Darrell why her trip to Jake's had taken so long. All the other young women in the pizza parlor seemed to be interested in engaging in conversation with the young man but he sat and talked to Senida until she left. She remembered that he ran out of Jake's to remind her that they had not exchanged numbers. Hesitant at first, Senida wrote his number down on Jake's receipt but did not give him her number. Weeks later, after a fight with Darrell, Senida called the young man and he quickly became her lover.

Jake also remembered that same day when he let Senida come to the front of the line he'd watched the entire conversation closely. When she walked in that day, Jake was busy taking orders but he noticed Senida before she even walked through the door. Jake had a small crush on Senida. He liked the way her hips curved out and dipped back into her body. He enjoyed watching the sway in her back and the movement of her backside. He'd imagined resting comfortably on top of her butt many of nights.

The only flaw that Jake noticed about Senida was her small breasts. Jake liked a woman with more than a mouthful of breasts. All of the Italian women that he'd dated in his thirty-four years of life had large breasts. It was the flat butts that Jake could not tolerate. Just as much as he liked large breasts, he liked large, robust butts. His mother told him not to judge a woman on her looks alone. She wanted him to get married and more than anything she wanted grandchildren. He was the only son. His two sisters produced only girls. The family was counting on him to carry out the name, but he was not married or had the desire to be.

When his father died and left him the pizza business, his passion for women seemed to take second place to keeping the family business alive. His heart ached many times when he thought about how his mother pleaded for him to get married. That was all she wanted to see before she died. And he couldn't even give her that much. She died shortly after his father. At the funeral he was the only over thirty person that was unwed.

Senida knew when she met Jake that he was special. Not special like he needed psychiatric help, but special like he needed love. The day she met her lover in Jake's, he'd warned her and she should have listened. By this time, she and Jake were close associates and he often gave her advice on her problems in life. But Senida knew that Jake didn't know what he was talking about in this situation.

Jake had watched from afar as the young suave, debonair brotha coolly walked up to Senida and slid his body in the booth next to her. At first he thought she wouldn't go for his charm but Senida seemed to melt with every word he spoke. Jake knew the young man was trouble. He'd seen him in his pizza place before talking to different women, each time exchanging numbers. There was even a confrontation with a few of the women, but it didn't seem to stop the attractive, young man.

Jake looked at his watch when he saw Senida turn her burgundy Honda Accord into the back of his parking lot. He knew her work schedule and he knew she must have gotten off work early; another subject he had lectured her about. It was still early and the small building only had a few people seated. Jake watched Senida carefully as she walked past the mirrored walls and through the front door, making the little bells ring as she walked into the place.

Senida wore an expensive looking business suit and a white lace shirt underneath her suit jacket. Her high heels matched her suit and her earrings were simple diamond droplets. Jake strained hard to get a glimpse of her backside but she was now standing directly in front of him. Her broad smile lightened his mood and he decided not to lecture her about leaving work early. Besides, he thought to himself, she smells so damn good, if I get close to her I might bite her. He smiled.

"Hey Jake. What's up?"

"Oh the lovely Senida. You are up. Or should I say, you make me get up," Jake responded in his Italian accent.

He reached his arms across the counter and gently caressed her hand before he raised them both to his mouth. Jake planted a sweet, slow, sensual kiss to Senida's hands. She liked Jake, but he usually made her feel a little uncomfortable when he made such a big deal over her. She didn't understand why the black men in her life couldn't take lessons. Now that's whom she needed to make big deals over her, her black men. Senida felt the Excedrin that she had taken earlier take effect. Her head was not pounding as hard and her vision was not blurred anymore.

"What can I get for my favorite beautiful lady?" Jake asked as he gave Senida back her hands. He pulled the white towel out of his apron pocket and slung it onto his shoulder. His once white apron was now yellow from the corn meal and the powdery dough of the pizzas.

"I'll take two slices of pepperoni."

"Yo, Sal. Get Senida two of the best pieces of pepperoni you can make."

"Oh you don't have to make a whole 'nother pizza for me..."

Jake put his finger to Senida's lips to quiet her. "Nonsense. Only the best for you. You are my favorite customer." And then he looked over his shoulder again and yelled at Sal to put extra pepperoni on her pizza. He rang up her order, collected her money and wiped down the counter with the towel from his shoulder.

"So how's your family doing?" he asked in the Italian accent. He leaned his body to one side as he watched her lips part in answer to his question.

"They're fine. I talked to my mother the other night."

"And the love life?"

"Fine," she lied.

"Come on Senida. What's that look for?"

"What look?"

"The look on your face."

"No reason."

"Senida." Jake leaned forward so she would be the only one to hear him. "When are you going to stop messing around with these men that treat you bad and get with me? Huh? When are we going to go out?"

"Jake. Your family would kill you if you went out with a Black woman."

Jake laughed. He looked over his shoulder to see if Sal was close enough to hear. He had been lusting over Senida since the first day that she walked into the little pizza joint.

"We don't have to tell them. It could be our little secret. Let me show you how Italian lovers do."

Sal walked up behind Jake and slapped him on the back. Jake jumped to attention and took the pizza out of Sal's hand. Senida smiled at the now nervous Jake.

"Yo' grease head, Senida don't want no little Italian lover. She wants a real Italian lover. With a real Italian sausage."

"And I guess that would be you?" Jake asked as he turned to look directly at Sal.

"Yeah. Ain't that right Senida?" Sal looked at Senida, who reached for her pizza and smiled. She was not getting caught up in some Italian macho conversation. She had made the mistake before and she learned her lesson. Her mama didn't raise no fool.

She tried to stay out of conversations that were laden with testosterone.

"Good-bye guys. See you later," she replied and walked out of the pizzeria. The two men stared at her until she had sat in her car and they couldn't see her body anymore.

The pizza was gone before Senida pulled into her parking stall. She didn't realize that she was that hungry. Hunger must have been the reason behind her headache earlier. Senida waltzed into her apartment and dumped her workload onto her couch. She would be posted there until the next morning, filing through Mr. Mortin's facts. She showered and slipped on her old, torn, sweat pants and a pretty white bra.

Oprah kept Senida's attention for the first part of the afternoon and then she flipped through channels in between sorting through her work. Tomorrow she would have more work to sort through because she knew that Mandla would come through on his part of the deal. He had a passion for law and would surprise Senida with the amount of work that he put into the Mortin case. Sometimes Senida would have to leave the office because she was thinking about his long, lean thighs. Her hormones would get the best of her. They always did. If he didn't work for her, she would have taken him for a test drive a long time ago. Senida smiled to herself. It was time for her to put these papers down and get her some loving. She hadn't talked to any of her men in such a long time, she thought she might have to get a new batch.

Senida's apartment buzzer awakened her out of a deep sleep. She hadn't realized that she'd fallen asleep. She looked around at the papers that surrounded her as she slept. The buzzer sounded again and Senida jumped to see who was stopping by her house without calling. As she dashed to the intercom on the wall, she glanced at the clock and realized that five hours had passed since she'd started her paperwork. Senida pressed hard on the intercom with an attitude.

"Yeah?"

"Hey Ms. Johnson?" the voice was low and sexy.

"Who is this?" Senida asked as she leaned her ear closer to the little box, trying to recognize the voice.

"It's me. Mandla Jackson from Smithers' Law Firm."

Senida frowned. He was the last person she would be expecting. She didn't even know he knew where she lived.

Senida pressed the button to allow him to come in. She ran into the bathroom, threw on a shirt, and slicked her hair down with some water and lotion. She then wiped the sleep out of her eyes and dabbed a small amount of brown lipstick on her lips. She wanted to look as though she had been looking good all evening. Senida jogged into her bedroom and sprayed some peach smelling spray on her shirt, on her arms, and in between her legs. Before she could gargle well with some Listerine, she heard Mandla's knock at the door.

Senida's heart dropped when she opened the door. Mandla was wearing a pair of dark blue jeans and a baggy shirt, with an Oakland Raiders cap on backwards. He had a brown leather backpack hanging from his left shoulder. His young appearance held a sex appeal, as he walked his long legs into Senida's apartment. His smell almost took her breath away. The cool smell of men's Obsession filled the room. Senida took in a deep breath of his scent. He was definitely a sexy, young man.

Mandla looked around the apartment, paying special attention to the pictures of Senida and her family on the mantel. He turned to her with a smile, waltzed over, and planted a kiss on her cheek.

"Nice place you got here," he replied, ignoring the shocked look on Senida's face. She had to get used to the quick, seductive kisses that he stole from her, every time he saw her. Mandla reached into his backpack and pulled out a stack of papers.

"Mandla, what are you doing here and how did you know where I lived?"

"I've known where you lived a long time ago. I brought some information to you about Ms. Latimore," he said still looking around the apartment. Senida figured she might as well offer him a seat, since he didn't look like he was leaving anytime soon. She actually liked the fact that she had company over, besides Darrell and Maya.

"And why did you just pop up like that? How do you know that I didn't live with my man or something?"

"I knew," Mandla said as he followed Senida's lead and sat on the couch. He still held the papers in his hand.

"Well, what do you have?"

"Here's a list of places that Ms. Latimore worked in the past ten years. Each employer has had some type of problem with her, which has resulted in a settling of monies." Mandla handed Senida the pile of papers, placed his bag on the floor next to the couch and sat back, crossing his legs. Senida looked through the papers and then looked up at Mandla, who was staring at her.

"Oh, I'm sorry. Would you like something to drink?"

"What do you have?"

"Umm," Senida had to think hard. She hadn't been grocery shopping in awhile. But then she remembered the bottle of red wine that Darrell bought for her a few months ago. "I have some red wine."

"That would be fine. But do you have any beer?"

"No."

"Oh. Well I guess the red wine will have to do."

"I guess it will." Senida got up from the couch and walked into the kitchen, with Mandla following behind her.

"I like the space in this apartment. It's pretty big," he said as he sat on the stool at the breakfast bar. Senida didn't understand why he was following her into the kitchen.

She turned to him and smiled as she broke ice cubes out of the tray. She reached into the cabinet to get the bottle of wine and pulled out two glasses with the bottle. Mandla talked about the differences between Atlanta and Washington D.C. He went on to tell Senida about what he's been doing in Atlanta. He seemed to be a regular at the Atlanta clubs.

Senida poured wine in his glass first and handed it to him as he continued to talk. She then poured herself some wine and leaned against the breakfast bar to listen to Mandla. She enjoyed the chatter that came from his sexy mouth. His gray eyes bounced with excitement as he told her about his mother and all of his "potnas" in Washington D.C. Senida slowly sipped her wine and Mandla gulped his down quick. He held out his glass for another fill, but did not miss a beat in his story. Senida reached behind her to fill his glass with the red liquid.

"So have you and your man made up yet?" he asked, as he took his second glass full of wine and headed towards the den to sit on the couch. Senida followed him, wondering whose apartment they were in. She seemed to be the guest. She watched as he sat on the couch with his legs gaped wide open.

"I shouldn't be telling you any of my business. But no we haven't." Senida sat on the floor in front of the couch with her legs crossed Indian style.

"Ummm," Mandla responded. He drank the rest of his wine and let his head fall back onto the couch. "So what do you do in your spare time? Do you go out?"

"Not really. Sometimes I might hang out with my best friend."

"Is that her in the picture with you?" Mandla asked as he pointed to the picture on the mantel of Senida and Maya.

"Yes."

"She fine."

"That's what they say," Senida took a few more sips from her glass. Mandla walked into the kitchen, poured himself another glass of wine and plopped back down on the couch. Senida looked at her glass. She was starting to feel a slight buzz and she was still on her first glass.

"So Mr. Jackson, why hasn't somebody tied you down yet?"

"I haven't found a creature capable of doing such a thing."

"Oh really? And what type of creature would be able to do that?"

"I usually date older women because I've had my share of little chicken heads. They're cool for fun. But an older woman has a little more stability in her life. She doesn't like to play all the games that the younger women do."

"Uh hum."

"So do you know any older women available?"

Senida smiled. She was feeling bold, but not *that* bold.

"I might. If I see them, do you want me to give them your number?"

"Please do. And don't forget to tell them that they'll be dealing with a real man." Mandla drank his third glass of wine in two large gulps and set the glass on the coffee table.

"Have you dated any younger men?"

"Yes."

"Recently?"

"Yes. Why do you ask?"

"Just taking mental notes."

"For you or for someone else?"

"Oh, for me. Fo' sho'. You can believe that," Mandla grabbed his leather pack and stood up. "I'll be seeing you soon Ms. Johnson."

"You're leaving now?" Senida asked as she stood. She wasn't quite ready for him to go. They had only talked for a short while. She wanted to hear more about his life and learn more about his personality. The alcohol made her want to find out if the large bulge in the front was truly a blessing, or a figment of her imagination.

"Yeah. I got some business I got to take care of. I just stopped by to give you that information," Mandla started walking towards the door.

"You have a date tonight?" Senida let the words slip out of her mouth before she realized that her thoughts were out in the open.

Mandla smiled. "Business. I handles business Ms. Johnson." He opened the door and walked out shutting it behind him.

When Senida went to look out of the window, to ask him how he got to her house, he'd disappeared. She opened the door quickly and looked up and down the hallway but she didn't see him. In the short time that she'd known Mandla, he had managed to get under her skin in a good way. She thought about him on a continual basis and anticipated work, knowing that she would have him all to herself at Smithers' Law Firm. Senida closed the door and went back to her position on the floor. After finishing her wine, she felt a feeling come over her that could not be controlled. She let her head fall back onto the papers, closed her eyes and went into her fantasy world.

FLOWERS AND BRACELETS AND CARS, OH MY!

"Of course these are for you," Stephen said as he sternly placed the vase of flowers on top of Maya's desk and waltzed out of her office.

This was the second consecutive week she'd been receiving flowers. Maya had no idea who was sending them or why. There was never a card. She eyed the beautiful arrangement that sat on her desk. The pencil she held in between her fingers rolled around, as she sat and thought of where the flowers could possibly be coming from. She didn't think Donald was sending them because it wasn't his style. And Michael was the type who needed recognition for anything that he did. Without a card attached, he could not take all of the credit for sending them, so it couldn't be him.

Maya sat back in her chair and dug her hand deep into her large purse. She pulled out her tiny black phone book and began leafing through it. She could not think of anyone who would be sending her flowers. She reached over her desk and pressed number one on her phone. Automatically, Senida's office number began to ring.

"Hello, Ms. Johnson's office."

"Hi Lacey, it's me Maya."

"Hey girl! How you doing?"

"I'm fine. How are you?"

"I'm doing good."

"That's good. Is Senida busy?"

"As a matter of fact, she's getting her stuff together for a meeting. Do you want to talk to her real quick?"

"Yeah, it won't take long."

Lacey transferred the call through to Senida, who reluctantly picked up the extension.

"Senida Johnson."

"More came today," Maya said into the phone.

"More flowers?" Senida asked quickly, catching on to her friend's voice.

"Yes girl. I'm starting to wonder if I'm not being stalked."

"Have you gotten a card with any of the flowers?"

"No. And they haven't just been flowers. I've been receiving some expensive gifts. I haven't the slightest who is sending them to me."

"Girl. That's a little on the spooky side to me."

"Oh Senida."

"Well what else have you been getting?"

"Yesterday I got a gold tennis bracelet. Do you know how much those things cost? Then, last week I got a bouquet of flowers with an entourage of balloons."

"Maybe somebody's sending them to the wrong address."

"Well hell, it's too late now. I've already gotten attached to that tennis bracelet." Maya laughed as she swiveled around in her chair and looked out of her office to see Stephen moping around the halls.

"I don't know if I'd keep them."

"Shit! The hell if I don't. If it *is* a mistake, then it's not my fault."

"You know you can get in trouble for stuff like that. I tell you this all the time."

"And what ever happens to me? Nothing. You need to chill. Don't forget that you ain't no saint either."

Senida sucked her teeth. "And you say you asked Michael?"

"Yes. I've asked Michael, who is acting just as peculiar as you are and I've asked Donald. Neither of them said they sent me anything. The way Donald acts at times, I wouldn't be surprised if he sent me dead flowers."

Senida laughed out loud at her friend's comment. She pictured Maya receiving a vase full of dead flowers from Donald. They were always arguing over something. Senida didn't know why Maya, or both of them for that matter, wasted their time trying to make their relationship work. Both Maya and Donald were seeing other people anyway. They claimed they had no commitment to one another, but they carried on as if they were already married.

"Well chile, I got to go. I have to meet with Mr. Mortin again today. Call me later when you get home." Senida hung up.

Maya sat holding the phone. She swiveled around in her chair and placed it in its cradle. She thought hard. Who in the world could be sending her all of these gifts? Flowers, candy, balloons, and an expensive bracelet? Such unusual gifts from a stranger. Yet, beautiful women receive unusual, expensive gifts from men all of the time. Why not her? She was extraordinarily attractive.

She decided to take the rest of the day off and do a little shopping. She still had to stop at the mall and she didn't want to be caught out in the dark. Maya called for Stephen and after a short time of him sucking his teeth, rolling his eyes, and sighing, she headed out to the MARTA station to go home. The air was crisp and clean...chilly. But it was a beautiful day. Birds were chirping and clouds were floating. Maya watched a squirrel dart in and out of cars, as it tried unsuccessfully to cross the street. She closed her eyes to erase the sight of the poor, little, flattened creature twitching and flapping, trying to hold on to life. Maya boarded the train and was soon on her way to the mall.

She refused to give in and he refused to give up. Maya could not figure out for the life of her how Jelani got her phone number but when she picked up the receiver, he was on the other end. Over a month passed and the red-faced mechanic told her that she would have to total out her car. She was stranded! She had neither the money nor the insurance to fix her car. He had been sending her little messages but she was not trying to play around with him. He seemed to be popping up everywhere she went. Maya couldn't shake him.

"Meet me at Kroger," his voice boomed.

"Who is this?" her irritated voice boomed back.

"This is J.R."

"Who?"

"Jelani...Jelani Ransom," he replied incidentally.

"How the hell did you get my number?"

"I got friends in high places," he laughed.

Maya hung up and was about to turn off her ringer, but hesitated. How dare he *look* her up? Did he think that she would just forget about her car and go out with him? His arrogant ass probably thought she would jump at the chance to go out with him. Well he was fine, but not *that* damn fine. She wouldn't be able to date him anyway because every time she would look at him, she would think about how she had to catch the bus at six in the morning. When he called back, she was ready to cuss him out. She picked the phone up on the first ring.

"Don't hang up. I want to talk to you about your car," his desperate voice kept her interested. Plus, he was talking about her car. "I talked to my insurance agent today. He told me that your car was totaled out."

She waited. Silence. He was obviously waiting for her to respond. She didn't have the patience.

"Make this good and make this fast," she responded in a cool, low voice.

"Is that any way to treat your future husband? Meet me at Kroger. I promise, you won't be sorry."

"My future husband wouldn't have left me stranded," she pouted.

"Meet me at Kroger."

"No."

"Come on Maya. I know we started off wrong but baby you just so fine! Seriously, meet me at the grocery store. Trust me on this one sweetheart." Jelani pleaded. He strategically planned to get her attention and hold it. Maya did not respond, leaving Jelani to believe that she was considering meeting him. "I'll only take up a little bit of your time. Or, I could come over there?"

"Not even close."

"Come on Maya."

"What is so important that you can't tell me on the phone?"

"I need to tell you in person. It *is* important. How long will it take for you to get there?"

"I didn't say I was coming."

"Please. I don't normally beg, but please."

"What time and for how long? I don't see why you can't tell me over the phone. If it doesn't have anything to do with my car then I really am not interested."

"I promise, it will be worth your time. I'll meet you in the parking lot in about an hour?" Jelani sounded like a child on Christmas day.

"Yeah," she responded flatly and hung up.

Maya hated herself for wanting to go. She sat for a minute thinking. She could tell that he wanted more than to talk about her car. Maya turned on the shower and let the water run. She undressed and stood in front of her floor length mirror. Her mind drifted into wander. Why was it urgent for Jelani to see her? Why did she even want to go? Why couldn't she just turn on the television and turn him off in her mind? She was not up for any games so if he dared say something stupid or let that fat ass ego of his get in the way, she would leave. Why am I even going?

Maya groaned to herself as she looked at herself in the mirror. There was something in his eyes that caught her attention when she saw him at Kroger's. Some type of mystery that kept her curiosity flowing. As much as she hated to admit the truth, Jelani had gotten under her skin in a bad way, but good. Maya leaned her naked body against the mirror. Why was life so complicated? Just a few months ago, she was riding on cloud nine. Now she was on cloud two, or lower.

*****

Jelani stood by his car with flowers and a card. He wanted to apologize to Maya for the inconveniences that his insurance company put her through. He patted his right front pocket insuring the biggest surprise. Everything had to be perfect. All of the begging he did on the phone could not go to waste. His feelings for Maya were growing at a rate that scared him. She would be perfect once he could show her that he was true. His ego would have to be put aside for the remainder of the ride. It was a task that was not easy for J.R. since he was used to the women falling over him. They would follow him home, look his number up in the directory, and show up at places that they knew he frequented. But Maya was different. Just her strength of being able to say no to him was enough to prove that she was not after his money.

It seemed as if Maya floated across the lot in her sheer tan floor length dress. Her face was twisted in her meanest look she could muster.

"Please make this fast. I am not in the mood for any of your games today Jelani."

"Please. Call me J.R. All my friends do." Jelani flashed a perfect heart-melting smile.

"I'm leaving." Maya spun around on her heels. Jelani reached out to grab her but pulled back. He counted quickly backwards from five to one.

"Please! Maya! Here. These are for you." He held out his right hand full of flowers. She turned and looked at the flowers and the card sticking out and then looked at him. "Please take them. I'm truly sorry for any inconvenience that my insurance company caused you and I want to make it up to you."

Maya stood looking at the flowers but did not take them.

"Are you the one that's been sending me flowers and presents?" she asked.

"Yes."

"How did you get my address and how did you know where I worked?"

"I got friends in high places." He smiled but she did not smile back. She was not the least bit amused. "At least let me take you to dinner."

"I don't have time for this Jelani. I need to figure out how I'm going to get around." Maya's exasperated look tugged at Jelani's heart. She turned and headed for the bus stop. Jelani remembered the special gift in his pocket. He planned to give Maya the special gift during dinner but that didn't look feasible at this point.

"Maya, before you leave. At least take this with you. I spent a lot of time and money buying this gift for you."

"Jelani it is not about money. I am stranded. Now I know you can't understand that but I'm not rolling in a fly Range Rover. I'm taking MARTA and bus! I don't have any more insurance and I definitely don't...don't...have...any...any money."

Tears welled in Maya's eyes and she cursed herself for letting him see her cry. Usually she was stronger. Jelani reached out and wrapped his arms around her. Stroking the back of her neck, he reached into his pocket and pulled out the large bracelet case. He wiped the tears from her face and carefully placed the velvet box in her hand. Maya looked at the box and then to him.

He didn't get it. She wanted her car not some cheap little bracelet. She opened the box and pulled out a set of car keys attached to an alarm. Her mouth dropped.

"Press the alarm," he said grinning. He could barely contain himself. "Press the alarm."

Maya pressed the button at the bottom of the little black gadget and lights flared and sirens roared from behind. She turned to see the commotion coming from a brand new, red, convertible BMW. Maya stood in shock with her mouth open.

"Oh my God...what...what...?"

"It's for all of your inconvenience. What's the matter? Cat got your tongue?" Jelani gently intertwined his fingers in her small hand and led Maya over to her new car. Jelani pushed his finger on the alarm and turned it off. She eyed the car and then him. And then she looked back at the car and back at Jelani. She was speechless. Everything did not register for Maya at once.

"What do you do?" she finally asked, still holding the key ring at a distance from her body, like she was about to set off the alarm again.

"I work. Hard. Like every other black man on this planet."

Jelani took the keys from Maya's hand and opened the driver's side. He started the ignition and pressed on the acceleration pedal. The red BMW gave a loud roar and then a soft purr. With the engine still puttering, Jelani got out of the car leaving the door open.

"Get in, let's go test it out."

Maya stood staring at Jelani in disbelief.

"Okay I'll drive. Get in on the passenger's side." He gently pushed Maya toward the passenger's side.

Maya walked around the other side of the car like a zombie. Maya sat in the BMW and put on her seat belt. She could not believe that this man bought her a car. Jelani sat down in the driver's side and shifted into first gear. He pulled out of Kroger's parking lot, headed toward Interstate 285. Maya sat not moving as Jelani shifted into third. He drove the car as though he was making love, smooth. Jelani's one passion besides beautiful women, were cars. He could drive all day, every day. Sometimes he would drive to Florida, just to get away from the life of Atlanta's metropolitan city. Florida allowed Jelani to relax.

The car purred like a big kitten under his soothing

fingertips. Entering the freeway, Jelani and the car seemed to be as one. Through harmonious fluctuations of shifting gears, Maya could have sworn he'd forgotten that she was in the car.

Easing her nerves, she finally opened her mouth to speak.

"You bought this car for me?"

Jelani seemed to have snapped out of a trance. He looked over at Maya as if she'd just appeared in the seat. His gentle smile made Maya ease up more.

"Yeah, baby. When I talked to my insurance man last week, I decided that we can't have you riding around at night, taking the bus and shit like that. You too fine to be on public transportation. That's for them ugly broads. Plus, it was my fault that you walking anyway. So it's the least I could do."

"But, how could you afford to just buy someone you hardly know a car?"

"I can. It's not like I hardly know you...I been trying to talk to you since that first day I saw you. You was just tripping. Trying to act like you all that."

"I wasn't tripping. I was just mad because you wrecked my car."

"Well, that's all over now."

Maya looked out of the window.

"Where are we going?" She had just realized that she got in a car with a perfect stranger.

"Are you hungry?"

Her stomach was growling and she didn't have any plans for later that night. Now that she thought about it, she hadn't eaten all day. Her stomach started to growl louder, as if on cue, when she thought about food.

"Yeah."

"Where do you want to eat?" Jelani watched Maya as she thought. She twisted her face and tilted her head to the side. She was gorgeous. He knew once she had an opportunity to see the real him, she would give him a chance. Now all he had to do was spin her around his finger before she caught word about him.

"Let's go to Charlene's."

Charlene's was a small seafood restaurant in College Park. It was a black owned business that specialized in Cajun seafood. Maya had only been twice. She loved the food, but could not always afford to spend the kind of money that Charlene was asking.

"Are you sure that's what you want?"

"Yes."

"We can go to a more elegant place."

"No. Charlene's fine. I haven't had seafood in awhile," she responded as she turned to look at him.

Jelani nodded and switched lanes. Jelani turned up the radio. He was listening to light jazz. Maya was impressed. Did this arrogant man have a soft side? He seemed cultured. There was something there that she must have missed earlier. They both rode in silence, listening to the sounds of the music pouring from the speakers. Jelani hummed along good-heartedly. His voice was as smooth as chocolate liquor. Maya could tell he was in a good mood. He did not say too much to her until they reached College Park. He pulled the rear view mirror down at the red light and smoothed out his mustache with his thumb and index finger. He then tilted his head to the right, to get a better view of himself. The sight was comical to Maya.

"So what do you think of the car?"

"I like it."

"Like it?"

"I love it." She smiled.

Jelani reached over and slipped his fingers in between her left hand. His calluses scratched her palms, as he rubbed the top of her hand with his fingers. He smiled but did not look at Maya. Did she finally meet her match?

Maya thought she might be dreaming, but decided that if it were a dream, she didn't want it to end. She would deal with reality later. She couldn't wait to get home to call Senida and tell her about Jelani. Especially, now she knew he was the one sending her the flowers and small gifts. Senida would flip! *She* was tripping. Maya still could not believe that *he* bought her a *car*. A *car*. Not a bracelet. Not a ring. Not a box of candy. A car! And not just any car, but a convertible BMW! Her dream car!

Her blood was pumping through her veins and her heart raced in her chest. She was beginning to feel light headed, so she rolled the window down. And it has power windows! Leaning towards the wind, Maya could not figure out what was really going on. What did he want in return for this car? Was it really for her inconveniences with his insurance company? Even if it was, you don't give cars away for inconvenience, you give people *cards.*

Jelani sat quietly until the waitress took their orders and left. He seemed nervous, like it was his first date.

"So I finally got you to go out with me. If all it took was a car, then I would have done this a long time ago." His laughter was contagious and Maya soon found herself joining in on the joke about her.

"I'm sorry for giving you a hard time, but..."

"But, you're worth it."

"How do you know I'm worth it?"

"I can tell. I've dealt with many women. You're different. Special." His eyes held a dreamy appearance. They bore into Maya's soul, causing her uneasiness. She smiled a weak smile, letting her fingers fumble with her cloth napkin.

Jelani reached across the table and held her hands. He looked deep into her large brown eyes, causing temporary dizziness. Maya felt as though she were swimming in a deep pool of darkness. His handsome face was stern, his eyes unblinking. He could tell that he'd finally trapped Maya and she was beginning to become one of his victims.

Maya could not help herself. He charmed her with those eyes. She did not move...watching, waiting, to see what his eyes would tell. His spell kept her attention and they sat staring at each other in silence.

The waitress interrupted the two, by putting the salads on the table. Maya delved into her salad for fear of getting trapped by his eyes again. Jelani took his time, watching Maya as she tried her best to ignore his gaze.

"So how long have you been here in Atlanta?" he asked munching on his salad.

"Since my senior year in high school," she said, easing a bit.

"Really? That long? Did you go to college here?"

"What do you mean that long?" Maya smiled jokingly.

"I mean..."

"Yes. I graduated from Douglas and then I went to Spelman. How about you?"

"I was born and raised here. But I went to the University of

Michigan."

"Oh really? What was your major?"

"Women. With a minor in football." His response made Maya look up from her salad, long enough to join in with his laughter.

He wasn't so bad, she thought. She was a sucker for a man with a sense of humor. Maya and Jelani continued eating and laughing throughout their meal. His charisma wove itself around her, making her feel as if she'd known him for awhile. Maya's beauty expressed to Jelani what he'd been missing all of these years, a good woman. He could do this forever. Dinner was topped off with a cup of coffee. They were both having such a good time getting to know each other that they did not want the night to end. Jelani drank three cups, trying to stall the irritated waitress from clearing the table.

"I understand. I used to be a cheerleader. Sometimes, I'd have to remember that *my* major wasn't cheering."

"I bet you were one of the prettiest cheerleaders."

"*I* thought so."

They both laughed.

"Our cheerleaders were tired. I think they recruited them from deep in the woods. I even think one of them had a wooden leg."

"That's terrible," Maya shrieked.

"I think the waitress is getting mad at us. What do you think?"

"I think that I really don't care."

"Good answer. Me neither."

"So what about your family?" Maya began.

"What about them?"

"Where are they from?"

Jelani's answer was cold enough to cause an ice storm. "I don't talk about my family." A wave of despair and anger swept across his face.

"I'm sorry. I just..."

"If you want to remain my friend, don't ever ask me shit about my family. I'm ready to go. Are you done?" Maya nodded her head and slowly got up from the table. Jelani noticed how disturbed Maya looked. "I'm sorry. I just don't talk about my family. It's a subject I'd rather not discuss."

They walked out of the restaurant. Maya hoped she hadn't ruined a perfectly good evening by asking about his family. Everything was going well up until this point. Their ride back to Atlanta was silent, despite the soft music floating from the speakers. Toni Braxton belted out the words that seeped through Maya's heart. "Oooh I get so high, when I'm around you baby. I can touch the sky. You make my temperature riiiisee. You making me high!" Sing it girl, Maya thought to herself. Toni was the queen of sad love songs and Maya was feeling the bite of the J.R. bug.

He insisted on driving behind Maya when they reached the Kroger's parking lot. She was not quite sure she wanted him to know exactly where she lived yet, but decided that he would find out sooner or later. When they arrived at her apartment complex, she parked the red BMW in her spot and he parked behind her. Jelani walked Maya to her front door.

"Thank you so much for dinner. And the car. I still don't know what to say."

"Say you'll give me a chance to get to know you better." Jelani leaned with one arm extended on the wall behind Maya.

"Oh it's cool," she responded nervously. "I would like to get to know you better too."

"So I'll give you a call tomorrow?"

"Yeah. I get home from work usually around six thirty."

He bent slowly and pressed his lips to hers. In one smooth motion, Jelani wrapped his hands around her head and kissed her hard. His sweet tongue darted in and out of Maya's mouth, wrestling with her own tongue. Their bodies melted together as he pressed his body closer to hers and wrapped his arms around her tiny waist. Maya felt his middle harden, as he pressed harder against her body. He was breathing hard and tasting every inch of her mouth, kissing her face and ending by gently kissing her hand.

"I'll call you tomorrow?"

Maya could not respond and nodded her head.

"What's the matter? Cat got your tongue?" he laughed, brushed the back of his hand down her cheek and left.

First thing Maya did, when she walked into her apartment was called Senida.

"Girl! Guess what?"

"Ahhh..."

"I got a new car!" Maya's excitement could not wait for her friend to play the guessing game.

"A new car? How? I thought you said you didn't have any money for a new car."

"Jelani bought it for me."

"Who?"

"The guy that ran into me. He called today and told me to meet him at Kroger's. And then he sprang this brand new. Are you ready for this shit?"

"What. What?" Senida screeched.

"A brand new red convertible B-M-W! He bought me a car, girl!"

"What? And you accepted it?"

"Hell yeah! Remember, *he* ran into *me*. That's why I didn't have a car in the first place."

Senida did not know what to say to her friend. She still could not shake the eerie feeling she got whenever Maya mentioned his name. Maya continued with her story, ignoring her friend's silence.

"Turns out that he's a cool person after all. We went to dinner and I think I might have to keep this one."

Maya rambled for about thirty minutes. Her excitement overpowered her usual keen sense of judgment. At the end of their conversation, Senida told Maya she would call her at work the next day. Maya prepared to get herself ready for the next day. That night Maya could not sleep. She tossed and turned, periodically walking to her window, to make sure that she wasn't dreaming. She would definitely have to send him a thank you card and some flowers. Men usually don't expect women to send them flowers. It showed them that you were unorthodox.

PICTURE PERFECT

Jelani looked over at Donnie. They wore identical frowns. The attorney looked from one man to the other. His tie matched his suit and the wire rimmed glasses made him look a little older than Jelani figured him to be.

"It's up to my brother," Donnie finally said. He looked from the attorney to Jelani.

"Keep him in there." Jelani replied without blinking.

"Fine." The white man stood and gathered his papers from the table. He stuffed them firmly into his brief case and snapped the two clasps on either side.

"Good day gentlemen." He said as he shook both of their hands and walked out.

Donnie ran his fingers through his hair and Jelani rubbed his hands down his face.

"Man, do you think we're doing the right thing?" Donnie asked breaking the silence.

Jelani stared into the wood of the table. He pictured his father. He pictured his mother. He pictured Donnie as a young boy. His face frowned and he narrowed his eyes. There was no way in hell that he would allow his father to roam free again. There were too many people that he'd hurt. Jelani sat for a moment thinking about his dear mother. How much he loved her. He thought about how much he missed her. He thought about how much she influenced him. He was sure that his mother would have loved Maya. She was fond of the pretty women that Jelani would bring around the house. His father, however, would usually look close at them and make rude and inappropriate comments to them.

"Yeah." Was all he said and he stood up.

"Are you sure?" Donnie asked. He began running his

hands through his hair.

"Donnie, the man used to beat us. He committed a heinous crime. He needs to burn in hell. I owe it to my mother *and* your mother to make sure he stays his crazy ass in jail."

"Yeah, I guess you're right."

"I know I'm right. All throughout my life I've been affected by his actions."

"I just don't understand that mothafucka'. How could a man be so cruel?"

"Some people don't have the kind heart that you have."

"Or you."

"Thanks. Now, I got a date with Maya. My first *real* date and I'm not about to let *him* ruin it for me. So I'll talk to you later." Jelani walked out of the building. He did not wait for Donnie like he normally did. He got into his black Range Rover and drove away.

Jelani shifted gears and turned the corner headed towards Maya's place. He'd written the directions on his miniature clipboard that was stuck on the front of the window. As he drove, he thought about how he really wanted to impress her. Maya's magnetic personality captured his soul and he could feel that she wanted him too. The way she moved, the way she smelled, the feminine way she tossed her hair or the way she crossed and uncrossed her legs that night they went to dinner. A woman like this hadn't turned on Jelani in a long time. It was more than just physical. It was more of a spiritual type of attraction.

Maya stood in front of the mirror. She looked stunning, but something wasn't right. Jelani told her that she could dress casual because he had a surprise for her. Maya turned to the side and looked at herself in the mirror again. She then just waved her hand at the air and walked into the kitchen. She wouldn't eat because she knew for sure Jelani would buy her dinner. That was the typical date. Her stomach churned and she strolled into the den to sit on the couch. She was dressed early and decided to watch a little television before Jelani arrived. She hoped the directions were okay.

Maya thought about how he looked when they went to dinner. His presence made her feel comfortable and secure.

Maya figured his bark to be worse than his bite. She knew underneath all of that egomaniac, pompous attitude, that he was a big teddy bear. She could see it in his eyes. Maya was still in the process of getting to know him and she was a little nervous about her date. Her mind was swarming and her body tingled. She couldn't wait to see him again.

"That's Rembrandt right there."

Maya's gaze followed the length of Jelani's finger to the direction of the painting. She was impressed. His surprise date showed that he understood her and took the time to understand what she liked.

"And that's Monet," he said as he turned to the left, placing his hand on the small of her back and guiding her turn. His gentle touch electrified her spine and she looked back into his eyes unable to concentrate on the fabulous painting. Maya turned to face Jelani and slipped her arms around his waist squeezing her chest against his body.

"I'm impressed. Did you learn all of this for me or are you really into art?" she asked smiling at him with a slight bend to her neck.

"Baby I'm cultured," Jelani responded with his face twisted in mock insult. "Thought you knew...plus it says so right here in the little brochure." He smiled as he retrieved a small art brochure from his back pocket.

Maya laughed and Jelani joined in. She let her head fall back indicating that she wanted to be kissed. Jelani bent and planted a quick kiss on her lips and squeezed her tighter into his arms.

"I'm so glad you brought me to this art exhibit." She smiled. Her brown eyes encircled his attention and captured his heart. Jelani's emotions confused him at times. He didn't think he was capable of caring for anyone else the way that he was beginning to care for Maya. It had been a long time since he was even close to caring for a woman...a real woman.

"Really? I thought you might like to see some art. I'm glad you came," he responded as he bent to kiss her on her lips, oblivious to the other art on-lookers. Her head fell backwards accepting his kiss allowing her hair to flow down her back, brushing the top of his hands that were now positioned at the top part of her back.

The High Museum was bombarded with art gurus, critics, and just plain ole' ordinary people who liked pretty pictures. Maya could tell that many did not know what they were looking at by the way they cocked their heads to one side and frowned. The abstract paintings received most of the turned up noses. Jelani however, seemed to know more about art than Maya gave him credit for. The date had been a wonderful surprise. He planned the entire day for the two of them, not letting her participate in the actual planning process. Maya was afraid that he would take her to some sporting event or movie, like most men that planned their own dates.

Georgia's weather complied with the ambiance of the outing. Sun sprayed down upon the earth, warming but not scorching everyone below. A gentle breeze floated amongst the people outside and cooled certain hot spots. "This weather feels like California," Maya remembered saying earlier that afternoon. Jelani's well shaped, slightly bow legs shined from the Vaseline that he applied to his knees to run the ash away. Maya had never seen him in shorts and the sight was making her thoughts wander. She wore a yellow sundress with highlights of brown and orange. In the dark halls of the museum, she caught the attention of many of the other people. When Jelani picked her up from her apartment, he complimented her on the way she looked and could not keep his eyes off of her during the entire exhibit. His small touches only made Maya fantasize, as she could tell he was trying to be a gentleman in her presence.

"Do you want to eat after this?" he asked and responded to his own question in one sentence. "Houlihan's is right up the street. We could walk there from here."

Maya did not respond but just looked up at Jelani with a wide grin on her face. She then nodded and nuzzled her head into his chest.

They walked hand in hand enjoying each work of art. Maya would catch Jelani staring at her as she stared at a particular painting. He smiled each time she looked up at him. The row of unbelievably straight white teeth glowed in the dim lights. Jelani tried to peer at Maya in the dark halls. He shifted his weight from one side to the other watching Maya carefully from the side.

"So why is it that a woman like you don't have no man?" he asked as he lightly squeezed her hand.

"I guess I haven't found the right one yet."

"And what does the right one have to have?"

"Ohhh, he has to be nice and possess ambition and drive. He has to be able to make me laugh and he has to respect me."

"That's not a whole lot to ask for."

"Well the list grows as I grow, but off the top of my head, those are the basics. Why don't you have a woman?" Maya asked as they entered another hallway full of paintings.

"Guess I ain't found the right one either." He looked vacantly at one of the paintings.

"Maybe you haven't been looking in the right direction."

"Maybe." He looked at her. "Had I known you were in the East, I would have been concentrating on that direction."

"Why the East?"

"That's where the sun rises."

She smiled. They continued through to the end of the exhibit and walked down Peachtree to Houlihan's restaurant. The sun smiled over them as they slowly walked and talked. Jelani could feel his emotions reaching out to Maya. She was the epitome of beauty. He knew with her, he would have to take it slow and play by her rules. He watched her risqué cat steps. He liked the way her smile was contagious. When he looked at her, he saw a female version of himself. That's how Jelani knew that she had to be his soul mate. He knew they would be good for each other. He could feel it in his bones that the universe had meant for them to meet. And as twisted as it sounded, he was glad that he'd gotten into the car accident with her.

THE GOSPEL TRUTH

Tressy was pleased and shocked at the same time when Jelani called earlier that week and asked her to go to the mall. He needed her to help him pick out a nice outfit to wear for Maya. He'd taken out the time to pick Tressy up especially for the occasion. After their shopping spree, Jelani treated Tressy to lunch at her favorite restaurant. When she suggested that the four of them go to dinner, Jelani seemed ecstatic. She was looking forward to meeting the woman that caught Jelani's attention for more than a week.

"What time did you want to meet?" Jelani asked as he chewed his food.

"At seven. And Jelani, please be on time." Tressy stared into his eyes.

"Always, sis-in-law. At Chev Marlons?"

"Yes."

"Remember. Not a word about me playing football."

"I remember." Tressy took a sip from her glass. "I don't see what the big deal is."

"I want her to love me for me. Not for my money. I'm a person worth getting to know. No frills, just me."

"You really like this one, huh?"

"Yeah." Jelani smiled.

"Well I've got to meet this woman. Do you know that you've never had a real relationship since I've met you?"

"Thanks for bringing that up."

"Oh I'm sorry. It's just that, you were so wild."

"I know. But that was the old Jelani. I've grown a lot since..." he paused.

"Since your mother died?" Tressy gazed at Jelani.

"Yes. Since she was murdered."

"I understand."

"I don't think you do Tressy."

"Donnie has told me about your father, your mother, his mother. He's told me about your whole family."

"I still don't think you know what I'm feeling." Jelani sounded irritated.

"Who do you think holds Donnie in the middle of the night when he *still* has nightmares about his mother? Me. I may not know what you're going through personally but Jelani, I've lost people in life also. My family wasn't the Huxtables. We've had our share of problems too."

"I'm sorry Tressy."

"It's okay. Just remember, I'm family too. Donnie may be your brother. But he's my husband. And I love him immensely."

"Okay." Jelani reached across the table and caressed Tressy's hand. She smiled. He smiled. He understood how Donnie had fallen in love with her. Jelani let go of Tressy's hand and continued to eat. She picked through her eggplant dish.

"What's wrong?" Jelani looked up from his food.

"Nothing."

"Tressy. Listen, you can tell me anything. Just like you said, Donnie is my brother. I love him too and I want the best for him. Now, what's wrong?"

"He was a little upset with me yesterday and I think he's still mad."

Jelani stopped eating and put his fork down.

"Tressy, Donnie is a very sensitive person. He doesn't know how to deal with a lot of emotions. Neither one of us do. Unfortunately, that's something we learned from our father. Maybe you should try to talk to him."

"I have. He doesn't want to listen to me." Silence. "Do you know what's wrong with him?"

Jelani swallowed hard before he answered her question. "Nah."

"Jelani, don't lie," Tressy said narrowing her eyes.

Jelani sighed. He didn't want to get involved. But he did drag it out of her.

"Tressy, what have you been doing on the corner?"

"What!"

"No, no, no. Who have you been meeting on the corner of Ashby?"

Tressy thought. How in the world could Jelani know about that?

"He knows about that?"

"All he knows is that you've been meeting some man on the corner."

Tressy put her fork down and wiped her mouth with her cloth napkin. Then she did something that Jelani did not expect. She started laughing. Tressy laughed uncontrollably for at least ten minutes. Jelani sat and watched her the entire time. When she finally calmed down, Jelani raised his eyebrows.

"And what is so funny? My brother has been going crazy trying to figure out what's going on."

"Jelani. I've been paying for a trip."

"A trip?"

"For our anniversary. Donnie has always wanted to go to the Bahamas. You know I don't have any money. How am I supposed to account for hundreds of dollars missing from our joint checking account? I've been sneaking around doing little odd jobs and saving money to take him on a vacation."

"So what does that have to do with the man on the corner?"

"He's my travel rep. He gave me a good discount. I don't have a car. How am I going to drive anywhere? So he meets me on the corner."

Jelani smiled. "You went through all of that trouble to surprise Donnie?"

"He's my husband. Of course I did. I love him."

"How much more do you have to pay?"

"About four hundred more."

"Here." Jelani reached into his organizer and pulled out his checkbook.

"Ooh no. I want to do this myself."

"Tressy take the money. I want to help. Consider it an anniversary gift from me to you."

"No Jelani."

"Take it. You can use the money that you've saved up to spend while you're in the Bahamas. I want you guys to have a good time. You know I can afford to do this. I'm learning that

money is important to live in this world but it's not everything."
He filled out the check, slid it across the table, and kept eating.
"I'm glad my brother married you."

"Thank you Jelani." Tressy blushed. Her red freckles
brightened as she slipped the check into her pocket.

Jelani and Tressy finished their meal and Jelani dropped
her off in front of her house. They rode and talked the entire time.
Jelani enjoyed Tressy's company and Tressy found herself
enjoying his company. She understood why her brother was so
crazy about Jelani. He'd shown her a whole new side of Jelani.
Ever since he'd been seeing this Maya woman, he's been much
more likable.

"Are you coming in?" Tressy asked Jelani as he pulled up
into the driveway.

"Nah. I got to meet with my coach. I'll see you guys
tonight."

"Seven at Chev Marlons. Don't be late." Tressy scolded.

"I won't. Tell Donnie, I'll holler at him later."

"I will. And Jelani..." Tressy looked down at the ground
and then smiled. "...Thanks for the check. I really appreciate it."

"No problem. I should be thanking you for taking me
shopping today. I needed a woman's opinion."

"Your welcome. Bye"

"Tressy!" Jelani yelled out. "If you ever need anything.
Don't be afraid to ask. Remember, we're family!" And with that,
Jelani sped off to meet with his coach.

Tressy went into the house and threw her sweater onto the
couch. She was home alone. Donnie had to work and the twins
were at her mother's house. She figured she would shower and
clean the house. Donnie would be walking in the door soon.
Tressy picked her sweater up and decided to get the check out of
her pocket so Donnie wouldn't see it. When she pulled out the
check she noticed that Jelani had made a mistake. He made the
check out for one thousand dollars! In the corner of the check he
had drawn a smiling face with the words, "Love Jelani."

*****

Maya fingered the small invitation. The border was made

up of little yellow rattles, light green baby shoes, pacifiers, and little yellow baby ducks. In the center were the date, time, and location. Maya sat her pen on her desk and thought to herself. She knew exactly where the street was so that there shouldn't be any problems finding the house.

Stephanie, thirty-seven, was having her first baby, which would make her perfect life even more perfect. Stephanie had the perfect husband, the perfect job, and the perfect car. She had the perfect life. An old schoolmate of Maya's and co-worker of Senida's, Stephanie would constantly brag about how perfect everything and everybody were in her life. She would brag to Senida about how she and Jaleel waited and planned for their baby, based on a financial scale that they both drafted to fit their perfect lives.

Maya looked at her watch. She told Senida that she would pick her up around two-thirty and it was close to one. Stephanie and Maya never seemed to have problems, even when Stephanie continued to gloat about the euphoric bubble in which she lived. However, Senida would spit venom just about anytime someone mentioned Stephanie's name in her presence. Senida held plenty of jealousy in her voice when Maya received her invitation in the mail and Senida didn't. Senida ranted and raved about how Stephanie was a witch and that's why her perfect little life would crumble and fall. It got so bad that Maya finally called Stephanie and asked her about Senida's invitation. Stephanie called Senida and apologized, explaining that her invitation must have gotten lost in the mail. With that, Senida was satisfied and ready to roll to the shower where she would eat, drink, and find new people to talk about.

In the corner of her study, which was actually just an extra bedroom with her desk, computer, and bookshelf, was an old worn beanbag. The black beanbag reminded her of the one she used to share with her father. When she was about five, she would cuddle close to her father on the bag. Eating popcorn, the two would watch movies, read books, tell jokes, and even tell secrets. Maya remembered that her father's skin, in contrast to her own color, would almost blend into the deep bag color. That was one of the reasons why black was her favorite color. It felt powerful, yet sexy; strong, yet gentle; dependable, yet flirty. It reminded Maya of her father. Many nights Maya would snuggle on the beanbag and think. Her thoughts were usually about her day, her past, and her future. Lately it had been more about her future.

Fingering the invitation gave Maya a sinking feeling. At the end of the year she would be turning thirty years old! Maya had never heard her biological clock ticking but she could have sworn that she felt something that first night that Jelani kissed her. Faint as it could have been, however, she heard it ticking. She just hoped *he* didn't hear it ticking. Things like that tend to make men run fast and far away. And although she wasn't quite sure what she wanted to do with Jelani, she would find herself thinking about him constantly. Maya would think about his smile while she sat at her desk at work. She would think about his eyes while she was driving the brand new car that he bought her, the one she had told her Aunt Setty she didn't accept. She found herself thinking about his body while she lay in bed alone. Each time he called, her heart would pound a bit harder. Maya hated herself for slowly falling in love with Jelani but he seemed to haunt her thoughts every minute of the day.

With Stephanie's baby shower less than an hour away, Maya was hoping that Senida would be on her best behavior. Although Senida was not quite fond of Stephanie, Maya knew that Stephanie didn't like Senida's bad attitude. Maya looked again at her watch. She had been daydreaming for over forty minutes. She grabbed her black satchel that was draped over the back of her chair and stopped at the mirror in her bedroom, to get one final look.

With one spin, she made a mental note to get a facial next weekend and to get her ends trimmed. She also made another mental note that those *Weight Watchers* dinners were starting to pay off. Since she'd started eating them, she'd lost five pounds. And really that's all she needed to lose. Maya's weight was proportioned in all the right places. It was just the extra five pounds that seemed to jump on her body when she turned twenty-eight and wouldn't leave her alone for a year. Well she'd shown those pounds, they were off for good. Maya locked her front door and headed to the perfect baby shower for the perfect woman.

Stephanie's mother, Mrs. Jacobson, greeted Maya and Senida at the door. Upon entering, they were both handed a clothespin and a nametag. Mrs. Jacobson took the gifts away from them and placed them on top of the pile of growing baby presents, in the corner of the room. As soon as Maya sat, she crossed her legs and a young woman took her clothespin. Senida sat, legs intentionally gaped, arms stretched out onto her thighs, so she wouldn't cross anything. She lived for winning. Maya didn't care one way or the other, as long as she had fun. Stephanie was still in the back room getting dressed. Mrs. Jacobson kept the party going until her only daughter came out of the room. Each woman was told to cut a certain length of yarn and keep it for a future game.

Stephanie's large house was filled with a bunch of chattering women. Her beige walls were elegantly decorated with different hues of African-American prints. Her exquisite vases were imported from Nigeria; many handcrafted especially to accommodate her decorum. Plants lined the walls, hung from the high cathedral ceilings, and sat on top of stands. In the corner of the living room was a beige baby grand piano. Stephanie did not know how to play but Jaleel would sit for hours on the matching marble stone bench and stroke the keys as if they were parts of a woman. Maya had seen him on occasion play. His talents were many. Sometimes at gatherings, Maya could sense a little jealousy from Stephanie when Jaleel received too much attention. Usually, unless asked, he would play the background for his attention-craving wife.

"Isn't that Betty?" Senida bent over to ask Maya.

"Yeah," she responded as she looked in the direction of the woman.

"I heard she was pregnant too, but her husband thinks it's by another man." Senida raised her eyebrows and turned her head away from Maya, indicating that it had to be the gospel truth.

"Now who told you that?" Maya asked, not believing a word Senida was saying. "We just walked in here and you trying to start some stuff already. At least wait until we well into playing some games."

Senida laughed. "Girl. I'm just saying. She don't look too happy over there. Where's her husband anyway?"

"You right. She do look a little upset about something."

"And what's taking Stephanie so long to bring her pregnant ass out here? I'm ready to get this shower on a roll."

Senida looked around the room. Most of the women there

were friends and associates of both Senida and Maya. Mostly, friends of Maya and associates of Senida. Maya spotted Jaleel coming out of the kitchen and waved to him. He looked a little out of place with the room full of women. He was the only man in the big house. Senida hated to see couples who act like they couldn't spend a minute apart from each other. She didn't want any men at her baby shower. The affair was for women only. Maya, however, was excited that Jaleel was there. Her and Jaleel shared the same interests in art. As a matter of fact, Maya had once pointed out to Senida, Jaleel decorated their home by himself.

When Jaleel saw Maya his smile widened. This particular smile was genuine. His face hurt from fake smiling the entire afternoon but he didn't mind smiling in pain for Maya. Ever since Maya had become Stephanie's friend, Jaleel found himself unusually attracted to her. He'd never dream of cheating on Stephanie, but if he ever did, he would hope it would be with Maya. Jaleel and Maya seemed to have much more in common than he and his wife. He made his way over to Maya and Senida, just as Senida finished asking Maya what he was doing there.

"Hey, Maya. I'm so glad you could make it. Stephanie's going to be ecstatic when she sees you. Oh, hi Senida. How are you?" Jaleel said just noticing Senida.

"Hey," she responded in her cool-I-don't-care attitude.

"How are things going down at the gallery?" Jaleel pulled an extra chair closer to Maya and sat down.

Senida lightly kicked Maya on the side of her foot but Maya ignored her.

"Fine, fine. I'll be going on a California trip soon," she beamed. Her smile was large and bright. Jaleel stared momentarily at her beautiful teeth.

"Great. California. I've never been."

"What!" Senida chimed in with Maya. "You've never been to the West Coast?"

"Nope. Born and raised right here in Georgia. I'm a southern boy. But I hear the weather is beautiful out there. One of these days maybe I'll make it out that way. They say the best things come from California," he said looking directly into Maya's eyes.

"Well I tend to agree. But then again I'm biased," Maya responded. Maya and Jaleel laughed.

"I'm going to have to come down to that gallery and get some new paintings. You get any new frames in? Cause I want to redecorate the guestroom. Now that I'm done with the baby's room, I need something to keep me busy."

"Yeah, we've got some really nice hand-made frames. You should come down and check them out. I'll pick out a few and they'll be waiting for you. Call me first to make sure I'm there because with my trip coming up, I'll be running around like a chicken with its head cut off. You do still have my card, right?"

"Yeah. Stephanie has one around here somewhere."

"Okay."

"So what plans do you have in California, besides work? I know you have to make time for some fun."

"Excuse me Jaleel. Could I please have a glass of water? Thank you," Senida interrupted.

Jaleel gave Senida a strange look and excused himself to the kitchen to get the guest some water. Maya turned to Senida shaking her head.

"Why do you always do that to him?"

"Because he wants you, and he's married. Plus he was getting on my nerves. You guys constantly talking about art. Knowing that's not what y'all want to talk about."

"What are you talking about?" Maya smiled at her crazy friend.

"He wants you. Can't you get that through your thick head? I saw it a long time ago. He don't even have deep conversations like that with Stephanie. I know 'cause I've been watching. She wants everyone to think her marriage is perfect. Well if it was so perfect, why is her husband always up in your face at every function?"

"Senida, you are tripping."

Senida laughed and Maya had to join in with her laughter.

Before Jaleel had a chance to get back to Maya, Stephanie waltzed out of the back room and pretended to be surprised at all the people who showed for her baby shower. She put her hands in front of her mouth as if she didn't know anyone was in the house. Senida sucked her teeth and Maya rolled her eyes at Senida.

"And you wonder why I can't stand her sometimes," Senida said to Maya.

Jaleel made his way to their side of the room and handed

Senida her water, which she sipped and sat on a coaster on the entertainment center. He then went back to the other side and stood by the kitchen, periodically smiling at his wife and eyeing Maya when no one noticed.

After going around saying hello to everyone, Stephanie made her way to Maya and Senida. She wiped at a few happy tears and wrapped her arms tightly around Maya. She gave Senida the same hug, just not as tight.

"I'm so glad you made it. I was just telling Jaleel that I was really looking forward to seeing you," Stephanie said as she sat in the same chair that Jaleel left empty. "How's everything at work?" she asked Senida.

"Oh everything is going smooth. I'm working on the Mortin account now."

"Wow. I bet that's exciting. Is he your first high profile case?"

"Yes," Senida replied thinking to herself that Stephanie knew it was her first high profile case.

"I remember my first high profile case. I was representing Marlon Tiggs, the famous basketball player. I was so excited it was hard for me to contain myself. I know it must be hard to contain yourself. And then one time I represented Sheila Thompson, the singer. We still keep in touch today. She was supposed to come today but she had a concert in Europe."

Mrs. Jacobson came over to retrieve her daughter. She was a short, stout woman with graying, red hair. Her smooth, bright skin and light green eyes contrasted her daughter's deep, dark eyes and dark, smooth hair. Stephanie stood at least three or four inches taller than her mother and her frame was much thinner, except for the large round belly. Her pregnancy was in her belly. Stephanie hadn't gained much weight in her hips, legs, or her breasts. Mrs. Jacobson slipped her arms in between her daughter's arms and began to lead her away when Stephanie turned back to Maya.

"Are you still going to be able to stick around after and help me clean?" she asked.

"Yeah sure," Maya responded. Mrs. Jacobson made the announcement that the shower was about to begin.

Senida turned to look at Maya.

"You didn't tell me all of that. Now I'm stuck here too?"

"Yep. That will give you plenty of time to get to know

Stephanie better." Maya smiled.

All of the women laughed and cooed at Stephanie. Senida had to admit that she was an attractive pregnant. Senida hated to see borderline attractive women get pregnant and turn ugly. That's what Maya and she called an ugly pregnant. Or those women who were ugly from the beginning and worsen while their bodies are going through the hormonal changes. Senida filled Maya in on all the gossip about everyone that she had dirt on, in the room. Both Senida and Maya participated in the name game, the string game, the clothes pin game, and the guess the pregnant woman's weight game.

The cotton ball game was the last game that the women played. Senida volunteered to go first. Once she was blindfolded, she took the big spoon and scooped a few cotton balls. Every cotton ball she got on her spoon, however, she ended up throwing over her bowl. When the blindfold was removed, she realized that she'd only gotten two balls in the bowl. She laughed at her misfortune. Although Senida was big on gossip, Maya could tell that she was enjoying herself. They rarely hung out with groups of women. It was usually Maya and Senida, or the two of them with their men. Maya thought about the time when she would have her baby shower. She wondered whom she would invite. She knew that Senida would be the one to give it for her. Maya looked at her watch. Jelani usually called her about this time. She wondered if he would even though he knew she was out.

Stephanie did not serve the typical baby shower food. Being the type of woman that craved attention, Stephanie had a layout that would put Oprah to shame. There was shrimp salad, crab cakes, and finger sandwiches. The little sandwiches had toothpicks with green olives stuck to them. Brie with crackers sat on a silver platter next to the stuffed mushrooms in wine sauce. In the middle of the table was a large watermelon rind that had been decoratively cut in half. Inside of the watermelon rind were chunks of watermelon, honey dew melon, cantaloupe, green and red grapes, apple chunks, orange slices, and slices of peaches all covered in a yogurt sauce. Maya's eyes widened. And that was just the finger food.

For dinner, Stephanie had a layout of seafood quiche with crab-real crab, not that imitation stuff. There was a combination of pastas. Bow-tie pasta with marinara sauce, a vegetarian pasta dish, pasta with beef for the meat lovers and seafood pasta were all arranged in a neat, little order. Stephanie also had a big bowl of green leaf salad with tortilla chip strips and walnuts, lightly sprinkled with a low-calorie dressing and parmesan cheese. Her cake was a two layer strawberry shortcake with real juicy, thick, red strawberries and strawberry sorbet ice cream to go along with the cake. Sistah girl showed out! She had so much food that most of the guests were seen unsnapping their pants and skirts after the food was served.

Senida noticed that Stephanie would periodically walk to the window to see if Jaleel was back. Throughout the shower, she would send Jaleel to the store. He looked tired from the trips back and forth. First to get some more ice, then to get some more drinks, then to get some more paper plates, because Stephanie had no idea that so many people would show up. Then, he forgot to get some aluminum foil the first time he went to the store. Senida wondered why he decided to stick around for the event. Strictly for the women, Senida thought, as she had watched Jaleel leave the house on the fourth run to the store for Stephanie.

Now she watched as Stephanie frequented the window, waiting for him to return. Mrs. Jacobson looped her arms in between Stephanie's and led her to the chair seated by the gifts. The guests were still eating their cake, when Mrs. Jacobson announced that Stephanie would be opening her gifts. Stephanie put on a fake smile and began sifting through the smaller gifts. Each gift that she opened, she announced who it was from, and said thank you. The women oohed and aahed over the tiny clothes and little things.

At the end of the day, the women filed out of Stephanie's large house and arbitrarily went their separate ways. Mrs. Jacobson stood with Stephanie at the door waving, hugging and thanking the guests for coming. Maya was picking up used cups and plates and tossing them into a large plastic bag. Senida sat on the couch and flipped through one of Stephanie's magazines. She was watching Stephanie and Mrs. Jacobson. All the other guests were gone and Stephanie and Mrs. Jacobson were conversing at the front door. Senida could not hear what the two women were saying, but she assumed it had to do with the fact that Jaleel had not made it back from the store yet.

Stephanie turned and closed the door behind her. She

joined Maya in picking up the extra trash. Mrs. Jacobson went into the kitchen to start on the dishes. Senida finally got off the couch and started putting the food away when Maya gave her a crazy look. Stephanie seemed to be in a good mood. She laughed and joked with Maya. Her deep dark eyes bounced up and down when Maya asked her about baby names.

"Well I was thinking about Daria, if it's a girl. Or Ashante. I like that one but my mother likes Jasmine. Jaleel wanted to name her Maya. He really likes your name." She bent to pick up a plate off the floor. Senida gave Maya a strange look and started smiling. Maya ignored her.

"And if it's a boy?" Maya asked.

"Oh...probably Jaleel."

"Well I like that name," Maya responded.

"I do too," Senida added with a smile. Stephanie was totally oblivious to Senida's under jokes.

"So Maya, tell me about this new man in your life." Stephanie sat on the couch and rubbed her stomach. Maya continued to busy herself, while Senida joined Stephanie on the couch.

"Well, his name is Jelani," Maya began.

"Forget all of that. Get to the good stuff. What does he do, what does he look like? That kind of stuff. Is he good in bed?"

"Steph!" Maya screeched.

"Well. When you're married you have to live vicariously through your single friends."

"I thought married people have sex every night," Senida chimed into the conversation. She was obviously trying to get some information from Stephanie, now that they were away from an audience.

"No. Once you get married, the sex slows down. Me and Jaleel used to be wild, but now...we don't seem to have the time to put romance into it." She stopped when she realized that her statements weren't feeding into her perfect life. "But back to Jelani."

"He's really good looking," Maya started again.

"He's fine," Senida offered

"*Is he good in bed*?" Stephanie asked again.

"We haven't had sex yet. I'm waiting."

"For what?" Stephanie rubbed her swollen belly.

"I'm just tired of having casual sex. I want my intimate interludes to have meaning and substance."

"Oh that's so special." Senida said sarcastically while smiling.

"It is," said Stephanie. "I don't know how you do it."

"Do what?" asked Maya.

"Not have sex," Stephanie responded.

"She meditates," Senida interjected.

"And I make trips to nine and a half weeks. The sex store."

"What!" Senida and Stephanie both squealed.

"Yep. On those lonely nights when Michael had to be at the hospital, I just whipped out my trusty friend."

"I'd expect that from her but not from you." Stephanie pointed to Senida.

"Excuse me?" Senida squawked. Stephanie ignored her.

"Seriously." Maya jumped in. "We're not getting any younger. Stephanie, you already have a husband and a baby on the way. At our age, we should be looking for serious relationships."

"Oh, you're just saying that because you've found a prince," Senida shifted in her seat.

"No really. I've been thinking long and hard since I've met Jelani. I'm no spring chicken. Eventually, I *do* want to settle down."

"Do you like Jelani that much?" asked Senida.

"I'm getting there." She smiled.

"He's the one that bought you the BMW, right?" Stephanie's eyes brightened as she waited for a response.

"Yes."

"Where is it now?"

"It's outside."

"I've got to see it," Stephanie wobbled to the window and looked out. "Oh my God. It's beautiful. He has to be an educated man to buy such lavish gifts."

"He has a bachelor's degree in marketing."

"*And* he's good looking. All that and brains too, huh?" Stephanie laughed as she sat back down on the couch and rubbed her stomach.

"Yeah. And he's wonderful. I haven't been interested in someone like this in a long time."

"What about Michael?" Stephanie asked still rubbing her

stomach.

"Michael was definitely a learning experience. That's a road that I don't want to travel down again, ever."

"Does he still call you?" Senida asked.

"Damn near everyday. I wouldn't trade him for Jelani though. Jelani is so perfect right now."

"Kind of like Jaleel," Senida added with a smile.

Stephanie ignored Senida, but both Senida and Maya knew that she was still worried about Jaleel. He'd been gone for over three hours. He didn't call to let Stephanie know he was alright or anything.

"Speaking of which, I don't know where that man could be. This is so out of character for him. He usually calls if something happens. I hope everything is okay." Stephanie stood and began picking up more napkins and wrapping paper from the gifts. She had a far out look in her eyes.

Senida shot a strange look at Maya. Neither of them had known Stephanie to slip and tell anybody that her marriage wasn't perfect. Maya continued to clean the living room and eventually walked into the kitchen, to see if Mrs. Jacobson needed any help. Senida picked up another magazine and flipped through the pages, as Stephanie fumbled with cups, paper, and plates. Senida felt guilty for not helping but the feeling quickly subsided as she remembered that *she* wasn't the one volunteering to clean. It was Maya that got her into this mess.

Senida turned to an article in *Essence* magazine. The article showcased a few young sistahs who were doing their thing. They were all beautiful, smart, and entrepreneurs. One day soon, Senida thought, that will be me with my own law practice. She had read half way through the article and had forgotten that Stephanie was still cleaning in the living room.

"I just don't understand," Stephanie said as she sighed and walked over to the window. Senida looked up from her article. She watched Stephanie gaze out to the left of the window. Senida continued to read the article.

"It's so unlike him," Stephanie turned to look at Senida. Senida again looked up from her article.

"You don't think anything bad has happened?" Stephanie walked across the room and sat next to Senida. It was rare for Senida and Stephanie to be alone, talking. Stephanie was more

Maya's friend than Senida's.

"No. I'm sure he's okay," Senida responded as she closed the magazine and tossed it back onto the coffee table.

"But he's never done anything like this before. It's so out of character for him to just leave and not call. He's such the perfect husband, that I don't understand the irrational behavior he had today."

"Stephanie, maybe he felt a little uncomfortable about being the only man here. Does he have any men friends that he spends time with?"

"Well, one. He's an old friend from high school, but I've never met him. That's really about it, besides the people from work. And he hardly ever spends time with them."

"Does he have any hobbies or anything else that he likes to do?" Senida asked the questions but she really didn't care about Stephanie and her perfect life. Jaleel leaving was just a minor obstacle for Stephanie. She didn't even understand why Stephanie was talking to her about her problems. Why didn't she just wobble her big, round belly into the kitchen and talk to someone who cared, like Maya or Mrs. Jacobson? But Senida thought that she would humor her to pass some time, until Maya was done doing her deed for the day.

"Oh yes, he loves to paint. He also decorated this entire house."

"Oh. That's nice. Steph, how long have you two been planning this baby?"

"Well Jaleel wanted to have children before he turned forty. So he's been planning to have kids for at least six years."

"And why did it take so long? If you don't mind my asking."

"I wasn't ready. I still had to finish my law degree. I wanted to work in the field for a while. I also want to start my own law firm." Stephanie leaned back on the couch and crossed her arms over her large stomach. "But now all that has got to change."

"Why does all of that have to change?" Senida asked.

"Because now I have to have this baby for Jaleel. I won't be able to start my own firm until the baby is at least a year old. I have to take time off work. And all because he wanted this damn baby. And now look! He's run off and left me already."

Stephanie was close to yelling. Her words were laced with venom. Senida sat up and moved closer to Stephanie. Now this is what she was talking about, raw, up close gossip.

"So you don't want this baby?"

Stephanie looked over at Senida. She'd almost forgotten that she was talking to Senida. Maya had told Stephanie that Senida liked to bump her gums about other people's business. Stephanie stood and looked down at Senida. She had to think of something quick, to get this bloodhound off of her back. She couldn't believe that she allowed herself to show her true feelings to Senida.

"No I didn't say that. I love this baby and I love my perfect husband. I just wanted to wait a while. But I guess Jaleel was right. My biological clock is ticking." She smiled at Senida. "It's like Maya said, we aren't getting any younger. You better start thinking about your clock too, Senida. How old are you? Thirty-three?"

"I'm thirty. And I'm not worried about my damn clock."

"Well I'll be in the kitchen helping out my mother. Make yourself at home," Stephanie sarcastically said to Senida, as she slipped behind the kitchen doors.

"And Maya wonders why I can't stand her sometimes," Senida said out loud to herself. She picked up the magazine and continued to read the article.

Shortly after, Maya and Mrs. Jacobson strolled out of the kitchen. Maya had two plates wrapped in aluminum foil in her hands. Senida stood as the two women entered the living room. Maya and Mrs. Jacobson were about the same height. And when Senida stood, she slightly towered over the two until Stephanie entered the room. She was at least three inches taller than Senida. She looked like an amazon with her height and her added weight.

"Senida, I made you a plate to take home," Mrs. Jacobson said as she hugged Senida. "I'm glad you could make it out." She smiled. Senida smiled and returned her hug.

"And I'll be talking to you soon. I'll be sure to call you when the baby arrives," Mrs. Jacobson said to Maya as she hugged her tight.

Senida made her way to the door first, then Maya, then Mrs. Jacobson, and last Stephanie. Stephanie waved and hugged Maya, and even hugged Senida. She thanked them both for coming and said she would call when the little addition arrived. Stephanie stood in the doorway looking down the street. Both Senida and Maya knew she was looking for Jaleel. Senida and Maya walked to the car. Maya was tired and wanted to get home to rest before Jelani came over. Senida wanted to get home so she could finish working on the Mortin case. She had a stack of papers a mile high in her room. No sooner than they put on their seatbelts, did Senida go into her new news.

"Did you know that Stephanie doesn't want this baby?"

"Who told you that?" Maya looked surprised.

"Stephanie."

"Senida, Stephanie wouldn't tell you the time, let alone her personal business."

"Well she slipped up today. I think she just needed someone to talk to. And you were in the kitchen with her mother, so she spilled the beans to me."

"That's possible. She doesn't like telling her mother about her marriage. Said she couldn't hold water," Maya looked over at Senida.

"Oh shut up. I can hold water." Maya looked at her again. "I can. If it's important and personal I can keep secrets. Have I ever told any of your business?"

"You know better."

"Well alright. I can hold water and keep my mouth shut if I wanted to do so. And that's the gospel truth." She smiled at Maya and they both started laughing.

"What are you wearing tonight?" Senida asked Maya.

"I'm not sure yet. This will be the first time that I meet any of his family members, so I wanted to make a good impression. I was thinking of wearing my brown pants suit."

"So they won't think you a hooch, huh?"

"Exactly."

"If you were a little taller, you could have worn this new outfit I just got from BeBe's. It's cute. It's a long, elegant dress and the back is out. But it's long on me, so I know it'll be dragging on you. What time is he coming to pick you up?"

Maya looked at the clock on the dashboard of her brand new car. It was six! Jelani was supposed to pick her up at seven thirty. She wouldn't have time to take her nap. Maya wanted to have a clear head when she met Jelani's brother and his wife.

Usually she had no problem with the family members liking her, but she was always nervous when it was time to meet them.

"Seven thirty," she responded without looking over at Senida. Maya turned the steering wheel and pulled her car into the driveway in front of Senida's apartment complex. Senida grabbed her plate of food and hopped out of the car.

"Call me later and let me know how it went." She slammed the door shut and waved to Maya as she briskly walked into the building.

Maya had approximately one hour to get herself together before Jelani arrived. As soon as she hit the front door, she went into action. She showered, shaved her legs, lotioned, and perfumed. Still uncertain about what she would wear, Maya stood in front of her floor length mirror, wearing her soft, pink, terry cloth robe. Her hair was a full mass of curls. She was smelling good and feeling good.

After spending all day at the baby shower, a nice hot shower had done her some good. She ran her hand through her clothes. What would be appropriate for tonight? Maybe she would go ahead and wear the brown suit like she had intended. As Maya began putting on her make-up, the doorbell rang. Her heart began to race. He was early! Maya looked at her watch. It was only seven; he was a half an hour early. Damn it Jelani, she thought to herself. She hoped he wasn't planning on trying to seduce her before the dinner, because she wasn't about to be late.

When Maya snatched the door open, Jaleel stood in the frame. He took in her entire body with one smooth look and smiled. Maya gathered the top of her robe, to make sure there was nothing for him to see. His eyes were red and despite the silly grin he had on his face, he looked sad. Jaleel was quite a tall man. Maya had to look up to see him. He stood about six feet, three inches. Although very attractive, Maya didn't think he knew of his natural beauty. She gave him a weak smile.

"Hi Maya. Can I come in?"

"Jaleel what are you doing here?" She did not move to allow him to enter.

"I needed someone to talk to. You seem to be the only one that understands me. Can I please come in? I won't stay for long."

Maya stepped aside to let Jaleel in her door. She didn't know what to say to him, or what he had to say to her. She looked again at her watch. Jelani would be strolling over to her apartment soon. How would she be able to explain? Jaleel made himself at home. He sat on the couch and reclined, letting his head fall back. The poor man looked like he had a lot on his mind.

"So what's up?" Maya asked sitting down next to Jaleel.

"Stephanie. She's been driving me crazy."

"She has, how? I thought everything was...perfect."

"I'm just tired of dealing with her selfishness. I've been dealing with it for a few years now. She only thinks of herself. And she's too preoccupied with what everyone else thinks. Plenty of times, I've been tempted to leave her."

"Is there another woman, Jaleel?" Maya gathered more material on her terry cloth robe. Her belt wrapped around her waist was beginning to slip aloose.

"Yes and no."

Maya looked confused. "Have you been drinking Jaleel?"

"Just a little. I had a few drinks."

"Well what do you mean yes and no? Is there another woman?" Maya switched her position on the couch. When she turned her knees toward Jaleel, it seemed as if she was sitting closer to him.

"There is another woman...but she doesn't know it yet. I've been physically faithful to Stephanie throughout our entire marriage. But we don't have anything in common. I constantly think about other women. Well, mostly this one particular woman." He looked at Maya. He noticed the light make-up and the terry cloth robe. It looked as if she had just gotten out of the shower. "Did I catch you at a bad time?"

"Actually Jaleel, you did. I'm about to go out and my date will be here soon."

Jaleel obviously didn't get the hint, because he continued to sit next to Maya. Even when she stood, he continued to sit.

"Oh, yeah, well I understand. A beautiful woman such as yourself probably has a lot of dates."

Jaleel stood. He looked directly into her eyes. She could see the alcohol redness in his stare. Jaleel edged closer to Maya and wrapped his left arm around her tiny waist. Before Maya could protest, Jaleel softly touched her face and kissed her passionately on the mouth. Maya's first mind told her to stop the process, but Jaleel's mouth felt soft and warm against her trembling lips. She could feel his heart racing with her hers. Maya could not think straight. She knew what she was doing was wrong, but his touches felt so good.

Jaleel slipped his hands inside of her robe and squeezed her breasts. Maya moaned. It felt so good, she thought, as he continued to kiss her and rub his hands down her stomach. Why did everything wrong feel so right? Jaleel became excited. Maya was fighting the feeling, but the more Jaleel touched her, the more she couldn't help herself. Jaleel thought about how good Maya felt. He'd dreamed of touching her for years and now he finally had the chance. He smelled her perfume and felt her soft skin.

He thought about Stephanie and how she would have stopped him by now. Stephanie only seemed to want to make love when it was convenient for her. Because Stephanie never wanted to make love or even have children, Jaleel would often think of other women. When they came over to visit Stephanie, he would secretly lust over how their bodies moved. It was when he met Maya that he knew that she was the one for him. She was the soul mate that took too long to find him. He would daydream of Maya on many occasions and dream about her at night, while laying in bed next to Stephanie.

"You are so beautiful Maya. I've always wanted to tell you that. Not only on the outside, but on the inside as well. I think about you all the time. I think about how it would have been if I had met you first." He kissed her again.

Maya knew she was wrong. She thought about Stephanie, her friend. The friend who trusted her. She couldn't believe that she was enjoying the soft touches and warm tongue of this *married* man, *Stephanie's* man. Maya thought about Jelani, *her* man. Jelani. Jaleel's touches were as soft and warm as Jelani's touches. Maya panted as she heard Jaleel's breath in her ear. He kissed her again and easily untied the belt on her robe. Her pink terry cloth robe hit the ground with a thud and Maya stood in Jaleel's arms, nude. Jaleel ran his hands down her chest to her stomach. He bent to kiss her soft plump thighs, running his tongue up the right leg. Maya's head fell back and she could have sworn she heard bells. Then she heard the bells again. Bells! Her door bell. Jelani! Jaleel stood quickly.

"Someone's at your door," he whispered to her, grabbing her robe and tossing it to her.

Maya looked at her watch. It was seven thirty! Her heart sank in her stomach and she began to panic. Jaleel saw the frightened look on her face and grabbed her by the shoulders. His voice had changed from the deep sexy voice, to a manly controlling whisper.

"I'll hide in the closet in your bedroom. How long do you think it will take you to get out of the apartment?"

Maya stood with her mouth open. It seemed as if Jaleel had done this plenty of times before. He was calm and cool. She couldn't speak. Her mind was racing at what would happen if Jelani caught them in the den, doing what they were doing. She quickly thought about Stephanie. Poor Stephanie.

"Did you hear me? When you leave for your date. I'll wait for about fifteen to thirty minutes and then I'll slip out of your apartment. Now you need to get out as soon as you can, okay?" He slipped into her room and into the closet as the doorbell rang for the third time. Maya heard Jelani shift his weight behind the door, as he began to knock loud and hard.

Maya tied her robe on tight and opened the door. Jelani looked irritated as he walked in and looked around. His tall body loomed over Maya. He had on a pair of olive green slacks and a slightly lighter colored shirt. His hair was freshly cut and his sideburns were edged perfectly.

"What took you so long to answer the door?" he asked, as he sat down on the couch that Jaleel just got up from.

"Umm...I was still in the shower. I didn't hear you at first. I'm sorry I'm running late baby. Let me just throw my clothes on and I'll be ready in a minute," she stammered as she planted a soft kiss on his cheek. Maya went into her room and checked in the closet, where Jaleel was crouched down in the corner. He gave her the okay signal with his hand and she shut the door. Maya pulled out her stockings from her drawer and picked up her dress off the bed. Jelani walked into her room and kissed her on her neck. Maya's eyes widened, as she thought about Jaleel in the closet. Jelani pressed his lips hard onto Maya's lips. He began passionately kissing her. Her eyes were still wide open.

"You think we got time for Superman to meet Wonderwoman?" he said as he slowly began untying her robe. Maya grabbed his hands and kissed them.

"Sweetheart. I need to hurry up and get dressed," Maya

looked over at the closet door, which was still shut. "I don't want to be late, my first time meeting your family. Tell Superman to wait until Wonderwoman has time."

"Does Wonderwoman even want to get with Superman? She always seems to have an excuse."

"She does. It's going to take some time I promise." She kissed him on the cheek and softly pushed him out of the bedroom door. "Now let me get dressed, please." Maya quickly dressed and rushed Jelani out of the front door. She was praying that Jaleel would leave and lock her door behind him.

A FAMILY AFFAIR

Tressy thought of a way to tell Donnie about her surprise. She couldn't continue to have him tormented. Since he'd been home from work, she could tell that he was still mad. A little voice inside told Tressy to just tell him. So she decided that once he got out of the shower, she would lay it on him. It would still be a surprise. It would just be sooner than she'd planned, she thought as she ironed Donnie's shirt. She could hear Donnie in the shower. A couple of times she heard him drop the soap.

Her house was clean. All she had to do was put on the dress that Donnie picked out for her. It was a simple dress. One that she would not have picked herself but felt compelled to wear because Donnie took the time to buy it for her. When he surprised her with the dress for her birthday, she could not help but to think of the surprise that she had in store for him. She smiled. They had been through a lot together. He took care of Tressy when the difficulties of having the twins were too much for her to go back to work. She thought she would wither away at the thought of becoming a housewife but Donnie supported her and allowed her to feel comfortable in her new role. She loved Donnie.

When Donnie came out of the shower Tressy wrapped her arms around his waist from behind. Donnie jumped because he didn't expect Tressy to be in the bathroom. She kissed his back and nibbled on his ears. Donnie was surprised at how frisky Tressy had become. Usually she complained about being on time. He was usually the one trying to get some lovemaking in before an outing. It was a rare treat to have the house to themselves and

Tressy and Donnie took advantage of the treat. Tressy whispered in his ear. She told him about her surprise and he became ecstatic.

Donnie unwrapped Tressy's bright orange, silk robe. She squealed in delight as Donnie ran his fingers through her loose red hair. He could see the freckles on her face glow brighter and brighter with each kiss that he gave her. It had been a long time since they made love to one another. With all that Donnie had been hearing about Tressy meeting the man on the corner, he could not bring himself to be romantic with her. But tonight, it was different, he knew. This particular night there was love in the air and it seemed to make both Donnie and Tressy in the mood for *amore*.

Jelani looked at his watch. Tressy was hardly ever late. He looked over at Maya. She was ravishing. Her dark curls were pinned up with a few strands hanging in her face which made her look innocent, yet alluring. Her cream dress fit her every curve and the pumps made her butt look higher than usual. Jelani was instantly turned on when she finally came out of the bedroom at her apartment. She never ceased to amaze him with her looks. Her natural beauty was enough but when she accented her features, she became a stunning beauty to behold.

Chev Marlon's was an upbeat jazz club/restaurant on the outskirts of Atlanta. Jelani had frequented the large place during his off-seasons. Chev Marlon's had two levels. The bottom level was for the group that came to party, dance, and sweat. The top level was the restaurant that had the best Italian food that Jelani had ever tasted. There was a jazz band that entertained the patrons while they were eating. Jelani spent most of his time on the top level since he'd turned thirty. All through his twenties, he was known to be on the bottom level getting his groove on. Jelani looked at his watch again.

"Are they usually on time?" Maya asked. Jelani check his watch for the thirteenth time.

"Yes."

"They'll be here." She intertwined her arms into his and gave him a sweet peck on his cheek.

"Are you nervous?"

"A little. Should I be?"

"Yeah."

"Yeah?" Maya unwrapped her arms from him and looked directly into his eyes.

"My brother doesn't like artists and his wife hates all my ex-girlfriends."

Maya looked at Jelani. He looked at his watch.

"I'm just playing, sweetheart. They'll love you."

Maya smiled.

"Do you ever think about marriage?" she asked.

"Constantly." He kissed her on her hand. "Did I tell you that you look absolutely gorgeous tonight?"

"Yes. But it feels good to hear more than once."

"Well you do. You look damn good tonight."

"Thanks. You don't look too bad yourself."

"You like?" he asked pulling on his clothes and smiling.

"Yes, I like." Maya laughed.

"What's on your agenda for next weekend?"

"Ahh. Nothing why?"

"Leave it open. I got a surprise for you."

"What is it?"

"If I told you, it wouldn't be a surprise, right?"

"I guess."

"Where are they?" Jelani asked looking at his watch again.

"They'll be here." Maya assured him, rubbing him on the back of his neck.

Tressy and Donnie walked into Chev Marlon's hand in hand. Tressy's freckles were bright and her face was glowing. With the big smile that Donnie had on his face, Jelani could tell that they had frolicked in the bed before they came to the restaurant. He smiled. It was good to see his brother feeling good about his marriage again. Maya knew who the couple was when they walked into the restaurant. Jelani had described Tressy as eccentric with bright red hair and bright red freckles. He didn't lie. Both Jelani and Maya stood when Donnie and Tressy walked up to them. Jelani and Donnie hugged. Jelani hugged Tressy and then stood back to introduce Maya.

"Tressy this is Maya. And this is my brother Donnie." They both shook Maya's hand and said how nice it was to finally meet her.

Shortly after the two arrived, Jelani motioned for the host

to seat them. The two couples got one of the best seats in the restaurant. Their table was in the corner against a large window that overlooked a man-made lake. The sky was dark and clear with a few stars but not too many. Jelani thought the view paled in comparison to Maya's beauty. He'd been thinking about her a lot lately and decided that she was the type of woman he wouldn't mind spending the rest of his life with.

Tressy and Donnie were as giddy as two teenagers on their first date. She ordered his meal and he ordered their wine. They were both smiling and cooing at each other. Jelani hadn't seen them act like that in such a long time that his heart fluttered.

"So Maya, what do you do for a living?" Donnie asked her in between Tressy's kisses.

"I supervise a small art gallery outside of Atlanta."

"Do you like it?"

"I love it. What do you do?"

"I'm a mechanic. So if you ever need a car fixed, I'm the one you need to talk to," he smiled.

"Well I sure needed one when your brother ran into me."

"Hey. I think you ran into me," Jelani said looking up from the menu. He kissed Maya on her hand.

"Tressy, what do you do?"

"I'm a housewife."

"And a damn good one," Donnie added. He smiled at her. She coyly looked away.

"Yeah, Tressy is one of the best cooks I've ever met," Jelani added.

"And you should know, as many times as you've been over to eat," Tressy replied. They all laughed.

"Tressy, do you guys have any kids?"

"Yes. Twins. A boy and a girl. Jah and Jahrina." She smiled.

"Oh how sweet."

"I have pictures." Tressy reached in her purse and pulled out a picture of her children.

"Ooh they're so cute," Maya lied.

"Thanks." She put the picture back into her purse.

"I guess *we* need to order now, huh?"

Maya watched as Jelani tried to make up his mind about what he wanted to eat. She noticed the strong similarities in Jelani and Donnie's appearances. They both had strong, defined, jaw lines and broad shoulders. Donnie's hair was darker, thicker, and curlier. His eyes were also deeper and darker, with a slight slant. Jelani, however, had eyes that told secrets of his thoughts. When Maya looked into them, she saw pain and hurt, caring, and sometimes a hint of insecurity. Donnie's eyes were solid as opals. She couldn't figure out what he was thinking. However, she could tell that he loved his red-haired wife tremendously. Both were extremely attractive men.

"I think I'll have the T-bone steak," Jelani finally said, placing the menu on top of the table. "What are you getting?" he asked Maya.

"I'll have the fettuccini parmesan."

The waiter scribbled their orders on his small notepad and scurried off to place their orders.

"Tressy. You look beautiful tonight," Jelani said as he smiled at her.

"Thank you Jelani. You two look wonderful too. You make a gorgeous couple."

Maya blushed. She felt guilty for the scene that happened at her apartment earlier with Jaleel.

"So Tressy, where are you originally from? Most people in Atlanta are from somewhere else." Maya shifted herself in her seat. Tressy was definitely from another planet, but she was attractive in her own way.

"I'm from Flint, Michigan."

"How long have you been in Atlanta?"

"Oh, for awhile. About twelve years. Cause me and Donnie been married for six years."

"Wow, six years. Where did you guys meet?" Maya leaned forward on the table. She loved to here of romantic first encounters.

"I brought my car into the shop where he worked..." she began.

"When I first saw Tressy, I knew I couldn't let her go without getting her number. But she didn't want to give it to me," Donnie chimed into the conversation.

"So what happened?" Maya grabbed Jelani's hand under the table.

"He kept my car for a whole week. He kept telling me that

there was more wrong with it than it actually was. And when I told him that I couldn't afford all of the work, he said I could pay it all off, if I just went out on one date with him," Tressy continued.

"I knew once she saw me outside of my greasy environment, I could persuade her to go on another date."

"And that's how it happened. He was so charming and nice that I couldn't help but to fall in love with him."

"Well, *eventually* she fell in love with me. It took her a little while to get used to me coming around." Donnie smiled as the waiter brought their salads. He carefully placed everybody's salad in front of them.

"Is there anything else, Mr. Ransom?" The waiter stood by Jelani's side.

"Everybody okay?" Jelani looked around the table at everyone. They all nodded. "We're okay, Tom. Thank you."

"Wow, you're pretty popular aren't you? You've been getting the royal treatment since we've gotten into this place." Maya stuck her fork into her salad. She was oblivious to the looks that Tressy and Donnie shot to Jelani. Jelani did not respond to her question. They remembered their promise to Jelani. Neither one of them were allowed to mention that Jelani played for the NFL, until he let Maya know himself.

"Maya's taking a trip to California soon." Jelani offered.

"Really? Do you have relatives out there?" Donnie asked.

"Yes. I'm originally from there. But I'm going out there on business. I have to negotiate prices and sells with an art gallery in San Francisco."

"That sounds exciting," responded Tressy. "I love art."

"Maybe next time we could all go to the High Museum. They're having this big art exhibit." Donnie offered. Jelani and Tressy looked at Donnie. "What? I'm cultured. I know about the High Museum."

"We've already been." Jelani stuck his fork into his salad.

"I'd like to go to Stone Mountain Park to watch the fireworks." Tressy said, as she picked her tomatoes off of her salad. Donnie picked them up with his fork and ate them.

"Y'all can go. That's for women."

Tressy flung her cloth napkin at Donnie and playfully hit him on the arm. "How could you say that?"

"Uhh oh." Jelani stuffed green leafy forkfuls in his mouth.

"I mean...watching the fireworks, and..." Donnie tried explaining.

"Don't even try to clean it up." Tressy said.

"Toast to family!" Jelani interrupted as he grabbed his glass. They all raised their glasses and clanked them together.

"Toast to friends..." Tressy added.

"And to wives..." Donnie kissed Tressy on the cheek.

"And lovers." Jelani smiled at Maya. They all drank.

The night was filled with laughs and conversation. Maya enjoyed Tressy and Donnie. They allowed her to see the soft, family side of Jelani. Her heart was opening more and more to the thought of loving him forever. In the middle of dinner, Jelani grabbed Maya by her hands and led her to the dance floor. She was reluctant to leave the delicious food. But when she heard them playing "Superfreak" by Rick James she couldn't pass up the opportunity. Shortly after they danced to three songs, they looked over and saw Donnie and Tressy dancing to their left. Donnie and Jelani danced a lot alike. Tressy had her own style, much like her own style of dress and look. But she was adorable on the dance floor and Maya could see why Donnie was so in love with her. Her smile, hair, and freckles were lighting up the dark dance floor.

"Go J.R! Go J.R!" Donnie yelled

Jelani broke out and did some type of dance that practically made the entire dance floor laugh. Maya was having the time of her life. Donnie and Jelani did the bump and Tressy and Maya did the Smurf.

The crowd slowed and a few dispersed as the DJ played, "If This World Were Mine" by Marvin Gaye and Tammy Terrell. Jelani sang Marvin's part and Maya sang Tammy's part. Maya was surprised to hear Jelani's sweet, mellow voice. He could actually sing! He let the words slip into Maya's ears.

Maya closed her eyes and pictured them dancing on a glass floor. She in a long, white dress and he in a nice, black tuxedo with a stark, white shirt would glide across the floor. Jelani tightened his grip around Maya's waist and pulled her closer to him. The rhythm of his heart beating echoed with sweet harmony through her body. Maya kept her eyes closed and imagined that the dance floor was in the middle of the Bahamas, on the water. When she opened her eyes, they were still in Chev Marlon's, but it didn't matter, as long as she was with Jelani.

Maya's phone rang three times before she could get the key in the door. She rushed to pick up the receiver as Jelani locked her front door. He turned on the C.D. player and put in his favorite Al Green. He began slowly undressing and dancing towards the side of the den, where Maya was on the phone with Stephanie.

"Maya. Jaleel still has not made it home. I'm worried. Do you think I should call the police?" Stephanie was letting her hormones get the best of her. Her voice was frantic. Maya's heart sank. She wasn't sure what to say to the woman on the other line.

"Ummm, I don't think you need to call the cops yet, Steph. Maybe you should wait a few more hours. I'm sure he'll turn up soon." Maya pulled the phone into her bedroom and shut the door behind her. She could hear Jelani plop down on the couch. She would have to make up with him soon.

"But he's never done this before."

Maya closed her eyes and took a long breath before she opened the closet door. She prayed that Jaleel was not still in her closet. When she opened the door, she smiled. He was gone! Maya sighed a breath of relief. She turned to sit on her bed when she noticed a pair of men's shoes at the foot of her bed. She knew they were not Jelani's shoes. Maya quickly kicked the shoes under her bed. The hard, loud pounding in her chest intensified. She could sense that Jaleel was still somewhere in her apartment. She knew she had to get Jelani out fast. Jelani walked into the room with a disturbed look on his face.

"Are you going to be on the phone long?" he whispered in her ear. She shook her head. He leaned his body against her.

"What are you doing? Do you have company?" Stephanie heard Jelani talking in the background.

"Yes. Me and Jelani just walked in the door." Maya pushed Jelani off of her. He began tickling her and she tried hard not to giggle while Stephanie was on the phone.

"Oh well, I'll let you go. I'll call you tomorrow."

"Okay, Stephanie. Don't worry. I'm sure Jaleel will turn up soon."

"If you happen to see or hear from him. Please tell him to call home."

Now why would she expect me to see him? Maya thought.

"Yeah, I will. Bye."

"So what's up?" Jelani asked as Maya hung up the phone.

"Oh Stephanie is looking for Jaleel, he..."

"No, I'm talking about us." He interrupted. "Tonight?"

"It's that time of the month," Maya responded as she slipped out of his embrace and sat on the bed. "I'm sorry." She looked around the room, hoping that Jaleel was not still there.

She felt bad. As long as they'd been dating, she still hadn't engaged in sexual intercourse with Jelani. The most they'd done was kiss and a lot of heavy petting. Each time she said no, he would get more and more frustrated. She knew he would get tired of it soon. Tonight was supposed to be the night for them, but right now, she had to get him out of her apartment. She would have to give in soon; her thoughts of him were starting to become X-rated.

"Last time you were on your period, and the time before that you had another excuse. What's wrong? You don't want to have sex with me?"

"No sweetie, it's not that. It's just that I don't want to have *sex* with you. I want to wait and *make love* to you," she grabbed his hands and held them in her hands. Jelani got up from the bed and began dressing.

"Well I'm going home. Just call me tomorrow." Maya sat on the bed and watched him walk out of the bedroom.

"Jelani, I'm sorry." Maya pleaded.

"Yeah, whatever. I'll see you later." He grumbled from the den. Maya heard him grab his keys and shut the front door. She sighed and laid back on her bed.

Once she was sure Jelani was in his car, Maya began calling out Jaleel's name. She heard noise in the kitchen and she went in, just in time to find Jaleel coming out of the pantry. He looked around and smiled at Maya. She could not believe that he was still in her apartment. His presence suddenly enraged Maya and she was on the verge of exploding, before Jaleel tried to quickly explain.

"I know you're mad just let me explain. I was going to leave right after you left but I ended up falling asleep. When I woke up, I was about to leave but I went into the kitchen to get me some water first. That's when I heard the keys in the door, so I hid in the pantry. I hope you're not mad." Jaleel smiled again at Maya but she didn't smile back. She opened her mouth to speak but could not find the right words to say. Jaleel reached for Maya.

"Maya..." Jaleel started again. But Maya quickly found her tongue.

"Get out. Jaleel, Stephanie has been worried sick over you and you need to go home to your pregnant wife."

"But Maya, I want to be here with you."

"How can you say that? Stephanie is your wife. You are married. How the hell can you want to be with me, when you're married and about to have a baby?" Maya was irritated with Jaleel.

"When we kissed, I felt sparks. There was chemistry between us. You felt so good when I held you, Maya. You don't know how many nights I've laid in bed waiting for the chance to do that."

"What about Stephanie? What about the baby?"

"Stephanie?" Jaleel laughed and put his hands on his hips. "Stephanie doesn't want that baby! She never wanted that baby! Shit, it's like I'm trying to give birth my own damn self. She's so damn set on not having this baby. She claims that the baby will ruin our lives. How can a woman actually believe that a child could ruin someone's life?"

Jaleel plopped down onto Maya's couch. She did not move. She was ready for him to leave. Jaleel was her friend, but she felt uncomfortable allowing him to be in her home at such a late hour. Her conscious had already gotten the best of her. For allowing him to taste her skin and feel her body earlier that night. How would she be able to face Stephanie, knowing what she knew? Jaleel grabbed Maya's arm and pulled her down onto the couch. He kissed her on the mouth, but Maya pulled away from him. He tightened his grip and rubbed his hands up her legs. Maya pushed his hands away and attempted to stand, but Jaleel's grip was tight.

"Jaleel it's time for you to go."

"Maya, I want you. I've wanted you for a long time. Just one night, one time with you and I promise, I won't tell Stephanie, I promise. It could be our secret. And if it's good, we can keep it on the under." There was a strange look in Jaleel's eyes. His grip tightened and Maya became scared. This was not the Jaleel that Maya was used to seeing.

She wrestled her way out of his grip and slapped him

across his face. Jaleel was stunned. He jumped up from the couch and stared at Maya. In a matter of seconds, Maya could see the change in Jaleel's eyes. The monster eased its way out of his soul and Jaleel was back. Maya felt as though she was back in control of the situation. Although her heart was pounding and her hands trembling, she tried her best to make her voice steady and stern.

"Jaleel go home! If you don't leave now, then I'll have to call the police."

Maya could see the hurt in Jaleel's eyes, when she threatened him with the police. She turned to look away. Despite the way she was feeling, she knew that Jaleel was a gentle, loving man and he was a good friend. Jaleel walked past Maya into her bedroom to get his shoes. When he walked back by her and to the door she did not look at him. He slowly closed the door without saying a word. Maya dashed to the phone to call Jelani on his car phone but he did not answer, so she left him a message.

"Hey baby. I'm sorry. Please forgive me. I promise real soon, Superman will be able to meet Wonderwoman. Call me, bye."

AFTER WORK PROJECT

"Listen to this," Mandla said to Senida, as he eyed her waiting for her response. They were sifting through the information on the Mortin case. Both were tired and had put in long hours on this Thursday to ensure some progress by Monday, when they would meet with Mr. Mortin. It was well past 11:30 p.m.

"It says here, that Ms. Latimore claims that Mr. Mortin made crude comments during her hours at work. It then says that he would stay after work late, so they could be alone." Mandla flips the page and continues to read. "While they were alone she said that Mortin would stand behind her as she sat in her chair and would slip his left hand into her blouse and fondle her left breast." Mandla put his finger on the last line that he read and looked up at Senida waiting for a reaction.

"So where's the discrepancy?"

"She said he used his left hand to fondle her left breast from behind, while she sat down in a chair."

"And...?"

Mandla stood up and walked behind Senida's desk. He then reached around her left shoulder and placed his left-hand inches away from her right breast. Senida sat waiting for his explanation.

"To slip his hand down her shirt, he would have to fondle her right breast. The elbow curves downward to the right. As high as the backs are in his office, it would virtually be impossible to reach straight down and slip his hands in her blouse, on the left side."

Senida rubbed her chin. He had a point. The chairs in Mr. Mortin's office did have high backs. With his current back problems, he made sure that all of his employees had proper back support. Mandla walked back around to the other side of Senida's desk and picked up the paper again.

"There's also another discrepancy. It says that he reached over her chair with his left hand..."

Senida sat waiting for him to finish. Mandla took off his glasses and rubbed his eyes with the back of his hand.

"So where's the other...oh, wait a minute...Mr. Mortin can't use his left arm."

Mandla smiled at Senida and nodded.

"Right."

"He can't use his left arm to do anything. Back in 1991, he had a stroke that paralyzed the entire left arm, including his hand." Senida could not believe that the pieces were starting to fit together like a jigsaw puzzle.

"You know what I'm saying," he responded with a big smile. He then nodded his head and did a little dance.

Senida smiled and continued to flip through her information. Mandla sat back down and flipped through more of his information. He put the pen in his mouth and held it like a long stemmed rose. Mandla looked over at the clock. It was after midnight. His eyes were burning and his stomach was growling. I guess this is what being a lawyer is all about, he thought to himself. Gazing across the desk, Mandla watched Senida as she took notes and read through the rest of the files. From the first day that Mandla laid eyes on, Senida he knew he had to play it slow to get next to her. She was much older and much more experienced. But his confidence overshadowed that.

"You smell good," he said sniffing the air.

Senida did not look up from her papers. "Thanks," she mumbled. She was determined to find more discrepancies in the case. If there were two obvious discrepancies, then there would be more subtle discrepancies.

"What kind of perfume is that?" Mandla ruffled through his papers, not looking up when Senida glanced at him.

"It's an African oil," she said and then glanced back down at her work.

Her tiny office fell silent, absent the ruffling and flipping of papers. Senida could sense Mandla looking at her every time he flipped through another page. She had to admit that he was an extremely attractive man, but she had her hands full with enough problems. She looked at him. Senida took in all of Mandla. His appearance was now mangled. His once organized business suit was a mockery of hard work. His tie was loosely undone and hung about the opened buttons of his shirt, which though still tucked in, was flaring at the pants area. He'd taken out his contacts and was wearing his wire-framed glasses, which sat on the bridge of his nose and hid his gorgeous gray eyes.

"How old did you say you were again?" he said breaking her concentration.

"I didn't."

"Do you mind me asking?"

"Didn't your mother tell you that it was impolite to ask a woman how old she is?" Senida joked.

"Yeah. But a woman as young and attractive as you shouldn't mind, right?"

She put her pencil down on the desk and slightly leaned forward. She raised her eyebrows and smiled at Mandla.

"I'm thirty."

"Oh." Mandla continued to take notes from the files onto his notepad. Senida retrieved her pencil and jotted more notes onto her legal pad. "I think you might be too young for me," he said without looking up.

Senida giggled to herself and they both erupted into laughter. Laughter bounced from the walls of the empty little office. Their sounds could be heard down the halls and through the other offices. The laughter stretched long and loud as they both released long awaited, pinned up tension.

Senida reclined in her dark mahogany colored, office chair. She needed a good laugh. She sure hadn't had one in a long time. Mandla reached across the desk and grabbed Senida's hands. They were smooth, soft, warm, and moist. His long fingers gently slid themselves around the top of her hands and pulled them open, exposing her palms.

"Have you ever had your hands massaged?" A hint of seduction lingered in his gray eyes.

"Oh, no..." Senida responded as she tried to pull her hands back. Mandla's strong hold forced her to resist pulling away.

He smiled at Senida and let his fingers do the work. Mandla's long fingers caressed the middle of her palms, sliding up and down, constricting and releasing. Tension and stress build-up flowed to the tips of Senida's fingers. He then took each finger and pressed gently, loosening her joints and making her wrists limp. Each motion was laced with sexual overtures but it was feeling too good for Senida to order him to stop. She fell into his gray eyes and stayed there until he let her go.

Her head whirled as he hypnotized her soul and invaded her thoughts. His breathing deepened as he kept his eyes locked on her emotions. He could tell she was losing her battle. Once he massaged the fingers, he worked his way up to the wrists, rotating them and flexing and relaxing her hands. Senida relaxed and let his fingers soothe her aching joints. Weeks of pressure were pushed out by Mandla's long caressing fingers. Her heartbeat dropped from her chest and into her underwear. The throbbing pulsated, making her squeeze her legs tight together. He paused momentarily, long enough to walk behind her chair and start on her shoulders.

"Mandla I don't think this is a good idea."

"What? I'm just helping you to relieve some of your stress."

His fingers gripped her shoulders and pressed and released. Senida could feel her muscles ache and loosen. Mandla's magic hands rubbed through her blouse. He rotated her shoulders and leaned forward when he applied pressure on her clavicle. Senida's inhibitions melted away and Mandla placed his hands on her bare skin. He continued to rub and squeeze the top of her shoulder blades. Senida's gyrating arms matched his rotating motions. Darrell never gave her massages and her lover never took the time. Mandla had the magic touch. His fingers felt like gold to Senida's aching body.

Senida leaned forward and Mandla rubbed up and down on her back with his knuckles, then the balls of his hands, then his fingers. He skimmed her sides and Senida thought she would die when his finger tips accidentally nicked the sides of her breasts. He continued un-noticing. Each time his fingers brushed the sides of her breasts accidentally, her heart raced faster. Her back stiffened and Mandla bent over to whisper in her ear.

"Why are you getting tense all of a sudden?"

"No reason," Senida lied. She could smell his cologne lingering in the air.

He pushed her chair back and bent right in front of her and kissed her. And she let him kiss her. He was not Darrell but she let him kiss her. He was not her lover but she let him kiss her. He was delicate. She couldn't do this. Yes, she could. No...no...no. They worked together. Her business would be all over the office. She could possibly lose her job. But it felt so good. His hands, those fingers, that tongue. She had to stop him...right after he got done licking her neck. Then she would stop him. Yeah, that's when she would stop him, right after he finished nibbling on her ear. Or maybe she'd wait and stop him when he was done kissing the upper part of her chest.

Senida quickly unzipped Mandla's pants, which immediately fell to the floor. She unbuttoned his shirt, her fingers swiftly looping in and out of the small holes, releasing the pinned up plastic. He rubbed his hands up and down her back. He squeezed her breasts and licked on her ears. Mandla slipped his hands under her skirt and pulled down her stockings, ripping them as he hastily pulled and tugged at them in an effort to free her. Senida could feel him rub against her. He was hard and his breathing was fast in her ear. He was breathing faster and faster. She could see his face distorted into a hurried look. He almost bounced up and down trying to unbutton her skirt and then decided to just pull it up over her thighs. He was breathing harder and faster and faster and harder. Mandla could barely contain himself. He was like a kid in a candy store, excited and hungry, craving the candy, licking his lips and salivating at the mouth. He was ready...but she couldn't do this. She grabbed his hand and held it there for awhile.

"We can't do this here," she said, exasperated.

"What...what...why...huh?" Mandla looked as if he would cry. Mandla looked around the room and then directly behind them. He pushed everything off the desk in one arm's swoop. "Okay. What about here?"

"No, no you don't understand. Did you forget that we work together?" she asked as she began to button her shirt.

"I didn't forget. I don't give a damn. You seem to be the only one tripping."

"Believe me, I do want you, but...I just don't think this is right. I'm not sure you can keep your pretty little mouth shut," Senida said, as she rubbed her fingers down his chest.

"Girl, I don't hardly talk to these white folks and you know it."

"It's not the white folks in this office that gossip."

"True dat. Do you think that I would actually jeopardize getting seconds, by opening my mouth?" He kissed her again. "Come on baby. Loosen up."

Senida kissed him back. This time they were both much more calm and gentle. She lay down on top of the desk and he lay down on top of her. She welcomed him into her world and found out just how much stamina young Mandla had in his body that night.

*****

"You and Jelani have been going out a lot lately."

"Yeah, I know. I like him. I think I want to keep him." Maya balanced the phone on her ear and her shoulder. She sat Indian style in the middle of her bed. Her red fingernails were almost dry. Next she would have to do her toenails.

"That's good girl. Where are you guys going to tonight?" Senida asked.

"I don't know. It's supposed to be a surprise."

"Oh. That's so sweet. Can I get a duplicate of him to go please?" Senida giggled over the phone.

"Speaking of men, how are things going with you and your trio?"

"Me and 'you know who' are through. Me and Darrell only argue when we talk. He's pretty mad at me. And me and Mandla, I'm not quite sure what we're doing."

Maya stopped clipping her toenails long enough to laugh. Senida laughed with Maya.

"Girl, I was trying to keep it on a professional level. It's hard."

"Sex?"

"What?"

"Have you had sex yet?"

"Chile yes. How about you and Jelani?"

"Not yet. I'm actually impressed with his staying power. Most men would have given up by now. He's actually turning out to be the total opposite of my initial impression of him."

Senida started laughing.

"What's so funny?"

"You *still* holding out."

"I'm cool. But I think it might happen tonight."

"Ummm chile."

"Do you ever think you and Darrell will get back together?"

"I don't know. For a time, I wished for it everyday. But now, I'm not quite sure." Senida sighed. "I'll tell you one thing though, you never know how good you've got it 'til it's gone."

"Yeah. You never miss the water 'til your well runs dry." Maya added. "My father always used to say that and I never knew what he meant until I got older."

"Take it from me. I am the epitome of dry wells. You just better hold on to that good man."

"I thought you didn't like Jelani?"

"It's not that I don't like Jelani. I don't even know him. I just love you and I want you to be careful. So far, he's only made you happy. And that's all that counts to me."

"Auhhhhh."

"Don't get me wrong. I still have my doubts, but he's proven me wrong thus far."

"So far everything is perfect."

"Speaking of perfect, have you talked to Stephanie?"

"Last week. She had a little girl. They named her Maya."

Senida laughed. "What ever happened with Jaleel?"

"I guess he never told Steph how he felt. Since the baby's been born, he's been the perfect daddy."

"Until the novelty wears off. Jelani never found out about that night?"

"Girl no! Thank goodness. He would have flipped! Hold on a minute, that's my phone." Maya clicked over to her other line.

Senida thought about Darrell. She did miss him tremendously. However, she was having fun with Mandla. She confused herself at times. Her skills with the men were definitely not one of her best qualities.

"Speak of the devil. That was Jelani," Maya gleamed as she got back on the line. "He's going to be a little late."

"Is he going to buy you a house for your inconveniences?" Senida laughed hard and long.

"Shut up chile."

"Maya. Did you ever figure out what he does for a living?"

Maya twisted her face while she thought. She'd been having so much fun with Jelani that she didn't question him anymore about how he got his money.

"You, know. I sure haven't. I'm assuming he's into real estate. That's what his card said."

"Well it still bothers me. You should find out what he does tonight."

Maya waved her hand in the air. It must be the lawyer in Senida that makes her investigate everything. She's been questioning Maya about Jelani for months. Maya decided that it was time to steer the subject from herself and onto another person.

"So is Mandla still giving everybody the blues around your office?"

"He's giving me the blues. Sometimes, I can't concentrate with him around. It's those eyes. I think he can hypnotize people with them."

"Sure sounds like he hypnotized your crazy ass." Maya peered at her clock. She had plenty of time before Jelani arrived. Spreading out her legs in front of her, she wiggled her toes and prepared to paint them.

"All of the little clerks come around the office now. Now, Maya, you know they don't have no business in my area. All of a sudden they need to borrow staples, tape, legal pads."

"Girl seems like you got a handful."

"He's quite a character though. When we go to our business lunches, he seems to loosen up the tension in the atmosphere. You know most of my colleagues are stuffy, old, white men, and Cindy. And she's even begun to ask too many questions about Mandla."

"What ole' Cindy trying to get her some Mandingo meat."

They both laughed.

"So are you going to go out tonight?"

"Nope."

"So what are you going to do?"

"Nothing."

Maya felt sorry for Senida.

"Do you want me to come over after my date?"

"Nah, I'm going to rent me a movie and eat some popcorn and ice-cream."

"You sure?"

"Positive. Go have fun with that man. And find out what he does."

"Alright. I'll call you in the morning?"

"Yeah. Have fun and be careful."

"I will. Bye."

Maya hung up. She finished her right foot and continued on to her left foot. She looked down at her feet. She'd done such an excellent job on her own personal home-based pedicure that she would have to wear her sandals tonight. She wasn't sure where she and Jelani were going. All she knew was that she enjoyed being with him.

Dropping her robe to the floor, Maya slipped on her silky panties and her matching, silky bra. She and Jelani had not engaged in sexual contact but just in case, she wanted to be prepared. She played around with her hair, trying to figure which way would look best for the night, up or down. She reached into her closet to take out a pair of slacks and a silk blouse. Maya placed the clothes carefully onto her bed and sat at her vanity. Her vanity allowed her to escape into the world of Maya. Her perfumes, make-up, hair accessories, and other important women stuff were assembled in front of the mirror.

She reached for the odd shaped bottle and dabbed the top on both sides of her neck, the insides of her elbows, and on her chest. Darrell bought the perfume for her on her birthday. He told her that men loved the smell and so far he'd been right. On their first date, Jelani could not stop sniffing the air. Maya caught him standing over her sniffing her hair, when she saw him in the reflection of a window.

When Jelani arrived, he was casually dressed. He wore a pair of loose jeans and a plain, white T-shirt. His Nike sneakers matched his Nike baseball hat. Maya immediately felt overdressed in her slacks and silk blouse. Jelani did not seem to mind the inconsistencies in their attire for the evening. He grinned and gently kissed Maya on her lips.

"You're going to like where we're going." He looked around the floor and scanned her living room. "Where's your overnight bag?"

"I need an overnight bag?" Maya questioned.

"Yes," he responded with a grin. Maya eyed him suspiciously. "But it's not that type of party. You might want to pack something comfortable," he said to Maya, as she walked back into her room to gather some things. "Like some jeans, T-shirts, G-strings and some lingerie."

She stopped in mid-stride and glanced at Jelani, as he settled onto her couch, pretending to read an upside down magazine.

"Just kidding," he said smiling as he turned the magazine right side up. "But you should pack some jeans and T-shirts. And at least one going out dress."

Maya went into her room and changed into her loose fitting, black jeans, slipped on a thin, white T-shirt and stepped into her Reeboks. She then unpinned her hair, by loosening the bobby pins and fluffing it out with her fingers. She reached into the back of her closet and pulled out her old Spelman baseball cap and placed it on top of her head, sliding the rest of her hair in the back through the hole, creating a loose ponytail. If he wanted casual, then that's what he was getting. Nobody had to tell her twice to wear some jeans. She was a Jean kind of girl anyway.

Maya finished changing and threw a few articles into a duffel bag. From her vanity table, she removed a small sample of the perfume she was already wearing. She then filled the bag with brushes, lipstick, mascara, and all the other essentials she felt she needed to keep this man interested. Pulling her long, black slip dress from her closet, Maya packed it into her garment bag. After putting her toothbrush and toothpaste into her duffel bag, she zipped it up and hiked it onto her shoulder. She turned off her bedroom light, but did not go into the living room. Instead, she flicked the light on again and opened her bottom drawer. From it, she pulled out a soft white, chiffon gown. Just in case, she thought. She also pulled out a package of condoms from the same drawer and tucked them both deep under her other clothes.

When she returned to the living room, Jelani stood to take her bag and they both headed out of the door. Maya made sure that her kitchen light stayed on and her doors were locked. Jelani climbed into a red Jeep Cherokee and tossed Maya's bag into the back.

"Whose is this?" she inquired as she climbed into the passenger's side.

"It's mine," he responded casually, as he backed out of the parking space.

"How many cars do you have?"

"Four."

"Four! What kind? I know you have the Range Rover, this jeep..."

"I have a Porsche and a Mercedes Benz." He did not look at her. He drove the jeep to the main street, headed for Interstate 285.

"What did you say you did for a living again?"

"I work...hard...like every other black man on this planet."

"I need to know what you do, cause if it's illegal..."

"Oh baby it's all legit...so don't worry. I've earned all of it and I pay taxes on the shit." He smiled at her as she turned to concentrate on the road.

Maya turned back to Jelani. She watched his strong hands grip the steering wheel of the jeep. His masculine legs flexing and relaxing as he pressed on and off of the accelerator and brakes. His handsome face had a slight midnight shadow where he needed to shave but it only added to his strong, square jaw line, which twitched as he chewed the gum.

"Where are we going?" she asked, smiling at him.

"Florida."

"Florida? How long does it take to drive there?"

"A few hours. But we're not driving. Not this time. Maybe next time. I have to go out of town on business in a few days, so I want to spend every waking moment with you in Florida, and not trying to get there."

"Oh." Maya sat back and enjoyed the air coming through the holes in the jeep. "So we're flying?"

"Yeah, baby girl." Jelani looked directly at Maya. "We're flying." He stared into her large brown eyes. Damn she was gorgeous, he thought to himself.

Jelani was glad that Maya was enjoying herself with him. He could tell that she was beginning to feel for him. He'd been searching for a relationship with a woman like Maya for years now. And ever since his run-in with Shatina, he vowed to clean up his act and stay celibate until he found the right woman. He had to admit that the first few weeks were the hardest, especially the celibacy. But he managed to hold out, making him feel stronger than he'd felt in years.

Instead of engaging in his old habits, he would spend his days and nights working out in his personal gym at home. He wouldn't frequent the health clubs that he was famous for attending. He dropped from the scene, much to everyone's dismay. He was usually the life of the party; the one that got everything started. But after the incident, he changed for the betterment of his life and the children he planned on having in the future. No use letting his perfect genes go to waste. And now he found the perfect woman to match his genes. His hardest task would be convincing her in enough time, to love him. Jelani felt as though he was working against the clock. It would be a matter of time before she found out and he had plans to have her hooked by then. Which is one of the reasons that he tried to spend every free moment with her.

*****

Waves crashed on Vero Beach and echoed in the night air. Water grew higher and higher, effortlessly bending and floating down in a bell curve fashion, eventually colliding onto the sand with insurmountable force. The roar of the waves and the swoosh of the water, rushing back towards the dark background, soothed Maya's nerves. She was slightly tense, from agreeing to spend the entire weekend with this man alone. She would call Senida as soon as she got in the house, to let her know where she was.

Maya swore she saw a falling star from the limousine window as the driver parked on the deck. Jelani stepped out first, pulled at his pants, and took in a deep breath. He looked over at his house and then out over the sea. This was going to be a great trip. The excitement on Maya's face attested to that. He bent and looked into the limo. Maya's large brown eyes were focused on Jelani. He reached in and offered her his arm. She smiled and accepted.

"This is gorgeous." She sighed as she looked out over the sea.

"Yeah, baby. That's my house over there." He pointed to a two-story beach house sitting on the sand.

The enormous home sat dark and still. Large windows revealed a spacious living area. The tan outside held speckles of red that matched the red shingles on the roof. Palm trees surrounded the house, separating it from the other two houses on either side. They offered little to no privacy, but accented the gentleness of the home.

"We can go put our stuff in the house and take a walk on the beach," Jelani said to Maya, as he looked out over the water and back at the limousine, still parked behind them.

Maya smiled up at Jelani. Vero Beach's atmosphere was euphoric. Jelani looked extremely handsome. Gazing directly up at him, Maya realized how large and physically fit he was. She stood watching, as his jaw line flexed and relaxed from his constant gum chewing. Her feelings for Jelani transpired over the course of a few months. Initially, she would have laughed if anyone even claimed that she would be dating the egomaniac. But Maya realized that she'd finally met her match. Although her sweet arrogance was often viewed as strong confidence and cute, she realized that between the two, they had a lot in common.

Jelani waltzed into her life and had taken control of her emotions. She hadn't seen Michael or Donald for quite some time. And for the most part, Jelani took up the majority of her free time. Jelani seemed to have a secret plan of monopolizing Maya's time. He called every day at lunchtime, to make sure she didn't want for anything. He made sure she made it home from work everyday, and he showered her with roses, gifts, and other small representations of his fondness.

Maya grew to expect the phone calls and the special attention. She thought she was dreaming. Jelani was handsome. He knew how to show a woman a good time. He was smart and funny. And although the ego still existed, he seemed to care about other people's feelings. Aunt Setty approved of him from what Maya told her over the phone. But Senida constantly warned Maya about Jelani and the strange feeling she got when Maya said his name.

Jelani tipped the limousine driver and pulled the bags out of the back seat.

"You don't need to carry them up for us, thank you. We'll see you on Sunday," he said, turning to the tall man that hopped out of the front seat to retrieve their bags.

The moon's reflection lit the sand, causing a glow around the water. Maya hadn't seen a scene like this since she'd been to the Bahamas. Jelani walked in front of Maya, periodically to make sure that she was okay. Her Reeboks sunk in the soft, white sand; deeper and deeper with every step she took towards Jelani's house. There were two small palm plants sitting on either side of Jelani's porch. Although they were beautiful, they looked like they needed some water and a little tender loving care; much like the plant that Maya was trying to nurse back to life in her office. Jelani unlocked the double doors and stepped in first.

"Wait right here," he instructed as he put a finger up to her face and left the bags sitting next to her feet.

Maya turned her attention back to the beach. Stars were out in full effect. The dark velvety sky twinkled with specks of bright stardust. Every so often, Maya would see another falling star.

"My parents must be telling me something," she said out loud to herself.

She smiled. She would enjoy this special weekend with Jelani. All games aside. If he wanted to have sex with her, she would be more than willing. She, herself, was interested in finally seeing the big bulge in front of his pants, up close and personal. Many nights Maya would dream of the rock hard thighs wrapped around her waist, as they both grunted and groaned in the dark. His body was unbelievably structured, like a God-like sculpture from the Greek times but even better than those puny little statues. Jelani had the kind of looks that would make a woman drop her drawers in a hot second.

However, Maya played it safe. He may have been one of the finest specimens of a man that she's laid her eyes on. Men approached her on a daily basis. She met them in the malls, the movies, the grocery stores, anywhere and everywhere. And she was positive that if she was having dreams about him, then he *had* to be having dreams about her.

Maya peeped her head in the door and saw an upstairs bedroom light go on and off. Shortly after, Jelani glided down the stairs and turned on the hall light. He brushed past Maya and snatched up the bags. He looked at her and smiled, lightly brushing his lips across her cheek.

"I like to make sure everything's in check before I bring a

young woman into my house. I only come to this house on special occasions and I don't want nobody surprising me while I'm up here."

"Like who?" Maya inquired.

"Like my brother, my close friends, or burglars." He picked up the heavy bags with no effort. "Certain people have keys to this place. Every now and then someone comes and spends some time up here, or they just come and check on it for me. You know, make sure everything is okay?"

Maya nodded her head and followed Jelani into a magnificent home. High ceilings were draped with bright crystal chandeliers. Large picturesque windows opened from the ground to the ceiling, allowing the moonlight to spill into the home and crawl on the floor, causing a romantic effect. Jelani's walls were adorned with African-American portraits and Maya noticed some of the portraits that were hung in her gallery. She gazed at the huge fireplace sitting on top of a brick pedestal.

There was a slight flowing of the curtains through the living room window, as the breeze kissed her slightly on her face. His living room had old style antique furniture, from the late 1800's. The dark red color was accented by floral arrangements in expensive vases. Maya walked around the room, touching the frames of each hung portrait. His expensive taste impressed Maya. From the living room Maya could hear Jelani humming an old gospel song.

Jelani was in the kitchen, while Maya gave herself the nickel and dime tour of his downstairs. Maya could hear Jelani opening the refrigerator door. There was a slight squeak of the door that shot through the quiet room. Maya stood at the bottom of the stairs. His staircase spiraled upward into heaven, complimenting the fluffy beige carpet.

"Would you like something to drink?" Jelani said to Maya, as he came up behind her and wrapped his arms around her waist, nuzzling his head in the nape of her neck. He could smell her perfume and he inhaled deeply, to ensure that he smelled enough to keep in his memory bank.

"What do you have?"

"Baby, anything you want."

"I'll take a glass of red wine."

Jelani walked over to the entertainment center and flipped

on the CD player. Sounds of Luther Vandross crept through the speakers, from each corner of the room. Jelani slipped back into the kitchen. Maya could hear him taking the glasses out of the cabinets. They clanked together as he held them both in one hand and reached for the wine bottle. He yelled from the refrigerator.

"Make yourself at home. Take a look around. You can give yourself a tour if you want to." He poured one glass of chilled wine and searched the refrigerator for cheese and strawberries.

No doubt, Maya was way ahead of him, as she climbed the elaborate staircase towards the bedrooms. His master bedroom was immaculate. Delicate plants and flowers were strategically placed throughout. The bathroom held a walk-in tub sunk into the floor and two long, large wall mirrors. His bedroom had two large closets. Maya opened one closet and Jelani's clothes were neatly aligned, as well as his shoes. She looked out of the window. She could see the beach and other beach homes. The water bled into the dark background.

Jelani walked up to Maya and looked over her shoulder out into the night. Her sweet smell permeated his nose and infected his brain. Everything about Maya made Jelani wish that he could sweep her off of her feet and lay her on top of his bed. He dreamed of smelling her breath on him, of tasting the salty nectar hidden in between her legs. But he decided to take precautions with his process with Ms. Maya Dickson. She seemed to be the type of woman that didn't take no mess.

"Here," Jelani said as he handed her the sexy, feminine shaped glass full of red wine. Her delicately, red painted fingernails clanked against the glass as she gripped it.

Maya turned to face Jelani's chest. She looked directly up into his eyes. He smiled as she raised the glass to her lips and sipped. He held his glass to his lips and sipped also. Maya noticed that Jelani's glass was not red, but gold.

"Why aren't you drinking wine?" she asked.

"I don't drink alcohol," he said, as he reached for her hand and led her out of the bedroom and into the hallway, down the stairs. Seeing her in the bedroom, next to the bed, was too much for him to handle.

"Let's go for that walk now." Jelani bent and kissed her softly on her lips, leaving Maya with her head cocked and her lips partly open, waiting for more. He pulled her gently through the front door and onto the soft cool sand.

Maya smiled up at Jelani as they began walking along side the waves. He sipped from his glass and watched the water intently. He held her hand in his, but seemed to pay more attention to the motion of the waves. Maya walked and smiled to herself as she felt the sand slip in and out of her toes. Her fingernail polish was now covered with tiny grains of white colored salt. Vero Beach was dark and serene. Jelani and Maya were the only two in eyesight. Jelani continued to walk and sip and stare off into the dark water, with the assurance that she was still attached to his hand.

"Beautiful isn't it?" Maya asked breaking the silence.

Jelani turned to her as if she'd just appeared by his side.

"Yeah." He sighed. "I used to come out here a lot and just sit and watch the waves. It's a good place to meditate." He smiled down at her and squeezed her hand.

"Thank you for bringing me out here." She smiled and looked past him, out over the water. "This is the first time I've ever been to Jacksonville."

"No problem baby. Thank you for coming. You seem like a pretty special woman. I just thought you might have needed some time to get away from all the work you're always doing."

"Tell me about it." Maya sighed and rolled her eyes. "Sometimes I don't even have time for myself."

"That's not good. You supposed to always have time for yourself." Jelani's expression was stern. Maya could feel his grip tighten.

"I know. But it just seems as though I always have something to do," she said as she gulped down the last of the red wine and handed Jelani the glass, which he slipped into the pocket of his jacket.

"You're a little Ms. Busy Body that's why. You need to start taking better care of yourself. If it's one thing I've learned in life, it's to care for self."

"I understand what you're saying but don't you think that's a little selfish?" Maya asked.

"No. I'm not the least bit selfish. I have so much and nobody to share it with that I sometimes have to find people to share my wealth."

Maya stopped walking and Jelani looked directly at her.

"What do you do for a living?" Maya asked sternly.

"I told you baby. Why you keep asking me the same ole' question?" He was obviously irritated.

"Because I need to know!" Maya stood still and pulled her hand from his and crossed her arms over her chest.

Jelani sighed and looked directly at Maya. She was a stubborn woman if he'd ever met one. He concentrated on her small jaw line jutting out, as she tried to appear forceful. Her arms were tightly crossed over her chest and Jelani figured he'd better tell her something to keep the right mood for the trip.

"I invest. I own a few homes like the one here, okay? I buy them and then I sell them after I fix them up. Is that all right with you?" he growled as he gulped down the last of his drink and put his glass into his other pocket.

Maya looked around, trying not to show Jelani her impending smile that she had finally gotten her way. She grabbed his hand back and continued walking down the beach. They had been walking for almost thirty minutes and were far from Jelani's house. Maya trusted Jelani enough to know that he knew where he was going and knew how to get back.

"Is that why you're always gone on business trips?"

"Sometimes." Jelani did not smile or even look at Maya. She decided to let that subject rest.

"So...do you have any kids?" She tried to strike up another conversation.

"No." He looked straight ahead.

Maya said cocking her head to one side. "Do you want any?"

"Eventually. Right now I'm taking care of five little boys."

Maya stopped, forcing Jelani to look at her. Her eyes searched his.

"Five little boys?" Her puzzled face made Jelani loosen up a little, as he stretched his arms and arched his back.

"I volunteer for a young boy's mentoring program," he said pulling her, forcing her to continue walking.

"Oh. Kinda like a big brother program?" she inquired. Maya enjoyed hearing black men talk about children. Children always seemed to bring out the best in anybody.

"Yeah. Exactly like a big brother program. Just that I have five little brothers, instead of one." Maya smiled at him and he returned her smile.

"I figure, since I had such a fucked up childhood, that maybe I can prevent somebody else from going through the same shit that I did as a kid," he continued as his smile faded. Jelani looked back out over the water.

"You want to talk about it?" Maya carefully asked, tilting her head, assuring him that she meant no harm.

"Talk about what?"

"About your childhood."

"No," he answered with a vindictive edge.

Maya remained silent as they walked up onto some rocks and sat on the top, overlooking the water. Jelani had his arm wrapped around her shoulder in an attempt at keeping her warm, but he did not say a word. He was deep in thought and Maya thought it best to wait until he was ready to continue their conversation. For some reason, Jelani did not want to discuss his family.

"You ever want kids?" he finally asked.

She smiled and snuggled her head into his chest.

"Yes."

"How many?" he said as he kissed her lightly on the top of her head.

"Two."

"Do you like working at the art museum?"

"I love it," she said as she lifted her head and turned to look directly at him. "It's my passion."

"So what exactly do you do at the museum?"

"At the Art Gallery," she corrected him. "I run its entire operation. I determine everything that is bought, sold, hung, and presented there."

"Does it get stressful?" he inquired.

"Oh yeah. I 'm in charge of everything. So if nothing goes right, then I'm liable."

"Ever think of leaving it and doing something else?"

"Something else like what?"

"Like a housewife?" He smiled.

"Hell no. I've always been an artsy craftsy type of person. I love what I do. Art is my life."

"Ever want more in your life?" His serious tone forced Maya to think. She did want more in her life. She wanted a husband to love her, like her father loved her mother. She wanted children, eventually. And she did miss the closeness of having a one-on-one partner that understood her wants and needs.

"I...I...never thought about anything else but art," she lied. She looked away. She did not want him to see the longing in her eyes.

Jelani pulled her face to his and kissed her. His warm mouth thawed her cold lips. Every part of her face was cold, except her lips. Jelani moved his tongue in and out of her mouth. He rubbed his hand up and down her back, stopping momentarily at her bra strap, as if he were contemplating unsnapping it. His hand slid around her waist and he gently squeezed her breast, sending chills down Maya's spine. Her body began to respond to his hands rubbing on her breasts. Her nipples poked out through her bra. Her deep breathing accelerated her heartbeats.

Jelani pulled his tongue out of her mouth and kissed her on her lips softly. He held her chin in his hand and looked deep into her large brown eyes. He didn't want to mess things up with her, so he decided to wait for her to make the move. He knew she was the type of woman that would let him know when it was time.

"You ready to go back?" he asked, trying to make his hard muscle go down with mind control.

"Yeah. It's cold out here."

"You looked a little hot to me," he said as he smiled and helped her up from the large rock.

He took off his jacket and draped it around her shoulders. Goosebumps instantly appeared on his arms and Maya wrapped her arms around him, to keep him warm, as they walked back to his house. Jelani slipped the key in the lock and sprawled out on the couch, with Maya in tow. There they slept in each other's arms, until the sun came up the next day.

WHEN WE SIN

"Let the church say, Amen." Reverend Breelow stood in front of the congregation. Sweat dripped down his thick sideburns and onto his black and red robe. His thick Afro leaned slightly to the right, as he jumped and hopped from side to side. "Hallelujah. The Lord is my Savior."

"And Tyrone is my barber," Mandla whispered into Senida's ear.

Senida and Mandla's secret love relationship had been going strong since their after work project. And the two times that Senida had brought Mandla to her church, he would talk about Reverend Breelow's hair and sideburns. Senida giggled at his joke and poked him in the ribs with her elbow. She looked around to see if anyone else had heard Mandla.

"Mandla please behave." Senida smiled at the two older women sharing their pew.

"How much more time do we have to listen to Reverend Sideburns?"

"At least another hour. Now be quiet."

"How 'bout you say we blow this joint and get into something a little wetter," Mandla said out the side of his mouth, while pretending to flip through the bible.

"Mandla you are terrible."

"Well?" Mandla smiled at Senida.

"Well what?"

"Let's...you know?" he said rolling his eyes.

Senida laughed.

"We aren't going to have time today, are we?"

"Baby I always make time for *that*."

"I don't know." Senida hesitated.

"I'm going to the restroom. Meet me in the lobby so we can discuss this."

Mandla excused himself and climbed carefully over the two older women, who rolled their eyes and shook their heads. They heard Senida and Mandla's entire conversation.   Mandla straightened his suit as he walked down the aisle to the lobby of the church. Eyes of young women watched each meticulous step he took. The people in the congregation already had their gossip sessions about Senida and the man that was too young for her. They watched for the past two Sundays at how she would parade him around and how giddy she would act, while the good Reverend Breelow was reciting his sermon. Mandla didn't care for the church or the people in it. He hated that Senida had bribed him to attend with her.

Mandla did not have to wait long for Senida to slip out of the church and into the lobby. She looked around to see who was listening and who was watching. As long as she'd been a member of the First African-Methodist Church, she had been in the loop of gossip. Mostly spreading the "good" word but sometimes the bad. But now it was she who was the topic of the gossip. Mandla pulled her to the side of the restrooms.

"Baby, I know it's Sunday but I want to taste you." He slid his hands up and down her back.

"Taste me?"

"Now."

"But you know I got to take Sister Bertha home."

"Damn," he said and then looked up to the church ceiling. "Sorry."

"And you know the church picnic is after service. That will probably take all day."

"And I got some things I got to do tonight," he said, thinking.

"Sorry Mandla. Maybe tomorrow," she said about to walk away. Mandla grabbed her arm. He looked around the lobby and spotted a small closet door in the corner of the building.

"Come here," Mandla said motioning to her with one hand, as he pulled her with his other.

He opened the small door quickly and pulled Senida in behind him. The inside of the closet was dark, but Mandla knew what he was reaching for. Senida could feel him reaching for her.

He pulled her tightly and placed his mouth to her mouth. He began kissing her, forcing his tongue in and out of her mouth and licking her lips. He ran his hands down the sides of her arms and tugged and pulled at her dress. He managed to unbutton the back and the dress fell swiftly to the floor with a soft thud. Mandla unsnapped her bra and pulled it up over her breasts. Senida could hear his breathing intensify. She couldn't believe what she was about to do in her church. The choir could be heard singing at the top of their lungs. Good, Mandla thought, now the congregation won't hear Senida hollering.

Senida began to loosen up when she felt Mandla's warm mouth on her breasts. He carefully took each one in his hands and licked around the nipple and then put the whole breast in his mouth. He slid his tongue up the center of her chest and she held on to his head, as he brought his tongue back down to her belly button. Mandla got on his knees and began licking the insides of her thighs. She could feel the soft touch of his tongue through the silkiness of her pantyhose. He fondled the middle of her pantyhose until he could feel her grip tighten on his head.

Mandla slid the silky undergarments down, until he got to her feet. Then he took off her shoes and slipped the hose off of each foot. Senida could hear him unzipping his pants and could feel his fingers gently rubbing her inside. She could not see anything in the closet, except for the small crack of light that came from the hinges of the door. But she could hear Mandla's breathing, his movements, and the choir singing, "Eye on the Sparrow."

Senida felt Mandla's breath on her pubic hairs. Her heart began to beat faster as she felt his warm, soft tongue slide across the small, thick, swollen tissue in between her legs. He caressed it with his lips and tickled it with his tongue. He held it in between his mouth and licked around the outside and the inside, until he heard Senida's soft whimpers. Mandla stuck his finger into his mouth and pulled out the silky looking finger. Gently and slowly, he slid it in between Senida's lower flaps, as her head fell back in ecstasy. Moving his finger in and out of the tight muscle, as it gripped around the long brown finger, Mandla pulled out and licked the creamy milk from his fingernails.

Once he was done, Mandla turned Senida around, by guiding her with his hands and body. With all the ease of a conscientious lion, Mandla skillfully eased his hard muscle, first touching tip to tip, and then thrusting softly, until he had worked his way in, as far as he could go. Senida let out a soft sigh and groan. She felt the sweet sensation rush over her body. She trembled slightly, as Mandla shifted his hips from side to side to guarantee a snug fit and ensure enough room to do what he had to do. He bent forward and gently kissed her on her back. His smooth lips caressed a little bit of skin and then let go, with a sliver of the wet tongue. Small beads of sweat began to form on Mandla's brow. He started to push inside of Senida. Her soft sighs, moans, and groans excited Mandla. Her whimpers became louder as Mandla stroked a few times, getting faster and faster. Senida rolled her head.

"Oh Mandla," she softly cried. This only made Mandla stroke faster, as he felt the turmoil brewing in his stomach and then in his loins.

"Shit girl!" he yelled out, as he held onto the back of Senida's head.

Mandla pulled on her shoulders, helping her to come quicker with him. Sweat formed on her back and slipped under each grip. Mandla grew louder and gripped harder as he stroked faster, until he exploded on top of Senida's back. She put part of her fist into her mouth so no one would be able to hear her. But Mandla's long, strong strokes were all she could handle. The more he stroked, the louder the choir seemed to sing, and the more Senida knew that she would scream out Hallelujah! And she did, right along with the congregation.

"Hallelujah! Yes! Oooooh!"

Mandla leaned on Senida as he tried to bring down his breathing and his heart rate. He reached under Senida's bent body and fondled her breasts. Her nipples were still erect and he rubbed them, adding more sweat to their already sweaty bodies. Mandla slipped slowly out of Senida and they both fell to the floor of the closet to rest. They could hear the choir singing outside of the closet door. Both were still trying to regulate their breathing and heart rates.

"You know we need to get up?" Senida said as she thought about how long they'd both been gone.

"Yeah, I know. Your ole' gossiping hens are probably talking about us right now."

Their eyes had adjusted to the darkness and Senida could see Mandla's silhouette. He was searching for her dress and his pants, when all of a sudden the door to the closet opened and a flood of light poured into the tiny box, exposing Senida and Mandla's naked bodies. Sister Ma-bell's reaction was almost comical to Mandla. The old lady held her chest and started to hyperventilate. Her eyes became as big as two flying saucers and she almost fell back out of sheer shock.

Mandla reached up and quickly snatched the door shut. They scrambled to put their clothes back on, but Senida could not find her stockings. Buttoning up her dress, she quickly went out of the closet door to check on Sister Ma-bell. She had fainted and was laid out flat on her back. Mandla came out less than two seconds after Senida and looked over the old woman's body. Senida became frantic.

"Sister Ma-bell! Sister Ma-bell!" Senida was holding Sister Ma-bell's head in her lap. She was kneeling next to the woman's plump body. "Mandla call 911!"

Senida began to cry as Mandla raced to the pay phone. To the left of the phone was a small kit with red letters indicating the emergency kit. Mandla quickly opened the kit and pulled out a small white capsule of smelling salt. He cracked open the little capsule, knelt down beside Ma-bell and waved it under her nose. Her eyes fluttered and she looked up at Senida with disgust.

"Ma-bell are you okay?" Senida asked as she continued to hold the old woman's head.

"I saw what was going on in there!" Ma-bell said as she sat up and looked from Senida to Mandla and back. "I saw what you was doing to disrespect the house of the Lord! How dare you bring this young heathen up in our church and disrespect my Savior's house?"

Ma-bell looked over at Mandla and turned her nose up at him in a huff. Mandla let his head drop. He knew the older women in the church did not approve of him. He also knew that the older women didn't like him because so many of the younger women did. He felt like laughing at the old woman but instead continued to let his head hang.

"Sister Ma-bell...I'm sorry...I don't know what got into me..." Senida began.

"I know what got *into* you! That heathen over there, that's what got *into* you!" Ma-bell spat as she snatched her arm away from Senida and looked over at Mandla, who had stood and was now leaning against one of the walls.

"Please forgive me Sister Ma-bell. I know I've sinned..."

"You need to ask for forgiveness from the Lord, not me. What you did was a disgrace. I can't believe you allowed that devil to come into your life and turn you against the workings of the Lord."

"Are you going to mention this to anyone, 'cause..." Senida didn't know how to phrase the question. She didn't want Sister Ma-bell to run her mouth to the other church members. If they got word of what just happened, she would never be able to show her face in this church again.

Before Sister Ma-bell could respond to Senida's question, a few people began to file out of the church and crowd around Senida and Sister Ma-bell. Mandla answered all of the questions of the congregation with quick short answers. Ma-bell stood up slowly with the help of Senida. Ma-bell looked around at the crowd that had gathered around her.

"Sister Ma-bell are you okay?" one of the members asked, as he stepped closer to help the old woman.

"I'm fine!" Sister Ma-bell hollered.

"Have you been taking you heart medicine, Ma-bell?" an older church member asked.

"I said I was fine! I just had a shock that's all!" Sister Ma-bell started walking from the lobby back into the church, swinging her arms at anyone who tried to help her. "Now are we having church or are we having a stand-around-and-look-at-Ma-bell service?" she yelled as she let the doors to the church slam behind her. All the other members followed Sister Ma-bell back into the church. Senida and Mandla were once again left alone in the church lobby.

"Boy, that ought to be good conversation at the church picnic today," Mandla said as he walked closer to Senida. He could tell she was feeling bad and he wanted to try to lighten the mood.

"Mandla that's not funny."

"I know. I'm sorry."

"Sorry for what?" Senida was irritated.

"Sorry for wanting you at the wrong time. Sorry for getting

the goods in church. And I'm sorry mostly for getting caught." He smiled. She didn't. "Do you want to go back in?"

"Heck no!"

"What about Sister Bertha?"

"We'll wait for her in the car."

"How about we go get some coffee and come back and pick the old hag up? You know Reverend Sideburns is going to talk over, like he does every Sunday." Mandla took Senida's hands in his and gave her a sideward glance. She held her head down in the same position since the incident had occurred. "I promise we can go around the corner and be back in about thirty minutes."

"Yeah. I think that would be best 'cause Lord knows I sure don't want to go back in there right now." Senida smiled as she looped her arms into Mandla's arms. They began to walk toward the door leading to outside. "Do you think she'll tell anybody?" Senida asked as Mandla held the door open for her.

"Who cares? Those old biddies act like they've never had sex. If sex is so bad, then how the hell do they think they got here?" Mandla used Senida's keys to open the car doors and slipped into the driver's side. He had been driving her car for so long, that sometimes he would have to remind himself that the vehicle did not belong to him.

"I guess you're right," Senida sighed as she watched Mandla start up the car. "I sure hope you're right."

*****

"You need to put another log on the fire," Maya yelled to Jelani. He didn't understand why she wanted him to build a fire, but he obliged her request.

"I'm way ahead of you baby." Jelani walked into his living room with an arm full of wooden logs.

"I wonder what all the people in Atlanta are doing?" she asked, leaning her back against the couch. Maya was sitting on the floor drinking a glass of white wine.

"What people?" Jelani dropped the logs into a pile next to the fireplace. He immediately tossed in two logs and a flare of fire rose and quickly died down.

"Like Senida. And her new friend Mandla."

"Who cares?" Jelani responded as he joined Maya on the

floor. "Right now the only two people that matter are me and you." He pointed to Maya. She smiled.

"That's sweet."

"I like your hair. It looks nice." He ran his fingers through her hair.

"You're messing it up now," she snarled seductively. He continued to finger through her hair. "But thanks."

"Have you ever thought about cutting it short?"

"I'm just now growing it back. It was real short a few years ago."

"How did you look with it short?"

"Good. Just like I do now."

"Excuse me, Mizz Thang." Jelani snapped his fingers in a circle.

A spark jumped out of the fireplace and onto the tile. It died quickly. Jelani kicked the little black clump of wood back into the fireplace. Maya lay down and snuggled into Jelani. He stroked her hair.

"We got one more day before we got to head back to Atlanta," he said.

"Don't remind me. I'm not quite ready to go back."

"We can come up here again. You just let me know. Anytime you want to come." He bent to kiss her forehead. "Have you been having a good time?"

"Yes."

"What did you like the best?"

"The walks on the beach at night. And I also like the restaurant we went to last night."

"If you like that, wait 'til tomorrow night. I'm taking you to this restaurant on the water. Next time we come out here we'll take a ride in my boat."

"Damn, you got a boat too?"

"Uh-huh."

"What don't you have?"

Jelani thought. He didn't quite have *her* yet. But he was working on it.

"I *almost* have everything I want."

"Must be nice."

"It is." He watched as the light danced and flickered off of her face. "Damn. Something about the way that fire glows off of your face..."

"What?"

"You are such a beautiful lady."

"Thank you," she blushed.

"Not only on the outside but on the inside as well." Jelani stood and pulled Maya up by her hands. "Let's dance."

"Dance? Right here?"

"Can you think of a better place?"

"But there's no music."

"Let's just dance to the rhythm of our hearts."

She allowed him to take her hand and he led her to the middle of the living room where he pulled her close and squeezed her body into his. The perfect mesh of her curves into his grooves melted into a beautiful blend. Maya pressed her head into his chest, feeling the racing of his heartbeat. She could smell the sweet alluring scent emanating from his shirt with every step and twirl he did with her still intact. Jelani took Maya on a magical journey. When Maya danced with Jelani, she felt as though she were floating. Ever since the first night they danced together at Chev Marlon's, Maya's heart would beat extra fast when they danced again.

*****

Senida smiled to herself as she watched Mandla talk to Lacey from the open door of her office. Lacey was trying to give Mandla a hard time about his reports but Mandla wasn't having it. He slightly bent over Lacey as she frowned at his work. Lacey had been in a bad mood all morning and she was taking it out on Mandla. She shook her head whenever he tried to convince her that his reports were right. Senida did not know why Lacey didn't like Mandla. She mostly mumbled about how men like him would end up breaking someone's heart.

Senida remembered the first night they had sex. He was gentle and caring. When he was on top, he looked her directly in her eyes. She liked the slow, low move of his hips. She still got chills when he walked into her office. And although Mandla sent chills down her spine, Senida still often thought of Darrell. She thought for sure when she and Darrell met that he was her soul mate. But lately her soul mate would rarely talk to her and would

not return her phone calls. Hard as it was for Senida to face up to
it, she and Darrell were through. She missed him dearly but she
knew somehow that she'd fucked up. She didn't think her
comments to him were bad enough to end their relationship.

Senida shifted her files from one side of her desk to
another. She looked at her watch. She would probably take a long
lunch today. Her mind was too full of situations that she needed to
sort out.

"What's up?" Mandla appeared in Senida's doorway.

"Hey. Is Lacey giving you a hard time?" Senida smiled as
Mandla sat in the chair opposite of her desk.

"Yeah. That's what I wanted to talk to you about. You
didn't tell Lacey about us did you?" he asked. Senida rose from
her desk and went to shut her office door.

"Of course not. Why would I tell Lacey of all people?
You know she runs her mouth like a faucet. Why? Did she say
anything to you about us?" She wandered back to her desk and sat
down.

"Nah, but she's tripping off of trivial stuff."

"Oh, she's been having some personal problems lately.
Don't worry about Lacey. She'll be alright."

Mandla leaned over the desk and gave Senida a quick peck
on the lips. Senida quickly looked behind him to see if Lacey was
looking through the window. She wasn't.

"Are you still coming over tonight?" Mandla asked.

"For your party? Yeah, I'll be there. What should I bring?"

"Bring some condoms and come early," he responded as he
slipped out of the door and back to Lacey.

Senida smiled. She couldn't believe that she was actually
dating, well sleeping with, someone from her office. She was even
more surprised that her business did not get out into the office.
She would hate to ruin a good working relationship and a good
sexual relationship with Mandla. She enjoyed spending time with
him. He taught her how to be young again. The other day they
went to Six Flags Over Georgia. Mandla had never been and
Senida only once. She had the thrill of a lifetime. He seemed to
really enjoy himself also.

Senida was a little nervous about meeting Mandla's friends.
She was sure that she would be the oldest person in the room,
unless his mother came. Senida picked at her nails. She would

have to stop by the store and get her some fingernail polish to get rid of the chipped red coats that she'd been wearing for the last week. She pulled her purse out of her desk drawer and headed towards her door.

"I'm leaving early for the day," she responded to Lacey and Mandla. Mandla winked at her indicating that he would see her later that night. She smiled and Lacey continued to fuss at Mandla.

The dirt was as stubborn as an old mule. Mandla had been scrubbing the floor since he came home from work but it just didn't look as clean as he wanted. That was the one thing that he didn't like about his new apartment, the white kitchen floor. But he had to make the apartment look spotless. In a few hours, he would have a house full of guests. His very first get-together. He was excited. He only wished his mother and sisters could be there to share his joy. Earlier he talked to his oldest sister. She informed him of the latest gossip happening in their "hood" and in their home.

Mandla didn't have a chance to talk to his mother. She started a new job that required her to work nights. Mandla wanted to tell her that there was a good chance that he might be coming back home to go to law school. He'd been receiving letters from various law schools that were impressed with his LSAT scores. As soon as he heard from the law schools in D.C., he would be relocating back home. He had been in Atlanta for a few months and although he liked the city, it just wasn't D.C.

He hadn't told Senida or Todd about his plans of moving. As a matter of fact, Mandla only recently made up his mind to go. The night before he went out with Todd, his mother called. She sobbed over the phone about how they were low on money. Mandla listened to his mother's cries in silence. He hated to leave her by herself. Most of his friends didn't understand why Mandla needed to be so close to his mother. Whenever Mandla was more than fifteen minutes away from his mother, he would have flashbacks on the night of terror.

The blood was smeared on the walls and the porch when Mandla came from the party. His sisters away out of town at the time were not informed until later. Mandla's mother lay on the stretcher as he ran to the ambulance to see the stab wounds and the blood seep through the white wrappings over her chest. There had been plenty of break-ins in their neighborhood but Mandla never expected his family to be victims. He had a good reputation with everyone in the "hood." Later, finding out that the people who robbed and stabbed his mother were from another area, Mandla had a hard time leaving his mother alone. And Mrs. Jackson was just as paranoid as Mandla to stay at home alone. The reasons for him to go back home were adding up fast. There was too much history in D.C. for him to leave behind.

Mandla rinsed the dirt from the floor. It was starting to look better. He went into the den to turn on the music. He needed to get a sense of party in the apartment. He continued to clean every room in the apartment except for his bedroom. Nobody would need to go in there anyway.

*****

Senida did as she was told. She arrived at Mandla's apartment building four hours early and she brought a box of condoms. He was anxiously awaiting her arrival and began undressing her as soon as she stepped foot into the apartment. They both rolled around playing and kissing, sucking and licking. Senida was on a natural high.

Mandla held Senida tight in his arms and growled in her ear. She loved when he was in the heat of passion. She liked the way he whispered in her ears of how beautiful she was, how good she smelled, how soft her skin was, how smooth her hair was, how shapely her thighs were, of how he didn't know what was brighter, her smile or those eyes. Whispers that were intoxicating as they seeped through his gritted teeth and into her ears like maple syrup slow, smooth, creamy, and sweet. She'd become quite fond of Mandla.

"Girl you too much," Mandla said rubbing his hands across her bare back.

"You ain't too bad yourself," she replied.

"Shit baby. You ain't got to tell me that I'm the bomb."

"Are you excited about your get-together?"

"Yeah."

Senida's expression became serious. Mandla noticed and

commented on her sudden change.

"What's wrong with you?" he asked stroking the side of her face.

"I'll probably be the oldest one at your party tonight, huh?"

"Is that what you're worried about?" He smoothed at her hair. "You won't be the oldest person tonight."

Senida's face lit up. "I won't?"

"No baby. I think my grandmother's coming." He laughed. Senida's face dropped but she had to laugh with him.

"You make me sick."

"Don't worry about age. I'm not tripping and you shouldn't trip either." He held her face in his hand. "Okay?"

"Yeah, you're right."

"I know I am. Now I'm taking a shower." And with that Mandla bounced to the restroom.

Senida let her head sink into the large soft pillows. She rubbed her hands across the sheets. Her fingers felt light under the smooth softness of the sleek, silk sheets. Her short opaque nails complemented the color. Her head rested on the fluffy pillows and her hair, cut short and neat was slightly out of place. She deeply inhaled allowing her cavities to be filled with the alluring smell of his Obsession cologne. Her body still tingled as her brain remembered the feelings of his tongue on her skin. His touches had slid and glided across her sensitive layers of skin. It was more than she imagined. The aloofness of his routine and the ego filled confidence of his skills were becoming. His handsome face as he looked down at her, as he looked up at her, as they faced each other, and then as she looked behind herself at him.

The feeling made her smile. The thought made her unhappy. She didn't understand why Darrell couldn't have been like Mandla. She looked about the room at the assorted bottles of cologne on the dresser, a different scent for each day. She sighed and rolled over onto her stomach letting her body slide and allowing the crimson colored material to brush against her bare nipples. She could hear him singing in the shower. His powerful voice boomed over the running water and she could just imagine his mouth swung open wide, belting out the sounds to Sam Cooke's "When a Boy is in Love." A sense of complacency mulled over her and lulled her into a deep sleep.

Senida dreamed of Darrell. Since her and Darrell's break-up, Senida's dreams had become more rampant. Most of her dreams did not make sense but most of them showed Senida how difficult it would be to get Darrell back into her life. Senida tossed and turned as she dreamed. Her dream seemed so real.

She stood on a cliff and he stood on the other side. She reached for him and called out his name but he would not respond. He looked directly at her but did not respond to her calls. Senida cried and yelled until she leaped over the cliff and perilously fell through the air spinning.

It had been at least an hour when Senida awoke with a jolt. She could only see the illumination of the clock in the darkness. Frantically, she rubbed her hands across the sheets feeling for another body...nothing. She scrambled to the side of the bed and swung her legs over the side. Stumbling, she found the light switch and flipped it on with vibrancy. She was alone in the room. Senida reached for his robe, quickly tied it around her waist and threw the sheets and covers back onto the bed. She slipped on his house shoes and headed for the living room. Outside Mandla was setting food on the tables. He smiled when she came stumbling out of the room. He wore only a pair of boxers and Senida could not help but to stare slightly at his washboard stomach.

"So you finally decided to wake up huh? I thought you'd sleep forever." He walked over to her and wrapped his arms around her, pressing his lips to her mouth. She pulled back.

"Why didn't you wake me up? I slept for over an hour." Mandla stepped back and raised his hands as if to surrender.

"I'm sorry. You looked so comfortable I didn't want to disturb you."

"I thought I was supposed to help you get stuff organized?"

"Everything is under control. You just sit down and relax," he said with a smile.

"How many people are you expecting?"

"Oh a few. Not that many. My apartment only holds so many people. Just some friends from home and some from here," he said as he continued to arrange the food on the table.

"I think I'm going to take a shower before the guests arrive."

Senida showered and quickly dressed, trying to beat the first guest from surprising her in her birthday suit. Mandla followed after Senida and dressed for his guests. She could tell he was very excited. He wore casual looking slacks and a crisp white shirt. Senida had to admit that he was looking quite handsome. She had to control herself to make sure she didn't jump on him again.

An hour later, the first guests arrived. The couple was young and Senida's fear of being the oldest person began to sink into her head. The girl was very cute and very young. Her husband was just as young and Senida didn't really have a lot in common with them to talk about. She smiled a lot and helped Mandla as much as she could to keep herself busy.

More guests arrived. Some of Mandla's classmates from Howard and some people that he knew in passing since he'd been in Atlanta. Senida mingled with many of the guests and introduced herself as one of Mandla's co-workers. He introduced her as his boss. He was as affectionate in front of his guests as he usually was when they were alone. But Senida didn't mind too much, she just felt a little awkward...like she didn't belong. Mandla mingled with his guests and would check up on Senida from time to time. It wasn't until the doorbell rang for the umpteenth time that the fireworks began to fly.

Todd and a young, attractive woman entered the room and the festivities began. Senida walked out of the living room and stopped dead in her tracks. The young woman cocked her neck and shot daggers with her eyes in Senida's direction.

"What the hell are you doing here?" Todd said breaking the silence between the three of them.

"I was invited. What the hell are you doing here?" she retorted.

"Bitch, you owe me money for my tires. I ought to beat your ass right here." The young woman practically yelled, causing others to look in their direction. Her stomach was poking out.

"Who invited you?" Senida asked Todd. She ignored the woman.

"Mandla. Who in the hell invited your crazy ass?"

"It don't matter who invited who. Do you know how much money I had to pay for four new fucking tires?" the young woman yelled again. She rubbed her swollen belly.

Other guests stared and a few got quiet. The music still blared but the young woman yelled a few decimals above the music. Mandla came out of the kitchen to see what the commotion was about.

"What's going on here?" Mandla asked, looking from Senida to Todd and then to the young woman. "Todd? Man what's up?"

"That's the bitch that slashed my tires man. The crazy one I used to mess with."

Mandla stepped back from Senida. He looked at her with questioning eyes.

"Yeah...and the bitch owe me money for my tires," the woman said. Mandla put his hand up to the woman's face to silence her.

"You ain't gon' call me too many more bitches," Senida replied and the young woman shot her a dirty look.

"Senida what's up with that? You used to mess with my man Todd? You the one that slashed his tires?" He looked sincerely hurt.

"I didn't slash his tires...and we only dated..."

"We fucked!" Todd interrupted.

"...For a little while," Senida continued. "Mandla it's not what you're thinking."

"Mandla, man we was fucking for a while. She was cheating on her old man cause he couldn't keep it up."

The young woman started laughing out loud. The other guests were watching closely. Senida was steaming. She'd never been in this type of situation and didn't know how to get out. Mandla shook his head and distorted his face. Senida could tell he was mad. She tried to touch him on his arm but he pulled away from her.

"Mandla..." Senida stood trying to think of what to say.

"Mandla come here man," Todd said as the two of them walked a few steps away. He was watching Mandla's expression. "Look potna. I used to fuck with her so take it from me. She's crazy. Look at what she did to my jeep. If you keep fucking with her, you won't be able to get rid of her."

Senida walked over to the two men with the young woman right behind her.

"Mandla...I..." Senida began but couldn't find words to finish her sentence.

"I think you need to leave right now." He looked directly into her eyes.

"Let's go in the back and talk about..." She pleaded.

"I'm not in the talking mood right now Senida. Just go."

"Yeah, get to getting," Todd said twisting his face. His dark skin was shiny and flawless.

Senida went into Mandla's bedroom to get her purse and walked quietly to the door. The other guests were staring at her and others tried to pretend as if they didn't know there was a commotion. She hopped in her car and was about to turn the ignition when she heard screaming. Shortly after the screaming she heard glass shattering when she realized that the young woman was breaking her windows with a baseball bat. Senida hopped out of the car covering her head with her arms to prevent glass from getting into her eyes. People from the party began to congregate outside as Senida grabbed the young woman by her arms trying to stop her from hitting the car more.

"That's for slashing my tires. And that's for messing with my man," the young woman yelled as she swung the bat each time stressing her point.

Mandla and Todd ran outside and made their way through the now formed crowd of guests who watched and shook their heads. Todd stood back and began laughing at the sight of the two women struggling while Mandla ran to break up the catfight. The young woman was still trying to swing the bat but Senida now had a tighter grip on her arms and was wrestling the bat out of her grip. Mandla stepped in and pushed both women out of the way as he grabbed the bat from the young woman.

"What the hell is your problem? Two grown women out here acting crazy. Senida I thought I told you to leave. Get in your car now and leave!" he yelled. Senida obeyed. She was embarrassed enough to know that she did not want to stick around.

As she drove away she could hear the young woman yelling obscenities at her and she could see Mandla in the rear view mirror pulling her by the arm into the house. Senida drove home. She couldn't find it in herself to cry. She was in too much shock. She lay in bed staring at the ceiling. She couldn't call Maya because she was in Florida with Jelani, so she tried calling Darrell but his answering machine came on. She didn't leave a message.

SEXUAL HEALING

The entire weekend had been a restful dream come true for Maya. She felt refreshed, relaxed, and in love. Her heart had longed for another heart to simultaneously beat with. And she thought she found that heart in Jelani. To her surprise, Jelani had been the perfect gentleman throughout the trip. So Maya took it upon herself to make the first move. Besides, they would be leaving the next afternoon and she didn't want to miss the opportunity. Her plan had been devised since the first night when they slept on the couch together. No sex. It felt so right being there in his arms. Like her body was made specifically to mesh with the bumps and curves of his body. They both slept soundlessly that night and now Maya wanted to feel the other parts of his magnificent body. Her heart overpowered her brain when it sent messages to her aching hips, her upright nipples, and her swollen behind. Now was the time. She knew it and she was sure he felt it also. His plans of taking her to dinner were going to be spoiled tonight, if she could help it.

The smooth silky white chiffon gown felt soft against her skin. Checking her reflection in the mirror, she noticed that her butt poked out far behind her. Maya smiled nervously at her reflection. The white chiffon clung to her breast and her nipples poked through the material, causing a tickling sensation. The white G-string that she purchased from Victoria's Secret a few months earlier had never been put to use. She ran her finger across the front of the panties feeling the rough lace.

A soft breeze blew a few curls in her face. Maya turned her head sideways to the left and then to the right to inspect the raggedy hair-do that she was sporting from her previous shower. She unpinned her hair and a mass of soft curls fell onto her shoulders. Brushing through the thick mane she stroked down on both sides. Maya slicked her sides down and reached around the back of her head to twist the rest of the hair into a French roll.

She wanted a sexy but manageable look. Her delicate fingers glided in and out of her hair as she held bobby pins in between her lips. She looked about the room for a hand mirror and checked the back of her French roll. Maya walked to the window to feel the breeze float over her body. Each ripple of air gently fluttered her white chiffon gown.

Jelani was out on the beach meditating. Maya could see him sitting in the sand from the guest bedroom window. He was transfixed on the motion of the waves. His bare feet were buried in the sand and his arms were wrapped around his knees. He still wore the blue shorts that he had on all day. His large body appeared diminished in contrast to the large body of water. But his back was solid. Strong. He sat like the rock of Gibraltar.

Jelani reminded her of her father. How his back swayed just a little to the back as he walked. His thick dark wavy hair that stayed in place as the wind blew around him. Yes, he was much like her father. How his large strong hands engulfed hers when he held them. The strong white solid teeth. Both were handsome men. But her father was a slightly smaller build than Jelani. Her father's cinnamon brown complexion clashed, but meshed so well with her mother's deep mocha brown color. The couple was the epitome of perfection. They married young and he had to work soon after, delaying his college plans until he was well into his forties. Their small wedding was rushed as Gladys' white wedding gown barely fit over the swollen belly. But their love was new and fresh and mutual respect kept it that way.

Maya walked slowly back to the mirror and grabbed the small bottle from the dresser. She would be dressed before he even got in the shower. Maya dabbed the perfume top on her neck and on her thighs. She then dabbed her wrists and slid it down the front of her neck. She hoped she wasn't making a fool of herself.

By the time Maya finished cleaning the room and pulled on her long leather coat, Jelani was stepping out of the shower. Maya caught a glimpse of him standing with a towel wrapped around his waist as she walked past the room headed for the stairs. Her eyes became transfixed on the chest and bulging thighs protruding from the split in the towel. He had his back to her as he searched

through his dr_____ _____ ___ __ _ ___ ir of briefs. A couple of
different outfit_ ___ ___ _____ __ ___ _____ ʒed. When her black heels
clicked to a _____ d floor hallway and then
simultaneousl_, _____ he staircase, Jelani looked
around, catching a glimpse ᴏ__ _____ ᴛ.

"You don't have to go," Jelani called behind her, stepping
through the door into the hallway. She stood at the top of the
staircase prepared to go down and wait in the living room.

"Come in and keep me company," he said. "Don't act like
you don't want to see my body." He smiled at her and turned to go
back into his bedroom. She followed close behind him. He was
right. She did want to see his body and that was not all she wanted
to see.

Maya rolled her eyes towards the ceiling and smiled at his
arrogance. She sat on Jelani's bed and wrapped her arms around
her body enclosing the leather coat. Maya watched Jelani pull
more clothing out of his closet. He moved from one part of the
room to the next, organizing his belongings and hypnotizing Maya
with his perfect body. The ripples in his stomach rolled for miles
like a washboard.

"Are you having a good time?" he asked as he went into the
bathroom to get the bottle of lotion. Maya could hear him
squeezing the lotion out of the bottle and wiping it onto his body.
Her imagination got the best of her and she crossed her legs to
contain the thumping feeling rising between them.

"Yeah. I'm having a great time. I'm glad I came. I needed
a get away," she yelled and then smiled to herself as she ran her
fingers across the comforter, smoothing out the wrinkles.

"That's good. I just want you to be able to relax and have a
good time. Any time you feel like you need to come up here...you
just let me know," he yelled from the bathroom. Maya could still
hear him rubbing lotion onto his skin.

"Thanks...I'll keep that in mind."

"I'm going to take you to a nice place tonight. Are you
hungry?" he asked as he walked back into the bedroom with a
shiny chest and the same towel pressing against his body and much
of it. He looked over at Maya. She sat smoothing out his
comforter. Jelani thought she looked a little nervous.

"Yes. I'm *very* hungry," she responded as she turned her
huge brown eyes up to look over at him. Maya rose from the bed

and walked across the room to Jelani. His eyes widened as she got closer to him. Maya stood directly in front of him.

Jelani's mood changed from angelic to seductive. And as if he could read her mind, he bent down and kissed her on her mouth. He pushed his tongue in and out of her mouth and guided her head with his hand. His grip tightened and Maya hoped he didn't loosen her French roll. She could feel the towel grow from his large muscle and impending excitement. Maya stopped kissing Jelani long enough to look at him. She took a few deep breaths and gazed at how handsome his face was. She tilted her head to the side. She tried to read his mood before she tried her stunt.

"Do you really want to go out tonight?" she asked as she opened her leather coat. "Or do you want to stay in?" She dropped her coat and exposed her chiffon gown.

Jelani could not believe his eyes. Was it really time? Was she going to let him get a taste? Shit she looked good in that skimpy, little, see-through thing. He was ready. And damn near starving, for love.

"What's the matter?" she asked with a sly smile on her face. "Cat got your tongue?"

Jelani smiled as he reached for her.

"Nah, he ain't got my tongue. You do," he said as he kissed her hard and long.

Jelani pressed his hard midsection against Maya and began to grind. He gently kicked the coat out of his way and picked her up to carry her to the bed. Maya's body went limp as Jelani laid on top of her and forcefully kissed her mouth. His breathing became deep and low. Jelani slipped his hands up and down the sides of Maya's breasts. She took in a deep breath and arched her back. His calculated movements became faster and he touched and caressed her as if he were in a trance.

"Ummm...damn baby, I've been waiting to get some of you for a long time," he managed to say as he continued to kiss her neck, her breasts and then her belly.

Jelani's body stiffened as he ran his fingers across Maya's bare shoulders. Her skin was as soft as a baby's bottom. Jelani marveled at her perfect body, how the curves were all in the right places. There were no scars or marks on her smooth, caramel complexion. Jelani ran his fingertips across each groove of her body. His hands slid down the center of her chest to her G-string.

Slowly he slid the thin material to the side and inserted his fingers. Maya's eyes rolled into the back of her head and she grabbed Jelani's hand. Carefully he bent down and rubbed his face on the inside of her thigh. Jelani licked the inside of Maya's thighs, running up and down and stopping at her middle. He lifted his head to look at Maya's response. Her eyes were closed and she bit down on her bottom lip. She concentrated on the feeling and the potential feeling to come. He lifted his head up. His tongue circled around her belly button as he sucked and licked. Maya responded with soft moans and sighs. Jelani's tongue was sending her into a world of ecstasy. She gyrated her hips to the motion of Jelani's tongue. The room spun whenever Maya opened her eyes. She could not believe that Jelani was capable of producing such pleasure.

Emotions rushed through her veins. Sweet smelling air swept through the room from the opened window. Maya could hear the faint sounds of the waves crashing on the beach through Jelani's heavy breathing. Salt air frizzed her bangs and Jelani played with her French roll causing the pins to loosen and fall out of her hair. The thick mass spread out on the soft white pillowcase. Crisp, white sheets and Jelani's fluffy, white comforter were strung onto the floor. Sweat glistened on Jelani's forehead and chest and dripped down the side of his face. He had not yet removed the towel from his body. Maya waited in anticipation to receive his thick, hard muscle. His hands and tongue roamed her body like familiar long, lost friends. Jelani slipped his hands under Maya and lifted her butt into the air. He gently kissed the insides of her thighs again and licked his way up to her soft world. She could feel his warm, soft tongue make her moist. She grabbed the back of his head and pushed it toward her, rotating her hips in accordance with Jelani's lead. The moisture of his tongue caused Maya to erupt into convulsions.

After allowing Maya to enjoy the bountifulness of his tongue, Jelani picked her up and carried her across the room to retrieve a condom from the drawer. Maya wrapped her legs around Jelani's waist and held on to his neck. He carried her back to the bed and cocked his head to the side to get a better view of the gorgeous body in front of him. He bent down and rubbed his face in the soft brown hair between her legs. He inhaled and she knew that he could smell the sweet scent of the feminine spray. He then slipped on the protection and looked deep into her eyes. He wanted to make sure she wanted this as much as he did. He wanted her to look into his eyes and see what she was getting herself into. He was ready. Not only for her body but for her soul, for her commitment. He had seen enough of life to know that he was ready. And he wanted *her* to see that.

Jelani concentrated on the way her small nose sloped upward and how her full, thick lips were fixed in a pout. She closed her large brown eyes and he could see them roll to the back of her head. In this position, Maya seemed vulnerable, like she was not in control of her feelings. Jelani was used to women in this position. But this particular time was different for him. He watched her carefully. He liked the way she licked her lips and ran her tongue across her teeth when he entered into her body. Maya's body rocked up and down as Jelani held her tight and supported her as he controlled their entire motions. Maya dug her fingertips into Jelani's back, squeezing gently, yet viciously peeling at his top layers of skin. The feel of her nails in his back was an aphrodisiac for Jelani and he thrust faster.

Pumping. Grinding. Sweat. Maya called his name a few times and he responded. Their breathing intensified. Wet and hot, faster, now slower. Touching tender spots. Right there...no, don't move from that spot...yeah...yeah...okay...right...there...that feels good. Does it baby? Yeah. How does it feel to you? Yeah...Damn good. Wait...don't...move...faster...faster...faster oooh...ooooh...oooooh. Shit girl, you feel good as hell! Uhmmm baby you feel good too! Give it to me J.R! I want to feel all of you. Oooooh, yes! Uhmmmm...ooooh...ooooh...ahhhhhh! Ooooooh baby! Yes! Baby! Yes! Ooooooh...ooooooh...ooooh!

The scene on the bed was reminiscent of an opera symphony. High notes and low tunes echoed through the room. Souls connected and bodies were locked. Maya's breathy moans intensified Jelani's excitement. Rolling in unison, their sweat drenched bodies joined in pandemonium simultaneously. Jelani collapsed on top of Maya. She struggled to hold up his weight and she gave her last ounce of strength to support his physical shell. She could feel his breath on her neck as he fought to control his bodily functions. They both closed their eyes.

Waves could be heard crashing through the window. The salt air hung like a thick blanket wrapped with the sweet smell of sweat, musk, and sex. Emotions, feelings, and love clung to this blanket and both souls rested, regaining strength for the future.

Jelani awoke first. He had been up a few times since they'd fallen asleep. He wasn't much of a sleeper, never had been. Maya slept soundlessly in his bed. He smiled to himself as he watched her from his chair. He had worn the poor woman out. It had been such a long time since he'd had sex that he almost forgot about the power he held in his groin. From previous experience, he knew that she would be out for at least two or three hours. The moon shone on her face. Her angelic smile was unlike her previous distorted face of pleasure displayed during their sexual interlude. Jelani thought about the quality time that he'd spent with Maya. It was unlike that of any other woman he'd been with. He wondered how he would be able to tell her about his horrible past. He could imagine her face twisting up in disgust and anger.

Jelani sighed and looked out of the window. The waves were calming and peaceful. He hadn't planned to fall in love with Maya, it just happened. It was something about the way she smiled. Her contagious laughter spread with ease. Her genuine personality filled with compassion and a zest for life brightened his gloomiest days. The fire in her brown eyes illuminated life. He glanced back at Maya sleeping. His eyes followed the contours of her body under the white sheets, the motion of her breathing, the smooth color of her skin. The moon cast a gray-like shadow on the dips and curves, which danced off of her body. He reached over and rubbed the side of his hand across her cheek. He had waited so long to touch her smooth, caramel skin. He could taste her in his mouth even before he had the opportunity to perform the actual act.

Jelani rose from the chair tiptoed his way out of the room and down the stairs into the kitchen. He poured himself a glass of milk and headed into the living room. He hit number three on his C.D. player and waited for Najee to escort him to another place. Jelani turned the volume down low and relaxed in the reclining chair. He closed his eyes and let his mind wander. He thought of his mother and his family. He thought of Maya and how she made him feel. He thought of his past and his future. But most of all, he thought of love. Something he'd never had a chance to really experience. Of course he loved his family, dysfunctional as they were. But he'd never truly been in love and the feeling made him feel a little giddy. Time had flown since the car accident that introduced him to Maya. He finished his milk and held the empty glass in his lap. Jelani closed his eyes and rested...still thinking.

An hour later Maya came strolling down the stairs wrapped in one of Jelani's thin white sheets. Her face glowed and Jelani could have sworn that she was floating on air. Her hair was a mass of beautiful curls and Jelani resisted the urge to run up half the stairs and whisk her back to his room. When her eyes adjusted to the darkness of the room, he saw her smile in his direction. Damn, she was beautiful, Jelani thought as she gracefully moved closer to him.

"Hey, you. Why are you down here by yourself?" she asked, straddling over his large legs. He could see her erect nipples through the sheet that clung close to her body. And when she bent to kiss him, he felt her heart beating fast.

"I didn't want to wake you." He stared into her large brown eyes. They were hypnotizing with special mesmerizing powers. He took her hand and slipped his fingers in between hers. Slowly he began to lick each finger and suck them as if they had barbecue sauce on them.

"That's mighty noble of you." She smiled.

"It is isn't it?"

"I've really enjoyed myself this weekend."

"Good. I've enjoyed myself also. I mostly enjoyed you though."

She blushed.

"Let's go on the beach." Maya wrapped her arms around Jelani's neck. The sheet fell to her waist and Jelani licked his lips at the sight.

"It's a little chilly out there," he said still focusing on her breasts. Jelani smoothly reached around to the back of Maya's neck and sensually massaged her nape.

"And?" she responded rolling her head around allowing the good feeling to seep into her soul.

"And I wouldn't want you to catch a cold." Jelani pulled Maya closer to him. He flicked his tongue and rubbed around the tip of her nipples.

"Uhmmm, now we really need to go outside," she said standing up. She pulled his right arm trying to lead him to the door.

"Where you going without your clothes on?" Jelani pulled Maya's arms gently and hugged her tight. She wrestled out of his grasp and retrieved the sheet from the floor.

"Outside."

"No you're not. There's no telling who's out there."

Maya gave Jelani a wicked and seductive smile. Her eyes narrowed into dare-me slants. He'd seen this look from her before and knew that what he'd just said, went in one of her ears and out of the other.

"Let's go!" she yelled as she ran out of the front door, sheet flying behind her body. "Live a little J.R. Live a little! Whooo! Enjoy life Jelani!"

Maya ran through the sand onto the beach. The thin sheet still clung snugly to her glorious body. The closer to the water she got, the more loose the sheet seemed to become. Maya flung her arms in the air and allowed the sheet to fly away to the sand. She ran through the shallow part of the water and ducked her head under the water once it had reached waist high. Jelani watched from the doorway, amazed at her zesty personality. He smiled to himself. What was that saying? If you can't beat them, join them. Jelani stripped quickly down to his birthday suit and ran to meet Maya in the water. He was hoping that none of his neighbors were watching.

Maya came up for air and stood straight up in the water. When Jelani got close to her, she playfully splashed water at him and tried to swim away. Jelani grabbed her and dunked her head under the water and then pulled her quickly out of the water. She squirted water into Jelani's face through her hands. He wiped his face with the back of his hand and splashed her back. They played water games until Maya accidentally brushed her legs against Jelani's growing muscle.

Jelani grabbed her gently and pulled her close to him. Maya stopped fighting his attempts and gave in to his mouth. Jelani pressed his tongue deep into her throat. A tingling sensation welled up between her legs and she passionately kissed him back. Her hands found their way around his body and he held her tightly as she roamed her fingers up and down his back muscles. Jelani picked her up and carried her back to the beach. He laid her down on the sand and wildly kissed her. He could feel the sand gather under his knees. In a fluid motion, Jelani caressed Maya's right breast and licked her left breast. Maya moaned in delight and giggled when Jelani tickled her nipples.

"You wanna do this here?" Jelani asked, as he looked around to make sure nobody was looking.

"Yeah. Why you scared?"

"No. I just want to make sure you know what you're doing and what you're getting yourself into."

"Oh I know what I'm doing. And just what am I getting myself into?"

"You're getting yourself into some serious trouble," Jelani responded, kissing her chin and then her neck. He ran his fingers down the side of her face, leaving a trail of sand on her right cheek.

"What kind of trouble?" she inquired, smiling at how handsome he looked in the moonlight. Her *own* sexual prowess excited her.

"Something that you need to be aware of."

"Like what?"

"Like love."

"Love?" Maya sat up, forcing Jelani to get up. "Do you love me?"

"I'm definitely getting there."

"So that's what I need to look out for, love?"

"Yes love," Jelani forced her back down in the sand and began kissing her again.

Maya allowed Jelani to take her heart. She purred like a meticulous feline as she slowly moved her body back and forth, awaiting the impending thrust of the ever-growing muscle. Maya's soft, low purr emanating from her chest only heightened Jelani's arousal. He kissed her neck, her ears, her nose, and her breasts. Maya softly moaned and Jelani could tell that she was ready for him. He slowly entered her walls of paradise and rocked in unison with her body. Sweat formed around Jelani's mustache.

The second time was much better than the first time and he found himself falling in love with Maya all over again. He felt small grains of sand in between his buttocks as a surge of energy ran through his body and he began to pump faster. Maya's loud moans inspired Jelani to perform his best. He rocked and she rolled. Both enjoying the feeling of each other's bodies, until a surge of orgasmic power crept up on both of them.

I'M INNOCENT!

Tension in the small office cracked through the air like a whip. The air was so thick that one would need a knife to cut through the frowns and wrinkled brows. Senida looked over at Mandla, who concentrated on the words of Mr. Mortin and Mr. Bochamp. He seemed absorbed in what the two men were discussing. Although Senida was supposed to be just as absorbed, she couldn't stop thinking about Mandla and the look on his face that night. Soon they would be moving from the small office, back into the courtroom, where Senida would have to advert her mind and give undivided attention to Mr. Mortin and his case. The case was open and shut but Senida lacked the confidence that spawned within her earlier that week. She could not believe the effect that men had on her personal and professional life. She thought for sure, that she was able to separate the two, until she met Mandla. She hated herself for allowing him to invade her thoughts every minute of the day. His presence stifled her ability to think on her toes.

"Personally I'm tired of being drug in and out of court. We've been at it for two weeks now. It should be open and shut. Just like that," Mr. Bochamp stated, tossing his pen on the desk. He was obviously disgruntled.

"I understand," Senida started.

"I don't think you do Ms. Johnson. I am aware of your abilities and what I've seen in this courtroom does not display your capabilities at all. You are on this case by default as it is. Smithers recommended you as one of their best attorneys. So far, I haven't seen that attorney. I don't know what personal ties you have to this case or to Mr. Mortin but all I know is if you don't get it together out their in that courtroom, I won't be giving you good reports. Do you understand *now*?"

"Yes."

"Our job is to defend our clients. You still have yet to do that. And truthfully I'm getting tired of coming down here. Now please Ms. Johnson, regroup. I have faith in your abilities as a defender of Mr. Mortin. And I'm sure that Smithers does also or they wouldn't have recommended you for the case." Mr. Bochamp stood and left the office.

Before court was back in session, Senida excused herself to go to the restroom. Inside, she applied more lipstick and touched up her eyeliner and face powder. She ran her fingers through her short-cropped hair and looked directly into the mirror.

"You can do this. Quit worrying about Mandla and do your job," she said to the reflection.

The judge listened to the plaintiff and the defendant. Each lawyer had a turn to appeal to the jury. The people in the audience listened intensely as Daphnee Latimore gave a teary statement about how Mr. Mortin fondled and exploited her in the workplace. The judge seemed unmoved, keeping a straight face throughout Ms. Latimore's testimony. The jury, consisting of mostly women, seemed to be moved by the very attractive and persuasive Daphnee. Senida flipped through her notes and jotted down a few statements that Daphnee mentioned. Occasionally, she would look back to see if Mandla was paying attention. His primary focus was the judge and the other lawyer. He watched the skillful mastery of manipulation turn the case into a horrific scene of jury appealment.

During Senida's chance to question Daphnee Latimore, she paced back and forth in front of the stand. Her face was hard and stern. She concentrated with every inch of muscle in her body and decided that she would win this case for Mr. Mortin because she felt without a shadow of a doubt that Mr. Mortin was innocent. However, Daphnee was very convincing to the predominately female jury and the audience whose hearts went out to her. Senida brought up the points about Mr. Mortin's left arm being paralyzed and the high-backed chairs. But Daphnee had done her research also. She knew about the left arm and the chairs. She wiped her eyes with her pink handkerchief and put one hand to her mouth as if she couldn't control herself. She'd worn a very innocent looking pink dress, which went way below the knees and high up to her neck. Her curves were hidden from the naked eye. Her make-up was light. Her hair pulled back into a neat ponytail. She even had the nerve to wear some fake glasses, Senida thought.

Daphnee continued to cry when Senida interrogated her. She dabbed here and there until she had to pull out another handkerchief. Senida did not go easy on her. But Miss Daphnee was sharp. She told the jury that it could have been his right hand, she was so shaken up that maybe she forgot.

Senida gave the case her best shot, but in the end, the jury found Mr. Mortin guilty. She'd lost the case. Senida's heart sank into her stomach. She steadied herself against the table as the audience began filing out of the courtroom. She looked over at Daphnee who was smiling and hugging her lawyer and a few of her friends. Mandla stood and was headed towards the door when they made eye contact. Her pleading eyes were much too much for him to endure, so he continued to the lobby. Mr. Mortin lowered his head as the officers placed handcuffs around his small wrists. He looked at Senida with pleading eyes.

"You do believe that I'm innocent? I'm innocent."

"Yes, Mr. Mortin. I do. Don't worry, we'll get you out of there soon." She managed a quick smile. He was escorted out. Mr. Mortin's son, George Mortin approached Senida in a huffy manner.

"I can't believe you let my father go to jail. What kind of lawyer are you? It was an open and shut case and you weren't even performing well enough to win such a simple case." He spat his words with venom. Senida felt beaten.

"Listen, Mr. Mortin. Here's my card. Call me first thing tomorrow morning and we'll work on a plan to get your father out of jail."

George snatched the card and shoved it into his pocket. "Like hell you will! We'll be looking for another attorney. *I* could have represented my father better." He briskly walked out of the courtroom.

Senida could not sit down fast enough on the hardwood chair. Her head ached. Not only did she lose the most important case of her career, but she could still possibly lose her job. And as far as her partnership possibilities, she could forget those. She slowly rose from her chair to head back to the office. The case was over which meant she could go home and sulk in private. She didn't want to go to the office, but she had no choice. She had to delegate duties to Mandla and Lacey, do follow-up work on the Mortin's case and prepare to get him out of jail. And since Mandla told her that he would be leaving in three weeks, to go to law school back in Washington, D.C., she had a few personal matters she wanted to discuss with him. She would swing by the office for about an hour and then go straight home and straight to bed.

*****

It felt good to be at home. Maya felt relaxed and calm. She decided to take the day off and pamper herself at home. She turned her ringer off after she checked her messages and heard Senida's frantic voice. Senida had gotten herself into more men trouble and Maya was not in the mood to deal with the drama. She was feeling so good from spending all of her spare time with Jelani that she didn't want to come down from her high. So she embellished. She ran a tub full of hot, steamy water and filled it with bubbles. Next, she lit candles throughout the bathroom and burned her favorite incense. She then took a carton of ice cream and ate out of the box while she soaked in the tub.

Since Jelani was out of town on business, she would be alone for another couple of days. He'd already called to let her know that he made it safely to the West Coast. He'd bought tickets for them to see the risqué musical *Cats* that was coming soon to the Fox Theater. Maya was thrilled considering that she'd never seen *Cats* but always wanted to go.

After her indulgence, Maya decided to call Darrell. He'd left a few messages over the weekend and she had been meaning to check up on him anyway. Darrell let the phone ring four times until the answering machine picked up.

"Hey Darrell it's me Maya, give me a call when..."

"Hello Maya?" Darrell snatched up the receiver and turned off the answering machine.

"Hey D. What's up?"

"Girl where have you been? I've been calling you for about a month now."

"I know. I'm sorry, I've been so busy."

"Busy?"

"What's up, everything okay?"

"Yeah. I was just thinking about you and wanted to see how you were doing."

"I'm fine." Maya dried herself with her towel.

"So who is he?"

"Who?"

"The man. Who is he?"

"Darrell, what are you talking about?"

"Any time you say you've been busy, it involves a man."

Maya laughed. He knew her all too well.

"I'll tell you about him later. How have *you* been?" She lotioned her body.

"Fine. Have you talked to your girl?"

"Senida? Not in a couple of days. Why?" Maya braced herself for bad news.

"She called me last night. She wants to get back together."

"Well Darrell. You two obviously still love each other. Are you going to give it another try?" Maya unwrapped her hair and sat down at her vanity table.

"Hell no." Silence. "At first I thought about it, but I decided against it. I've been dating lately so I've been meeting a lot of women who have appreciated my kindness. Plus...I found out that Senida was cheating on me when we were together."

Maya stopped brushing her hair. How did Darrell know? She didn't respond to his statement. She didn't know what she would say if he asked her about the affair. Although Senida was her best friend, Darrell was a close friend also. They'd all grown up together in California as children.

"Yeah, she was cheating on me almost the entire time we've been in Atlanta. The guy's name is Todd. Young mothafucka' too. Only twenty-two or three or something like that," Darrell continued.

Maya sat listening to Darrell ramble about what she already knew. She dared not interrupt him.

"His uncle is a good friend of mine. We've done some consulting work together and just in conversation her name came out of his mouth. Now Senida is not a common name, so I started inquiring about how he knew her. He said that his young nephew was messing with her. Ain't that about a bitch?"

"Damn," was all Maya could say.

"So that was the straw that broke the camel's back. I gave

her plenty of times to confess since we've been separated and she won't admit to nothing."

"Well Darrell..." Maya started carefully. "Of course she won't admit to something like that because she knows that she's wrong."

"So are you saying that she really did have an affair while we were together?"

"Uhhhh..."

"Why else would she feel bad if she didn't do it? Was she cheating on me?"

"Darrell...I'm not saying that...I'm"

"Well you tell her when you see her, that..."

"...No Darrell. I'm not getting in the middle of this. You call her and let her know exactly how you feel. You two need to work this thing out. I love both of you and I'm not trying to get stuck in the middle. It's not fair to me."

Darrell thought for a moment.

"You're right. I don't want to bring you into this craziness. So let's switch subjects. Where have you been this weekend?"

Phew! Maya smiled. She picked her brush back up and continued to brush through her damp hair.

"Florida."

"Florida? How was it?"

"It was won-der-ful."

"You went with a man, hunh?"

"Yes, it was with a man. And Darrell, I really like this one."

"You actually like *one* man. I mean just one?" he teased.

"He's great."

"And what does he do for a living?"

Maya shifted her weight. She stood and walked into her kitchen.

"He told me that he invested in housing or something like that."

"Housing? That's a good business to be in. Real estate. What's his name?"

"Jelani Ransom." Maya put her teakettle on the stove.

"Jelani Ransom?" Darrell thought for a minute. "Hummmm."

"What's that for?"

"What does this Jelani Ransom look like?"

"Fine."

"Maya."

"Okay, okay," she laughed.

"Do people call him J.R.?" he continued.

"Yeah, how did you know?"

"I wonder if it's the same one."

"What, Darrell? Spit it out."

"Is he from Atlanta?"

"Yeah."

"'Bout my height, my color?"

"Yeah. Darrell *spit it out*."

"He plays professional football."

"Football? Are you sure?"

"Positive. Jelani is not a common name. You're dating Jelani Ransom?"

"Yes."

"Umm."

"What?"

"The guy has a bad reputation. You don't remember reading about him a few years ago?"

"No. Bad reputation?" Maya took the teakettle off of the stove and turned the fire out.

"He's a great player but the boy's been in a lot of trouble with the law. Just a few years ago."

"A football player?" Maya could not believe her ears. Darrell couldn't be serious. No wonder he could afford to buy her all of those expensive gifts. No wonder he was so secretive about his family and what he did for a living. He lied to her. Their whole relationship was based on a lie. Her mouth hung open in disbelief.

"What type of trouble Darrell?"

"Mostly drugs, beating up women. He used to be a real partygoer. Was in the newspaper all of the time, on the news. He has a lot of family problems too. Why didn't you tell me earlier that you were dating him?"

"I don't know."

"Well did he try anything while you guys were in Florida?"

"No. What else have you heard about him?"

"I haven't heard anything bad about him in the last year or

so. I only heard that he was trying to turn his life around. I played against him a couple of times in college. He's a cool brotha. He just has a lot of problems. You might want to be careful. I take it he's on the West Coast right now?"

"Yeah. How'd you know?"

"'Cause he played earlier today and they have another game coming up in New York. Maya just be careful, *very* careful."

"Yeah. Okay. Thanks. I will." Maya didn't feel too well anymore.

"I hate to be the one to tell you the bad news."

"It's not your fault, Darrell."

"He didn't tell you about his past?"

"No."

"What are you going to do now?"

"I don't know. What do you think I should do?"

"Leave him alone."

"That's what I was thinking."

"Well, where did you guys meet?"

"He was the one that ran into me when I had my car accident."

"He's the one from the accident?"

"Yes. Look Darrell, I'm gonna go now I'll call you tomorrow."

"Okay little sister. You take care of yourself. Bye."

Maya sat perplexed. She couldn't believe that Jelani had such a horrible past. How could she fall in love with a person that beat women? He seemed so gentle and safe. He seemed like the perfect man.

"I can't believe he lied to me," she said out loud. "He lied to me."

CONFESSIONS

"Yes! I knew my baby would come back to me!" Mrs. Jackson yelled into the phone.

"Ma, please." Mandla held the phone tight to his ear.

"Lord knows that I've prayed for you to come home. And I know you've been working hard to get into law school. Baby both our prayers have been answered. Now you can go to school here and still live with us." Mandla's mother was as excited as he'd imagined she would be.

"Yeah, I know."

"What about your job?"

"I've already talked to Dr. Cardell. He told me it was okay since I've been accepted. The only problem is that I won't be getting those last paychecks for those months."

"It's okay. With the Lord's help we gon' find a way."

"I'm going to leave my furniture here with Todd along with some other things. He said he would sell some of it for me."

"Do you think you gon' miss Atlanta?"

Mandla thought for a minute at his mother's question. He shook his head. "Nah, not much. I'll miss Todd. But I'll be back to visit him."

"Well, we will be at the airport to pick you up. I gotta get out of here. Little man has a doctor's appointment."

"Okay ma. I love you."

"I love you too baby. Talk to you later."

Mandla stuffed as many clothes into the suitcase as he could. When he tried to fit a few pairs of shoes in it, the suitcase would not close. He sighed and looked around to see how much more packing he had to do. There was still at least a week's worth of stuff that needed to be boxed, shipped, sold, given away, and packed. He looked at his watch. Senida would be over in three hours. He didn't want to talk to her, but decided that since he was leaving for good, he would allow her to speak her peace. He told himself that when she came over, he would not look at her curves. They were too dangerous, and would only get him into trouble. But since he had been working those long hard hours on the Mortin case, he didn't have time for other women. Usually he would go to work, research, stay at the office late, and come home in enough time for his body to give in on the couch. Mandla sat on the suitcase and snapped the two buttons on the side. He sat there for a minute, thinking of his short stay in Atlanta.

Senida pushed down on the pedal hard. She knew that she was going over the speed limit. But she was in a hurry to get to Mandla's house, before she forgot everything that she wanted to say to him. She didn't think that he would ever talk to her and when he agreed to let her come by, she hopped in her car and sped down the streets. Interstate 75/85 was congested so she tried to take Peachtree Street as far as she could. It had rained earlier that day and she prayed that if she had to stop suddenly she would be able to do so.

At the red light, Senida turned the radio up. There was an accident on Interstate 75/85 North, at Wesley Chapel and on Interstate 285. She was glad that she decided to take the street. Before she turned down Mandla's street, she made a left and stopped at the little gas station on the corner. She bought a yellow rose, which signified friendship. Senida parked her car along the street and slowly walked up to the apartment building. Her nerves made her heart pound and her knees shake. She couldn't believe that a twenty-two year old could do this to her. But somewhere in between the office, the courtroom, and the sheets, she'd fallen for him. Now her mission was to convince him that there was nothing *really* going on between her and Todd, that bastard.

Mandla answered the door, sweating. Senida could tell that he had been doing some type of physical work. He wiped his mouth with the bottom of his T-shirt and moved aside for her to enter. He didn't smile or give her a hug or a kiss like he usually did. Senida pulled the rose from behind her back and held it out to him. Mandla stood there looking at the rose and then shut the door and walked back into the living room. Senida just put the rose on one of the boxes near the door and followed him.

"So what did you need to talk about?" he asked as he sat down on the couch.

"I...I... wanted to talk about what happened that night at your party."

Silence. Mandla raised his eyebrows but did not speak.

"I'm sorry for the commotion. And I'm sorry that..."

"That I found out that you were sleeping with my potna?"

"Yes, I mean no. I'm sorry that you had to find out that way. Listen Mandla, there was nothing really going on with me and Todd. It was more like a misunderstanding."

"You were sleeping with him and cheating on your man. So you were sleeping with two men at one time. And your nasty ass suckered me into that fucked up love triangle."

"I'm sorry, it wasn't what you thought. Yes, I cheated on Darrell. And yes I slept with Todd. But so what? You've never slept with more than one woman?" Senida fought back tears as her anger made her nose flare. Mandla sat cool on the couch acting as if nothing was bothering him. He hadn't raised his voice or shown any emotions. "I was desperate at the time. Can you forgive me? I really do care for you and I enjoyed the times that we've spent together. Why can't we just let the past be that...the past?"

Mandla sat with his legs gaped open and his elbows resting on his thighs. He did not respond.

"Mandla. I'm sorry." Senida allowed one tear to fall for effect.

"Yeah, you sorry alright."

"Please, Mandla. I thought we were better than that?"

"We were! Don't forget Senida, it was you who was skeezing around. So anything that happened between us, you can *blame it on yourself.*"

"But I'm here now, trying to make it better. I want this to work. I want to at least remain friends. And then maybe later we can move back to the way we were before."

"I don't think we could ever move back into that position."

"But Mandla. I said I was sorry."

"It doesn't matter now anyway. I'm leaving. So you might as well just let it go. I'll forget about it and you forget about it and we'll move on with our lives." He stood. "Is that all you came over here to say? 'Cause I got some packing to do."

She wasn't saying anything that he wanted to hear. All that fake drama shit and the one tear. Mandla wasn't falling for that. He was going back home where the women were real. He knew of a few women that were trying to get with him before he left and they would definitely be trying now that he was going to law school. He'd have to beat them off with a bat.

Senida stood and walked in front of Mandla as he started for the door. Suddenly Senida turned in a frenzy and flung her arms around Mandla's chest. He pushed her off of him and stepped back.

"What the hell is wrong with you?" he yelled.

"I can't lose you Mandla. I can't lose another man. Please. I've lost Darrell, and...And I've lost Todd. I can't lose you. I need you. Please. I need you," she pleaded as she held tight to his shirt with her fists.

"You *need* help," Mandla said as he tried to pull her tight grip off of his shirt.

"But I told you that I was sorry. I've proven to you that I care. And I do."

"Look, I ain't got time for this. Just forget it. Forget that we ever existed. You fucked up and I had to get rid of you. It's as simple as that. Now get over it."

"How dare you get rid of me? You need me too. I can't believe that I allowed your young ass to trick me like this. You and Todd knew all along what was going on."

Senida cried hysterically. She did not look like the same woman that had poise and class in the law office. This was probably what Todd was talking about. Senida held on tight as Mandla yanked her fingers open and held her by both of her forearms. She was still crying, loud.

"I knew I shouldn't have messed with you young fools! You'll regret this!" she yelled.

Mandla pushed her and was about to shut the door when she reached out and slapped him. In one quick reflex, Mandla reached out and hit her square in her jaw. She stumbled and grabbed her mouth as she cried out louder. He could not believe that he hit her. He'd never hit a woman before. Then again, he'd never been hit by a woman before either. He reached out to stop her from stumbling and she pulled away running through his lobby out to her car. Before he could reach her she was gone down the street in the burgundy Honda Accord.

Mandla felt bad. His mother had taught him to never hit a woman: and he never did. Mandla looked around to see if any of his neighbors had seen. Nobody came out of their apartments, so he went back into his apartment and closed the door. Inside, he sat on the couch and waited for Todd to come and take some boxes to his place. As he sat, he thought about his experiences in Atlanta. He couldn't wait to get back to D.C. That plane couldn't come quick enough.

*****

"Hey sweetheart, did you miss me?" Jelani's voice was shady through his cell phone.

"How was the game?"

Silence.

"Jelani, why didn't you tell me?" Maya was the angriest she'd ever been with him.

Jelani's heart started beating faster than he could handle. He knew she would find out eventually. He'd hoped that she would have fallen in love with him before she had a chance to find out.

"Tell you what, Maya?"

"About your record. About the arrests. About the drugs and the women and the abuse, Jelani. The abuse...why didn't you tell me about all of that?"

"I wanted you to give me a fair chance. If I had told you about my past, would you have gone out with me?"

"A fair chance? Hell you didn't give me a fair chance. You didn't let me decide if I wanted to date you."

"Maya listen...If you knew that I was a football player with a past would you still have dated me?"

"Hell no! And it's not the fact that you're a football player...it's the fact that you lied to me. You lied to me for the past few months. Something told me not to trust your ass. And then come to find out that you beat women. I don't play no shit like that! I don't know what the hell you thought this was going to be," she spewed in the phone.

"I don't beat women..."

"That's not what all of the newspapers said. You were arrested for drug abuse, woman abuse. How could you Jelani? You lied to me. I can't believe that you used to be a drug addict and a woman abuser!"

"Where are you getting all of this shit from?"

"From a reliable source. Are you denying it?"

"Listen Maya...I've changed."

"Are you denying it?!" Maya yelled.

"Denying what? That I have a fucked up past? No I'm not denying that. But I'm not living that past anymore. I don't do those things anymore. I've..."

"I don't give a damn what you do anymore because it doesn't even concern me anymore. I don't ever want to see you again. I trusted you *and* I cared for you. And how do you repay me? By lying! I should have known something was up with you. I can't believe that I fell for your shit! Well J.R. you can kiss my ass!"

Maya slammed the phone into its cradle with as much force as she could find in her body. The phone chimed and fell to the floor. She kicked the phone across the room and began to cry. It was the first time since she'd heard the news about Jelani. Her heart cracked in a thousand places. She threw herself onto her couch and sobbed into the cushions. Why was love so hard to deal with? She'd finally found someone she could love and he turned out to be one of the biggest losers she had ever dated. Life was hell. Right when you're feeling good, it comes right along and pulls the rug right from under your feet.

Her phone let out a loud interrupted dial tone, letting Maya know that her phone was off of the hook. She walked back over to the stand where the phone lay at the bottom, placed the receiver onto its cradle and turned off the ringer. Just then her answering machine picked up.

"Maya...Maya...Please pick up the phone. Maya please. I need to talk to you. Maya pick up the phone! Look Maya I really want to talk to you. I've changed. I haven't acted that way in over two years. All...I need...is for...you...to let...me...explain." Jelani's voice broke up on his cell phone. It cut off.

Maya sat staring at the answering machine. No sooner did Jelani's voice record, did the answering machine click again.

"Maya pick up the phone. Maya this is hard enough for

me. Just let me explain. Maya pick up the phone shit! Stop playing around! Fuck! Pick up the phone Maya. I know you're there, so just pick up so I can talk to you. Look I care a lot about you. I wouldn't hit you, now pick up so we can talk. Damn! What the fuck am I supposed to say to you, huh? I love you? Well I do. I care about you? Well I do. Pick up the phone Maya so we can work this out." Silence. Jelani sighed into the phone. He was silent for a minute. Maya could tell he was getting angry.

"Well if you want to play these childish games then fuck it!" he yelled as he clicked off his cell phone.

Maya wiped her eyes and brushed the curls from her face. She slowly walked into her bedroom and sat on the floor with her back against the foot of the bed. She cried. Her heart poured out all of its feelings and emotions into her tear ducts and they ran down her face and fell onto the carpet. Her soul ached. She desperately needed to talk to someone but didn't know who. Senida was busy with her own men problems and Aunt Setty was a little too old to know about dating in the nineties. Maya suddenly felt alone. She hadn't realized how much time and energy she had spent with Jelani. And although she vowed to never see him again, she felt a loss...a void. One that would take another lifetime to fill.

SPILLING GUTS

"My plane leaves at 9:10 a.m.," Maya said to Aunt Setty. "I'm taking a cab from the Oakland Airport okay?"

"All right baby. I'ma make a big ole' country style dinner for you. Now what time you 'spose to be getting here?"

"I'll be there at four thirty-five. I have a layover in Denver."

"Okay. Aintee'll see you tomorrow."

When Maya placed the phone in the cradle, the doorbell rang. She looked at her clock. It was nine forty at night. She wasn't expecting anyone. She quietly and slowly walked to her door.

Jelani stood staring at Maya through the screen door. Her expression revealed to him that maybe he shouldn't have come. She was gorgeous and he regretted the terrible things she'd probably heard about him. And the terrible things he'd said to her. He could tell that she was in the middle of packing because she held undergarments and other clothing in her arms. He watched as she threw the things onto the love seat. But she still did not say anything, just stood there like she'd seen a ghost.

"Can I come in to talk to you?" he said calmly.

"No," she replied shaking her head slowly from side to side.

"Maya please. I don't normally beg, but girl you been having me beg since I've met you." He tried to crack a weak smile but Maya's emotions did not change from her terrified look. She'd expected him to call but she didn't expect for Jelani to show up at her front door.

"What do you want?"

"I want to talk to you."

"You can talk to my answering machine."

Maya motioned to close the door and Jelani reached out and yanked on the screen door, knocking the little hook from the wall. Maya's shocked expression terrified Jelani.

"Maya, baby I just want to talk to you. I would never hurt you."

Maya walked backwards into the living room.

"Jelani if you touch me I'll scream."

Jelani stopped in the middle of the living room. He sensed that he shouldn't go any further.

"Maya please. Let me explain." He had to let her know how he felt. He had to defend himself from what she'd heard. He couldn't let her leave the state thinking that he was some sort of monster. He wasn't. And he truly believed that she knew that he would never hurt her.

"Explain what?" she yelled. "Explain that you lied to me. That you abuse women?"

"That's the old Jelani. I've changed. And I really didn't lie to you. I just wanted you to get a chance to know me, so you could realize that I'm different now."

"Different from who? The rest of those womanizing motherfuckers! All of you football players are the same. You're looking for groupies! Well I'm not the one! You need to go find one that's going to let you push 'em around. 'Cause I swear Jelani, if you ever hit me, you'll regret it!"

Jelani put his hands down and lowered his head. He'd hoped it wouldn't come to this. He actually thought that he loved Maya. And that was not something easy for him to say or feel. Jelani took a few steps towards Maya and she let out an ear-piercing scream that could have awakened the dead. Jelani, shocked, reached for her to keep her quiet. He didn't want the neighbors to call the cops. Then he would be right where he started. All his hard work flushed down the drain.

He grabbed her arm firmly but did not hurt her. Maya stopped screaming long enough to look at him. He could feel the fear pump through her veins as he held on to her arm. Her eyes were large and round, larger than normal. He didn't want to scare her. He didn't want to hurt Maya the way he'd hurt the other women in his life. He cared for Maya. Jelani didn't want her to be afraid of him. But he could not let go of her. He didn't want her to run. He didn't want her to hide. He didn't want her to scream again. He wanted her to see *him,* for who he was, not who he *used* to be. He'd worked too hard to get to the point where he was now. He had to make her understand without her being afraid of him.

"Please Maya." His pleading became a soft whimper. "I care about you. I want to sit and explain what went on in my life to make me do the things that I used to do. But I assure you that I am a different person. Please. I'm begging. At least give me the opportunity to explain...and if you still don't want to see me, then I'll be heartbroken but I'll understand...please?"

Jelani's expression soothed Maya despite his having a firm grip on her arm. His eyes revealed soft emotions. She saw a little boy when she looked into his eyes. He guided her to the couch still holding firmly onto her arm. He sat down gently pulling her down onto the couch next to him. Jelani looked longingly into her eyes and took a deep breath.

"A few years ago I was arrested, repeatedly for abuse...drug abuse and battery..."

He let go of her arm and put his hands together, intertwining his fingers. After what seemed like hours, Jelani continued his story.

"...I partied, hard and long with my teammates. There was always alcohol, weed, coke, and always plenty of groupies..."

Maya sat in silence waiting for him to continue.

"All my life, I watched my father beat my mother. I never cared that he beat the shit out of me but he used to hurt my mother...bad...I remember wanting to kill him. He was my father and I loved him, but I hated him."

Jelani rang his hands, breathing slowly and evenly as if trying to control the thoughts. He was silent for a moment. Maya could see the expression on his face change with every sentence.

"She tried her damnedest to hide it from me, the black eyes, the swollen lips. She would comfort me and tell me that I was her special little man. She tried so hard to protect me. She would try to hide the bruises with make-up. I knew she didn't wear that much make-up unless she'd got into a fight with my father."

Jelani's mind drifted back to when he was five years old.

He squeezed his eyes tight as if trying to forget a bad memory. Maya watched him, but dared not say a word. He could see his mother's face. Blood was dripping from the corner of her mouth. She was holding her left eye and tears were squeezing through her cupped hand. Her long hair was crumpled about her head and she sniffed and dabbed at the blood coming from her nose. She cowered in the corner of the kitchen. Jelani could remember seeing her from this angle. He was as tall as she was bent on her knees. His father's loud voice boomed out at her as he slammed the door behind him. His mother noticed Jelani standing and hiding behind the door and briskly scooped him up assuring him that everything was going to be all right, as she kissed him and wiped away his tears with her blood stained hand. She promised to bake him some chocolate chip cookies for being such a brave little boy as soon as she cleaned herself up.

"I loved my mother...she was the only thing I had in this world," he said breaking out of the spell. "She was the only person that understood me. I didn't have no real brothers or sisters, no grandparents, and certainly no father. My family didn't care about a damn thing. They never came around. My older sisters were too busy getting high and pregnant."

"What about Donnie?" Maya whispered.

"I didn't meet Donnie until we were both teenagers. While I was growing up, my mother was the only one who had a heart. She was the only one who cared."

He stopped talking long enough to look at Maya. He wanted to read her expressions but could still only see fear in her eyes.

"When I grew up, I only knew how to deal with women in one way. And once I started playing pro ball...I didn't see them as humans. By watching my father, I learned that women deserved to be hurt. But when that motherfucker..."

Jelani stopped. He did not look at Maya. He did not ring his hands. He was spaced out from his own thoughts.

"But when that motherfucker killed her...I knew it was time for me to change. There was no way in the world that I would end up like him. No way that I would even think of him as my father."

A single tear slid down Jelani's cheek. Maya watched it as it slowly glided down around his chin. Her fear superseded her urge to wipe the tear from his face. She remained motionless.

"All throughout my life he caused my mother pain. He hit her and beat her and caused her pain. He made her life a living hell. Until one day he hit her so hard...he killed her. He took the only person that I cared about away from me. He killed her and I lost my whole world. He made me want to kill him." Jelani paused and Maya could see his face change from sorrow to rage.

"And do you know what that motherfucker said? Do you know what he said to me when I asked him why he did it? When I asked him, *why* he killed my mother?"

Jelani turned abruptly towards Maya, taking her off guard and scaring her slightly. She could see anger and hatred in his eyes. Of the months that she'd known Jelani, Maya could not remember ever seeing such rage form in his body. His gentle and caring body turned into a furious body of spit and fire, blood and tears.

"That motherfucker said I was just like him. I'll be damned if I ever end up like him!" Jelani punched the air with his right fist as more tears streamed from his eyes. His lips were pursed tight and the large veins in his neck bulged out uncontrollably. His red, bloodshot eyes were damp and he wiped at them with the back of his fists, which were still clenched tight.

"Ever since that day I decided that I would never end up like that motherfucker. I swore if it was the last thing I would do in life, I wasn't going to end up like him."

Jelani looked back down at the floor. Maya felt helpless as she sat transfixed. She didn't know what to say or do. She'd never thought that such a terrible secret was eating away at Jelani and it scared her silly. She watched silently at his hunched over body. He seemed tired as if he'd been fighting with his thoughts and emotions for an eternity. He didn't seem like the same arrogant Jelani that she'd met in the beginning, nor did he seem like the same caring Jelani that she'd grown to know and love. His posture mirrored a scared little boy. A man who never knew how to accept love or love himself. Maya watched him clutch his head in between his hands as he sat bent over forward. He seemed oblivious to where he was or whom he was with.

Maya thought of her own parents, she'd never thought of how lucky she was to have had such caring and loving parents until now. Although she'd lost them early in her life, she realized that her father adored her mother and vice versa. And between the two of them, they loved her unconditionally. She looked up at the ceiling as if she could see her mother and recited a small prayer to herself.

"Jelani, why didn't you tell me this from the beginning?" She tested by asking.

"Would you have gone out with me if I told you all of my family and personal problems? Would you have given me a fair chance to get to know you?" He lifted his head and concentrated on her expression. Maya looked down at the floor in thought.

"I didn't think so," he said when she did not respond. "I get so goddamned tired of people judging me for what I did in the past. I'm a changed man. Everyone is always talking about giving someone a second chance but nobody is willing to do it."

They sat in momentary silence. Maya was scared to move for fear of breaking Jelani's concentration. He sat unmoving, trying to calm himself. He knew Maya was scared and he did not want to scare her anymore than he already had. His intentions were not to scare her but to let her know how he felt and to make her understand him as a new person...a new man. Words swarmed through his head. He leaned back onto the couch and then as quickly, sat straight up. His eyes remained unmoved as he stared out into space. Maya waited. She didn't want to make any sudden moves. Jelani, eyes still fixed out in space, spoke without moving.

"So I started therapy." Silence. "At first all the guys on the team talked shit about me. Said I was getting soft 'cause I decided to stop drinking, smoking weed, doing coke, and I stopped kicking it with them nasty ass groupies." Jelani looked up at the ceiling. "It's been two years going on three since I been in therapy. I've learned to control my temper. I've learned how to communicate with women better. Since I've been going to Dr. Carson, I've learned a lot. She was the one that told me to pursue you," he said looking at Maya from the corner of his eye.

"She told you to pursue me?"

"Yeah. Every since that day we got into that car accident...I knew that you were special. And that's part of the reason why I didn't tell you about my profession...or my past. I knew that if I gave you the chance to get to know me, Jelani, for the person that I am, that you would see that I *am* a good man."

Maya frowned and sat back on the couch. She couldn't think. There was too much for her to digest. A murder, a battered boy, drugs, media. It was a far cry from her quiet, little, artsy world.

"Why do you care what I think about you?" she finally responded.

"Because baby." He sighed. "I don't want you to leave here thinking I'm some kind of monster. I'm not. Don't you believe that everyone deserves a second chance?"

Maya could not think straight. Every muscle in her body tensed, waiting for flight. Her heart pumped a thousand miles a minute. She'd slowly fallen in love with Jelani but no matter how much she loved a man she always loved herself more. She looked at Jelani. His eyes were wide as if he was waiting for a response, but Maya had none. They sat until Jelani finally stood up and left. Before he walked out of the front door, he turned to her.

"Some things are best left untold. But you've always wanted to know about my family and now you know. I wanted to tell you when I was ready and not when I felt forced to. But just remember, I'm still the same man that you went and spent the weekend with in Florida. I'm still the man that's been coming around and spending nights with you and you with me. I'm still the same man that you've been kicking it with for the past few months. And I'm still the man that loves you. I want to work this out if we can. While you're gone, you think about that and I'll be here when you get back." He didn't look back, he didn't try to kiss her, he didn't try to touch her. He just left.

Maya cried. She cried the entire time she packed and even cried herself to sleep. Her plane was leaving in the morning and she had to get some rest. She didn't think she would have to deal with Jelani so soon. Her sandman came quickly that night as her soul was tired.

Maya stepped out of the front of her apartment building. Atlanta was cold. Winter was coming, soon. The cool, crisp air brisked through her wool sweater, chilling straight through to her bones. She shivered, rubbed her gloved hands together and pulled her coat tight. Atlanta's weather was too cold for Maya. Each time she filled her lungs, she could feel the cool air entering her chest. And each time she exhaled, a warm cloud of mist would emanate from her mouth and nose. Snow had fallen the night before and she hoped that this white slush would not interfere with her flight plans to California.

Tree leaves were heavily covered with the white flakes. The ground that was usually the color of brown and red was purely white. It was an unusually cold winter for Atlanta. The small, little creatures that scurried about in a constant rhythm were now buried deep in their burrows under ground where it was warm. She looked at her watch. It was still early. Her ride wouldn't pick her up for at least another hour. Maya enjoyed the crisp air as she deeply inhaled. Looking at the large white blanket that covered most of her block, she waved to Mr. Miller. He was out receiving his paper in his pajamas. Nobody else on the blocked seemed to be awake. Her neighborhood slept. The quietness and serene of the block calmed Maya.

A squirrel ran across the street and into the white bushes. Just as quickly, another ran out in the middle of the street and stopped. It twitched it's tail around and wrinkled it's nose. Maya could see the beady little eyes as they darted from left to right looking, for the other squirrel. Noticing movement in the bushes, the squirrel scampered the rest of the way to the bushes scaring the other squirrel out. Maya watched intently as the two squirrels jumped from the bushes, ran across a grass lot and scurried up a tree.

It reminded her of the times she spent with her father at the park. He would tell Maya that she could earn a dollar if she caught one of the many squirrels that ran amuck. He would yell for her to run faster, as he laughed at his daughter's light heartiness and determination. Although she would come close, Maya never won the dollar. But afterwards, her father would take her to McDonald's or to the little store at the city mall and buy her whatever she wanted. Then, the dollar didn't seem to matter much.

A breeze blew the thoughts of her father away and her thoughts darted back to Jelani and the night before. He had surprised her by dropping by her apartment. He had given her a whole new light on the situation that she was involved in. And this morning when her heart told her to do one thing and her mind told her to do another, she just shook her head vigorously and commenced to cleaning her apartment.

When the thoughts were too overpowering, she dressed and went to stand out in the cold, hoping that she would and *could* come to some resolution, soon. She did not want to take her problems home to California to Aunt Setty. She didn't even want to tell Senida what happened. She wanted to handle this "thing" by herself. She cared for Jelani deeply. Hell sometimes she really believed that she loved him. And that he loved her. She couldn't keep him off of her mind. She thought of him during the day and dreamed of him during the night. And when he was out of town...away playing football, she waited for him to return. And if that ain't love, then what is?

But all in all, Maya was scared. Scared to take a chance. Life was like a large checker game; you never knew when you would be jumped. And love was an even harder game...something like chess. Who knew when you would hear those dreadful words..."check mate?" Oh why did love have to be so complicated? She shifted her position as the snow was beginning to seep through her boots. But she didn't go into the house. She stood, thinking...of him. Of her. Of them. And there she stood in the cold, until her ride appeared to take her to the airport.

California. Sun, water, a cool breeze, and Maya. These were the kind of winters that she was used to having. Maya walked past the small shops on University Avenue in Berkeley, California. Her long, sexy legs were a sight to see, even on her small frame. She took quick glances at her reflection in the windows, smoothed at her hair and kept strutting. Her flight from Atlanta to Oakland was long but she finally made it to California safe and sound. Aunt Setty had waited up almost the entire morning for the yellow cab to pull into her driveway. And before Maya could put her bags down good, Aunt Setty was all over Maya, smothering her with kisses and hugs.

For the first three days, Maya stayed in the house with Aunt Setty, eating, laughing, and gossiping. They ordered Chinese food and pizza, much to Aunt Setty's dismay. She was used to an old fashion country meal. But Maya had convinced her not to cook for the first three days so they could spend the extra time together. Aunt Setty had asked a lot of questions about Senida and Darrell, about Maya's job, about the white boy Stephen, and of course about Jelani. Maya exposed everyone else's business but when

Aunt Setty asked about Jelani, Maya was short and straight to the point. Aunt Setty didn't mind. She just continued to ask more questions.

Now, nearly a week into her California trip, she was enjoying the sunshine and walking down University Avenue to pick up Aunt Setty from the hair salon. When Maya made her way to the shop, Aunt Setty was just getting out of the hairdresser's chair. Her hair was an attractive array of loose silver ringlets. They neatly bounced when Aunt Setty laughed. Her copper brown skin gleamed as she smiled. From the neck up, Aunt Setty was *glamorous*. Her wardrobe however, consisted of the same old rumpled, frumpy dress that she wore on her days out. Maya was determined to change that during her trip. She planned to take Aunt Setty to get her hair done, shopping, and to lunch. Maya looked over at Aunt Setty who waved and smiled at her while she stood in the lobby waiting. Her hair was glorious. One down and two to go thought Maya.

"Ready to go baby?" Aunt Setty asked as she hugged and kissed the hairdresser.

"Chile you need to let me put some streaks in your hair. It's so thick and pretty. I can make you look as good as Oprah," the hairdresser said touching Maya's hair.

"Thanks, but I think I'll keep it like this."

"Suit yourself. Bye Mizz Setty. I'll see you in two weeks," he said and switched off.

"Whew!" Aunt Setty laughed. "Don't mind ole' Antwoine. Folks say he got diabetes." Aunt Setty headed for the door.

"Diabetes?" Maya inquired.

"Yeah. Got a little sugar in his tank."

Maya laughed. But Aunt Setty was serious. That's what she'd heard a few people in the shop say. That Antwoine had sugar in his tank. So naturally, Aunt Setty thought of diabetes. Poor Antwoine, she would say.

"Where we gon' eat?" Aunt Setty clutched her large purse to her bosom.

"Cafe Valencia. It's an Italian restaurant."

"I don't know why you eat all dees crazy kinds of foods. We can get on home now and I can cook us up some good ole' cornbread and some oxtails."

"No thank you Aunt Setty," Maya responded as she hugged

her aunt. They were about to cross the street. "It's right up the street. We can walk. It's such a nice day."

"Sho' is, baby. Sho' is."

Familiar sounds of laughter and conversation floated across Cafe Valencia. Loud, rambunctious rolling from chests echoed throughout the restaurant. A vibrant lunch hour crowd filled the small cafe and spilled out onto the patio. Floor plants were delicately thrown into each corner, allowing the warm California breeze to creep its way through the people, kissing each one slightly on their cheeks. Aunt Setty's eyes lit up when they entered Cafe Valencia. Maya knew that she didn't get out much, except for bingo night.

"Dis here is a fancy place. I sho' shoulda worn my Sunday dress."

The hostess sat Aunt Setty and Maya, handed them menus, and left.

"She ain't gon' take our orders."

"No. She's the hostess. Our waitress will be here shortly."

"I sho' am glad you could make it out here. Aunt Setty miss ya."

"I miss you too Aunt Setty."

"Now when you 'sposed to do that work. You been here 'bout close to a week. And I ain't seen't you do no work. Don't let me git in the way a yo' work."

"I'm not. We start negotiations and biding tomorrow. I just wanted to spend as much time with you as I could before I actually had to work. So I came a few days early. Most of the other buyers aren't even here yet."

Maya studied her menu. She knew that she would probably have to order for her aunt.

"Hello ladies," the waitress said placing napkins onto the table. She was a tall lanky white woman with long brown sandy-colored hair. She looked like she could have been a student working her way through college. Aunt Setty smiled at her. "What can I get for you today?"

"I'll have the Sicilian special," Maya responded.

"And what would you like on your salad?"

"Ranch, please."

"And for you ma'am?" she asked Aunt Setty.

"What she got," Aunt Setty responded with a large smile

and pointed at Maya.

"She'll have the same thing but on her salad...what type of dressing Aunt Setty, blue cheese?" Maya asked her aunt.

"Oh no chile. Dat blue cheese don't too tough agree wit' me." The waitress smiled. "Let me git the same thang Maya got."

"And something to drink?"

"Water is fine." Maya answered. The waitress looked at Aunt Setty and she shook her head in agreement.

"Okay, sounds good. I'll be back shortly with your salads and drinks." The waitress disappeared behind a pair of double doors.

"You know ole' Margaret beat me at bingo last week?"

"Sounds like you're slipping."

Aunt Setty laughed. "Yeah, sounds like it. It's okay tho'. I'ma git her next week. I been practicing my quick draw hand."

"Aunt Setty what's a quick draw hand?"

"It's when I can grab da chip to put it on my sheet fasta dan Margaret."

"You and Margaret been friends for quite some time, huh?"

"Yeah. Been knowing Margaret 'bout forty some odd yearns. Speaking of friends. You say Senida and Darrell broke up?"

"Yeah. They're not together anymore. I never thought *that* would happen."

"Umm chile. An' you don't hear from dat doctor no mo'?"

"No."

"But you say you like dis Jamal person?"

"Jelani."

"Uh-huh."

"Yes, I do."

"Plan on gittin' married?"

"Aunt Setty!"

"What? Your ole' Aunt Setty know what's going on in today's society." Then Aunt Setty leaned over the table to whisper to Maya. "I ain't no virgin, ya know."

Maya laughed and Aunt Setty laughed with her.

"I doubt it."

"You ain't gittin' no younger."

"I know, I know."

The waitress brought out their salads and their water. Aunt

Setty blessed her food and so did Maya. They enjoyed each other's company.

"Yes, Lawd. I'm sho' glad you could make it out dis way Mizz Maya. Aunt Setty sho' did miss you. And I love you," she said in between bites of her salad.

Maya looked up from her plate and smiled. "I love you too Aunt Setty."

WHAT TA DO? WHAT TA DO?

Darrell looked good in his dark blue jeans and his sweater. He wore his glasses, something he rarely did. His face was stern, yet relaxed. He looked as though he had been sitting for a while. There was a small plate with remnants of chocolate cake in front of him and he sipped from a mug of hot coffee. From where Senida stood, he looked serene and calm. Just the way she wanted him to be. She couldn't believe that he agreed to meet her at the small cafe. It took a lot of coaxing and begging but she felt that it might be worth the effort. She slowly made her way to the side of the table and Darrell looked up at her. He didn't smile. He just nodded his head for her to sit down. As soon as Senida sat, she went into conversation.

"Hey." She tried to smile. "I'm glad you decided to meet me. Did you order something already? Everything is on me today."

"I had a piece of cake." His emotions did not change.

"So how have you been?"

"Cut to it, Senida."

"Okay. I miss you and I want to get back together."

Darrell drank from his mug. He looked straight ahead, avoiding Senida's eyes. He thought for a minute, letting the words digest into his brain. He couldn't believe she had this much gall.

"I don't think that's going to work."

"Are you seeing someone else?" she asked still focused on his eyes.

"As a matter of fact, yes. I'm dating. I have a few women friends that I go out with."

"Darrell. I know things didn't work out right for us. But I hope you know that I do love you. I've always loved you and I always will." Senida took her coat off and sat it beside her. She motioned for the waiter.

"Senida. You know that I've been nothing but good to you. But *you* were the one who made the decision to end our relationship."

"How? I said some mean things but I didn't think that they would end our relationship. I was mad at the time. You said some pretty mean things too but I didn't give up on us. I thought we were better than that."

"It wasn't the things that you said. It was the things that you did. The things that you did ended our relationship." He sipped from his mug. The waiter came over to the table and Senida ordered herself a cup of black coffee. She had a feeling this would be a long conversation. She watched Darrell as he stared at her intently. He watched each word form and fall out of her mouth. He was waiting for her to confess or say the wrong thing again. He was tired of her bullshit and was trying to keep his composure.

"What could I have done that was so bad? I loved you. I cared for you. We grew together Darrell. We've been knowing each other since we were little kids."

"What the hell?" Darrell stopped, took another sip of his coffee, and looked around the quiet room. "Senida, do you think I'm stupid? I know what's up. I know about Todd. I know that you've been fucking around on me."

"Darrell..."

"I know that you've been fucking other men because of my..." he looked around to see if anyone was listening. "...Because of my problem."

"Darrell. I would never..." Senida was stumped. How could he have possibly known about Todd?

"Don't play stupid. I'm tired of this shit. I gave you the best relationship I knew how to give. I bought you anything that you wanted. I tried to be a good man but you fucked all of that up."

Senida inhaled deeply. She had to choose her words carefully. The cat was out of the bag. She knew that if she admitted to her crime, there would be no way of reconciliation.

Darrell's veins were popping out of his neck, indicating that he would explode on contact.

"Darrell. I didn't cheat on you. Todd is someone that I know. He's a friend. Where are you getting this information from anyway?"

"Don't worry about all of that. I got the information and I know that it's true. My contact knew too much about my personal life. Personal business that only you and I should have known." He sipped more coffee. "You're lucky I don't reach over this table and slap the shit out of you. I've never been so embarrassed and humiliated in my whole life, and by someone that supposedly loved me."

"I do love you." Tears welled in Senida's eyes.

Senida could not believe that she was losing him all over again. She'd spun an evil web of deception, mistrust, and infidelity that had finally caught up with her and was beginning to suffocate and squeeze the life out of her soul. Her head became hot and she could feel her eyes swell. Her heart was beating a mile a minute. She had to think quickly, of what to say. Her future relationship with Darrell depended on how carefully she picked her next few words. She was sure that she could get him to see how much she loved him. He *had* to see how much she loved him. Sitting there in that booth in a public place crying like a big baby should prove to him that she loved him.

"Darrell. I would never intentionally hurt you. I love," she cried as she reached over the table and grabbed his arm. Coffee spilled out of the cup. Darrell grabbed and dabbed with the napkins sitting on the table.

"Senida. Now look what you've done," Darrell stood up trying to stop the coffee from falling from the table and onto his pants. People in the restaurant stopped eating long enough to look up and see the small commotion. The waiter came over with more napkins and began dabbing the table and the seat. Senida was still crying. She couldn't lose Darrell. He was her last hope.

"Darrell," she said even before the waiter left the table. "I love you. Please give us another chance. I promise, I won't fuck up any more. I need you in my life. You've been such an important part of me, I don't think that I could make it without you."

Darrell reached in his pocket and threw a five-dollar bill

onto the table. He was furious now. He turned to look at Senida who was crying uncontrollably and clutching his sweater. The other patrons were watching intently, most of them white people.

"Senida you messed up. If you needed me in your life, then you would have acted right then. But you had to be sleeping around with every Tom, Dick, and Todd. I'm tired. I tried to give you everything. I used to trust you but now I don't think I can trust you as far as I can throw your ass. You should have been thinking about this shit before."

"Please Darrell." Senida was still clutching his sweater as Darrell pulled her arms away. He'd never seen her act as outrageous as she was now. He was going home. He refused to let her embarrass him anymore. She'd done it with his friends, with his co-workers, and now she was doing it in public. He had a feeling he shouldn't have met her at the restaurant. He was surprised that Senida did not come prepared with some type of logical reasoning for her infidelity. He was sure that Maya would have told her by now that he knew of Todd. Darrell snatched Senida's fingers off of his sweater and left her in the restaurant. She quickly followed him out to the parking lot.

"Please Darrell!"

"Senida. You've made your choice. The way I feel right now can never be fixed. I've moved on with my life. I advise you to do the same." Darrell got into his SAAB and started his car. When he accelerated out of the parking lot, he saw her in his rearview mirror, walking slowly to her car with her hands over her face, crying.

*****

Jelani's Cascade mansion sat quietly. Only sounds of his clock ticking could be heard inside. The loud ticking vibrated through Donnie's head because he was aware of the time. He looked over at Jelani and then again at his watch. His brother had been in the house for three days straight. Donnie could tell that his break-up with Maya was bothering him. Even his game was off. He didn't look like the same J.R. that the fans came to see play.

Donnie had scanned the house when Jelani let him in. Clothes and papers were strewn on the floor. Dishes filled his kitchen sink and the carpet looked like it hadn't been vacuumed in a month. When Donnie asked Jelani about the cleaning lady, he responded by saying he gave her a three-week vacation with pay.

A small painting covered the large hole in the wall, but Donnie could see it anyway. He tried not to let his brother know that he knew of the hole but felt compelled to say nothing after Jelani made no mention of its presence. He also knew that Jelani had punched the wall out of frustration. He knew that Jelani was going through a lot when he came over to his house late one night with blood shot eyes. He allowed him to spend the night and the next day Jelani left early before anyone else in the house had awakened. Now a few days before Donnie's trip, he was comforting the very man that usually lent the shoulders to cry on.

"I don't know what the fuck to do Don. I told her about the family problems. You know I don't usually talk about that." Jelani was ringing his hands together as he bent his head over. He sat with his elbows resting on his thighs.

Donnie was seated comfortably in the reclining chair. Jelani's large, five-bedroom Atlanta house held a feeling of despair. Jelani looked over at the love seat in the opposite corner of the room. He remembered when he and Maya made love on the small sofa. Her legs were spread eagle, one against the wall and the other, wherever he would guide it. He remembered that the next night she'd told him that she loved him. Words that he never thought he would hear from her sweet lips. He could even remember her smell. A sweet, musky scent. Her hair was tousled from their frenzied episode of lovemaking.

"Have you talked to her since she's left?" Donnie finally asked after watching his brother sit in agony. He had to get home before Tressy did. He'd promised her that he would cook dinner tonight and he still had to pick up the twins from Tressy's mother's house. Donnie looked at his watch, trying not to be too obvious.

"Man. I haven't talked to her since that night that I went over there. Don, you should have seen her face." Jelani rubbed his hands down his face. That's when Donnie noticed how much older than usual Jelani was looking. His face was not clean-shaven. The midnight shadow was getting thick around the sides of his face. Jelani's hair was not the usual groomed cut. His fingernails were usually short and clean but tonight they were long and full of dirt. Donnie hated to see his brother in such a pitiful state, but he'd been like this for a few days.

"You need to contact her and try to reach her. Remember what you were telling me about Tressy? Well man, you need to hang in there like I did. I could tell that woman loves you. I saw it in her eyes when we all went to dinner that night. She couldn't stop looking at you. And man, I've never seen you happier. She's probably sitting around going through the same thing that you're going through. You need to call her. Don't you love her?"

Jelani looked up at his brother. His eyes were focused waiting for an answer.

"Yeah. Fuck yeah. I love her ass. I think about her all day *and* all night. I miss her when she's not lying in bed next to me. I miss her when we're not making love. I miss her touches and her smile. Man she's the mothafucking bomb. I do love her." Jelani stood as if he'd just realized something. "I do," he said.

"You need to call her man. She's probably sitting in California feeling the same way that you feel. I'd bet on it."

"I don't have her number."

"Potna. Didn't you get her address *and* phone number before, when she didn't want you to have it?"

"Yeah."

"Well what happened to that fighter spirit? You need to get off yo' ass and go get your woman. Is she worth fighting for?"

"Yeah."

"Well then what the hell are you waiting for?"

"She ain't gon' take me back Don. I lied to her. She's scared of me. I saw it in her eyes. She ain't gon' never talk to me again."

"She will. J.R. man, she loves you. I'm telling you I saw it. She probably just needs a little time to think and she'll come around."

"I don't know man..."

"Trust me. She's worth going after." Donnie stood and walked into the kitchen. "And as for your cleaning lady, tell her to get her ass back to work. I can't even find a clean glass." Donnie fumbled through the cabinets and found a small shot glass and a plastic cup. He took the plastic cup and poured himself a glass of red wine. "I'm telling you the truth. You the best thing that's happened to her and vice versa," Donnie responded as he sat next to Jelani on the couch. He gulped the wine in two gulps and looked at his watch.

"I know you got to go pick up the twins. I'll be all right. I'll hit you later at home."

"You sure? I could call Tressy's mother and tell her that I'm going to be late."

"Nah. I think I'm going to lie down for a minute. Maybe watch the game or something."

Donnie stood and Jelani waved his hand at him when he tried to put the glass in the kitchen.

"I'll get that. Don't worry about it."

Jelani walked Donnie to the door. Donnie turned to his brother. He could see the bags under Jelani's eyes and almost did not want to leave him. The more he looked at Jelani, the more he could see his father. Both of them resembled their father. Their strong defined jaw lines, their deep dark color, and the sturdy builds of their bodies were reminders of their father.

"Look, J.R. I've met Maya. I've kicked it with her. We've had conversations about you. She loves you. She's just hurt right now. Give her a little time and go after her. Love is difficult. I tried to tell you it wasn't always roses and football." He smiled and gave his brother a hug.

"Thanks man. I'll call you later."

Jelani sat in the black Mercedes Benz for at least forty minutes before he got out and rang the doorbell. He hadn't seen Sheila in a long time. He wasn't even sure that she would let him into her house. He looked at his watch. It was still early and he noticed that her car was parked in the driveway. Jelani walked to the porch. Everything seemed to be unchanged. Lights were on in the living room and Jelani assumed that she might be reading, which was her favorite pastime. Jelani leaned his body on the doorbell and knocked twice. He knew that she would know it was he when he knocked the way he did.

Sheila was beautiful. Her round hips and red lips were provoking and sensual. She reeked of sexuality. Her deep chocolate skin was almost as smooth as a newborn baby's. Jelani remembered when they met those many years ago. Sheila was young and impressionable. She'd left home at the age of seventeen and met Jelani when he was playing arena football. The young

Jelani fell instantly in lust with her soft curves and sweet face. Many nights he would taste her milky, smooth skin and ravish her in his fire.

Poor little Sheila lasted only a few months once the abuse began. Jelani had moved her into his condo and would do what he pleased. Although she left after the abuse started. She always held a special spot in her heart for Jelani. She realized back then that he had a problem, but she knew the soft side. She remembered when he would leave rose petals on their bed, or when he would buy her cards and roses just because, or when he surprised her with candlelight dinners. She missed that Jelani and knew that he was there most of the time. The other terrible Jelani came out when he'd been drinking or when he was hanging with the other guys from the football team.

Sheila spoke first when she opened the door and saw that it was Jelani. She did not look surprised or scared. She didn't move away from the door, she just gave Jelani a weak smile.

"Hello." Her lips were beautiful. Almost as perfect as Maya's lips, Jelani thought to himself.

"Hey."

"Long time no see."

Jelani gave a slight nod.

"I'm surprised to see you. What brings you around?"

"I was thinking about you. I just wanted to see you for awhile."

"You wanted to have sex, so you decided to look me up, huh?"

"Sheila, it's not like that. I just need a little company."

"Have you been drinking?"

"I had a beer. That's it."

"I thought you stopped?"

"Well I did. This was the first one I had in over two years."

"I'm proud."

"I needed to talk to someone of the female persuasion. And since my mother's not around."

"Yeah, I heard about that on the news a few years ago. I'm sorry."

"Thanks. Listen if this is a bad time, then I'll leave," he said as he realized that he was still standing on the porch and she was still standing inside of the house with the door partially cracked open.

"Jelani why did you come over here?"

"I just need to talk. But I'll leave." Jelani turned to walk down the steps. He made it to the bottom of the porch and onto the grass when he heard her open the door all the way.

"Wait. J.R. You can come in to talk. But just talk. Nothing else. Are you going to talk?"

"Yes," he said walking back up the steps.

"Just talk," she said to him again although she knew in her heart that she was trying to convince herself.

Sheila knew as soon as Jelani walked into her house that he would sit on her couch and start talking. Then she would see the large muscles bulging from underneath his shirt and his pants. His deep dark skin would entice her and those large hands would tease her as he rubbed up and down her back or her legs. She knew the game all too well. She knew and he knew that she could not resist him. But she let him in anyway. She let him in, closed and locked the door. There was no use in playing games; she knew what he needed tonight.

Sheila's house held a familiar feel. It seemed to Jelani that everything was still in the same order as the last time he was there. Outside of a few new items, statues, and paintings, the house was the same. Sheila had the same furniture; the two long leather couches that he'd bought her when they were together. The same dining set was in the kitchen and the same bedroom set that they'd shared so many years ago. The big canopy was a fantasy of Sheila's and she had begged Jelani to buy it for her. At first he was hesitant, but when he found how easy it was to tie her to the bed with velvet ropes, he enjoyed the bed sometimes more than she did.

"Jelani," Sheila sighed as she sat on the bed next to him. She didn't realize that they had made their way straight from the front door into the bedroom. And when she did realize, she couldn't understand how easily he could manipulate her. She carefully sat at least an arms distance from Jelani.

"Why do you do this to me?" she asked finally.

"Do what baby? I just needed to talk."

"Well we need to talk in the living room where we can concentrate." Sheila stood and began walking back into the living room. Jelani followed. She sat and he sat on the couch next to her.

"Now what's the matter J.R?"

"Not too much. I was just thinking about you. And I was in the neighborhood. And I decided to stop by." Jelani reached for her hand but she pulled away before he could touch her.

"You were in the neighborhood at this time of night and you were thinking about me?"

He nodded.

"And what were you thinking about?"

"How we used to be. How we could have been."

"Uh huh. That's all you were thinking about?"

"Just thinking mostly about you. How much I missed you and how good you were to me. The good ole' days, when we used to be in love. When we used to have fun together making memories."

"Jelani. Those were not good memories for me. I don't know about you, but I sometimes still have nightmares of you choking me and hitting me." Sheila looked away. She could feel the water forming in her eyes. Her heart was beating fast. She wasn't sure if she should press the issue with him intoxicated.

Jelani rubbed his hands down his face. He didn't come to Sheila's house to be confronted about his past. He needed to release some tension and here she was building up more tension. He thought about Maya. Sitting there with Sheila made him realize that he'd struck out twice. He knew that Maya would never talk to him again. And when he left Sheila's house, he was sure she wouldn't be talking to him either. Jelani looked at Sheila from the corner of his eye. He knew she would start crying soon. She never could hold in her tears.

"Sheila. I didn't come over here to make you cry. You know that I've changed. I've gone through a lot but I've changed. I've put all of that behind me. You need to put it in the past and leave it there. It's time for you to move on with your life."

Sheila's face frowned into an evil stare. She was not staring at Jelani. She was staring at the floor as if she was remembering something terrible. She spoke in an even, monotone, calm voice. With each word, came new tears.

"Of course, you put it behind you. You weren't the one with bruises and broken fingers. You didn't have the black eyes Jelani. You can put it behind you because you were the one doing the hitting. I can't believe that you would say something like that."

"Look. I'm sorry but you're going to have to move on with life if you're to start the healing process. I know."

"You don't know shit," she replied still in her monotone voice. She was still looking at the floor. Jelani did not move. It was the first time that Sheila had expressed her feelings without fear. In the past, she would only cry and beg. She would never tell him that he was in the wrong. She would always make excuses to justify his behavior.

"You were never there for me Jelani. You didn't care about me. You weren't there when I went through the hard times..."

"I was there for you. We went through those hard times together..."

"Shut up," she said. All of Sheila's fears had vanished. There was something she had to tell Jelani and she thought that it should be now or never. Even if he killed her, she would have had a chance to tell him how she really felt about him.

"I've waited for a long time to tell you this." She still stared at the floor. "I loved you at one time Jelani. I loved the ground that you walked on but you took that love away. You took advantage of me when I was young. You stole my youth from me and I could never forgive you for that. I can't tell you how many nights I sat up on these very couches, wondering when you were coming home. I can't tell you how many days I've nursed an eye that you had blackened in your drunken stupors. You knew that I had no one else to turn to so you treated me like a dog. But even a dog deserves a little love. And even when I was carrying the baby..."

"Baby?" Jelani responded as he grabbed her arm. She winced and shook her head. Realizing that he was back to his old ways, he let her go and rung his hands together. He stood and paced the floor.

"Yes Jelani. We had a son." Sheila began to sob softly. She held her head down. Her sobs were uncontrollable.

"A son?" Jelani repeated as he stooped down to look Sheila directly in her eyes. He held her hands as she cried. Tears were dropping onto his knuckles. The soft flow of her hair to the back of her skull made Sheila look sexy. The way she bent her neck and softly rocked as she cried made her look vulnerable. Her deep dark eyes reminded Jelani of a little lost doe.

"A son," Jelani said again. "When? Where was I?

What..."

Sheila looked over to the row of pictures that lined the mantel over the fireplace. Jelani's eyes followed and landed on a few pictures of a smiling little boy. He slowly walked over to the fireplace and picked up the biggest picture. The little boy was smiling. He looked like Jelani did in his baby pictures. The nose that spread across his face was definitely that of the Ransom men. His smile was a smaller replica of Jelani's smile. The little boy wore a blue sailor's suit and had dark curly hair like Donnie's hair. Jelani could not peel his eyes from the adorable child. Memories flashed through his head. He saw his father and then his mother. He saw the mistreatment and the love and the little boy, looking for his father. Then he saw the little boy, wiping the blood from the cracks of the mother's mouth, helping her to pack the ice loosely in the plastic bags and place them on her swollen eye.

He couldn't believe that he had a son. A son! And Sheila never told him. He looked to be at least three months old. He looked like a happy baby. All the times that he was out partying and drinking, and he had a son to look after. He had a son to care for, and he was abusing the mother. He was using her for his pleasures, like he had intended on doing tonight. Jelani slowly turned back to Sheila. She was quiet. She did not move when he walked over to her.

"Where is he now?"

Sheila began to cry again. Her uncontrollable sobs irritated Jelani because she was not talking. She cried so hard that she was unable to form words to explain to Jelani. She was trying his patience. But he knew to get any information out of her, he had to be calm. Her silence was too loud and Jelani quickly became unbearably irritated.

"Where is my son, Sheila?" he yelled as he grabbed her by the shoulders and gave her one good shake.

"He died."

"Died? What the hell do you mean died? What happened? Shit!"

Jelani dropped to his knees and tears formed in his eyes. He'd quickly fallen in love with the tiny replica of himself and just as soon as he felt the bond, he'd lost him.

"He died of SIDS. When he was four months. About three days after he took that picture," she said as she looked over at the picture that Jelani held earlier.

"Why didn't you tell me?" Jelani's monotone voice was steady and deep. He did not move from his position on the floor.

"The doctor's said there was nothing we could have done..."

"We? You didn't even tell me that I had a son! *We* couldn't do anything because *I* didn't know. Why the hell didn't you tell me Sheila?"

"I knew you weren't ready for kids. You were still using that stuff and running around with different women."

"So you didn't tell me that I had a son? And what's worse, you didn't even tell me when he died. I swear I ought to..." Jelani jumped up quick and almost grabbed Sheila by her throat, but he didn't. He froze. She was wailing loudly, falling onto the floor and gripping Jelani around his shins. Jelani stood there for a minute thinking about his next move. He gently pushed Sheila off of him, walked over to the mantel, took the picture of his son, and left.

There is a large, brown field with nothing but acres. At night it seems to go on for miles and miles. On either sides of this field are houses. Both at least fifty yards in opposite directions. For some reason, city officials did not build any houses on the field. Some say it is an old superstition and other's say the land is not good for anything but looking. Many nights Jelani would drive out to the field and sit right in the middle of the dirt and think. Sometimes he would think out loud, but mostly he would think to himself and many times he would cry. Jelani drove straight from Sheila's house to his thinking field. He liked the serenity of the openness. Many times, he swore he felt the spirit of his mother coming down to guide him. Her spirit always brought a sense of belonging to him.

Jelani tightly gripped the picture between his arms and his chest. As he sat in the dirt in the middle of the field. Tears streamed down his face, mourning for the loss of a son never known. He didn't even know his name. The night air chilled Jelani but he continued to sit for at least four more hours. He thought about his mother, he thought about Maya, he thought about his son, and he even thought about Sheila. Thoughts continued to bombard his skull. Tears continued to flow uneased, until he eventually left, relieved that he'd had a chance to properly grieve for his son. His life was a turbulent ride of emotions. Jelani felt as though he had been on a roller coaster for the past few days. It was time for him to take control of his life once again, as he had before.

IT'S ON TONIGHT!

"Ahh yeah. It's on tonight!" Todd yelled from his jeep. Mandla heard him long before he turned down his street. Master P was bumping so loud that the bass rattled Mandla's windows. Todd began honking the horn loud. He was yelling and laughing at the same time.

"Man! Potna get your ass out here!"

Mandla poked his head out of the window and motioned with his arm, for Todd to come upstairs. He saw Todd roll his eyes but Mandla wasn't ready to go yet.

"I know ma." Mandla turned from the window, balancing the phone on his left shoulder and trying to iron his pants with his right hand. "Don't worry about a thing. When I get there, things are going to be okay. So don't you worry your pretty little head about a thing. Did you get the money I sent you?"

"Yes, baby," Mrs. Jackson replied.

"Good. There should be another check coming soon. How's little Jay doing?" Mandla asked, referring to his nephew.

"He's fine. You want to say hello?"

"Yeah, let me holla' at him for a minute." Mandla walked over to the front door and opened it just in time to see Todd appear in the frame with a bottle of Korbel in his hand. He wore a pair of dark blue slacks and had on a deep, dark sweater. His baldhead shined as usual and Mandla could tell that he was ready for a good time.

"Where are the bitches, 'cause I'm ready to pah-tay?!" Todd

hollered as he walked past Mandla. Mandla waved his arms to get Todd's attention and then mouthed that he was talking to his mother and pointed to the phone. Todd's eyes widened and he mouthed the word, "sorry"" as he went into the kitchen to get two glasses for the Korbel.

"Hey Uncle Man-Man!" little Jay yelled into the phone.

"Hey little man. What's the word?"

"Uhhh. I got a big person's bike. I rode it today."

"And who bought you that bike?" Mandla unplugged the iron and folded up his ironing board. He heard Todd in the kitchen breaking ice out of the ice-tray.

"Ahhh, my mommy."

"Really? You must have been a good boy lately," Mandla said as he thought about how much that big person's bike had cost him.

"Yeah. Uhhh, when are you coming home?"

"Soon. Why you miss me?"

"Yeah, are you far?"

"Yes."

"How far?"

"Real far. But I'll be coming home in two weeks." Todd handed Mandla a glass of Korbel. He sipped from the wide mouthed glass.

"How long is that?"

"Ask your mommy to show you on the calendar. Are you going to come pick me up from the airport?"

"Yeah! I'm, I'm going to pick you up on my bike okay?"

"Yeah," Mandla responded. He knew that his sister would have trouble explaining to little Jay why he wouldn't be able to take the bike to the airport. He smiled at how smart and determined his little nephew had become.

"Let me speak back to grandma. I'll see you when I get home. I love you."

"I love you too Uncle Man-Man." The little boy stayed on the phone. Mandla could hear him breathing into the phone.

"Put grandma on the phone."

"Okay." Mandla heard his footsteps running out of the room and him yelling for Mandla's mother. "Grandma! Man-Man want choo on the phone!"

"Hey baby," Mrs. Jackson sang into the phone.

"Ma. I gotta get outta here. Todd just came to pick me up."

"Where you two young men going?"

"To a club."

"To dance?"

"Yes, ma. I'll call you in a few days to tell you what time my flight is coming in." Mandla made his way into his bedroom and was slipping on his shoes. He looked in the mirror at himself. He smiled. He knew exactly what the women wanted, him.

"Alright baby. Y'all be careful out there. Call me and let me know when you coming. Tell Todd I said hello."

"I will."

"I love you."

"I love you too, ma. Bye."

Mandla threw on his shirt and brushed the little bit of hair that had grown. He smoothed down the sides of his mustache and looked through his wallet. He had all the essential necessities for a man of his caliber, money, I.D., and condoms. Todd was chilling on the couch watching television when Mandla walked back into the den. He had the bottle of Korbel sitting next to him on the small table and his glass in his hand. Mandla reached for his glass and sat down next to Todd. Todd poured more Korbel into Mandla's glass.

"What moms say?" Todd asked as he took a gulp from his glass. He flipped through the channels with the remote control.

"Just talking. She excited that I'm coming home." Mandla kicked his long legs up onto one of the boxes full of his clothes. His entire den was filled with boxes. Only the couch, his entertainment system, his bed and his kitchen were still in order.

"Dawg, I wish you was staying another week. My boy is getting married and we throwing him a phat ass bachelor's party."

"It ain't like I can't fly back. Shit I'm mainly going back because of money and moms."

Todd looked over at Mandla. "Moms having money problems again?"

"Mom's always having money problems. But I'll take care of it when I get there."

"Go on and take care of that family like the big dawg you are. You old man of the house mothafucka' you!" Todd screamed as he reached over and slapped Mandla on the back of his neck.

"Man quit fucking around." Mandla laughed. Todd flipped through more channels on the television. He poured himself another glass of Korbel and replenished Mandla's glass.

"Seriously, is there anything that I can do to help out? I got a little money stashed away if you need to get at it." Todd's tone was serious. Mandla knew that Todd had his back. When times were tough, Todd had always come through for Mandla. He was a good friend. Mandla looked over at Todd. He was going to miss his crazy ass. He would have to make a few quick little trips to visit once he got back to Washington, D.C. and got his family situated.

"Nah dawg. I can handle it. But thanks."

"You ready to go?" Todd finished off the rest of the Korbel.

"Yeah. Let's do this," Mandla said as he stood and felt his buzz.

Todd pumped the new Lyrical Giants CD and Mandla felt the music seep into his bones. He was ready to enjoy his last couple of weeks in Atlanta. Todd had plans for them just about every night. Mandla nodded his head to the beat. He was feeling good. He looked good, he smelled good, hell he felt good! He was also excited about going back home. Since he'd been in Atlanta, he'd had many of sleepless nights worrying about his mother and the girls. They all seemed so vulnerable when he wasn't around to protect them. The only other person in the house with testosterone was little Jay and he didn't have enough to light a candle.

First thing he would do when he got home was take his family out to dinner. It was a rare occasion for them to all be able to go out and eat at the same time at a nice restaurant. He thought about his last check from Smithers that he would get. It ought to be enough to buy his plane ticket and pay a few of his mother's bills.

"Potna. You ever talk to that bitch Senida?" Todd asked as he continued to pump his fist to the music coming out of his speakers. Mandla hated that Todd used that word when describing Senida. He had spent many nights with her and he tried hard not to admit the fact that he'd developed feelings for her. He was trying to forget about her and her crazy ass, and as a matter of fact, he had done a good job of it until Todd brought up her name.

"Nah dawg."

"Man remember that girl that was fighting Senida?"

"Yeah." Mandla turned to look at Todd.

"She gon' crazy too."

"Word? Is she still going to have the baby?"

"Yeah."

"Why you say she crazy?"

"That bitch cut up my couch and almost set my bed on fire." Todd flipped on the windshield wipers. Small drops of water formed on the front window.

"Why she do some shit like that?" Mandla asked, but he had a feeling he knew why.

"Same reason ole' girl slashed my tires. She caught me with another woman." Todd shook his head as if he couldn't believe his own words.

"Damn!" Mandla started laughing at Todd. "I thought she knew you was doing your thang anyway? I thought y'all had some type of agreement?"

"We did, but I guess that agreement didn't include her friends."

"Her friend?"

"Potna, her friend-z," Todd emphasized the sound of the s.

"Dawg?!" Mandla could not believe what he was hearing. He rolled the window down and let a few sprinkles of water hit his face. The jeep was getting stuffy and his buzz was intensifying because he hadn't had anything to eat.

"Ole' girl tried to set me up by having a couple of her girls try to get with me. That was last week at this club. Seems that your boy got more game than she thought. I had both of them women come over the other night! They didn't give a damn! Ole' girl rode by my house and recognized their cars and came busting in like APD." Todd laughed.

"What's ole' girl's name again?"

"Tracy. She crazy."

"Potna. We both afflicted. I get them crazy ones too."

"When you get back to D.C. hook up some of them honeys and I'll make a special trip so we can tear the town up. I got some vacation time coming up next month. I need to get up out of here for awhile."

"Potna, they crazy in D.C. too!" They both started laughing and then Todd turned up the volume and let Master P thump through the speakers.

"So what you got planned for work when you get back home?" Todd yelled over the music.

"I'm thinking about joining the reserves," Mandla yelled back. Todd gave Mandla a crazy look and turned the music down.

"Dawg?"

"Yeah. They're going to pay for law school. And give me a monthly stipend."

"What moms have to say about that?"

"She don't know right now, but when those checks come rolling in, she won't trip. I need to pay those bills and be the man of the house."

"That's cool. Do what you got to do. That's what a man's responsibility is, to take care of his family."

"Word. And I ain't trying to be like pops. My mama came through for me too many times. She's been there for me since day one and I swore if I ever had a chance to pay her back, I would."

Todd smiled. He envied Mandla's relationship with his mother. Todd's mother never attempted to take care of him. His grandmother raised him.

"How's your grandmother doing?" Mandla thought about Todd's close relationship with her.

"I talked to her today. She sounded pretty good. My cousin said she have her good days and her bad days. When I get my vacation time next month, that's one of the places I'm going to go, California. I promised her that I would come see her before the end of the year is up." Todd pulled the jeep into the parking lot of the club and parked. He took the keys out of the ignition, turned and looked at Mandla.

"Ready to get your groove on?"

"Potna. Am I cooler than a mothafucking polar bear?" Mandla asked as he opened the door and jumped out of the jeep.

Women were spilling in and out of the club. Mandla and Todd carefully watched butts, breasts, and legs. As smooth as they were looking, women were watching them carefully also. The club was tightly packed and the women were tightly packed in their clothes. Inside, lights were flashing and the music was loud. The dance floor was packed and sweat dripped from the walls. There were women of all shapes, sizes, colors, and bra sizes. Mandla scoped the room for potential dance partners and Todd scoped the room for potential bed partners. Todd smacked his lips and ran his tongue across his teeth.

"I need a drink. You want something?" Todd asked Mandla as he pulled the arm of a very sexy woman in a tight red dress. "How you doing? You want a drink?" The woman smiled and shook her head.

She followed Todd to the bar and Mandla watched as she leaned close to Todd. Todd began stroking the woman's arm and then her waist and moved his hands down her butt. She didn't seem to mind. Mandla looked around for someone to catch his eye. A young woman smiled at him from a nearby table. She was sitting with two of her girlfriends. Mandla smiled back and proceeded to walk to her table. The closer he got, the more her friends began talking and watching him.

"You wanna dance?" he asked.

She smiled and stood from the chair. She grabbed his hand and led him to the floor. After squeezing in through the crowd to the middle of the dance floor, she began to pump and grind fast, smiling as she pushed her butt into Mandla's groin area. His nature began to rise and he fought for control of his physical actions, but his old faithful friend won. After they danced for five more songs, they were both tired and Mandla had calmed down enough to walk off of the dance floor. Mandla and the woman walked back to the table. He sat in the only empty seat.

"My name is Mecca. What's your name?" the woman asked once they sat down.

"Mandla."

All three of the women turned up their noses.

"Manglo?" one of the women asked.

"Man-da-la," he phonetically sounded it out to them. He had been sitting for less than two minutes and already they were getting on his nerves. "Would you like a drink?" he turned to the woman that he danced with.

"Ah yes, please. I'll have a rum and coke." The other two women cleared their throats and looked over at her. "Can my friends have drinks too?"

"Yeah, if they buy 'em themselves." Mandla walked to the bar and ordered himself a Henley. He had no intentions of returning to the table.

Mandla walked over to the other side of the club drinking

his Hennessy. He spotted Todd and the girl he was with earlier on the other side of the bar. She was whispering in his ear and he was touching all over her body. Todd had a large grin on his face and Mandla knew what that meant. He might be taking MARTA home. After a few more attempts at the women in the club, Mandla had a feeling that tonight was not his night. He would dance with a woman for a few songs and then either he would buy her a drink, or they would ask for one, which was a definite turn off. He usually didn't have any problems with the women, but tonight was NFL night and the big "ballers" were in the house. Most of the women stood around waiting to be noticed by the men that played professional basketball, football, or baseball. Not only was it NFL night, but a few music celebrities were hanging out as well.

Todd walked up to Mandla at the bar with the same girl on his arm. She was an attractive young woman. Her slightly round hips swayed each time she walked and her ruby red lips matched her bright dress. She looked young, maybe about nineteen, but the make-up was making her appear older. Todd constantly rubbed his hands and fingers up and down her back, her legs, and her butt. Mandla could tell that he had been drinking all night because he was slurring and stumbling over the girl.

"Potna, this club is the bomb!" Todd yelled in Mandla's ear. Todd looked at Mandla closely. "You ready to go?"

"I'm cool. We can go when you ready. I'm just chillin'."

"Well actually, I found what I came here for. Baby is giving me mad play. I'll be in those drawers as soon as I drop your ass off!" Todd smiled at Mandla and started laughing. Mandla started laughing also. He couldn't believe Todd. If he knew any players, Todd was definitely the one.

"She riding home with us?"

"Nah, she drove. She gon' to drop her girls off and then meet me at my house." Todd turned to the girl and patted her on her butt. "Go'on and gather up your girls. And remember to keep the cutest one with you."

The girl nodded her head and walked off.

"Man, she got some fine potna's. You want one?"

"Nah I'm chillin'. I'm surprised that you've hung with one girl all night. What happened? Is the playa getting tired?"

"Nah. But she been hangin' all on *my shit* all night. So I

figured I'd do her a favor and show her what a real man got."

"Uh huh," Mandla continued to scope the room.

"Plus...I told her I played for the Falcons. Baby think I got money!" Todd fell over onto the bar laughing hysterically. Mandla joined him with the laughter.

Soon, the young woman walked up to Todd and Mandla with another tall, light complexioned woman next to her. She was lean and extremely attractive. In her heels, she was almost as tall as Mandla and Todd. She smiled at Mandla and commented on how pretty his eyes were.

"This is Tina," the woman in the red dress said as she snuggled next to Todd.

"Hi," Tina said as she held her hand out to shake Mandla's hand.

"I told you she was fine!" Todd roared.

"Do you want to dance?" Tina asked Mandla looking directly into his eyes.

"Fo' sho' baby you ain't said nuthing but a word."

Mandla pulled Tina onto the dance floor and began grooving. Tina moved her long lean body from side to side, trying not to split the tight black dress that she was wearing. Thirty minutes passed and Mandla had worked up a sweat. Tina continued to slide from side to side in a sensual movement, all the time smiling and putting her hands on Mandla's chest. Tina moved closer to Mandla and leaned against him as she planted a deep kiss on his lips. When she pulled away, she smiled at him and lowered her head as if she was shy. But when she looked up again, her eyes showed horror and fright. Mandla could not figure out what was wrong with this crazy girl. She quickly pulled him closer as if she were hiding from someone.

"What the hell is your problem?" Mandla asked irritated. He had met his share of crazy women tonight and he was beginning to get tired of their games.

"Please don't move. There's Yolawnda's man."

"Who the hell is Yolawnda?"

"The girl with yo' friend. The one in the red dress, my friend."

"Uh," Mandla said as he continued to dance. But Tina quickly stopped him from moving.

"What the hell is going on? You got something going on

with her man?"

"No."

"Well what choo worried about her man fo'? She gon' to be the one in trouble, right?"

"No, you don't understand. Ricco is crazy. He don't play. Him and his boys be shooting at people. We wasn't even supposed to be here. She told him that we was going to her mama's house. I bet he up here looking for her," Tina said still hiding behind Mandla as if she was hiding from her man.

"Look, me and my boy ain't got no time for no bullshit, so...I'm going to get my potna, and you go and get your girl and that will be that." Mandla began walking off of the dance floor. "I can't believe my luck tonight!"

"Yo Tina! You hear me calling you." A large, light complexioned man stood in front of Mandla and Tina as they tried walking off of the dance floor. "Where Yolawnda at? Hey what's *up* my man?" the man said as he looked Mandla up and down and side stepped to let him pass.

"Uh, I 'on know," Tina responded, trying to keep up with Mandla as he continued to walk through the crowd.

Todd and Yolawnda walked up beside Mandla. Tina pulled Yolawnda's arm but she resisted, staying attached to Todd's arm. Tina wanted to warn Yolawnda but it was too late. Ricco had already seen his woman hugged up under Todd and he made a beeline to Todd.

"What the fuck is this shit?!" he roared at Yolawnda who now looked like she had seen a ghost. She quickly let go of Todd's arm and stepped backwards as if she was truly scared of Ricco. "Is this the mothafucka' that you're fuckin'?"

But before Todd or Yolawnda could respond, Ricco hit Todd square in his jaw, causing Todd to stumble backwards. Ricco was on Todd in a quick flash and Mandla was on top of Ricco, pounding him in his back and on the side of his head. Tina and Yolawnda started screaming and Yolawnda picked up a glass from a nearby table and smashed it over Mandla's head. Women started screaming. Some people started to leave the club and others began gathering around the three men wrestling and fighting. Before things could really get out of hand, security was on the scene and kicked Mandla, Todd and Ricco out of the club. Ricco swore he would get Todd as he jumped in a waiting blue

Chevy Blazer and sped off.

"This is just not my night! What kinda luck is this?" Mandla squealed as they headed for the jeep. "Man, I know it's time for me to take my ass back to D.C."

Mandla touched the back of his head. There were mostly small cuts and a couple of bruises, from the small glass that Yolawnda cracked over his head. Todd looked at the back of Mandla's head before they got into the jeep.

"You want to go to the hospital for that? It's not bad, but you do have one deep cut that might need stitches."

"Nah. Take me home! I'll just soak in the tub. Forget that. I don't need to be out anymore!"

"I feel you baby boy. After that ordeal, I might need to go home and chill alone." Todd thought. "Damn...alone. I ain't chilled alone in awhile. I swear these women are a trip!"

"Well it's time you do!"

"Do what?"

"Chill the fuck alone!"

On the side street, Ricco and his boys were waiting in the blue Chevy Blazer. Ricco had caught Yolawnda sneaking around on him too many times and he needed to teach her a lesson. He'd told her that he would not have the mother of his baby seeing other men, especially as long as he was alive. With the lights off, the blue Chevy slowly began to follow Todd's jeep. None of the four men in the car had a plan but they'd all been drinking and smoking weed, so tonight, they were down for whatever. When Todd turned his jeep off of Peachtree Street, the blue Chevy pulled up beside them at a red light.

"What's up fools?!" Ricco had his window rolled down and all four of the men were looking into Todd's jeep.

"Mothafucka go on with that bullshit," Todd responded, he was exasperated.

"Who the fuck you think you talking to? We ain't from Georgia. We from Cali fool." Ricco pulled his 9mm from his lap and pointed it at Todd.

Without thinking, Todd pressed hard on the pedal and ran the red light. He drove fast with the blue Chevy Blazer close behind. Both Mandla and Todd's hearts were beating fast. Todd sped up and down the empty streets, dodging in and out of side streets to avoid any late night traffic. A few cars were cruising on the main street when Todd hooked a right and drove down a two-lane street. Ricco and his boys caught up with Todd and began shooting at the jeep.

"Ah shit! They're shooting at us," Todd screamed as he jerked on the wheel and swerved into the other lanes. He had to dodge the oncoming cars. Bright headlights came at them a mile a minute but the blue Chevy Blazer was still keeping up with Todd's jeep. Both Mandla and Todd were trying to duck low enough to avoid bullets but Todd had to keep his eyes on the road.

"What the fuck is wrong with them fools?!" Mandla screamed. He prayed silently that he would not get shot. Panic rose in both the men as the blue Chevy Blazer continued to stay on their tails. Sounds of bullets hitting and bending the metal of Todd's jeep could be heard throughout. Music still blared loud, but they only heard the quick, loud beating of their own hearts.

Todd turned the car full speed down a side street that he was sure would not be crowded. The one thing he didn't want to do was stop and give these guys a chance to pull up to the side of the jeep and shoot both him and Mandla.

"Oh shit! Oh shit!" Mandla yelled.

His life began to flash in front of him. He started regretting a lot of the bad things that he'd done in the past to people. He regretted playing with Chandra's life, he regretted that he did not want to visit his grandfather when he was on his death bed, he regretted the way things turned out between him and Senida. He wanted to tell his mother how much he loved her and to tell his sisters and little nephew that he cared.

A loud, piercing scream shattered Mandla's flashback of life. A small bloody red hole opened in Todd's neck. His head fell forward and his body slumped. The jeep accelerated and hit a bump, causing it to spin and slide off the side of the road. Todd's jeep toppled over a few times until it landed on its side.

Mandla was thrown around in the jeep, hitting his head on the windshield, on the dashboard, and then against the side window. Todd's jeep was turned over on its side and Mandla could hear more gunshots and then the blue Chevy Blazer screeching away.

Blood trickled from Mandla's head. He did not know if

he'd been shot or if he was bleeding from the car accident. He felt a warm tingling sensation in his stomach and noticed that he had blood all over his shirt. He couldn't tell exactly where the blood was coming from. Todd lay lifeless and unconscious as Mandla began to cry. He looked over at Todd. Please Lord don't let my man be dead, he thought to himself. His breathing became intense and he started to cough. Mandla coughed hard and pain shot through his body as he spit blood out of his mouth. He tried to call Todd's name but words could not find their way out of his mouth. He could see the blood where Todd had been shot and there was blood everywhere. He's going to be mad when he has to clean the blood out of his seats, Mandla thought as his head began to hurt and the tingling sensation turned into pain.

"Todd! Man, Todd wake up man! Please don't be dead!" Mandla screamed inside of his head. Todd would not move. His eyes were shut and Mandla couldn't even tell if he was breathing. Mandla heard vague sounds of sirens in the distance. His crying was making his head hurt worse and he became dizzy from the loss of blood. A swirling feeling overcame Mandla. He let his head fall to the side and waited for the paramedics to show up. He quickly lost consciousness.

*****

"Thank you Ms. Dickson, we look forward to doing business with you."

"Likewise, Mr. Grangent."

Maya shook the old white man's hand. She looked at her watch. She had been in negotiations and meetings for over two hours. She was sure that Aunt Setty was looking out of the window waiting for her. And she was right. By the time Maya made it home, Aunt Setty was all over her.

"How'd it go?"

"Great."

"Are we still go'in to tha' picture show?"

"Did you still want to go to the movies, Aunt Setty?" Maya smiled at the woman's shyness.

"Only if'n you feel up to it."

"There is nothing I'd rather do more, than to spend my last few days with my favorite Aunt Setty. What did you want to go see?"

"Dat new movie wit' that cute little thang in it."

"Denzel?"

"Dat's the one."

Aunt Setty grabbed her shawl and her purse. Maya freshened up a bit by reapplying her make-up and changing into a pair of comfortable jeans. On the way to the movies, Aunt Setty chatted about how her and Margaret were planning a trip to Atlanta to visit. Aunt Setty's plans excited Maya.

"Did you buy some nice art pieces?" Aunt Setty finally whispered, once they were in the movie theater.

"Oh yes, Aunt Setty. I have to pick them up tomorrow. Maybe you can go with me. And then you'll be able to see what I do, up close."

"Aunt Setty would love dat." She smiled and clutched her large purse.

"I needed this trip home. I was getting tired Aunt Setty."

"Tired of what?"

"Life."

"You should never get tired of life. You too young."

"Well I feel a lot better now. Now that I had a chance to visit you."

"I sho' am glad you came too. You know your Aunt Setty thinks 'bout you all the time."

"I think about you too, a lot. You're my only family. I cherish our relationship."

"Good. Now you gon' have ta be quiet. Da show is startin'. You know I can't miss nuthin' dat sweet little boy say."

"Denzel?"

"Yeah him."

Maya smiled and embraced her Aunt Setty's arm. They watched the movie in silence.

IT'S SO HARD
TO SAY GOOD-BYE

Senida watched as the partners to Smithers' Law Firm jotted down notes on their notepads. She sat at the end of a very long table waiting to hear their response to her plea to keep her job. She hated that the three of them held the fate of her future in their hands. Peggy Korwitz, Jonathan Crass, and Kevin Sumpter had begun Smithers' Law Firm in the early seventies after they graduated from law school together.

Senida had felt many times that her presence at the law firm was crucial, but not crucial enough to make partner. Peggy wrote quickly with her short fat fingers. She would periodically look up at Senida from the top of her glasses as Senida spoke. Kevin liked Senida and would try everything, he told her, to keep her at the firm. Jonathan had no feelings either way. He thought Senida was an excellent attorney but her performance on the Mortin trial had been disappointing to him.

"Ms. Johnson. My partners and I have decided to allow you the opportunity to stay with Smithers' Law Firm. After reviewing your trial record, your office performance, and listening to your convincing statement, we've decided that you are more of an asset to our business. However, you will be put on a probationary period until you can prove to us that your behavior in the Mortin trial will not happen again," Peggy finished her statement and peered again at Senida over the top of her glasses and cleared her throat.

Senida nodded. She could not wait until she was able to start her own firm. She would blow Smithers out of the water. But until then, she had to smile to the three and promise that her performance would improve. She was sure that they had caught wind about her and Mandla. That was probably the reason they felt the need to call a conference to discuss her professionalism in the workplace.

"Is there anything else that you would like to add before we adjourn this meeting?" Peggy asked.

"No. I've made my statement earlier Mizz Korwitz," Senida responded adding emphasis on the Ms., because she knew Peggy wanted desperately to get married. Kevin smiled, and Jonathan nodded his head without looking up from his notepad. Senida rose, said her good-byes and went back to her office.

Senida looked at her watch as she plopped down in her seat. She'd closed the door, because as surprising as it may have seemed, she was not in the mood for gossip from Lacey. It was ten o'clock and Mandla had not come to work again, nor had he called in sick. This made two consecutive days. Senida had been trying to call him all weekend long but he would not answer. His answering machine would pick up but he would not return her calls. Although it was his last week at Smithers, she was sure he would come into work.

Senida picked up the phone and dialed his number. His phone rang two times before the recorded message told Senida that the number had been disconnected. Senida twisted her face. She wanted to apologize to Mandla personally about her behavior at his house. Although they did not end on the best note, she still thought of him as someone special in her life.

No sooner than Senida picked up her stack of papers to do some work, did she hear a light tap on the door. At first she thought it might be Mandla, but when Lacey poked her head through the little crack in the door, Senida flopped back down into her seat.

"Come on in Lacey," Senida called out. She didn't want to hear about any office gossip. She had to straighten up her act so she could keep her job. Lacey had a somber look on her face and she held a box of tissue in her right hand. Senida saw tears welling up in her eyes and her heart began beating fast.

"Ms. Johnson, I just got a call from Mrs. Jackson, Mandla's mother." Lacey sat in the chair across from Senida's desk. She placed the box of tissue on Senida's desk and pulled a few tissues out.

"Mandla was in a car accident this weekend and he died

later at the hospital of gun shot wounds to the chest. Ms. Johnson, I'm so sorry," Lacey said as she began to softly cry.

"Shot?" was all Senida could say as she felt her insides twirl. Her head spun. Surely there must have been a mistake. Senida looked at Lacey.

"Yes ma'am. The driver, Todd, is in a coma. The doctors don't know if he's going to make it through. They say alcohol was involved. I'm so sorry."

Senida shook her head vigorously. "No, no, no. Lacey that can't be true. There's got to be a mistake! Oh my God no! Please Lord no! Lord no! Noooo! Noooooo!"

"I'm so sorry Ms. Johnson. His mother just arrived in Atlanta this morning. The funeral is Thursday. The family couldn't afford to fly the body home and it's not that many of them, so they flew into Hartsfield Airport this morning."

Senida flung her things off of her desk and began pounding on the desk with her fists. She picked up the glass paperweight from the floor and threw it towards the door. Glass shattered on the carpet. She threw the stapler and the tape dispenser. Senida yanked every piece of paper from inside of her desk and threw them at the floor. Lacey stood by as Senida took out her frustrations. Senida threw nearly everything that she put her hands on in the tiny office. With each throw, Lacey could tell that she was losing her energy. She finally fell to her knees and pounded the floor crying. Lacey flopped down next to Senida cradling her in her arms like a small child.

Senida's screams and cries could be heard echoing throughout the law firm. A few other attorneys rushed into Senida's office to see what the commotion was about. But Lacey shooed them all away as she held Senida. Her heart ached and she couldn't stop the tears from coming. Lacey began to rub Senida's back. Senida allowed sour tears to run down her cheeks and into her mouth. Heaving came in repetitive dry spurts. Her tears flowed and were absorbed into Lacey's large dress. She tried to hand Senida some tissue but she refused to take any.

He was so young and had such a future. How could such a terrible thing happen? Senida couldn't think straight. She didn't get to talk to him like she wanted. She would never see him again. She would never be able to feel his breath on her face or his hands on her back. Senida cried louder. She would never be able to tell him how she really felt about him. Senida cried for close to an hour with Lacey by her side wiping away at both of their tears. Mandla had become an important part of Senida's life and had become a part of the Smithers' Law Firm family. He would be greatly missed.

"Why Lord?! Whyyy?! Whyyyyy?!" Senida's body heaved as Lacey held her tightly.

*****

"I'm glad you sound better," Donnie spoke into the phone.

"I'm feeling a little better," said Jelani.

"Good. Have you decided what you were going to do?"

"Yes. I'm going to go get my woman."

"Now that's the J.R. that I know."

"I saw Sheila the other night."

"Oh yeah. What's she up to?"

"Same thing." Jelani did not want to re-live that night so he did not mention his baby to Donnie. That was something he would tell him later. "Since Maya's been gone I've had a chance to do some serious thinking."

"And what have you been thinking about?"

"About that fool."

"The one in jail?"

"Yeah."

"And what conclusion have you come up with?"

"He's haunted us for too long. Our father literally *murdered* our mothers. I've lived with that, we've both lived with that for years. It's a shame for two grown men to still be haunted by one crazy asshole."

"I agree. Do you talk to your therapist about this?"

"I talk to her about my personal problems with drugs and women. I've only touched on our father. She wanted me to open up more about him but I wasn't ready at the time. I'm more than ready now."

"Did you want to come to dinner tonight? Tressy's cooking your favorite."

"Greens?"

"Yeah that among other things."

"I'll be with the boys later."

"Taj and Randell and 'nem?"

"Yeah."

"Bring them. They can play with Jah and Jahrina. Then we'll have a chance to talk."

"That's cool. What time should I come by?"

"'Bout six."

"I'll see you then."

"Jay?"

"Yeah?"

"I'm glad to see you back to your old self," Donnie said.

"It's good to be my old self."

"I'll see you at six."

"Bye."

"Bye brother."

*****

Senida looked out of the passenger side window of Lacey's car. She watched the little children crossing the street when they stopped at a red light. It was the first time that she'd been out of the house since the terrible news. She could not believe that Mandla was gone. She would never see him again. A slow tear slid down the right side of her face. Another tear followed the first tear and then more fell. Streams flowed down the left and the right side of her face. Senida leaned her forehead against the cool window and put her face in her hands. Her body shook as she uncontrollably cried.

Lacey reached over and rubbed Senida's back. She let her emotions go and the tears flowed non-stop. Lacey continued to rub Senida's back until she had to turn the car. Then she would reach back over and rub her back some more. Lacey drove down Clark Avenue and made a left onto Peachtree Industrial. Saint Michael's Church sat on the left side in the middle of the block. People in dark colors were filing into the church. Many were crying and holding on to each other. Lacey parked across the street and turned off the car. She looked over at Senida who still had her face in the window. Lacey decided to wait until Senida was ready to go into the church.

Lacey missed the zany, colorful personality around the office. She had always been suspicious of Mandla and Senida's relationship. She had sensed early in the game that there was something more than just a work relationship between the two. Lacey had not mentioned her suspicions to Senida but she would observe them when they didn't think that anyone was looking. One particular time, Lacey overheard them talking in one of the supply closets. After listening at the door for a few minutes, Lacey swore she heard some moaning and groaning. Another time, Lacey saw Mandla bend over and kiss Senida when they thought she had gone to lunch. Lacey never mentioned these sightings to Senida, but she knew how she felt about Mandla. That was the main reason why Lacey volunteered to go with her to the funeral. Lacey let her head fall back onto the seat. She couldn't believe that such a young promising life was lost over some foolishness.

"We were having an affair," Senida said, breaking Lacey's concentration. Senida did not move from her almost fetal position in the corner of Lacey's car. Lacey did not respond. Although she enjoyed office gossip, this was not the type of gossip that she would participate in spreading.

"I know he was young...but there was just this air about him that attracted me to him. I knew we shouldn't have gotten involved, but..." Her voice trailed off. Senida started to cry again. Lacey was patient. She waited for Senida to tell her what she wanted. She didn't say anything. She just listened. Senida started again.

"I fucked up though. I messed up my relationship with Darrell, over these young ass men. I messed up with Todd because of fucking Mandla. I just can't seem to get it right with these men," Senida sighed.

"We had an argument. I didn't get to tell him how much I really cared. Do you think he knew?" she asked Lacey but did not look in her direction.

"I'm sure he did."

"I miss him. He was such a sweet person. He made me laugh. He brought out the child inside of me. We had great sex."

Lacey raised her eyebrows. That was a little more information than she thought she needed to know.

"I can't believe he's gone. I'll never see him again." More

tears streamed down her face. "Never."

Lacey rubbed Senida's back. She felt sorry for her. She seemed so together in the office. Now she sat in a clump, full of insecurities.

Senida sighed. She wiped the tears from her face and looked out of the car window at the people still going into the church. "Are you ready?"

"I'm never ready for something like this, but I'm ready when you are."

Senida got out of the car and straightened out her black skirt. Lacey walked to the front of the car. "I'm here for you. Whatever you need, you let me know." Senida smiled. It was the first time that Lacey had seen her smile since she'd heard the bad news on Tuesday.

Everyone in the church wore black or dark colors. The organ player was playing "Going Up a Yonder," when Senida and Lacey found their seats in the middle pews. A young woman was singing and with every phrase, mourners cried as they allowed the words to sink into their hearts and souls.

"If anybody asks yoouu, where I'm going, where I'm going..." As soon as Senida saw the casket in the front of the church and saw Mandla's body laying in the box, she lost all control.

"...I'm going up a yonder, I'm going up a yonder..." Senida's knees became weak and Lacey had to hold her up until they sat down.

"...To be with my Lord..." There were lots of Mandla's friends present and a few of his family members.

Senida's eyes were red and almost swollen shut from her constant crying. She'd taken a couple of weeks off of work and after the funeral, she was going to fly home to California for a much needed emotional and mental break. Cries from every corner of the church rang loud. Senida saw a small lady, three young girls, and a little boy sitting in the first pew. She knew right off that the woman was Mandla's mother and the other girls were his sisters.

The woman was bent over and the oldest girl was consoling her. She cried loud and hard. One of the other girls held a little boy, who couldn't understand why his favorite uncle was laying in the box. The other girl, who looked exactly like the one sitting next to her, was crying loud with the mother. The sight made Senida weep harder. She tried not to look at the casket, but her eyes kept averting themselves to Mandla. He looked at peace. She hated the fact that she would never be able to touch him anymore. She missed the way he smiled, the way he made her smile. She missed the youthfulness and adult ambition that attracted her to him. She cried as Lacey consoled her. She leaned into Lacey's large bosom and let herself go.

"Today is a sad day," the preacher began. "It is a sad day, because we've lost a loved one, Brother Mandla Jackson. A fine, young, promising man. And although his death was a senseless death, we know that Brother Jackson is with the Lord right now, looking down on us. He's in a better place. The Lord giveth and the Lord taketh away..." the preacher continued with words that pierced the hearts of everyone in the Lord's house.

Cries went up in the church. Mandla's mother fell out onto the floor and threw herself onto his casket. The girls cried louder and tried to contain their mother. Senida cried loud. She felt his mother's loss. She'd lost a dear friend, who was important in her life. After the preacher's sermon, the organ player played Cooley High's song, "It's So Hard to Say Good-bye to Yesterday," and a young man about Mandla's age, sang.

"Hooow doooo I saaay good-bye to what we haaad, the good tiiimes that made us laauugh out weighed the baaad..." The people in the church walked past the casket in a single file line.

"...I thoouught we'd geeeet to see foreverrrr, but forever's gone awayyy..." Each person touched Mandla, kissed him or fell over the casket crying.

"...It's sooo haaarrd to saay good-bye to yesterdaaaayieie..." Senida didn't think that her legs would make it to the casket, but Lacey walked her through the process. Mandla looked calm and made-up. He didn't look like the same smiling Mandla that Senida was used to spending her time with.

Loud piercing screams echoed throughout the church. Mandla's mother had fallen into the casket and wouldn't let go. Her daughters had to physically pull her away from her son's motionless body. She fought with her daughters as all three tried to control their mother. The little boy was sitting on one of the pews crying, alone.

"...If weee geeeet to see tomorrrooow, I hope it's worth allll the pain and soorrrooow, it's sooo haaardd to say good-bye to yesterdaaaayyyieie." The young man wiped a single tear from his eye and placed a rose on Mandla's casket.

Before leaving out of the church, Senida introduced herself to Mandla's mother and hugged the little lady. She sat on the first pew of the church, staring at the casket. Her body was thin and fragile. Bags looped under her bloodshot eyes and her hair was a rumpled mess. She calmed down a bit, from emotional fatigue. Despite the current circumstance, she was quite a pleasant woman.

"I'm so glad, you gave my Man-Man a chance to become a lawyer," she said in between sobs. "He would have made a fine lawyer too. He was such a good boy. I don't know why the Lord took him away from me. Why? Why did this have to happen to him? He was so good to me. Why Lord? Whyyy?!"

Mandla's mother cried hysterically and Senida wrapped her arms around the woman. They both cried together, in each other's arms, in front of the casket. Lacey stood to the side and cried out loud. The girls were still crying and the little boy was tugging on his grandmother's leg, crying for Uncle Man-Man. It was a sad day in Atlanta. It rained and thundered the entire day. Senida assured Mandla's mother that she would raise enough money from the firm to fly Mandla's body back to Washington, D.C. so he could be buried at home with her. Senida handed her one of her business cards and Mrs. Jackson put it into her purse. She thanked Senida again. They cried some more and departed.

Lacey pulled in front of Senida's apartment complex. She turned the engine off and looked over at her boss.

"I'm coming up with you," she stated sternly.

"Lacey, I appreciate it, but I need to be alone." Senida's wearily responded.

"My mother died five years ago. And it still seems like yesterday. I needed someone there for me so I wouldn't go crazy. This isn't the time for you to be alone, Ms. Johnson."

"I understand, Lacey. But really. I just want to go lie down. My head is pounding, my heart is aching. I just need some rest, alone. I promise I'll call you when I wake up."

Lacey gave Senida a stern look.

"I promise. I'll call you. Thank you for everything. I appreciate it. I'll call you." Senida staggered into her building and Lacey drove off. When Senida made it to her apartment, she threw herself across her bed to grieve, alone. She allowed streams of tears to flow into her pillow.

*****

Maya's weeks went quickly. It was time for her to return to Atlanta to finish her work. She finished her negotiations with the gallery in San Francisco and talked over the phone with Stephen twice. He actually seemed thrilled with Maya coming back to Sanfords. He must have gotten a taste of everything that entailed being the "boss." The large strong man that monopolized her time in Atlanta, Jelani, was continually invading most of her thoughts. He'd become much more of an important part of her life than she wanted to admit.

After the four days of negotiating, Maya spent her last two days in California with Aunt Setty. Just the two of them, like it was in the beginning. Maya benefited from her rich sense of culture, her quick-witted tongue, and her wise knowledge of life and love. Their bond grew stronger with each hour that they spent talking and laughing. Maya's trip was not only one of business, but one of spiritual healing. Her tired little soul needed a rest from the stress of everyday living. But who didn't? She felt that she could go back to Atlanta with a new attitude and new insight on how to deal with her life, and Jelani. Senida, or Aunt Setty, she was sure, would not approve her decision. But one thing she learned on her trip back to California was that life was a wee bit too short. And her new motto was to "live it and learn."

The night before Maya's flight from California back to Atlanta, Aunt Setty sat down next to her real close. She had tears in her eyes and a dusty brownish-red book in her hands. Her white handkerchief was soiled, with what Maya did not want to know. She stared into Maya's eyes and brushed some of the soft curls out of Maya's face for her.

"The older you get, the more and more you remind me of your father. How I do miss my brother James." Her smile was one of admiration. "I only wish he was alive to see how pretty and smart you turned out to be." Aunt Setty dabbed at her eyes with her soiled handkerchief.

People called her Setty because she used to always "set" on the porch waiting for her father to come home from the cotton fields. Her real name was Jane. One day one of her uncles said, " you just little Miss Setty always settin' and waiting for your ole' pappy." Maya hated when Aunt Setty became emotional over her parents. She did not want to relive those years for anything in the world. "Yeah, you so smart and pretty, just like your mama too, God rest her soul. She was a pretty one. That's why my brother loved her so much."

"Aunt Setty, I have to finish packing my things," Maya said carefully.

"Well you can do dat. Dis ain't gon' take long. I just wanted to spend a little time wit you befo' you head back to Georgia." She held the book out to Maya who just looked at it momentarily. "Your father made me promise to give this to you when you was old enough to understand. He said, 'Setty if'n anythang ever happened to me, give this here book to my baby girl when you feel she old enough to understand.' How I do miss him."

Aunt Setty placed the dusty book carefully into Maya's lap. Maya looked down at the book and fingered the dust around the edges. She felt tension build in her neck and tears form in her eyes. She and her parents were so close; it hurt like hell when they died. Maya looked up at Aunt Setty.

"He told you to give this to me? My daddy did?" Maya said in between snot and tears, wiping her nose with the back of her hand, like she was a little girl.

"Yes child. Take it with you back home and maybe you'll understand the struggles that we all went through befo' you was born." Maya dusted off the top of the book and read the word "diary," in gold bold letters.

"It's his diary. I can't read his diary." Maya pushed the book back into Aunt Setty's lap.

"You can if'n he gave you permission. But if'n you ain't old enough to deal with it, then I'll keep it a few years longer. I just thought since you was gon' to be thirty at the end of this year that you might be ready for it. If'n you ain't, then Auntie Setty sho' understand." She took the diary and went through the double doors of the kitchen.

Maya sat there for over twenty minutes staring into space as tears rolled down her face. Emotions welled up inside of her. Maya heard Aunt Setty rustling around in the kitchen. She was sure that Aunt Setty was preparing to cook dinner. Noise from the double doors caught Maya's attention and Aunt Setty swayed her large behind through the doors.

"Chile you still in here crying? Aunt Setty didn't mean to get you all upset. I just thought it was time," she said as she sat down, pulled Maya's head into her big bosom and began to rock her like a child.

One of Aunt Setty's large hands rested on Maya's back and the other steadied her head into the breasts. Aunt Setty was a large soft woman. Her matronly shape contradicted with her smooth, young looking pretty face. Maya inherited the infamous, large, brown Dickson eyes from her father who had the same identical pair as Aunt Setty. All her life had been spent working in a dress factory. Her rough hands were scarred with pinholes and needle pricks. She continued to rock Maya allowing her to cry onto her dress. Heaving and gasping for air, Maya let years of frustration flow from her weary body.

"Yeah, baby, let it all out chile. I knew your grief and sorrow was in there somewhere. You ain't cried since you set foot on Georgia soil. I understand sometimes you have to go back to where you was raised to feel yo' parent's spirit." Aunt Setty began to hum. In between hums she would let out a few verses. The more she sang the more Maya cried.

Aunt Setty was right. Once Maya had left California and went to live with her aunt, she did not truly grieve over the loss of her parents. Her days were filled with her survival at Douglas High School and her nights, with empty prayers of another chance with her parents. Now her emotions flowed like the Niger River, endless, painful, flowing. She remembered her parents waving to her in the car as she stood on Senida's porch before going into the house. She remembered the kisses on the cheeks that her father and mother gave her. She remembered them saying that they would see her later. And they never did.

"Aunt Setty?" Maya wiped her face on the old woman's apron. "What does my father's diary say?"

"Honey I ain't the slightest. He gave *you* permission to read it, not me." She continued to hum.

"You mean all these years you've had the diary and you've never read it?" Maya was more shocked, because her curiosity would have gotten the best of her.

"Nope. I'm sure I know a lot of what it says. He was my

only brother. And since we was twins, we was closer than the otha' sisters."

"You said that if I read the diary, that I would understand what went on before I was born? Was that all the arguing that went on about my parents, when I was growing up?" Maya remembered the family gatherings when arguing would erupt because of something that happened in the past before she was born.

"Yes, chile," Aunt Setty said as she brushed curls out of Maya's face. "That's what dat was all about."

Maya ran her hand across the velvety feel of the book. She wished she could talk to her father about the feelings she was having. He was usually the one that she went to when she needed someone with excellent insight. Maya stood to go to the bedroom. Physically she was tired. Emotionally she was drained.

"Aunt Setty, I'm going to lay down for awhile. I'll talk to you in about an hour. Wake me if I haven't awakened yet." She walked through the living room as if she were dead, still carrying the little brownish-red book.

"Okay, babee. You go on and rest a spell. I'll wake you when dinner is ready."

Aunt Setty went back into her kitchen to prepare her meal. She hummed old slavery songs from her heart. Maya could hear the old woman's husky voice from the bedroom and the sounds lulled her to sleep. She slept on her back. One hand dangled over the bed and the other rested on top of the diary, which rested on top of her heart.

Smells of collard greens, chicken, yams, and macaroni and cheese woke Maya out of her sleep. Her stomach growled and rumbled all the way up to her chest. She rolled over to peer at the clock and realized that she had actually slept for two hours instead of one. She sat up in the bed, oblivious to the book that fell to the floor. The soft thud caught her attention and she hesitated before she reached for it. Instead of opening the book, she placed it on the nightstand by the bed and laid back onto the bed with her back to it.

"Daddy," she said out loud. "I'm not so sure I want to know what's in your diary. For years I've learned to live without parents. Although I know you've always been with me. But many times...I...don't...know what to do. Life has gotten unbearable at times." A small tear slid down her right cheek.

"Baby, you okay? Who you talking to?" Aunt Setty stretched her neck around the corner of the room. She still wore her apron, which now had grease spots and crumbs on it. She was wiping her wet hands on the apron. Her large body filled the entire space of the doorframe as she entered the room.

Aunt Setty sat her plump behind onto the bed next to Maya. She rubbed the wavy hair and brushed back some loose curls from Maya's face. Aunt Setty was a warm kindred spirit. Her eyes were filled with much more seen and experienced than Maya's. She pressed her soft hands on top of Maya's and squeezed.

"Aintee didn't mean to git you all upset count of your daddy's book. But I been keeping it for a long time now and I thought this was the best time to gives it to ya'."

"It's okay, Aunt Setty. I just miss them that's all," Maya responded as she stood to go into the kitchen. "Is dinner ready?" She smiled to reassure her aunt.

"Yeah, babee, come on. It's natural to miss yo' mama and daddy, they's the ones that birthed you." She rubbed Maya's back as they walked towards the kitchen. "By the way, some gentleman called looking for you whiles you was 'sleep, but he said not to wake you, he would call back."

Maya stopped in her tracks. Who in the world could be calling her at her Aunt Setty's house? She usually hid away from most people when she was in town. Maya turned to look at Aunt Setty.

"Who was it?"

"Said his name was Jamal or Malik. Somethin' like that. Some ole' kinda African type name." Aunt Setty continued into the kitchen with Maya close on her heels.

"Jelani?" Maya asked. Aunt Setty nodded her head. "What did he say when he called?"

"Said he'd call you back and fo' me not to wake you," she responded as she fixed both of their plates. She began to hum while Maya sat waiting for her to continue.

"Well...?" Maya's impatience rose.

"Well what chile?" Aunt Setty grew annoyed.

"What else did he say? How did he get the number? And

why was he calling?" She asked out loud, but more of rhetorical questions than direct questions to Aunt Setty.

"Didn't ask him all that. What you gettin' so hot 'round the collar fo'? Is that the man what bought you that car?" Aunt Setty sat across from Maya as she placed their plates on the table.

"Yeah..." Maya hesitated, because she didn't tell Aunt Setty that she kept the car.

"Well 'member what I tol' you 'bout them mens what buy you stuff. They think they own you if'n you let 'em do a little somethin' for you. Not like the men in my day," she said as she held up a piece of bread and waved it at Maya before she took a bite and continued her lecture. "Those was real men. Whan't all that actin' crazy, beatin' yo' wife and stuff. Folks had mo' respect fo' each other. We stuck together. 'Cause if'n we didn't, them white folks would tear us up. Yeah those was the days. I wouldn't change to being young today if'n you offered me a million dollars."

Aunt Setty paused long enough to take a sip of lemonade from her mason jar. She refused to use the new set of glasses that Maya bought for her as a gift. Said they weren't sturdy enough, just like everything else made now a day, cheap. Maya waited and just chewed her food. She knew better than to interrupt Aunt Setty once she got on her soapbox.

"Yeah, back in those days we used ta have fun." She laughed. "Could go out and party, have a good time wit out all that shootin' and mess. You don't know yo' Aunt Setty could use ta cut a rug. Not too much anymo' though, since ma' hip went out. But I used ta be a swinger back in those days..."

"...Me and yo' daddy used to go to the sock hop and show everybody up. They called us the dancing two-step twins." She laughed and this time Maya joined in on the laughter.

Maya enjoyed her moments with her aunt. Her vibrant personality shone through her not-so-bright eyes that had dulled from life. But Aunt Setty would tell you in a minute that she still had a few more years kicking before she was going anywhere.

Maya started thinking about Jelani and how much she did care for him. He surprised her by calling. And as Aunt Setty rambled on about the good-ole-days, Maya daydreamed about the good times that she'd had in the past few months with Jelani. It was going on almost a year since she'd met him. She had decided not to disclose too much information about him to Aunt Setty, as she probably would not understand what she was going through. But each time she thought about the future her heart would ache, first from love, then from anger, then from frustration.

She would wonder what she did to deserve the pain that she had to endure her entire life. Yes, she had much more than most people. And sometimes luck, and her pretty face, would get her a little farther than others. But she'd lost the most important things in life. The things worth living for. Not cars, or money, or homes. But parents, and friends, and loves. And many times she would thank the Lord for what she did have, like Aunt Setty, but would wonder why He took the other things she loved away, like her parents and yes even Jelani.

The phone rang and interrupted Aunt Setty from her lecture and startled Maya back into reality. Aunt Setty slowly rose to retrieve the phone, which was in the living room. Maya walked briskly behind her to catch up to the older woman. Aunt Setty placed her hand over the receiver and whispered loudly.

"It's that man. What you want me to tell 'em?"

Maya reached for the phone and waited for Aunt Setty to reluctantly leave the room. Her heart raced as she hadn't planned what to say to Jelani or even planned for him to call her. She held the phone to her ear but waited a few seconds before she said hello. His voice was crisp and clear as if he were in the other room.

"Hi." Jelani was apparently nervous.

"Hi."

Silence.

"Um...I know you're probably still mad at me. But there are a few things that I really would like to have a chance to say to you." Silence. "Hello?"

"I'm still here. Go ahead." Maya's heart thumped hard against her chest.

"First let me start off by saying that I miss you, a lot. I've been thinking a lot about us. About me. And my past. And you. And although I said that I loved you before, this time I can really feel it. I know I had a fucked up past. But there is nothing I can do about that now. I feel like an ex-con sometimes. Well, you know what I mean. But I feel like I've paid my debt to society. It's that nobody will give me a second chance to prove that I'ma changed man."

Maya stretched the phone cord over the small stand to sit

on the couch. She could tell this was going to be one of those long conversations. Plus, she had been doing a lot of thinking lately too. She had a few things that she wanted to tell him. Jelani continued uninterrupted.

As he rambled on Maya thought about the good times that they spent together. The times when she couldn't sleep without him by her side. The times when he would drive to her house to pick her up and take her back to his house, just so they could be together. Her mind went back to the time that they acted like two big kids and she hid in the closet waiting for him to find her in a water gun game of hide and go get it. She *did* miss him. She missed how safe he made her feel. Maya sighed. Life had been complicated for her since she could remember. It seemed as if every decision that she had to make was a major life-altering decision. But she'd put a lot of thought into this decision and was going to stick by her guns.

"How many times do I have to pay for the same crime? I'm only human and I made mistakes and now I've learned from them. I've made every attempt and took every step to try to fix what I did. But that's the past." He stopped. Maya decided that this was the perfect time for her to cut in.

"Listen Jelani. I care for you a lot. And what you did I think was inexcusable." He sighed as he listened to her speak. He had a feeling she was not going to let him live it down. "But I've been doing some thinking of my own. And I do think that you deserve another chance. We'll have to take it slow, real slow. But I think we can give it another try. You've never disrespected me and I would hope that you wouldn't start now. 'Cause I'ma tell you like it is. I don't play. I'll take off in a minute if you ever pull some shit with me."

She could hear him sigh and pictured him sitting on the black leather reclining chair in his living room, sipping orange juice from the feminine shaped glasses he loved. She pictured him smiling his bright, white smile and his legs propped up with bulging muscles, slightly bowed.

"I would never hurt you," he said. "Thank you. Not too many people have given me a second chance."

Maya swore she heard him choking up.

"Are you crying?" she asked.

"No. I got something in my eye," he responded. She

laughed. Jelani hadn't heard her laugh in a few weeks. It was like music to his ears. He wished he could see her and touch her. He couldn't wait until she was back on Southern soil so he could feel her and smell her sweet scent. Surprisingly to himself, he wasn't even thinking about sex. He was thinking about love.

"Like I said. We're going to have to take it slow, because I still need time to digest all that's happened. So you're going to have to be patient."

"I will."

"I saw you on ESPN the other night. You looked good," she said remembering when her and Aunt Setty stayed up late to watch his interview. Maya remembered Aunt Setty commenting on how handsome he looked.

"Thanks. I was thinking of you the entire time."

She smiled. He smiled.

"Maya. I swear. I'm not going to fuck up. I needed someone like you to give me a second chance. I knew when we had that accident, that I had to make you mine."

"Well, I knew when we had that accident, that I would have to do all of the driving." They both laughed.

"Maya."

"Yes."

"I love you."

It was the first time that he'd uttered the words and meant them. An awkward silence filled the phone. Tears welled in Maya's eyes as she realized that he *did* love her. And that she loved him too. She really did.

"I love you too, Jelani."

"Please. Call me J.R. All my friends do."

They both laughed out loud. Maya laughed, all the while, wiping tears of joy from her face. She'd found true love. Hopefully, love that would overpower whatever drama she had to endure.

Expecting a lot of yelling and crying, Aunt Setty poked her head around the kitchen door and smiled. She saw Maya smiling. She went back to cleaning her kitchen, a ritual that brought her inner peace. She was glad to see her niece happy again.

Aunt Setty was in the middle of drying the dishes when

Maya slid into the kitchen door. She smiled and gave Aunt Setty a big hug. Aunt Setty laughed and smiled back. Maya sat at the table as Aunt Setty continued to dry. The scene was reminiscent of when Maya was small, reporting everything to Aunt Setty about her day. She would sit with two big, fluffy ponytails, telling on the neighborhood kids. This time, however, she was telling Aunt Setty about adult stuff. She explained to Aunt Setty her whole relationship with Jelani and expected Aunt Setty to forbid Maya to see such a man.

But when Maya spilled her guts about the accident, the car, the vacations, the times spent, the abuse, the killing, and the jail time, Aunt Setty surprised Maya. Aunt Setty took the hot teakettle from the stove and poured steaming tea into Maya's cup. Every time Maya would tell her aunt something different, she would shake her head.

"Chile." She started. "The things chil'ren have to go through now-a-days. I wouldn't trade my days for all the days in the world."

"Well Aunt Setty. I've decided to give him another chance." Maya sipped from the mug of hot tea. Aunt Setty sat down and joined her, but she drank lemonade from her mason jar.

"Good."

Maya looked up from her mug. "You approve?"

"Has the man ever disrespected you?"

"No."

"You ever felt safe wit' him?"

"Yes. All of the time."

"Then what's wit' the surprise? Back in my day. Folks stuck together. Now yo' daddy wasn't no saint, God rest his soul, but your mama stuck wit' him 'til their graves. Folks today scared of everythang," she said as she pointed her finger and shook it at Maya. "Black men got it hard enough wit' the white man lynching and killing and drugging 'em. And I only see it being fit that we's they women, that we need to stick by 'em. Not to make no excuses fo' dat young man. But he's done proved his 'self more than once, so you say. So why not give him another chance?" She thought for a moment. "Hell I don't see how you gon' give him anotha' chance *anyway*."

"Ma'am?"

"He ain't never done nuthin' to you. So what you giving

him a second chance fo'?"   She took a long gulp from her jar and wiped the precipitation on the glass with her kitchen rag.

      Maya smiled as her Aunt Setty went on and on about the "good ole' days."   She felt whole again.   She felt a sense of inner peace that took an entire lifetime to feel.   She had her health, she had her best friend Senida, she had her Aunt Setty, had a wonderful job, and now she had Jelani.

PICKING UP
THE
PIECES

Jelani held the phone for a while. He could hear the dial tone but was not paying attention to the loud noise. Maya's good-bye held him suspended for a matter of minutes. He finally got up from the reclining chair, swallowed the rest of his orange juice and went upstairs to check on the twins. He tiptoed up the spiral staircase allowing his bare toes to sink in the fluffy beige carpet. He could hear Jahrina softly snoring behind the door. Her little sinuses were acting up all day from the salt air in Florida. She was used to the humid weather in Georgia and Jelani's house on the beach did nothing for her nose. He pushed slightly on the door and it opened. He flicked on the light and saw two small bodies with red hair lying side by side, asleep. He smiled. He loved his niece and nephew. He couldn't wait until he had a wife and children to make him proud.

He wanted to call Donnie bad, to tell him about his update news with Maya but decided not to interrupt the two. Donnie left the emergency number where they would be for emergencies only. Jelani didn't want to intrude on their anniversary celebration in the Bahamas. When Donnie told him the story of how Tressy surprised him, Donnie tried to convince Jelani that he knew all along that she was planning a trip and wasn't cheating on him. Jelani wished he could have been there when she sprung the island tickets on his brother. Now their marriage was paradise, as they celebrated their second honeymoon. Jelani just hoped they didn't come back with any more red head kids with freckles.

He crept back down to the kitchen. Maya would be flying

back to Atlanta tomorrow. He would still be in Florida for another week. Maybe he would surprise her and send her tickets to fly to Florida for the weekend and spend time with him and the twins. He missed her and couldn't wait to see her again. He was glad she would give him another chance. Jelani couldn't wait for Maya to come home so he could pick up the pieces and start working on their new and improved relationship. A relationship without untruths. He swore to himself that he would do her right. He would make her his wife when the time was right. The two of them would live happily together and he would have accomplished his goal to be married and happy. His nature began to rise and he knew he had to wait so he went upstairs to take a cold shower.

      Senida rolled over onto her side. She'd been in the bed for two consecutive days. Her plane was scheduled to leave in less than five hours. She decided not to call Maya until she was in California. She didn't want to depress Maya while she was trying to concentrate on her work. Senida's mother was waiting for her daughter to come home to visit. Mrs. Johnson hadn't seen her daughter in at least two years. She knew that her daughter needed some motherly healing and love. Senida waited until eight before she called her parents. She hadn't talked to Maya since she'd left for California. Maya didn't even know that Senida was coming to California. There were so many changes that occurred in her life in such a short period of time.

      She watched the clock. It was three minutes after eight and she still hadn't dialed her parent's number. She felt bad about losing the Mortin case. She felt as though she personally let him down as a friend. Senida knew the reason for her losing the case was not her ability, talent or her ambition, but her emotional dependency on the men in her life. She usually let them get in the way of her logical thinking. She was also feeling bad about losing Darrell, Todd, *and* Mandla all in one year. She didn't know what happened to her that night with Mandla or Darrell, but she just snapped. It wasn't the first time.

      She snapped that time when she slit Todd's tires, and she snapped that time when she fought the woman in the store that looked at Darrell. She snapped when she sat waiting outside of

Todd's house, and she snapped when she broke the windows out of one of Darrell's client's windows. When she thought she was losing love, she snapped. She could feel it coming. It was like a rush of blood to her head. Her fingers would start to tingle and she would end up doing something that she would regret later.

These were the situations that she never dealt with, her humiliation, her embarrassment, her defeats. She was too used to being the person to come out on top. She was so used to being the one that was victorious that she couldn't really tell a soul how she was feeling. Going home would be her way of getting her life back together. She would rest, return to Atlanta and pick up the pieces. Being home would allow her to heal without the interruptions of everyday living.

Senida swung her legs over the side of her bed. She sat for a few minutes and headed for the shower. Once she was dressed, she realized that she had to call her parents and let them know what time to pick her up from the airport. She'd hesitated on calling her mother because Mrs. Johnson could tell when her daughter was hurting. Senida knew that her mother would know instantly from her voice that things were not right in her life. Senida was afraid to start crying all over again. It took her close to a week to stop crying over everything that had happened in her life within the last year. She reached over and dialed her parent's number. Her mother answered on the second ring in her normal cheerful voice.

"Mom..." Senida began to cry.

"I'm here for you baby," Mrs. Johnson said. "Tell mama what's wrong."

The brownish red book practically burned a hole in Maya's hand as she held it on the plane. She'd promised herself that she would wait to read it, but her curiosity always got the best of her. A single tear ran down her cheek and she quickly brushed it away with the back of her hand. She slowly opened the book and noticed that two pages were folded down, one page in the middle and one towards the end. She flipped to the first page that was folded down and read the faded, dark brown ink. What she found made her heart stop. She had to take in air through her mouth. Her breathing intensified and she had to read the passage more than once, to make sure she hadn't made a mistake.

June 5, 1966

Happy days come and go, but today, despite the circumstances, is a happy day for me. My new baby boy looks exactly like me. I may not be able to be with him everyday, but he has brought joy to my heart. Angelo Dickson, named after my great uncle who did great things. He weighed 7lbs 2oz. Although his mother vowed to never let me see him, I will fight her for custody. Gladys cried her eyes out today. She threatened me with divorce and I can understand why. My mistake has ruined her life and made me look like a monster to her family. If I ever get another chance, I'll treat her like the queen that she is.

Maya then flipped the pages to the other folded down page and read.

June 25, 1968

Today was the beginning of a beautiful day. Today Maya was born. She's a beautiful 6lb, bouncing baby with my eyes. The delivery was long and hard, but Gladys made it through with flying colors. I haven't seen Angelo in over a year. His mother let me see him only once at the park. He still looks like me, but is taking on some of my father's characteristics. One day I will explain to my new baby girl, about her estranged brother. But me and Gladys decided to keep the secret of my infidelity out of her life. We've gone through a lot. I'm glad she took me back in her life. I swear under God, that I will never hurt her again.

She had a brother? Maya leaned back in the seat. She looked out of the window, down at the houses. She had been flying for a few hours and would be landing at Hartsfield Airport in Atlanta soon. She could not believe that she had another relative out there somewhere. She thought for sure that Aunt Setty was her only living relative left. As soon as she hit the ground in Atlanta she would have to call Aunt Setty and see if she knew anything about this brother.

Maya's body tingled. How exciting! How scary! A brother. And her father. He had an affair? And her mother forgave him? She forgave him. Just like what Aunt Setty was talking about. Second chances. The two of them, through love, picked up the pieces of their marriage and worked through the madness. Their situation reminded her a little of her relationship with Jelani. She smiled. She knew with the spirits of her parents behind her, and the strength of their love, she would make it through the tough times. She looked at her watch. She would be landing in a few hours. She would call Senida when she got to the airport. Maya had a lot to tell her when she got home. She wondered what Senida had been up to while she was gone.

When Maya got off of the plane at Hartsfield Airport in Atlanta, she prepared to take a cab. Instead of taking the little train to baggage claim, Maya walked the entire way. She waited among the rest of the passengers to claim her baggage. Through the thick crowd of people, she heard someone calling her name. The familiar voice sent chills up her spine. Her suspicions were confirmed when she turned to see Jelani standing with an arm full of red roses. There were two little red haired kids standing next to him. A large smile crept across his face as he walked closer to her.

"I'm not supposed to be here. Just last night we were in Florida," he said as he looked down at the two strange looking little kids.

"And so what are you doing here?" she smiled.

"I *had* to see you. I had to prove to you that I love you," he replied. The two little kids snickered. Jelani held his hand out.

"These are for you."

"Thank you," Maya said as she took the roses in her arms and smelled them.

"We have to fly back to Florida tomorrow so may I *please* drive you home and take you out to dinner tonight? We really need to talk." Jelani looked down at his niece and nephew. They were both looking up at him. "That's if you don't mind the extra company for a little while."

"I'd love to. And I don't mind the extra company at all. As long as I'm with you." Maya smiled. Jelani paid a skycap to take Maya's luggage to his jeep.

"Those are the sweetest words I've heard in a long, long time." He took her arm and Maya grabbed one of the kid's hands as Jelani grabbed the other's hand. All four of them walked out of the airport building.